D0909217

KILL FOR AN ORCHID

BY THE SAME AUTHOR

Deadly Slipper

The Orchid Shroud

A Twist of Orchids

KILL FOR AN ORCHID

A Novel of Death in the Dordogne

MICHELLE WAN

Doubleday Canada

Library and Archives of Canada Cataloguing in Publication has been applied for

ISBN: 978-0-385-66486-8

This book is a work of fiction. Names, characters, places and incidents are products of the author's imagination or are used fictitiously. Any resemblance to actual events or locales or persons, living or dead, is entirely coincidental.

Printed and bound in the USA

Published in Canada by Doubleday Canada,
a division of Random House of Canada Limited

Visit Random House of Canada Limited's website: www.randomhouse.ca

10 9 8 7 6 5 4 3 2 1

TO HOLGER AND WENQING. I WILL ALWAYS REMEMBER
THE MOUNTAINS OF YUNNAN AND SICHUAN.
AND, AS EVER, TO TIM.

ACKNOWLEDGEMENTS

I am grateful to many at home and abroad who helped me with this book. In France, my special thanks go once again to Michel Renard, Marie-Pierre Kachintzeff and Garry Watt for their linguistic and factual assistance; and to Robbert Kieboom, Dave McCrae and Helène Bougot for the wonderful recipe for *beignets des fleurs d'acacia*. In China, I am tremendously grateful to Holger Perner and Wenqing Gan Perner for their friendship and generosity—Holger, who unstintingly shared with Tim and me his vast knowledge of orchids, both on paper and in the mountains of Yunnan and Sichuan; and Wenqing for her many kindnesses and superb organizational skills.

Closer to home, I am grateful to Chris Young and Dr. Dwight Stewart for their kind help with things medical and chemical; to Taras Hollyer for his insights into the patenting process; to Tan Kok Chiang for his timely and generous aid with the intricacies of Chinese nomenclature; and to my agent, Frances Hanna, and my editor at Doubleday, Amy Black, for their critical inputs on the manuscript. To my sister Grace I send a great hug for her support and encouragement. And to my husband Tim, with whom I have walked many orchid miles, I return love for love.

Finally, I would be remiss in failing to acknowledge the wealth of information afforded me by the 1868–1870 diary of Abbé Armand David, whose description of his travels up the Yangtze provided me with many of the details I needed for

Horatio Kneebone's similar fictional journey. I refer interested readers to Helen M. Fox's translation, *Abbé David's Diary*, Harvard University Press, Cambridge (1949).

As always, responsibility for all errors of fact or interpretation are entirely mine.

AUTHOR'S NOTE

This fictional work takes place in the *département* of the Dordogne, southwest France, and Sichuan Province, China. The characters in this book are imaginary, and the landscapes are a concoction of real and invented places. All of the orchids in the book are real, except perhaps *Cypripedium incognitum*. But then, it still waits to be discovered, doesn't it?

PROLOGUE

The sun bled into the wrinkled surface of the bay. Through the open third-floor studio windows the sounds of the Arcachon Basin drifted up, the sharp cry of gulls, the dull thudding of craft riding gently against their moorings, the street noises of an unusually warm March day in this placid French seaside resort. The windows, large floor-to-ceiling affairs, framed shifting compositions of sky and water.

Sofia dropped her brush into a jar of turpentine and stepped away from the life-sized canvas. The painting, *Paraphernalia on Nude*, was finishing up well, the broken umbrella in the foreground lending its touch of madness to the piece. The nude, in real life a hairy youth named Gino who lay sleeping on a worn leather couch, appeared as little more than a backdrop of gawky arms and legs and genitalia. It was the umbrella that riveted the eye, made you hold your breath, waiting for an imminent crazy explosion of spokes.

"Humans are ridiculous," Sofia liked to tell the coterie of young artists who gravitated to her studio. "We walk imperfectly on two legs, our faces are squashed like pies, our knees are grotesque. But that is why God loves us. We are His private joke. And that is how we must paint the human body. As if the universe were ringing with His laughter." Tall, largely built, with wild, orange hair and a square face made arresting by huge Mediterranean eyes, Sofia dearly loved a laugh.

"Hey, gorgeous," she called softly.

Gino twitched but did not wake. Like all of her hangers-on, he was penniless and hungry, hungry for life, for a quick fix, for anything he could cadge or snatch. She had chosen him out of her flock eleven months ago because he was young, beautiful and as randy as a satyr. He was also proving to be wildly jealous of his position as her current favourite and already making trouble over that long-necked gazelle Antonia whom Sofia had decided would shortly take his place. For it was Sofia's practice to choose a model, male or female, from among her young friends to pose for her for exactly one year, after which she moved on to someone else. It was understood that she would pay them well, paint them exclusively and, despite the joke that was the human body, have sex with them. She herself was a bi-directional transgender female. Her operation years ago had left her with a scar, a need for regular hormone treatments, and no angst. She hadn't even had to change her signature. It was now, as it always had been, simply Ventura.

Let him be, she decided wearily. What she needed, more than a coupling, was a long, hot soak. The painting had sucked up all her energy, even to the point of destroying sleep. She felt almost bruised with exhaustion. Kicking off her sandals, she headed toward the far end of the studio where a door on the left led into the W.C. and a door on the right into the bathroom. A relaxing bath, she thought, followed by dinner at Bruno's. Hellishly expensive, but a good setting in which to talk to Gino about the transition to Antonia. In all her dealings Sofia was generous, and she hoped he would be reasonable.

The third door—more a crude, black representation than a door—surprised her. It stood where no door had ever been and seemed to have been cut into the outer wall. Or, she wondered fleetingly, perhaps Gino, as a prank, had somehow managed to paint it on her wall without her knowledge. Amused, she moved forward, reached out to touch its oddly intangible surface. With no resistance, it swung open into a blinding explosion of light.

The noise made Gino jerk awake. Seagulls, crying harshly, were swooping low over the rooftops. He sat up.

"Sofi?" He looked around and sat up. "Sofi?"

Her sandals lay on the floor. Perhaps she was in the bathroom.

The painting stood on its easel, nearly finished, the last she would do of him. He rose and went to it, drawn and repelled at the same time, wanting as he had for days to slash it apart, to beg her not to leave him like that, a mere *arrière-plan* to a fucking umbrella that seemed to say, "the laugh's on you."

Then he heard the babble of voices rising from the street below, someone shouting, "*Mon Dieu*!" And someone else: "Call an ambulance."

Gino went to one of the windows and stood, naked as a newt, looking down.

• 1 •

It was spring in the glorious Dordogne.

God's country, Julian Wood called it. He paused in his labours to raise his eyes to a sweep of wooded uplands and high blue sky, then threw his weight onto the spade, turning and lifting soil oozing with life. Mid-fifties, tall and lanky with a salt-and-pepper thatch, a long jaw framed by facial hair in need of trimming, he was a man at peace. A man who had long ago fled the damp cold of England to put down roots in this sunny, rugged corner of southwest France. He loved this place, its fields, its woods, its rumpled hills, its robust earthy wines and especially its hardy, good-humoured farming folk. Sadly, they were giving way to paler generations removed from the land and anxiously trying to squeeze out precarious livings in a *département* where good jobs were hard to find. A chronically underemployed landscape gardener himself, Julian was sure he contributed to the regional unemployment statistics.

But that was not a problem for today. Today the wisteria dripped like purple rain from the eaves of the houses, irises raised elegant flags against old stone walls, the air was heady with smells. Today was a day to set the old-fashioned annuals that he favoured—wallflowers and pansies—into the warm bosom of the earth.

Until Mara came out of the house with the morning's post.

"Mostly bills," she called. "Yours, I'm afraid."

Julian sighed, relinquishing his spade and his view of sky and forest. Nothing was perfect.

•

"Can we talk?" said Mara Dunn.

They were seated at the terrace table. He had his glasses on and was sorting through his mail.

"Fire away." He glanced at a notice from his bank. "*Merde*."

"Well," said Mara, leaning forward on her elbows. "I've been doing a lot of thinking." And when he did not respond, she added, "About us."

"Eh?"

Mara sighed. She was a small, slim French Canadian with a determined chin and large, intelligent eyes that were at the moment darkly serious.

"You and me. Life together. Do we stay as we are?" She paused, giving him time to absorb the question. "Or do we move on to something—well—more permanent?"

It was risky, where she was going. They were such different people. She, an interior designer, was accustomed to moving space and objects around, shaping everything to a timetable, a budget and a plan. Julian was happiest out of doors, planting and pruning, or rambling through woods and meadows looking for orchids, going nowhere in particular. They had come to the Dordogne by different paths, had met four years ago under peculiar circumstances, and had gone on to live together just as peculiarly in her house in Ecoute-la-Pluie with two dogs and no clear notion of where this would take them. And therein lay the difficulty. Mara needed to know where they were going. Julian did not seem to care.

Now he looked up. *Stay as they were*? *More permanent*? *Was there a difference*? Well, yes, Julian had to conclude, it was a bit awkward, this living out of two places. His cottage in Grissac, twenty minutes down the road (for sale; no buyers, not even any prospects to date), was where he still kept most of his belongings and where he dropped in occasionally to check on things, to pick up the odd phone message (he still kept his land line going; he refused to get a *portable*) and to collect mail that had not been forwarded to him at Mara's. These were his Times Out, when he wandered through his poky darkened rooms, touching his books (of which he had a great number), when he gave in to a secret desire to sit idly in his tattered leather armchair (it did not match Mara's decor), savouring with a sense of poignancy the remembrance of a time when he had actually lived there. But what exactly did she mean? For starters, could he bring his books? And his armchair? His eyes fell on a letter bearing a Canadian stamp. For a moment he thought it must be for her, but no, it had been addressed to him, care of his publisher, his name clearly typed, and redirected to him.

"Sure." His melancholy features broke into a boyish, lopsided grin. Life was good. He had no objection whatever to things continuing as they were for as long as she liked. "I'm open to that."

"You are?"

"Of course." Curious, he tore the envelope open. The letter it contained, postmarked March 25, 2007, had taken thirteen days to reach him.

Dear Mr. Wood,

I don't know how to contact you directly, so I am asking your publisher, Éditions Arobas, to forward this letter. I have just seen your book on wild orchids of the Dordogne. In it you show a drawing of an unknown Slipper orchid that you call Cypripedium incognitum *and that you believe grows locally. I happen to be writing a book on the life of my great-great-great-grandfather, the 19th-century plant hunter, Horatio Kneebone, whose expedition diaries I possess. Amazingly, one of them includes a sketch and description of an orchid that closely resembles your artist's drawing of* C. incognitum!

Mara watched in bemusement as Julian's jaw went suddenly slack.

Since Horatio had ties to the Dordogne, I think my ancestor might just hold the secret to the origin of this incredible flower. I plan to spend some time in your part of France researching Horatio's "Dordogne Period," and I would greatly appreciate a chance to meet you and talk further about what I'm sure is an area of mutual interest. If this suits you, please reply to the address or e-mail shown below.
Sincerely,
Charles K. Perry

"Julian," she burst out, "you do understand I'm talking about marriage!" Immediately she said it she was sorry. It had come out all wrong, sounding like a threat.

"My God!" shouted Julian, whose heart had made a sudden leap.

"Don't sound so appalled."

"Appalled?" Julian's eyes were starry. "I think it's absolutely brilliant!"

"You do?" said Mara, quite surprised.

•

Mara said a little sourly after she had read the letter—she had just proposed, hadn't she? And all he could think of was his orchid—"I don't suppose he realizes you've never seen this flower of yours and that your only proof it exists is an old, very bad photograph and an even older embroidery?"

"Who cares?" Julian snatched the letter back from her and kissed it. "You read what Charles Beautiful K. Perry wrote: his ancestor's orchid matches mine. There are diary entries on it. That means *Cypripedium incognitum* is not a phantom, Mara. It has a documented provenance."

It was true that Julian had never seen, never touched, his mystery orchid. It was totally unknown to him and to the botanical world, for his considerable research had turned up nothing like it. That was what made it so special. It was the bad photograph, brought to him by Mara at their first meeting, that had started it all. The antique embroidery, which had turned up later, showed a clearer representation—a stunning if structurally anomalous flower with a bright pink pouch flanked by blackish-purple, extraordinarily long, twisted lateral petals, and *three* sepals—not the two normally characteristic of *Cypripediums*—of the same hue. Since then he had been driven to find it, if truth be known, had lusted for it with all the desperation of an addict. Was it an extremely rare, indigenous species that grew only in an isolated spot in the Dordogne? An import that had managed to survive and propagate? If so, from where, and what was the history of this amazing flower's journey to his corner of southwest France? Now, out of the blue, he was actually on the verge of having his answer. All that remained was to find the flower itself.

So what was he doing sitting here? It was already April, things were blooming. He lurched involuntarily from his chair, propelled by the same old fear that always swamped him around this time, that a careless hiker or a bulldozer would wipe it out of existence. Worse, that someone else would find the orchid first. His unopened mail fell to the ground.

"You're worried about Géraud, aren't you," Mara observed with perfect comprehension. Living with an orchid freak had taught her to read his moods according to the seasons—spring was always a fraught time—although she had yet to understand his passion. She often wished more of it would find its way to her.

"That poacher!" Géraud Laval was Julian's arch botanical rival and, after Julian, the Dordogne's next best orchidologist. A retired pharmacist, he was a temperamental old goat with hairy ears and a habit of shouting. He also had a nasty reputation for acquiring orchids any way he could, which included the unthinkable crime of digging them up in the wild. "He's an outright menace." Julian paced restlessly to the edge of the terrace.

"Quite a dilemma," said Mara with a touch of sarcasm. "Which to do first? Answer Beautiful Charles Perry's letter, or rush out to find your flower before Géraud does?"

•

6 April 2007
> Dear Charles,
I'm astounded, intrigued, fascinated, gobsmacked—what can I say? Frankly, the search for C. incognitum *has taken over my life since I first found traces of it here in the Dordogne four years ago. Your news is an immense break in the mystery surrounding this incredible flower and I can hardly wait to learn more. Can you send me a copy of your sketch? I'm using a friend's e-mail, so you can reply to me care of her, Mara Dunn. She informs me you can send me a scan of the drawing. By all means, let's meet. I can't tell you how much I welcome ANY information you can give me on* C. incognitum.
Yours in anticipation,
Julian Wood <

"A friend's e-mail?" Mara felt hurt as she read his reply. It was an hour later, and they were in her studio, a converted building behind the house. Julian was at her computer. An initiate to the mysteries of electronic communication, he had to be coached through the process. "What's wrong with fiancée?" She assumed that's what they now were.

"For heaven's sake, Mara," said Julian, looking alarmed. "That's personal. I hardly know the man."

•

"Delighted," was Charles Perry's e-mail response the following day, although he made it clear that he preferred to defer any further exchange on *Cypripedium incognitum* "until their happy meeting." He gave an arrival date in a week's time, said he was in need of a self-catering short-term rental while he carried out his research in the region, and could Julian suggest anything? Absolutely, Julian fired back. His own cottage at a knock-down price. The offer was accepted. Perry insisted on paying a deposit.

"That's settled then," Julian said.

"He likes playing hard-to-get, don't you think?" Mara sniffed. Until their happy meeting indeed.

"Oh, I expect he's just being careful. After all, he doesn't know what he's getting into."

Mara forbore to comment, eyes wandering to the windows. Outside, a wind was building up, forerunner of those spring storms that blew in so quickly over the land. Once again, they were at her computer. Around them lay the detritus of her trade: architectural bits and pieces, old doors, a chimney hook, a collection of fanciful *épis*—the finials that decorated the roof ends of old houses—remnants she had salvaged from wrecking sites, junk shops and flea markets. The clutter, however, had its purpose. Everything would one day find its way into her many clients' re-remodelled environments.

A flash of lightning split the sky with an electrifying *crack*. Bismuth, Julian's rangy grey-speckled mutt, offspring of Edith the local pointer bitch, gave a howl of anguish and shot under the desk. He was terrified of thunder. Another dog, Jazz, Mara's tan-and-white pit bull and also Bismuth's sire, snored windily beside a roll of salvaged carpet.

"I wonder what you'll do," she mused.

"Court him, of course. Coax, screw, squeeze out of him everything and anything he can give me on *Cypripedium incognitum*."

"I mean, what you'll do if you ever find your orchid."

"You mean *when* I find it!" Julian declared. "Stand the botanical world on its ear, what do you think. Then throw the biggest blowout this side of Brives. You do realize that the discovery of an unknown orchid ranks up there with finding a new solar system?"

"Oh sure. But after that?" She paused, dark, straight brows drawing together in a velvet line of frustration. Rain was beginning to slash against the windowpanes. "This flower has ruled your life for as long as I've known you. It makes me wonder. Once you find it, once the mystery is solved, what then? Will it be over?"

"Will what be over?"

"I mean, will you be able to let it go? Or will you just look for something else to fill the gap?"

He said a little anxiously, "This isn't about how much time I spend looking for it, is it?" She had complained about that. She had complained about a lot of things.

"No." Mara pulled her cardigan a little tighter around her. The studio was inadequately heated. "It's about the lure of the unattainable." *Which I'm not*, she thought ruefully. *I'm Mara, available, on the downhill slide of forty-five, irrationally in love with an orchid maniac who thinks more about botany than he does me.* "And the fact that you're impossibly romantic. Where orchids are concerned, at least."

"Hey," he teased, seeing where she was coming from, "not jealous of a flower, are you?" And when she did not respond, he said earnestly, "Oh, come on, Mara. Surely you understand what a break like this means to me." He threw his head back gloatingly. "God, I can't wait to get my hands on Kneebone's diary. I can't wait to meet Charles Perry. I wonder what he's like."

She gazed at him sadly. "You sound like a man waiting for a mail-order bride. Maybe I *should* be jealous."

"Not a chance." He rose from the desk, drew her to him and kissed her on the nose. His face broke into its crooked, heart-tugging smile. "But if he brings me information on *Cypripedium incognitum*, I'll have to love him, won't I? Just a little bit?"

· 2 ·

Mara was having what the French called *une nuit blanche*, a white night. Normally, she slept like she worked—hard and flat out. But ever since she had said, *I'm talking about marriage*, and Julian had replied, *I think it's absolutely brilliant*, a disquiet had nibbled at the edges of her mind, spoiling her rest.

"Julian," she had pressed him at one point, "are you sure you really want to do this? Hitching up, joining at the hip, 'til death do us part?"

The look he had given her had been so impenetrable that her heart had dropped to her socks. She braced herself for him to say, *Mara, I was married once, as you know, and I'm sorry, I just don't think I can go there again.* She, who had also left a bad marriage behind her, would have understood.

Instead he had taken her in his arms and gazed earnestly into her eyes. "Of course. What do you take me for?" But his voice did not express conviction.

Mara sighed and shifted, making room for a bony canine rump. The bed was king-sized, but it had to do for four. She and Julian, plus Jazz, who snored and farted, and Bismuth, who liked to lie sideways, taking up most of the space in the middle.

Perhaps she'd got it right: it really did boil down to the lure of the unattainable. Julian longed not for her, but for what eluded him: his blasted orchid. And she wanted not just the bits and pieces that were left over after his obsession with *Cypripedium incognitum* was accounted for, but all of him, fully concentrated on her for once. Why is it, she wondered, that we always want what we can't have?

"Julian," she whispered in the darkness. "Are you awake?"

He wasn't. He slept deeply, chasing orchids in his dreams.

•

The Canadian proved a harder nut to crack than Julian had anticipated.

He declined to be met at Roumanière Airport, saying instead that he would pick up a rental car there and drive himself to the cottage, using a map that Julian, with Mara's help, had scanned for him.

On the day, Julian was there well ahead of him, had been, in fact, since early morning, airing out the place, cleaning, tidying. He had stocked the *frigo* with basics, put flowers from the garden in a chipped vase on the scarred dining table. He hurried outside as soon as he heard the crunch of tires on the road.

"Well!" Julian sang out enthusiastically. "You found it."

"Perry," said Charles, climbing out of the car and pumping Julian's hand. "Charles Perry. Charlie to my friends."

"Charlie it is!"

Julian sized him up: a solemn, shortish, squarely built man, forties, with round blue eyes and a beaky upper lip, somewhat resembling an owl. His head was even topped with fine brown hair that stuck out like feathers. There was something about him, however, a hint of underlying steeliness that warned Julian that Charlie was no downy chick.

Julian helped him carry his bags inside and gave him a tour of the cottage, explained the operation of the cranky heating system—nights could still be cold—where things were kept, what to do if the fuses blew, and so on. Charlie asked if Julian was on high speed.

High-speed? Julian wondered. *Surely the man wasn't talking about drugs*?

"I think you'll find the pace of life around here pretty slow," he offered. Maybe Charlie was one of those type-A personalities. "Oh, and there might be the odd person calling or turning up for me. The place is for sale, although I doubt you'll be bothered with floods of buyers. But I'm a landscape gardener, and even though I don't live here I'm still in the Yellow Pages under this phone number and address. Just direct them on to Ecoute-la-Pluie. I've stuck the information and directions on the fridge door. And of course, ring if you need anything."

"*Pas de problème*," assured Charlie. And then, neatly cutting Julian off, he declared, "Look, I'm feeling pretty whacked out. If it's all the same to you, I'd like a chance to settle in. After that I'd be glad to talk about your orchid."

"Oh, absolutely," said Julian, stamping down his disappointment. To be fair, the man did look exhausted. "But we—Mara and I—were hoping you'd join us and a few friends for lunch tomorrow? There's a new restaurant in Bergerac we want to try. It's Mara's party, actually. Do you like Chinese?"

"Why, yes," said Charlie with surprised enthusiasm, "it so happens I do."

•

They met at La Pagode, France's Newest, Most Authentic Sichuan Restaurant, situated below the old quarter of the city and opposite the quay with a view of the river. The friends were Loulou La Pouge, a former cop whose chubby, cheerful presence made him look more like an elderly baby than an ex-*flic*; Prudence Chang, a retired advertising executive from Los Angeles who spent her summers in a remodelled farmhouse near Belvès; and Patsy Reicher, a psychoanalyst from New York. Freckled, with crackling, iodine-coloured hair, Patsy and Mara's friendship went back to Patsy's mid-life career change as a sculptor in the Dordogne. Patsy had since returned to her practice in the Big Apple. Now she was back for the summer, trying out Prudence's new guesthouse, which Mara had reconstructed from a stable. Prudence was one of Mara's biggest clients.

Charlie, recovered from jet lag, made a good impression on them all. He introduced himself to Patsy and Prudence as "Charlie. A writer? From Toronto, Ontario?" ending his phrases in a pleasant, tenor updraft. He addressed Loulou in courteous, perfectly serviceable French and took the liberty of teasing Mara about her accent.

"Made in Montreal, eh?"

Mara reddened a little. Try as she might, she could not entirely suppress her accent, which ran syllables together, flattened vowels and released sibilants in tiny explosions against the teeth. Like bad hair, it had a way of springing up, irrepressibly, provoking curiosity, questions, even laughter.

But he redeemed himself by saying, "I like it. It has character. It smacks of where it's been."

He carried a thin, plastic binder under his left arm.

Linus Chen, the noodle-slim restaurant owner, seated them at a round table with a gas burner in the middle, put out small cold dishes to open the appetite and immediately poured green tea. "*Pas de vin*," he said. "Wine doesn't go so good with Sichuan food."

"I know this place," said Prudence. "Didn't it used to be a pizzeria?" A walking collection of designer labels, she pulled off Gucci sunglasses to take in a subtle surround of green and gold. "At least it no longer looks like a Roman brothel."

"It had better not," Mara muttered. "It's my decor."

"Yours?"

"That's why we're eating here and why you're all my guests. Linus had me do the work, then told me he couldn't pay me. I'm taking my fee in meals."

"Gee!" exclaimed Prudence. She addressed Linus. "You're buying her off in won tons? I hope your food is good. She doesn't come cheap." The place, apart from them, was empty.

Writhing ingratiatingly, Linus laughed. "Ha ha! No problem. You leave everything to Mama Deng. Today she makes you something *très special.*"

"Who's Mama Deng?" asked Loulou.

"Head chef," said Mara, waving at a dumpling of a woman in a hairnet who appeared from the kitchen at that moment, pushing a loaded trolley.

"*Bonjour, bonjour,*" said the dumpling, face puckered with smiles. Linus lit the burner. Together he and Mama Deng set on it a sizzling cauldron of dark, oily broth afloat with unknown ingredients and into which went shelled shrimp, scallops, long-stemmed mushrooms, paper-thin slices of chicken and pork, tofu cubes and a medley of chopped vegetables. A rich, pungent aroma swirled up to their nostrils.

"Sichuan hot-pot!" exclaimed Charlie in genuine delight.

"*Très authentique,*" said Linus with pride. "Mama Deng's the real thing." He waved at the colourful array of dishes now crowding the table.

"This," said Mama Deng, chopsticks fishing out something brown, the size of a pea, "is Sichuan pepper. Make your mouth go numb, but hot-pot not hot-pot without it. Can't get here. I got nephew in Sichuan, send special." The chopsticks plunged again, and she pincered up starter servings for them all. "Cook quick. You eat now. I come back."

"Looks interesting," said Julian, peering cautiously at his plate.

"Hey," declared Patsy, trying hers, "I like it."

"Wow," said Mara, coughing a little.

"Rather spicy. Otherwise *très bon.*" This, judiciously, from Loulou.

Julian was unable to comment because his mouth, rather than going numb, was on fire. Some of the interesting things that Mama Deng had dredged up for him were chilis as explosive as hand grenades. A frantic gulp of tea only further burned his mouth. "God in heaven!" he gasped. His voice had gone unaccountably high.

"Well, it *is* a hot-pot," said Prudence, munching on a harvest of shrimp with no ill effect. "The real thing. Excellent."

"And right in the middle of the Dordogne," Charlie enthused. "Unbelievable!" Joyfully, he popped a glistening payload of chicken and mushrooms into his mouth. "If you're ever in Toronto, any of you, I know a terrific Sichuan restaurant. I'll give you the name."

All of this left Julian to sweat and blow his nose and wonder if his taste buds were somehow developmentally challenged. However, once he learned to avoid the lethal flotillas of chili peppers that crowded the broth, he actually found the hot-pot quite good.

"So, Charlie," he said, when he was able to speak normally again, "tell us about yourself."

To which the Canadian replied, with a directness that warmed Julian's heart, "Don't you mean, tell you about Horatio Kneebone and the orchid?" The man sketched an impish grin. "That's what you're really asking, isn't it?"

"Not at all," assured Julian heartily.

"Yes it is," corrected Mara with her mouth full.

"Well," said Charlie, busy with his chopsticks, "Horatio Kneebone was born in 1820—English father, French mother—right here in Bergerac. I'm hoping to trace the actual house, if it still stands. So, you see, by extension, I'm a son of the Dordogne." He went on to say that his three-times-great-grandfather had trained as a plantsman with the Royal Horticultural Society in

England, travelling not only for them but also for the Museum of Natural History in Paris. As his reputation grew—Horatio enjoyed what he called the Luck of the Kneebones—he was contracted by private sponsors and nurserymen all over Europe. From India, Southeast Asia and the Philippines he brought back boatloads of exotic plants.

"But more than anything"—Charlie leaned forward so that none would miss the significance of what he was about to say—"he wanted to investigate the fabled flora of China."

Julian, hanging on the man's every word, fumbled with a scallop, dropped it twice and ended up skewering it on the point of his chopstick. "China," he breathed. "The home of *Cypripediums.* I should have guessed."

"In 1850 he got his chance with the English East India Trading Company in Canton. He spent the next seven years there, learning the language and customs of the people, and then, before the company folded in 1858, found other employment with the French legation in Peking. But he was always frustrated because he was allowed to make only brief incursions into the surrounding countryside. The Chinese authorities were very suspicious of foreigners, you see. Nevertheless, he discovered and sent back numerous plants unknown to Britain and Europe at the time. *Cornus horatiana* was named after him, as was *Lilium patellae.*"

"*Patellae,*" said Patsy. "I suppose that's a play on Kneebone?"

"Hey, very good!" beamed Charlie. "Then in 1861, after China was forced to open up its interior to foreigners and just before he had to leave the country, Horatio managed to put together the funds to make a trip up the Yangtze River."

"And that was when he discovered *Cypripedium incognitum* and brought it back to France?" Julian found that he was gripping the edge of the table.

"Correct," Charlie affirmed with all the solemnity the conclusion deserved. "He returned to Bordeaux, where he married and based himself. But he also moved around a great deal between Paris, London and Brussels—Belgium at the time was the orchid capital of the world, as you probably know—trying to raise financing for a return trip to China. Unfortunately, I have no information on what became of the orchid from that point forward—he managed to bring back only one living plant—if he sold it or to whom. That's the part of his life I'm here to research."

"And did he ever return to China?" asked Prudence.

"No." Charlie shook his head regretfully. "It's almost as if after leaving, the Luck of the Kneebones turned sour. Promises fell through. Sponsors pulled out at the last minute. There's some suggestion that he was the victim of a smear campaign by one of his rivals, a fellow named Tarquin Foster, but I haven't been able to find anything specific on it. Horatio was eventually reduced to poverty, estranged from his wife and children, fell ill and died under, um, unusual circumstances, leaving nothing but the clothes he wore and his trip notebooks, among them the log of his China expedition, which includes the sketch I mentioned."

"Unusual circumstances?" Mara stiffened like a setter on the point.

Charlie looked a little embarrassed, as if his ancestor had committed a social faux pas. "He hanged himself."

"*Ah, ça,*" murmured Loulou, professionally interested.

"It's that damned orchid!" Mara burst out, throwing down her chopsticks. "It's always wrapped around with violence!"

Charlie looked startled. "What do you mean?"

"I mean—" She broke off, remembering, and her voice dropped. "People associated with it die violent deaths." She did not elaborate, but Julian, Patsy, Prudence and Loulou, who knew the background stories, understood. "If I were you, I'm not so sure I'd want to dig into the history of this flower."

"Nonsense," said Julian, somewhat shaken. "It's a plant. There's nothing wrong with it. It's people who are evil. In any case"—he was not to be thrown off course—"I really need to see that drawing, Charlie."

Charlie, sobered by the sense of undercurrents he did not comprehend, tore himself from a fascinated study of Mara to say, "Oh, right. Of course. I knew you would, so I made you a photocopy. You can keep it." With a flourish, he produced the binder, unzipped it, removed a sheet of paper protected by a plastic sleeve, and handed it to Julian. "I'm no expert, but it looks identical to the one in your book."

Julian stared hard at a small pen-and-ink sketch of an orchid with appended handwritten notations:

A tall, magnificent plant bearing a solitary flower. Petals three, the vivid pink labellum being large and deeply saccate. Lateral petals exceedingly long, narrow and elaborately twisted. Sepals three, the upper overarching and blackish purple, as are the two oblong lateral sepals which depend separately. Leaves three to four, dark green, strongly veined, elliptic, glabrous both sides.

"You're absolutely right," he breathed reverently. "It's a perfect match." He passed the drawing around for the others to see. "It's all come together. China is a logical point of origin, and Charlie's ancestor was clearly the means by which my orchid got to the Dordogne."

Charlie said rather smugly, "That's why I wrote you."

"What does Horatio say about where he found it? He must have described the location, made precise notes on habitat."

To Julian's surprise, Charlie replied, "Afraid not."

"What?"

"Sorry. The only thing I have is the drawing." And when Julian continued to look incredulous, the Canadian reddened. "Look, I think Horatio purposely didn't put anything in writing in case his papers fell into the wrong hands, if you see what I mean. You have to remember the European fever for orchids exploded in the nineteenth century. There was huge money to be made. A single rare plant could fetch a fortune, and plant hunters and their sponsors weren't above playing some pretty shoddy tricks to outdo competitors. Hunters had to protect their finds from claim-jumpers. Some even went to extremes. One I know of found a fabulous orchid, took all the plants he could dig up and destroyed everything else in order to secure the monopoly for himself." For a second, Charlie's eyes seemed to flicker with an odd, blue light that only Julian saw. "Anyway, if the orchid grows here, the real story is its transplantation to the Dordogne. Why is it so important where in China he found it?"

"Everything connected with *Cypripedium incognitum* is important," said Julian firmly. "Look, Charlie, maybe if I had a look at the diary? I might be able to pick up something you missed. That is"—Julian sensed immediate reticence—"I wouldn't need to see all of it. Just the relevant bits."

Charlie looked profoundly uncomfortable. He hardly noticed that Mama Deng had returned and was sliding meatballs, shredded cabbage, noodles and thinly cut raw beef into the broth.

"You have to understand," he addressed the company at large. "The diary is my primary source of information. As a writer I really need to keep it under wraps." His gaze went from face to face, seeking comprehension from the other members of the party but finding only polite interest. "Look." He yielded to Julian's obvious yearning. "Let me think about it. No promises, mind. Although"—now he broke off sheepishly—"you'll probably think I've got a damned nerve, but there are a couple of favours I'd like to ask *you*."

"Name them!" Julian cried, prepared to barter his soul.

"First, I'd like any information you have on the history of the orchid in the Dordogne."

"That's easy. It's not much. The photo I included in my book was taken in 1984. As you saw for yourself, it's in terrible condition."

"Yes, it is. Where was it taken?"

"Er," replied Julian evasively, "somewhere in the region, but the exact site is unknown."

"Well, can't you ask the person who took it?"

"No, we can't," said Mara curtly.

"Oh," said Charlie, momentarily taken aback. "And the embroidery?"

Julian cleared his throat. "Well, it's nineteenth century, provenance unknown"—he avoided Mara's eye—"botanically exact, and extremely detailed—"

"So it must have been based on a living plant," cut in Charlie eagerly. "Which supports my theory that when Horatio was unsuccessful in arranging a second expedition, he ran out of money and sold the orchid as a last resort to someone in the Dordogne. You wouldn't have any idea who the purchaser might have been, would you?"

Mara opened her mouth to speak, but Julian stamped on her foot.

"No, I don't."

"Well, how about the embroiderer? Who she was—I assume it was a she—and where she might have seen the orchid?"

"Sorry, again no idea." Julian's expression was suddenly bland.

"Bummer," said Charlie, looking disappointed.

"And finally," Julian went on, "there's some indication that *Cypripedium incognitum* might have been something locals used to call *Sabot du Diable*, Devil's Clog, further evidence that it did propagate in the wild, at one time at least. Unfortunately, over the last century or so, owing to some kind of silly superstition, people dug it up wherever they found it and planted wolfsbane in its place. That, I'm afraid, is all I can tell you. What's your second favour?"

Charlie put down his chopsticks and shrugged. "Look, I'm a writer, but the bottom line is I'm pretty ignorant about flowers. In fact, my real background's chemistry, if you want to know the truth. I'd like you to educate me, take me around with you in the field, show me what orchids grow in the Dordogne and in particular the kinds of places where *Cypripedium incognitum* might grow. I'll probably be a damned nuisance, but it would mean a lot to me and will certainly enhance my book."

Julian said with feeling, "My God, if it's a crash course on orchids you want, you've come to the right man!"

3

By the time they got to the fortune cookies (Julian's read: *Momentous events lie just around the corner*), the conversation had drifted on to other things.

Sofia Ventura.

"Did you hear? Gino, the lover, has been charged with her murder," Prudence said. The case had dominated the news, offering titillating glimpses into lives driven by drugs, art, sex and violent jealousy. Prudence's interest stemmed from the fact that she owned a Ventura, *Nude on Bicycle*, that she had bought years ago. With a perversity typical of the art market, Ventura's paintings, now that she was dead, were worth five times what they had been when she was alive. "Although he swears he didn't push her. But how do you just walk out a window?"

Loulou shook his head. "And he was the only one with her at the time. I'm afraid our boy's looking at a good long stretch."

From Sofia and Gino, they moved on to Patsy's New York practice. She was feeling overworked, becoming more and more forgetful, losing concentration with patients, thinking of winding it down and retiring to an ashram in India with a fellow shrink named Stanley. Two years ago she had survived a trip to Nepal with him, searching for enlightenment and eating nothing but *daal bhaat*. Surprisingly she was still with him.

"Why an ashram? Why India?" Prudence smoothed an imperfectly arranged strand of hair with a perfectly manicured fingernail. "Why not retire to the Dordogne?"

"Stanley's terribly spiritual. France is too venal. That's why I'm here." Patsy sighed. "One last kick at venality."

"You're not serious!" Mara was agog at the thought of Patsy, who loved red meat, who changed men like underwear, living out her life in an ashram, subsisting on lentils.

"Maybe," said Patsy, looking troubled.

"Is this what you really want for yourself?" Mara was deeply concerned. The shoe was usually on the other foot, with Patsy asking the difficult questions, doling out wise counsel. "Will you be happy? Don't do something you'll regret."

"The only things I've ever regretted," said Patsy, "are the things I never did. Can we change the subject?"

They did: Mara's insomnia.

"I'm like the walking dead. I have bags like bladders under my eyes," she complained.

Patsy peered at her with a clinical air. "How long has this been going on?"

"Oh," said Mara vaguely. "Couple of weeks."

"Chamomile tea at bedtime," Loulou suggested. He winked. "Followed by a dose of cognac."

Patsy said, "Why not try BoniSom? It's the new herbal that hit the market last year. In North America it's called Xerafus. Over-the-counter, non-addictive, you can take it long-term with no side effects. I've used it since it came out, and I sleep like a baby."

"BoniSom?" Julian reared up in his chair. "Not on your life! Don't you know the active ingredient of BoniSom is an alkaloid extracted from an orchid that grows wild in Southwest China, and its commercial exploitation could wipe out the entire species?"

"Well, *pardonnez-moi*, I wasn't aware," said Patsy.

"It's an ecological disaster waiting to happen," Julian rolled on. "And another thing. Your wonder drug is also the subject of an international patents lawsuit: the Baixi people of China, who've traditionally used the orchid to make a soporific drink they call Sleep Tea, versus Bonisanté, S.A., the proprietors of BoniSom. The Baixi are arguing that Bonisanté pinched Sleep Tea, their intellectual property, and are profiting unfairly from it."

"Gee," said Prudence. "David and Goliath. What chance do these Buy-whatever have against a giant like Bonisanté?"

"Nil," admitted Julian glumly. "They're Europe's biggest herbal pharmaceutical company. Although a coalition of NGOs has got behind the cause, and they've engaged a patents lawyer on behalf of the Baixi. They're trying to overturn the European and North American patents. They also want to block further applications. At the very least, they hope to embarrass Bonisanté into some kind of settlement with the Baixi. But I expect it's like pissing in a hurricane."

"You seem very worked up about this." Charlie was interested enough to stop eating fortune cookies. He had five slips of paper lined up in front of him. *Your ready wit and charm attract many admirers* was one of them.

"Damned right I am. If Bonisanté has its way, they'll soon have worldwide rights over something they never created in the first place."

"Which, I suppose," said Patsy, "cuts the Baixi out from marketing their thing, if they had a mind to."

Mara said repressively, "The bottom line is Julian doesn't want anyone, Bonisanté *or* the Baixi, messing around with his orchids."

"They're not *mine*," Julian growled. "It's just that wild orchids can't sustain mass commercial exploitation. But it's also the principle of the thing. Big companies walk in, steal indigenous knowledge, tinker around a bit, then slap on a patent, even on the plant material itself, so they can monopolize the exploitation of it. It's nothing less than bloody biopiracy, and it's happening everywhere."

"Okay, okay." Patsy backed down. "Forget BoniSom. We'll all count sheep."

"But don't these companies spend a lot on R and D?" Charlie was not ready to let the matter go. "They're entitled to get their money back, aren't they? Without Bonisanté, the world would never have known of BoniSom. Those Baixi would never have done anything with it."

"It doesn't justify ripping people off," Julian retorted. "Or destroying a whole population of wild orchids. ActionTerre is the NGO heading up the action in France. They're based in Paris. I've been in touch with the director, fellow named Jean-Luc Jarry, offering to throw my concerns about the source orchids behind their campaign." He preened a little. "Jarry's asked me to act as their botanical consultant. Informally, of course."

"Right up your street," observed Loulou, picking his teeth.

"They're organizing a public demonstration against Bonisanté in Bordeaux sometime this month, and they want lots of people to show up. We should all go. Lend support."

"No thanks," said Prudence. "I don't have trouble sleeping."

"How do you manage that?" asked Mara, interested.

"Well, I just lie back and close my eyes."

•

Linus Chen and Mama Deng bowed them out.

"You like?" asked Mama Deng anxiously.

"Excellent," said everyone but Julian.

"Too hot," he answered honestly.

Mama Deng looked disappointed. "You want not so hot?"

"Less chilis," suggested Julian kindly. "Christ," he mumbled as he went out the door. "I'll be shitting warheads into next week."

•

The quayside across from the restaurant was busy with a travelling fun fair. There were rides, musicians and jugglers. A man on stilts doffed an enormous top hat to them as they strolled through the crowd toward their cars, the women and Loulou walking ahead, Charlie and Julian lagging behind.

"Maybe it's stress," said Patsy, reverting to Mara's insomnia.

"I'm not stressed," Mara denied.

"Well, something's bothering you. You have that pinched look. Is it Julian?" They had all followed Mara's up-and-down relationship with Julian, Patsy the most intimately because she was the one Mara poured her heart out to online.

"Not at all." Mara fought to keep a telltale edge of defensiveness out of her voice. "Things couldn't be better."

"Of course," soothed Loulou.

"Really?" asked Patsy.

They were approaching a colourful, hunchbacked figure, dressed as Punchinello, or, as the French called him, Polichinelle, strutting about on a little wooden platform. Billed as a *mime automate*, he was executing a jerky dance to old-fashioned hurdy-gurdy music, lifting his arms and legs in a series of stiff wind-up-doll movements. The performance attracted a lot of onlookers, and they also paused to watch. Mara thought it charmingly country-fair-ish, except that Polichinelle's ferociously hooked false nose, attached to his face by an elastic, gave him a somewhat threatening appearance. The music ran down and so did the mime. An appreciative audience tossed money into a cloth hat on the ground. The mime now stood inert on his stage.

"Don't sound so skeptical. For your information—but Julian wants it kept under wraps for now—we're engaged. Unofficially."

"Engaged? *Félicitations*!" exclaimed Loulou, opening his arms to Mara and giving her a kiss on both cheeks.

"My God," said Prudence bluntly. "Julian Wood finally popped the question?"

"No," admitted Mara. "I did." It cost her to own up to it, but there was no prevaricating with these three.

"What brought this on?" Patsy asked.

Mara shrugged. "It was the logical next step." She added, since Patsy's broad freckled face expressed doubt, "We're in no hurry, of course. Anyway, Julian's head's so full of Charlie-frigging-Perry and his orchid right now, he can't think of anything else."

"When has it ever been any other way?" murmured Prudence. "Don't get me wrong, Mara. I adore the man. But why marriage? You two are fine as you are, aren't you?"

"And is it really what you want?" pressed Patsy, turning the tables on Mara.

"Why would I have proposed if it wasn't?"

"Then why can't you sleep?" pursued Patsy and Prudence together.

"Hmm," said Loulou.

A speaker fixed to the side of the mime's stage emitted a wheezing sound, and Polichinelle began another dance, this time to a different tune. The four of them watched the performance until it ended, threw money in the hat, and walked on.

•

Julian and Charlie had stopped near the bumper cars, which seemed to interest Charlie even though he had to shout in order to be heard over the crashing and the amplified music.

"I said, what did Mara mean about the orchid being associated with violent death? I don't mind admitting it really gave me a chill."

"Oh that." Julian pulled the Canadian away from the noise. "It was her sister who took the photo. Twenty-three years ago. But she, um, died. Tragic circumstances. The embroidery was, uh, found by some workmen. On a dead baby. You shouldn't take Mara seriously. She gets a bit emotional about it."

"I see." Charlie's blue eyes were fixed on him. "Julian, are you being entirely transparent with me? Are you sure you really don't know where it grows?"

"Transparent? Oh, absolutely." Julian tried to look as clear as glass. "And no, I don't know where it grows. If I did, I would have found it. You see, my problem is I have no information about *Cypripedium incognitum*'s preferred environment or its pollinators. That's critical to pinpointing habitat. So"—he trolled shamelessly—"it really is too bad Horatio's diary gives no details. Which, quite frankly, I find strange. *Anything* would have been helpful."

If Julian was being sparing with the truth, he was pretty sure that Charlie also was holding something back. It was unthinkable that a dedicated plantsman like Horatio Kneebone would not have included detailed notes on the growing site. What it boiled down to was this: Julian wanted a look at the diary before having to disclose anything himself. And he was pretty sure that Charlie was manoeuvring for the same thing, only the other way around. A man who could consume a Sichuan hot-pot without breaking sweat was no pushover.

"I mean," Julian went on, "the slightest hint . . ." His voice trailed off as an unwelcome sight hove into view: a bulky figure moving toward them through the crowd, Géraud Laval, his *bête noire* where things botanical were concerned. Julian cursed the day he had foolishly told Géraud of *Cypripedium incognitum*'s existence. And now the last thing he wanted was for Géraud to get wind of Charlie or the Kneebone diary.

"Er, half a moment," he muttered to the Canadian. "Wait here. I'll be back." He hurried off.

Géraud spotted Julian and immediately adopted an aggressive posture, bandy legs widespread, arms tensed at his side, like some kind of squat, superannuated gunslinger. His bald head, skirted by tufts of white hair, gleamed in the sun. He liked Julian no better than Julian liked him. The two men came toe to toe in front of the *mime automate*'s stage.

"*Ah, c'est vous*," sneered Géraud. His tone implied that Julian was something the cat had dragged in.

"Always underfoot, aren't you," retorted Julian. His tone suggested that Géraud was something the dog had left. Fluent in French, he could trade insults competently with the likes of Géraud. "Have you been following me?" Géraud had actually had the nerve once to tail Julian on one of his searches.

"*I* follow *you*? You flatter yourself. Never will you go before me in anything, *mon ami*."

"I'm not your friend, and I hear Iris has dumped you again." Julian had not heard anything of the sort, but it was the lowest blow he could think of. Iris Potter, Géraud's live-in partner and an English watercolourist whom Julian liked very much (it was she who had done the artist's sketch of *Cypripedium incognitum* in his book), did periodically walk out on her temperamental paramour whenever his tantrums were past bearing, so the odds favoured Julian's guess. Indeed, he now had the satisfaction of seeing Géraud go purple in the face.

"It's none of your damned onions!"

Julian exhaled with relief as Géraud went stamping off. That had been close. He looked around. Charlie, still standing where Julian had left him, had obviously taken in the exchange with Géraud. Farther ahead, Mara, Loulou, Patsy and Prudence had stopped to watch a juggler.

Then someone spoke in his ear: "Hello, Julian."

He froze in place. The English was heavily accented, the voice husky, seductive, carrying with it hints of a remembered past that sent a shiver through him. Slowly, he turned. There was no one there, except the inert *mime* on the wooden stage.

"Don't tell me you've forgotten."

Julian stared at the grotesque figure before him in shock and disbelief. Slowly, almost obscenely, Polichinelle lifted the false nose and mask away from a face covered in greasepaint.

Julian's jaw dropped and his heart squeezed painfully in his chest.

"My God, it—it's you!"

4

It was midmorning, and the day was promising hot. Charlie, wearing Bermuda shorts and an "I ♥ Ontario" T-shirt, was busy in the kitchen of Julian's cottage. It was the room that offered the best working space, so it was there that he had set up his laptop and printer. Cables snaked across the floor toward the phone jack and electrical outlets. He had spent the last hour organizing files. Now he was sorting a stack of papers into two piles. He took the largest pile, checked it through page by page, squared it off and placed it in a folder. He squared off the remaining pile and slid it into a Ziploc bag, carefully pinching the seal closed and putting this in an even larger Ziploc bag that he also sealed. His actions were controlled, precise. The phone rang. He stood frowning for a moment before deciding to answer it.

"Hello?"

"Do you do pools?" the caller asked in French.

Charlie responded in that language that he did not and that Julian Wood could be contacted at the following number. It was the third such interruption since taking up his tenancy. One had been delivered in person by an irritated individual who said Julian still owed him for a Rototiller, and was he dead or simply not returning phone messages? Charlie disliked the disturbances and hoped they would not continue. If they did, he would have to speak to Julian about them.

He had barely hung up when the four ominous opening

tones to Beethoven's Fifth sounded from the table. He picked up his cellphone.

"*Oui*?" He listened for a moment. "*Non. Rien.*" He continued in French, "Nothing so far, but the hunt is young. It's just a matter of time."

The caller must have had a lot to say, because Charlie was silent again for a much longer time.

At last, he cut in, "What's to negotiate?" Then, impatiently, "I understand you may not like it, but you've brought me into it and you'll have to leave it to me—" He broke off to raise his head, listening.

"Look, someone's at the door. I have to go. Don't call me again. I'll be in contact. When? When I have news."

•

"*Ah, non. C'est pas possible*!"

The ragged hole in the wall gaped before her like a nightmare. Yet Mara knew she was not dreaming, even though she was asleep on her feet. It was late Tuesday afternoon, which, according to her timetable, meant she was in Prats-du-Périgord, stopping by to see how the renovation of the Billons' newly acquired country home was coming. The Billons were a Parisian couple who combined high expectations with a tight purse.

"Who told you to put the window there?" she choked out.

"You did," answered Smokey the Greek calmly. His real name was Aristophanes Serafim, but he went by Smokey because he was never without a Gitane. He spoke French with an accent as dense as a wedge of moussaka.

"Not *this* wall, *that* one, you cretin!" The word was out before she could bite it off.

"We're from Thessalonika," corrected Smokey's younger brother, Theo.

"East wall. It's what you said," Smokey assured her. "Right, Theo?"

"Yeah." Theo nodded solemnly. "Definitely. For sure."

"And is this the east wall?" Mara nearly screamed. "Do you two even know which side the sun comes up?"

"There," both men said promptly, pointing west.

Mara clutched her hair. "Why, oh why, oh why?"

The two brothers stood before her, mallets in hand, like barrel-shaped truants.

"Well, maybe," admitted Smokey, squinting through the hole they had just made, "we got turned around a bit. It's the fault of this house. Should never have been laid out the way it is."

"You two are a double disaster," she fumed. "You have all the finesse of a wrecking ball. Blueprints make no sense to you. You cannot follow instructions, you cannot be trusted—"

"Hey, you shouldn't say those things," said Smokey reproachfully. He touched his chest delicately with two banana-sized nicotine-stained fingers. "We're skilled stonemasons, we are."

Mara groaned loudly. "No, you're not. I tried them. They were all busy. You were what was left."

•

She told the Serafims to go home, to do nothing more until she could oversee them personally, and drove away from the work site in a fog of exhaustion. In the end it was her fault. She never should have hired the brothers. Her own experience told her that. She had worked—disastrously—with them before. Having hired them, she never should have left them alone.

It was her insomnia, she decided. It seemed to have settled in like an unwanted guest, leaving her cranky and out of control. Was it, as Patsy had suggested, down to stress? Mara had to acknowledge that it was strangely coincidental with her and

Julian's engagement. Having won his agreement to move their relationship forward, was she having doubts of her own?

Sunshine danced in the trees, shimmered on the road and hillsides, bloomed with wildflowers in the fields. Unseeing, on automatic pilot, she drove homeward toward the hamlet of Ecoute-la-Pluie. Nestled in its valley, it received her into its leafy embrace. Her house, double-storeyed, steep-roofed and built of honey-coloured limestone, was the last in a line of small holdings, some still working farms. Olivier Rafaillac, the artichoke farmer next door, trucked his produce to market in summer as he had done for decades, and Suzanne Portier's walnut grove across the road yielded annually a rich harvest of nuts that were sold in the ancient nut market in Belvès every fall. Mara parked next to Julian's vehicle and dragged herself into the house.

"Hello?"

Not even the dogs greeted her. It was too much to hope that Julian was off on a job; his van was outside. She worried about him sometimes. New landscaping clients were thin on the ground of late, possibly because he never bothered to call them back, and the ones who retained him—even Prudence—seemed to have less and less for him to do. He did not seem to care, however. Earning a living detracted from orchid hunting.

Wearily, she dumped her things on the kitchen table and wandered out to the studio. It irritated her immensely to find Julian there, crouched in front of her monitor, stabbing at her keyboard. She wished that, in addition to drumming up business, he would buy his own computer.

"I've found an online forum on Chinese orchids," he sang out enthusiastically as she entered. The studio smelled of the apple he was eating, a big red Ariane, noted for its tartness.

"I didn't know you read Chinese." Grumpily, she dropped into a chair.

"I don't. It's international, and everyone writes in English. I posted the scan you made of Horatio's drawing of *Cypripedium incognitum* along with his description, and I'm getting questions from orchid buffs around the world, even experts at Kew Gardens. A lot of people want to know how a Chinese orchid wound up growing wild in France."

"What have you told them?"

"Oh"—he munched juicily—"that it was likely brought back from China by a plant hunter following an expedition into the interior in the 1860s."

"You didn't mention the Kneebone diary or the fact that you have Horatio's three-times-great-grandson living in your cottage?"

"Of course not." He gave her a foxy look. "Don't want to give the game away, do we? There's a lot of interest in *Cypripedium incognitum*. Obviously, I need to manage what I release. But all that's nothing compared to this." He wiped his fingers on his T-shirt and paged down. "A woman named Ms. Hsu—she's a botanist with the Chengdu Institute of Plant Sciences who's doing gene mapping of *Cypripediums*—writes that *C. incognitum* strongly resembles a legendary Chinese orchid called Yong Chun Hua, literally translated, Eternal Youth Flower, which was reputed to have magical powers to restore the sick, elderly and dying to youthful vigour."

"Humph. Sounds like an old wives' tale."

Julian was reading onscreen now. "She says, 'In addition to a strong overall similarity, Yong Chun Hua, like *C. incognitum*, distinguishes itself by the same structural peculiarity. The lower sepals aren't joined to form a *synsepalum* but are clearly separate.' Her English is damned good, wouldn't you say? 'This could be a very important identifier, especially since Yong Chun Hua has never been found in modern times, although it is described, with drawings, in ancient Chinese pharmacopoeia and botanical treatises dating back to the eleventh century.'" He sat back, elated. "I've discovered a bloody living legend, Mara!"

"No," she corrected, "Horatio Kneebone did. He found it first."

"Well, yes, I suppose so," admitted Julian, looking slightly put out.

Mara was puzzled. "You know, there's something I don't get. If the orchid Horatio brought back *was* this legendary Eternal Youth Flower, why wasn't more made of it? You'd have thought his discovery would have been feted all over Europe. And you of all people would have read about it."

"Good question." Julian frowned, shoving his glasses up to the top of his head. "He mustn't have known what he had. And yet"—the frown became a scowl—"the flower itself is spectacular enough that it should have raised a frenzy of interest. Sponsors should have been tripping over themselves wanting to send him back to China. Which makes it even *less* believable that Horatio would *not* have made notes on habitat or location, because he clearly planned a follow-up expedition."

"Instead he ended up in obscurity and hanged himself."

"That, too." Julian studied the floor. "Unless"—now he squinted up at the ceiling—"Horatio really was afraid his diary would fall into the wrong hands and he needed to keep the orchid under wraps in order to manipulate the market."

Mara's eyebrows rose sharply. "How?"

"Simple. You release information on a new discovery to whet people's appetites. Ideally, you make a few plants available which you sell for fabulous sums. That really gets the public's attention. Then you follow up with the master stroke of putting enough plants on auction to ride the tide, making a fortune in the process. It happened with *Cypripedium spicerianum*, you know. At its peak, a single plant was valued at £9,000 in the 1880s, something like $45,000 in U.S. dollars. God only knows what that would be today. That unleashed a race across India to find where it grew and bring back more. But when rival suppliers started shipping back thousands of the things, the price dropped to a shilling a go."

"So you're saying Horatio would have wanted to keep everything a dark secret until he was ready to roll?"

"Exactly, because once the news was out, China would have been crawling with plant hunters following his footsteps, and the market would have been quickly flooded."

At this point, Jazz and Bismuth scratched at the door. Mara rose to open it for them. Jazz, big square body and gaping grin, shouldered his way in first. Bismuth followed, his melancholy jowls and drooping ears tipped with mud. Both dogs trotted over to poke their noses affectionately at the humans. Julian offered the rest of his apple to them. Only Bismuth accepted. Then he flopped down in the middle of the floor to clean himself. Jazz, satisfied with his day, curled up in a corner and went to sleep.

Mara, who was working through another line of thought, said, "You know, it's possible that Horatio never actually found anything."

"Eh?"

"Suppose he merely learned about the orchid from those—what do you call them?—pharmacopoeias? He read and spoke Chinese, didn't he? His annotated sketch could have been taken from them. Which means the only thing he brought back from China was not the plant itself but a drawing!"

"Nonsense." Julian looked indignant. "He must have brought it back. How else could it have been found growing in the wild here? Your sister photographed it. It was also probably the thing locals long ago called Devil's Clog. Then there's the embroidery. That's as botanically detailed a rendering as you could ask for. It had to have been based on a living plant."

Mara shook her head. "First of all, Bedie's photograph is unreliable, as you yourself admit. There's a stain right through the middle of it, which makes it hard to know what you're looking at. And Devil's Clog may be just another old wives' tale. There's no one alive today who can verify such a thing ever existed. As for the embroidery, don't you see that if Horatio *didn't* have a live plant to show potential sponsors, what more logical than for him to have used the drawing as a kind of promotional piece? Your embroidery could have been taken from that."

Julian stared at her aghast. "You're suggesting I've been chasing a phantom? That the embroidery was based on nothing more than Horatio's drawing, which in turn was something he copied from a sodding book?"

"It could explain why he was unsuccessful in attracting sponsors, Julian. Who'd want to lay out money for something he couldn't prove existed?"

Julian sat motionless, his face gone white. "There's only one thing to do. I've got to get my hands on that damned diary."

"Has Charlie changed his mind about letting you see it?"

"No. I talked to him about it again just yesterday. He's sticking to me delivering first on where I think *Cypripedium incognitum* grows."

"Then give the man what he wants."

"But what guarantee do I have that he'll play fair?" Julian pushed away from the desk and began to pace the studio.

The phone rang. Mara reached for it. "*Oui, allo*?"

"Mara?"

She recognized the accent of Géraud's live-in partner, Iris Potter. A comfortable little person with greying fly-away hair and periwinkle eyes, her voice was surprisingly cheerful, considering the news she had to impart. "I'm calling because Géraud and I have just had the most frightful row."

Mara almost said, *Again*? Instead, she said, "I'm so sorry, Iris."

"Don't be, ducks. You know how impossible he is. He intimates it's something to do with Julian. So is he there? I need to speak to him."

"For you." Mara handed the receiver to Julian. "It's Iris. She's had a fight with Géraud. Because of you."

"Hello, Iris?" Julian answered cautiously. "Well, yes, I ran into him in Bergerac, and, er, we did exchange the odd word." He listened for a long time, his expression exchanging caution for malicious pleasure. "You did? How'd he take it? Ha, ha! Well done, you. Absolutely. Okay, will do. And you stick to your guns, love. *À bientôt.*" He informed Mara as he hung up, "She's moving out and is staying with friends in Quercy. And she's given him an ultimatum: mend his temper or she's not coming back. Serves the bugger right." Iris's call had cheered him up to no end.

The phone rang again. Mara swept up the receiver, half expecting it to be Géraud, full of bluster, with his side of the story. Iris and Géraud were unabashedly public about their conjugal crises.

"*Est-ce que Julian est là*?" The voice, low and husky, was not Géraud's.

"For you again." Mara handed over the receiver resentfully. "You know, you really should get a cellphone. That way people won't have to keep calling you on my line."

"*Oui*?" Julian spoke into the mouthpiece.

A moment later she saw his face grow wooden.

"*Quoi*?" Then he said, "*Non.*" And again, "*Non.*" Then, hoarsely, "*Pas question*!"

What, she wondered as she watched him turn his back to her, *was out of the question*? A difficult client? He had a few of those. She watched him scribble something on the back of a scrap of paper and slam the receiver down.

"Who was that?" she asked as he stuffed the paper in his pocket. He looked unaccountably rattled.

"Problem," he muttered. "Nothing to worry about."

But later, when she was preparing dinner, he came into the kitchen and stood about aimlessly for a few minutes, focus inward, dark as a thundercloud.

Abruptly he said, "I have to go out."

"Out? Where? What about dinner?"

"Sod dinner," he said, and left almost at a run.

5

Le Verger, a town of 437 souls, was situated some forty minutes' drive away. Julian knew it because he sometimes bought morels in season from the woman who ran the gift shop on the main street. Her son collected them after a spring rain, leaving the dark, reticulated mushrooms in a basket outside the butcher's next door. The basket emptied fast—fresh morels were delicious fried in butter—and customers were quick to grab what there was. Everyone knew that you first took your morels to the butcher's to be weighed, then walked back to the gift shop to pay on the honour system.

However, he was unfamiliar with the network of small lanes that honeycombed Le Verger. It took him a while to find rue de l'Angle, which proved to be little more than an alleyway running behind the church. It was too narrow for parking, so he had to leave his van around the corner and walk in. Number 17 *bis* was at the very end.

He knocked, aware that the flaking paint of the door came away on his knuckles. Above a jumble of tiled rooftops, a violent sunset stained the sky.

A muffled voice spoke through the door. "*Qui est là?*"

"*C'est moi, Julian.*"

The door opened, framing a woman against a dingy, poorly lit interior. She was barefoot and wore a rumpled silk kimono that hung loose at the top. Behind her, dismantled and folded down into a handcart on wheels, was the *mime automate* stage.

"That was fast," drawled the woman in deep-throated French.

A slow smile widened her mouth. Stripped of the padding and greasepaint, her face and body were no longer that of Polichinelle but of someone Julian had not seen for almost thirty years.

"*Mais entre, alors, entre*!" She made a show of drawing the lapels of the kimono together as she beckoned him in.

Julian remained rooted to the doorstep. His expression, his very posture declared that he was there against his will, that he had no intention of engaging, that he knew the person standing before him was nothing but bad news.

"Okay, Véronique," he said angrily. "I'm here. What the hell do you want?"

"Oh, *cheri*," laughed Véronique with a gaiety that did not ring true. "What a way to greet your long-lost wife!"

•

She was obviously down-at-heel, otherwise why would she be living in a miserable bed-sitter at the back of a rundown house in a seedy part of town? Once beautiful, she still retained remnants of her good looks and a certain sexual allure that time had cheapened but not entirely eroded. It was evident in the way she held herself—she was a tall woman with a good figure still—in the way she tossed her head. Her hair, he noticed, naturally honey-coloured, was bleached platinum and looked as dry as straw.

"What do I want? Well, let me see. Quite a few things, as a matter of fact." Her gesture took in her surroundings. "Better to talk inside. The neighbours."

She moved back, pulling him in by the arm. Unwillingly he took a few steps forward. Now that he could see her better in the light of a dangling ceiling bulb he realized that she had aged badly, presenting a face that was hardened, drawn and sharply opportunistic. Her eyes, of a cornflower blue he had once admired, were dull, like water-worn glass. The air was heavy with stale cigarette smoke.

He jerked free. "This is as far as I go."

"*Oh là*! You needn't be rude. We haven't seen each other for such a time. I thought a little celebratory drink?"

"You and I have nothing to celebrate. Get on with it."

Véronique tried a pout. "All right. I'll cut it short. I want to come back. I want us to be together again."

Julian started, then gave a harsh laugh, almost like the bark of a dog. "Not a chance. You walked out on me, remember? We were finished a long time ago."

"Were we? But you never cut the tie, did you." She moved very close to him, letting the kimono fall loose again. Her musky perfume filled his nostrils. "Think of the good times we had, Julian. Admit it. You've carried a torch for me all these years. You couldn't even bring yourself to divorce me."

He shook his head vigorously, as if to drive away her scent. "You're delusional. If I didn't file for divorce, as I bloody well should have done, it was from sheer inertia. The truth is, I couldn't be bothered."

Véronique stiffened. For a moment she studied him. "You've changed," she said musingly.

"Damned right I have."

"*Bon*"—now she was all business—"if you won't take me back, you'll have to buy me off."

"Why the hell should I buy you off?"

"The fact is, I'm broke. I need to get away. I need a change of scenery. And because your *petite amie*, the one you plan to marry—Mara her name is, I think?—might take it badly when she learns that you're still legally attached."

He stared at her in mute astonishment.

She laughed harshly. "You see, I know all about your plans. Give me 10,000 euros and you'll never hear from me again. It's a bargain. You can divorce me, no contest, no fuss, and get on with your life, *bonne chance* to the two of you. Otherwise—"

"Ten thousand!" he exploded.

"Otherwise, I'll blow your wedding and your fiancée out of the water." She raised her chin. "I promise you, Julian, if I don't get my money, I'll make your life impossible. I'll get a sharp lawyer. I'll create a story that will drag you across the front page of every newspaper in the region. And I'll make sure sweet Mara never speaks to you again."

Julian squared up to her furiously. "You're raving. I was glad to be rid of you then, and I intend to stay rid of you now. I'm not going to let you mess me around again. Yes, I'll damned well divorce you, and don't even think about putting obstacles in my way because you don't have a leg to stand on. I'm warning you, Véronique. Stay away from me. And stay away from Mara. You try anything"—he gestured violently—"I'll wring your scrawny neck!"

Seething, he swung about and strode out the door. Moments later he was speeding off into the night. Kilometres down the road, he realized that he had no idea where he was going. He pulled off onto the verge, cut the engine and sat staring blindly into the settling darkness, trying to get his brain and his breathing under control. Véronique had rocked him to the core and left him feeling acutely vulnerable. He was also experiencing the beginnings of a stress headache. Thumpers, he called them, for they did just that, thumped his skull with the skill of a mad drummer. The van suddenly felt like a cage. He jumped out and walked, he cared not where, boots ringing on stony ground.

Not that he had any feelings left for Véronique, but he was surprised at how much anger still remained that time had scarred over but not healed. For a moment he allowed himself to relive the bitter sense of betrayal he had experienced each time he learned of her many affairs. In the end, she had run off with a second-string rugby player from Bordeaux—Bordeaux, for Chrissake! She really had no taste. That time she had stayed gone. He remembered his growing sense of relief and liberation as months, then years passed without word from her. She had simply faded from his life. If Julian had never bothered to formalize the break it was because he had always assumed Véronique would make the first move. At some point he had heard through a mutual friend that the rugby player had taken over the family's abattoir business and that she had moved with him to Les Eyzies; it gave him a sour satisfaction to think of her coupled to a dealer in dead meat. Also, never had he expected to be looking at matrimony again.

Nor would he be if Mara had not pushed it. Even now, he half believed it would never happen, that Mara in the end would be satisfied, as he was, to leave things as they were. He and she together, her house or his, he didn't really care, happy, untroubled by the yoke of marriage.

Now he pictured Mara's stupefaction when she learned that he was still tied by the nose like a bullock. Forget stupefaction—her blazing anger when she realized that he had kept his secret from her all this time, that he had let her go on about a marriage that, as things stood, was legally impossible. Mara had often criticized him for drifting with the current, for failing to be proactive, and in this case she was bang on. He had landed himself in a mess by default because he'd done bugger all, because he'd been too tired—or too lazy?—to cut himself free legally, because there was a side to him that would rather avoid than confront. Never had he imagined that Véronique would turn up suddenly like a rain squall on a sunny day, like an ugly blot on the pleasant landscape of his life. And he did not doubt that she was desperate and determined enough to carry out her threat if she didn't get her money. So how was he to come up with 10,000 euros?

What he needed was to buy time. Or somehow head Véronique off. Maybe he could talk her down, placate her with a smaller sum. Then he realized he was dreaming. In twenty-nine years Véronique could have found him any time she wanted by simply looking in the phone book or calling directory assistance. He had never gone into hiding. So why now, after so long? There could be only one reason: Véronique was well and truly down on her luck. The slaughterhouse owner—or maybe a string of them—had dumped her, and she was frantic to leech onto any source available. Once he started down that road with her, she'd bleed him white. Rationally, he doubted that even a sharp lawyer could mount much of a case against him. Pessimistically, he assumed the worst. Damn Véronique. Damn her! And damn his rotten luck. As he stormed back to his van, he found himself wishing she were dead.

•

Véronique lay on her bed, smoking. The kimono had come open, exposing pale, creased flesh. As she brought the cigarette to and away from her lips, her hand in the light of the bedside lamp cast a shadow that shrank and swelled grotesquely upon the wall.

All things considered, she did not think her meeting with Julian had gone badly. She had predicted he would kick at first, but she knew him of old. In the end he would cave in rather than fight. That was the trouble with him. Soft, with the backbone of a larva. Maybe, she thought with a surge of nostalgia, things might have been different if he'd had a little more *cran*. She didn't mind a man who pushed her around a bit. It showed he really cared. Her rugby player, for example. He had *cran*. Until he took over his father's business. After that he had settled into being the *petit bourgeois* he really was, counting his small change, coming home with the smell of animal fat on his hands, and in the end wanting her gone so he could marry the daughter of the local mayor. She shifted position. Worn bedsprings complained with the movement.

There was a knock on the door. She killed the cigarette in an ashtray, swung her legs over the side of the bed—the springs sang out stridently—retied her kimono and padded barefoot across the cracked linoleum floor.

"*Qui est-ce?*"

"César."

She opened the door. Her landlord, a rat of a man with long greasy strands of hair plastered over an unhealthy looking scalp, stood on the stoop.

"*Toi*," she said dismissively. "What do you want?"

His eyes roamed the deep V of her kimono, dropped to her bare legs. "I thought you wanted *me*." His tone was suggestive.

"Oh, that." She ignored his innuendo. "It's this door."

His eyes rose again to her cleavage. "What's wrong with it?"

"It doesn't lock properly, that's what's wrong with it. I want you to install a decent lock."

César Fargéas stepped inside and shut the door. He turned the lock and tested it.

"Seems all right to me."

"It's not all right. It's flimsy. Anyone could break in here. I'm a woman living alone, don't forget."

He snickered.

"What's that supposed to mean?" Véronique snapped.

César shrugged. He opened the door and worked the lock again, trying the handle from either side.

"It'd cost to put in something new. Good hardware's not cheap, you know. I'd have to pass the cost on to you. Your rent hardly covers the expense of having you here. Electricity, water, taxes. And then there's my labour."

"Hah!" Véronique's snort of derision told him what she thought of his labour.

"Of course"—César rubbed the back of his neck, studying the problem—"I could persuade the wife it was a necessary upgrade." He let this dangle.

Véronique tipped her head back and stared at him narrowly. "What's the if?"

"Well, if you were nice to me."

Véronique said in a low voice, "You *pauvre con*. And if I told the wife about your little games? If I told her you're always sniffing around my skirts?" She gave him a shove that propelled him backwards through the open door. "You get that new lock installed—*putain*!—and maybe, just maybe, I won't say anything to the fire dragon."

"You're a real bitch, you know that?" César cried out angrily. "You can sing for your lock."

Véronique, about to slam the door, pulled it open again.

"You think?" She turned persuasive. "Look, I'm not asking much. Just a little security. And your wife doesn't have to know a thing about what you get up to if I don't tell her. So is it a deal?"

"*Va au diable*!" snarled César.

"She'll eat you alive, you know," Véronique jeered as he stamped away.

•

"*Merde*!"

Véronique pushed the door to, securing the unsatisfactory lock, and turned back into the room. She wasn't joking. The thing really was a piece of shit. She lit another cigarette and sat down on the sagging bed, staring about her. *Mon Dieu*, what had things come to? Her glance took in an armoire the warped doors of which did not close, a rickety table covered with a torn oilcloth, a wobbly chair. The mime stage was the sturdiest item in the room. Her only source of running water was a tap that dripped into a stained ceramic sink. A food-encrusted hot plate stood on a chipped counter. The toilet, which smelled, was behind a curtained alcove at the back of the room. When flushed it gargled like an underground sewer in full spate.

"*Merde*," she said again, her body slumping in an attitude of defeat.

There was a soft knock on the door.

Véronique looked up. She rose, smoothing her hair and adjusting the fall of her kimono.

"*Oui*?"

She opened the door.

"Ah." Her voice took on new life. "It's you. Had a change of heart, did you?"

6

Julian stared moodily into the smoking pan. Two slabs of organ meat, topped with onions, were sizzling in butter. It was his turn to cook that night, and what he was preparing, curling up unpleasantly at the edges and starting to smoke, reminded him darkly of the mess he was in. Liver was not his favourite food, but it was something he had grown up with, and he cooked it partly out of habit, partly because he knew how. His repertoire, like Mara's, was limited. Now, as he lifted the liver onto plates, he shuddered at the thought of eating it.

•

Mara looked at her portion, cooked to a toughness.

"Pour me more wine, will you?" Surreptitiously she sliced off two large pieces that she slipped to the dogs, hovering hopefully. She did not like liver either. They were eating on the terrace. The air was warm, the sun lingering vividly above the horizon. Birds in the cherry tree overhanging the terrace squabbled noisily.

"Julian? Everything all right?"

"What?" He pushed food about on his plate.

"I said, are you all right?"

"Fine."

He did not look fine. He had been moody and tense, positively jumpy, since the phone call the evening before. The problem that had come up obviously had not gone away.

"Loulou called," she said. "He wanted to know if we're on this week." For several years now they had met their ex-cop friend most

Fridays for dinner at the Chez Nous Bistro. "He wasn't sure because he thought we might have other plans with Patsy and Prudence. I told him we're all on. I assume you want to include Charlie?"

Julian returned with an effort from an interior place. "What about Charlie?"

"Dinner Friday. I thought it would be a chance to introduce him to Chez Nous and Paul and Mado."

Chez Nous, run by other good friends Paul and Mado Brieux, served some of the best food in the Dordogne. Paul, despite having hands the size of hams, had a marvellously light touch with pastry; Mado's sauces were inspired. And the food was always fresh, bought from local growers and producers who still did things the old time-consuming way, with loving stubbornness.

"Who knows? Maybe Mado's cooking will sweeten him up enough for him to let you have a peek at Horatio's diary."

"I doubt it." Julian relapsed into gloomy silence.

After dinner he proposed a walk. Mara would have preferred a hot bath and bed. Following another mostly wakeful night, she had weathered another trying day with the Serafim brothers, and sleep was what she most craved. However, she slipped on a sweater and whistled for Jazz and Bismuth.

Beyond the house the unpaved road running through the hamlet dwindled to a narrow track leading up a forested slope. Here the dogs vanished into the undergrowth. The path was steep and rocky. Deer and wild boar lived in the shadows of the trees. Few people but themselves, mushroom gatherers and hunters came this way.

At the top of the rise they stopped. Below them, wooded hills and valleys fell away in zones of light and shadow. The dying sun held its own momentarily in a brilliant conflagration.

"Sit down." Julian pointed to a fallen tree, a century elm that had gone down in a storm a couple of years ago. "I want to talk to you."

"Oh?" Mara peered at him anxiously. Julian rarely said things like, *I want to talk to you.*

She hiked herself up on the massive trunk. He did not join her. Instead, he paced.

"I'm waiting, Julian."

He turned to face her squarely. "It's like this, Mara. I've, ah, run into a problem."

"What problem?"

"Véronique."

"Véronique?" She wrinkled her forehead. "Are you talking about your ex?"

"Yes. She was the Polichinelle at the fair in Bergerac."

"You mean the mime?"

"Needless to say, I didn't recognize her."

"Well, no, you wouldn't have. Not with a false nose and a hump on her back."

Julian said grimly, "But she knew *me*. And she heard you talking about our engagement."

Mara took this in, turning the implications over in her head. "Was that Véronique who called last night?"

He nodded.

Mara now understood why he had been upset, why he had left so abruptly. She, too, would be shaken if her ex, Hal of the Bottle, Hal of the Monumental Ego, unexpectedly resurfaced. She couldn't remember the last time she had thought of him. Briefly she wondered if he had managed by now to drink himself to death.

Mara said, "What did she want?"

Half of Julian's face was illuminated by the dying sun, the other half was in shadow. It made him seem as if he were gazing off in different directions. He was silent for a long moment before saying, "I have something to confess."

Then he told her.

He watched her struggling to take it in. Her eyes expressed puzzlement, disbelief and hurt. "All this time married, and you never told me?"

He gestured ineffectually, knowing that she would cry, hoping that she wouldn't. "It never seemed relevant."

"Not relevant?" she echoed faintly.

"I mean, I didn't see how it could affect our relationship. It—it was always just a technicality."

"Bigamy isn't just a technicality!"

"Well, yes, there's that. But to be honest, I wasn't sure you were really serious. About the marriage thing." It was his only defence.

"Not serious?" Her voice rose. "About the marriage thing? Julian, I've told everyone. My parents are asking about a date, Patsy wants it to be before she goes back to New York, Prudence has offered her house for the reception, and the Brieuxs are handling the catering. And all this time you've said *nothing*? Or is it that *you* weren't serious? That you hoped if you dragged things out long enough I'd eventually forget the idea and things would settle back to what they were?"

"Good God, no!" he burst out. "That's not how it was. All right, fair enough, in the early days marriage was the last thing on my mind. Yours, too, probably. But things have changed."

"Yes. Véronique has come wriggling out of the woodwork." Her skepticism was as weighty as a stone, her anger even heavier. She slid off the tree trunk. "I've always known you were absent-minded, Julian. Eccentric, obsessed even, about your damned orchids, but I never thought you were deceitful."

The dreaded tears came. He tried to hold her. She pulled loose.

"Please, Mara. Believe me—"

She turned on him in fury. "Believe you? How am I supposed to believe you? How can I believe anything you say ever again?" She stalked away.

He followed her back to the house in silence.

A car was parked in the driveway. As they approached, the doors opened simultaneously on both sides and two figures, one tall and thin, the other short and stocky, emerged. Startled, Julian realized that the vehicle was a police *break* and the figures were in uniform.

"What the hell do the gendarmes want?" he muttered.

"Monsieur Wood? Madame Dunn?" the tall gendarme called out. They recognized him as Laurent Naudet, the grandnephew of their friend Loulou and an up-and-coming young sergeant with the Brames Gendarmerie.

"You remember my partner, Albert Batailler?" Laurent gestured at his companion. They all shook hands. Laurent's arms, as usual, were too long for the standard-issue navy blue *pull* he wore. "Look," he said, "maybe we should go inside?"

Once in the house, the gendarmes exchanged significant looks. Albert took the lead. "Monsieur Wood, are you related to Madame Véronique Rignon?"

Julian felt his throat constricting. "*Oui*," he choked out. "Husband. Estranged. Many years. Look, what's this about?"

"Maybe you should sit down," suggested Laurent in a kindly tone.

Both Mara and Julian backed onto an art deco sofa that stood in the middle of the front room. The gendarmes remained standing.

"I'm afraid we have some bad news for you," said Laurent. He paused to swallow, his Adam's apple bobbing like a captive ping-pong ball. "Your wife is dead. I'm very sorry."

"Dead!" Julian stared at the officers. "*Mon Dieu*! What happened? Heart attack? Accident?"

Albert said quickly, "Sorry, we can't disclose the details. However, there's evidence of foul play. Her body was found in her apartment this morning by her landlady."

Julian sat speechless, a hammering in his head threatening another Thumper.

It was Mara who gasped, "Foul play! Are you saying it was murder?"

Albert replied uninformatively, "It was on the eight o'clock news."

"We didn't watch it," Julian muttered numbly. At eight o'clock he had been coming clean to Mara about his past. "How did you track me down?" Too late he realized the question made him sound like a man on the run.

Albert answered literally, "We went to your address in Grissac first and were directed here by someone who said he was your tenant."

But Laurent, understanding the question, said, "Papers among your wife's effects identified you as her husband." He coughed, looking uncomfortable, and stood up very straight. "I'm afraid I have to ask you this, *monsieur*: where were you between nine and midnight last night?"

Julian opened his mouth. No sound came out.

In the desperate silence that followed, Mara stepped forward.

"Here," she declared in a low voice. "With me. The whole evening and night. He never left the house."

7

Julian's mouth kept opening and closing and still no sound emerged. At last he croaked, "What—?" but Mara let him go no further.

"We were together all evening," she said staunchly. "We had dinner around seven, we watched television. There wasn't much good on, just those idiotic talk shows, so we read for awhile and went to bed."

Albert stepped forward. "And yourself, Madame Dunn? You didn't leave the house at any time?"

"No."

"Can anyone else corroborate this?"

"Why would they need to?" Mara, aware that her voice had gone shrill, added, "Look, why are you asking these questions?"

The stocky gendarme ignored her. "Monsieur Wood, when was the last time you saw your wife?"

Quickly, Mara answered for him. "On Sunday. At the fair in Bergerac."

Surprised, Albert asked Julian, "You were at the fair in Bergerac with your estranged wife?"

Julian blinked, as if coming out of a trance.

"What? No. Of course not. I mean, it was a chance meeting. She was one of the entertainers. She approached me. Well, not exactly approached. Made herself known. I didn't even recognize her. She"—he trailed off lamely—"she was disguised as Polichinelle. We spoke only briefly."

"I was there. I can vouch for everything he says," Mara lied again. It was only a half lie.

Albert pushed his kepi back on his head. "Okay. Just so we have this straight, you last saw your wife at the fair in Bergerac on Sunday, where she was a Polichinelle? And last night neither you nor Madame Dunn left the house?"

"Correct," said Mara.

"Right," croaked Julian.

Albert and Laurent swapped looks.

"I guess that's all for now," said Albert.

"Sorry about the bad news," said Laurent.

The two gendarmes left, but this time they did not shake hands.

•

After Laurent and Albert had gone, Julian turned to Mara in bewilderment. "Why did you do it? Why tell them that pack of lies?"

"For heaven's sake, Julian. Don't you know the husband is always the first to be suspected? If you had told them the truth, that Véronique had called here, that you had gone to see her, that she'd tried to blackmail you, they'd have arrested you on the spot."

"Maybe you're right, but, Christ, Mara, you've probably dumped me in even deeper water."

"I was only trying to help. So much for gratitude." She glared at him, and then said grudgingly, "You may be an untruthful bastard, but I'd like to believe you're not a murderer." She turned away. "I'm exhausted, and this has been a positively god-awful end to a bad day. So, if you don't mind, I'll sleep by myself tonight. If I can get any sleep, that is." She marched out of the room and came back with a pillow and a blanket that she tossed on the sofa. "Yours," she said unnecessarily, and stamped off into the bedroom and slammed the door.

•

The art deco sofa was hard and too short for Julian. He lay curled in a fetal position, sorting through a mix of emotions. Gratitude. Mara, despite everything, had stuck by him. Fear. He was deeply afraid of the case the police could build against him. Mara was right. The husband was always the first to be suspected. And he *had* been there. It would take so little to prove it, to bring Mara's alibi crashing down around his head. Had he touched anything while he had been in Véronique's bed-sit? Dropped a hair? They did all kinds of things with DNA nowadays. Then there was guilt. It was all his fault. He had landed himself—both of them—well and truly in it.

He turned over on his other side, and then on to his back. Somewhere in the darkness Bismuth whimpered in his sleep. Also shut out of the bedroom, the dog had no choice but to bunk in the living room with his master.

Julian groaned. Mara's facility for fabrication absolutely amazed him. He hoped he could remember the story she had concocted. The gendarmes would be back, would work on him until they tripped him up. He was certain Laurent and Albert had sensed that something had not rung true. Mara may have bought him a temporary reprieve, but what she had really done was to dig a yawning pit into which he would inevitably tumble, out of which he would be unable to crawl.

In the middle of the night, Mara woke him. Groggily, he moved over to make space for her on the awful sofa.

"Can't sleep?" he murmured.

"Did you kill her?" she asked, digging her elbow into his side as she pulled the blanket over her and off him.

Julian raised his head. "No! I swear to you, Mara, I never touched her!"

"The gendarmes asked about the time between nine and midnight. You left here around a quarter to eight."

"If you say so. I don't remember. That means I must have got to Véronique's around eight thirty. I barely went in, and I stayed no more than five minutes. As I said, she demanded money. I refused. She threatened to tell you and to create all kinds of misery for me. I warned her not to try anything, and I left. I'm sure I was gone well before nine."

"But you didn't get back here until after eleven. I was awake when you came in. If you didn't stay, what were you doing all that time?"

"Stewing. I drove around and parked somewhere trying to figure out what the hell to do, how to break it to you. Then I drove around some more. I'm telling you the truth. You do believe me?"

She made no answer.

Tentatively, he put his arm around her. Her body was stiff, unyielding.

"Look, I'm really sorry." He stroked her shoulder. "I know I should have told you from the start I was still married, if you could even call it that. But I didn't, and as time went by—well, it just got harder."

"It generally does when you're living a lie." She sighed and let herself roll slightly into him.

He was silent for a long moment. Then he drew her closer. "Can you forgive me?"

She spoke into his chest. "I'll think about it."

But she stayed the rest of the night with him on the sofa.

8

The murder covered the front page of Thursday's *Sud Ouest*. The body of Véronique Rignon, forty-nine years of age, resident of Le Verger, had been discovered the day before by her landlady, Madame Célestine Fargéas.

"I went to collect the rent," Madame Fargéas was quoted as saying. "She was behind as usual. But it was a shock, I can tell you, finding her like that in the middle of the floor, her things scattered all over the place." The landlady claimed to know little about her tenant except that Véronique had earned her living as a street performer.

The cause of death was blunt-force trauma to the back of the head by some kind of heavy round-edged object, possibly a wine bottle. The first blow had stunned her; the second had killed her. However, no wine had been found in her stomach, and no bottle had been found on the premises. The flat had been ransacked, suggesting that the crime might have been a burglary gone wrong. The perpetrator had simply taken the murder weapon away with him.

"Burglary!" Julian declared. He sat hunched over the newspaper at the kitchen table. "Now that's more like it." A moment later, he groaned. "However, it says here the gendarmes are questioning all known associates, including her estranged husband, me, whom they identify by name. Well, that's my reputation gone."

Mara looked across at him over the rim of her coffee cup and said nothing.

There was a knock on the front door. She went to answer it.

"Oh." She stepped back with a sense of what was coming.

This time it was not Laurent and Albert on the stoop but their boss, Adjudant-chef Jacques Compagnon. With him was a female gendarme whom Mara did not know.

"Madame Dunn," said Compagnon. His acned skin looked redder than usual in the morning light, and his pale protuberant eyes fixed her warily. He knew Mara and Julian from times past, and if asked, the adjudant-chef would have said the two always spelled complications. "This is Agent Lucie Sauret. May we come in?"

Mara stepped aside to admit them. Behind her, Julian's chair grated harshly over the kitchen tiles. For a mad moment Mara thought he was going to cut and run. However, he came forward to join her in the vestibule.

"I suppose," he said in a doomed voice, "you want to ask me more questions."

"It's just a matter of going through your statements one more time," Sauret said brightly. She was young and pretty and efficient looking, pen and notebook at the ready. The *bon* cop, Mara decided.

Compagnon did the questioning. "Monsieur Wood, in your statement to agents Naudet and Batailler, you said you last *saw* your wife at the Bergerac fair on Sunday. I'm now going to ask you when was the last time you had *any form of contact* with her?"

"What?" mumbled Julian stupidly.

"You were cutting the truth a bit fine, weren't you? Because, we now know she telephoned this number at around six thirty on Tuesday evening. The call lasted one minute and twelve seconds—"

"Actually, I took the call," Mara cut in. "I'm sorry. I should have mentioned it. It just slipped my mind."

"Slipped your mind, did it?" The adjudant-chef glared at her, then turned to Julian. "You spoke with the deceased?"

"Well, yes, but hardly," Julian gabbled.

"What did you talk about?"

He decided to stick as close to the truth as possible. "She wanted to borrow money. I said no. Then I hung up. It wasn't what you'd call a conversation."

"I see." Compagnon sounded mightily unconvinced. "She wanted money. You said no. And that was that?"

"Yes. That was that."

Compagnon's eyes shifted to Mara. "Madame Dunn, you said Monsieur Wood was with you all Tuesday evening? Do you stick to that? You're quite sure neither of you left this house at any time, say, to run a little errand that might also have slipped your mind?"

"Absolutely." Mulishly, Mara stuck out her chin.

"And you, Monsieur Wood, you hold to this?"

"Well, I—yes." Julian had an awful feeling that the adjudant-chef was measuring the rope with which he planned to hang him.

"Hmm." Compagnon's smile was not nice. "That's very interesting. *Very* interesting." He seemed to swell up in aggressive anticipation of what he was about to say. "Because we questioned your neighbours, and one of them, a Monsieur Boyer, claims he saw a light-coloured van very like yours go past his house on its way out of the hamlet at a little before eight on Tuesday evening. This is a dead-end road. How many light-coloured vans do you think go up and down this lane at that time of night?"

Julian said nothing.

Mara's stomach began a downward slide. Nevertheless, she rallied a weak defence. "Monsieur Boyer was mistaken. I told you, Julian was here with me all night. Neither of us left the house."

Compagnon drew himself up to his full, considerable height. "Monsieur Wood, I must ask you to accompany us to the gendarmerie for further questioning. Purely for elimination purposes, you understand. I assure you"—the bad cop's smile was now a ghastly grin—"your cooperation will be for the best. You'll have nothing to worry about as long as you're telling the truth."

Mara sat, head in hands, elbows propped on the kitchen table. Bismuth and Jazz, sensing her distress, moved in to nose her. The phone rang. She ignored it. The dogs lay down at her feet.

The gendarmes had marched Julian out of the house between them. All of the neighbours—those damned Boyers especially—had come outside to watch the police car with Julian in it drive past. They had each been interviewed by the police, and every one of them had undoubtedly drawn the worst conclusions. She imagined the wagging of tongues. Tomorrow they would read that Julian had been detained, questioned and formally charged with the murder of his wife.

"His wife." She spat the words out. Julian had sworn he had left Véronique's flat before nine. But he had not returned until after eleven. Was he lying? Again? She gazed hopelessly into her mug of coffee, gone cold.

"The bastard!" She flung the mug across the room. It bounced off the wall and hit the floor, shattering in a spectacular spray of liquid that made the dogs scramble for safety.

The phone rang. The neighbours, wanting to experience every frisson the awful situation had to offer. Again she ignored it. It went silent for a moment before starting up anew. She let it ring itself out. Ten minutes later, it sounded again. This time she snatched up the receiver and yelled furiously, "Leave me alone!"

"It's me—Loulou," said the normally cheerful ex-policeman, not sounding cheerful at all. "I just heard."

Mara burst into tears.

Loulou did what he could to comfort her. "*Tiens, petite. Calmes-toi.*" After she had subsided, he said, "I simply can't believe it of Julian."

Mara hiccuped. "That awful Adjudant-chef Compagnon can. He's convinced he has his man. It's significant he came himself today and didn't send Laurent and Albert."

"*Non, non et non*!" Loulou's negative was so vigorous that Mara could almost see his cheeks flapping. "I'm not talking about the murder. Of course he didn't do it. Julian's not the violent type. I mean, I can't believe Julian has been married all this time without telling you. It comes as a shock."

"How do you think it hit *me*?"

"*Ah, ça, alors*! On the other hand," Loulou pointed out, "look on the bright side. He's now a widower. As to his being detained, Compagnon's simply following routine procedures. You'll see. He'll be released in no time."

"No, he won't." Then she told him, with many starts and stops, about her false alibi and the eyewitness to Julian's departure from the hamlet.

Loulou was silent for a long moment. Then he exclaimed, "*Oh là là!*" After another pause he said severely, "You realize you've complicated matters badly? In a case like this, the gendarmes always favour *le crime passionnel*, which naturally implicates a lover or a husband, and your lies make Julian appear guilty even though we know he's nothing of the sort. And then it involves you. Did the two of you plan it—?"

"Of course not!" screeched Mara.

"Or are you simply an accessory after the fact?"

"Loulou, this is not helping."

"But that's the way Compagnon will see it."

"Oh God. Does he have to know?"

"Hmm, hmm, hmm."

Mara heard him tapping his front teeth with a fingernail.

"*Eh bien, petite*. Leave it with Uncle Loulou. At least I can find out where things are at for you."

"You'll ask Laurent?" Mara's hopes lifted slightly off rock bottom at the thought of the tall sympathetic gendarme.

"Laurent's a good lad," responded Loulou. "Smart. Discreet. But under the circumstances, I think I'll go straight to Compagnon himself. He owes Julian. Both of you. Adjudant-chef Compagnon would still be a simple adjudant and a few criminals short if it hadn't been for you two."

"He doesn't like us," Mara said pessimistically. "And anyway, he's not going to subvert the course of justice for Julian."

"Who's talking about subversion?" rejoined Loulou with spirit. "No one with a gram of sense would cast Julian as a killer."

But her hopes sank like a cement block when Loulou added, "All the same, I hope he has a good defence lawyer."

The next phone call was from Prudence and Patsy.

"We heard," said Prudence. "There's no other Julian Wood, is there? Oh Lord, that's what we were afraid of."

"You okay, kid?" asked Patsy on the extension. "Just say so if you want us there."

"Thanks," said Mara, truly grateful. "But for the moment, I really need to be alone."

"I hope you're not thinking of doing anything silly," Patsy broke in sharply.

Prudence said, "Of course she isn't."

"Look, she's already sleep-deprived. Something like this is enough to drive anyone over the edge."

"This is all Julian's fault," said Prudence.

"Because his ex-wife got herself killed?" Patsy sounded indignant.

"Not his ex-wife. That's the problem."

Mara broke into a conversation that was running away without her. "Please save your angst for Julian, not me. He could wind up charged with murder."

"Gee!" exclaimed Prudence, deeply impressed, at the same time that Patsy cried, "Holy shit! You don't mean they've arrested him?"

"As good as. He's been placed under *garde à vue*, which gives the gendarmes plenty of time to come up with a charge. They'll find a witness who saw someone resembling him leaving Véronique's place, and he or she will pick Julian out of a lineup, and it will be game over."

"But why would a witness finger Julian leaving Véronique's place?" asked Patsy.

"I hope you impressed upon the cops that he was home with you," said Prudence.

Mara took a deep breath. "Of course. Where else would he have been?"

•

Mara was on her knees, cleaning up the mess she had made with the coffee cup, when Jazz gave a sharp *gruff*. She heard a *rat-tat* at the front door.

"Nothing. I know nothing." Pushing herself to her feet, she steeled herself for an onslaught of nosy neighbours. "It's routine police procedure. Thank you for your concern. Go away. Go away. Go away."

She dried her hands and opened the door.

Charlie stood there, blinking in the sun. "Hi," he said. "Julian here?"

•

He wore hiking gear, running shoes and a slightly aggrieved expression.

"He was supposed to pick me up this morning for an orchid walk." Charlie followed Mara into the house, dodging Bismuth and Jazz who danced a welcome around him.

"I was expecting him at nine. It's now half past ten. I called, but you didn't answer. So I drove over." He looked around, as if expecting to find Julian hiding in a corner.

Mara said, "He was called away. Unexpectedly."

"Oh?" Charlie seemed suddenly aware of Mara's agitation. "Hey," he said, peering at her closely. "Are you okay?"

"Fine. I'm fine."

"You don't look fine. Wait a minute. This wouldn't have anything to do with a visit I had from the police yesterday, would it?" When she nodded, he said, "Damn. I figured it was something routine, like a traffic fine. Although why they'd send out the gendarmes for a parking ticket beats me. I hope I didn't land him in trouble?"

Mara's shoulders sagged. She collapsed onto the art deco sofa. "Then you really haven't heard?"

"Heard what?"

Mara took a deep breath. "Julian has been taken in for questioning regarding the murder of his estranged wife."

"Good grief." Charlie dropped down beside her, staring perplexedly into her face. "His wife? He murdered his wife? I thought you and he—"

"No, he did not," snapped Mara. "It's just that husbands and lovers are always the first to be suspected. So I'm afraid your orchid walk is off. Very much off."

"Bummer," said Charlie. He corrected himself, "I don't mean about the walk. I mean about Julian." For a moment he was silent, his beaky upper lip shaping to an even sharper point. Then: "Look, I'm really, really sorry to hear this. My God," his blue eyes swam with sympathy, and Mara found herself wanting to cry again. "This must be awful for you. And for Julian as well. I feel terrible that I'm the one who told the police where to find him."

Mara shook her head. "Don't blame yourself. They would have found him in any case. Véronique—his wife—called here. The police have a record of the call, and all they would have had to do was trace this address."

"I wish there were some way I could help. I mean, you've been so kind to me, inviting me out with your friends and all. You didn't have to do that. Would you like me to stay? For moral support?"

She smiled bleakly. "I'm afraid there's nothing anyone can do except wait and see."

"Okay," declared Charlie. "I'll wait with you. This isn't a time to be on your own, and we Canadians should stick together. No, I insist. Can I make you something? Coffee? Tea? A drink? How about food? I'll bet you haven't eaten a thing."

"Honestly, Charlie, I'll be all right. In fact, if you don't mind, I'd rather be alone. There are a lot of things I have to do." *Like find a crackerjack defence lawyer*, she thought.

Charlie nodded. "Right. I understand." He rose. "But, Mara, if you need anything, you'll let me know?"

9

Chez Nous was more than a bistro. It was the centrepiece of Paul and Mado Brieux's thriving business empire that occupied the ground floor of a large stone building situated in the middle of the village of Grissac. The owners lived with their two young sons on the level above.

One entered the bistro by way of the emporium, a conglomerate grocery store, bread depot, tobacconist's, news agent's and vintner's where you could buy wine *en vrac* if you brought your own bottles. There was even a special English section that sold things like Bird's Custard and Worcestershire sauce. Customers indicated what they wanted by where they positioned themselves at the long wooden counter. Nobody minded waiting for service because the local gossip was always good. If you were there to eat, you simply passed through a bead curtain on the left and sat down in the simply furnished restaurant at an available table. More and more, however, you needed a reservation.

The dinner on Friday night should have been a festive affair because of Julian's release from custody that afternoon. It was not. Julian, certain that Loulou, Prudence, Patsy and Charlie thought him a murderer, a cad, or both, was very subdued. Everyone wanted to ask about his experience at the hands of Adjudant-chef Compagnon but talked instead about the weather and the rising price of gas.

The bistro, as usual, was full. Not just with people, but with dogs. Bismuth slept under the table, Jazz by the bar. Bismuth's mother, the black-and-white short-haired pointer bitch Edith, joined them later when one of the other diners (a regular from the neighbourhood) saw her looking mournfully through a window and got up to let her in.

The food, as always, was extremely good. Loulou kissed his fingertips to Mado's fricassee of rabbit. Julian had a perfectly seared steak and *frites*; the women all went for the quail. An excellent filet of sole in butter sauce emboldened Charlie to say to Julian:

"You still owe me an orchid walk."

Julian closed his eyes. "I know, I know."

"I suppose you're going to tell me you were—ha ha!—unavoidably detained?"

No one laughed.

Dessert was chocolate gateaux served with a rare, old-fashioned treat, *beignets des fleurs d'acacia*, panicles of robinia blossoms, picked in the dewy morn, dipped in fluffy batter thinned with Grand Marnier, deep-fried and dusted with powdered sugar. It was a delicate work of teeth and lips, stripping the flowers from the stem. But even the *beignets* did little to dispel the gloomy mood.

By eleven when the bistro had emptied of all other patrons, Paul and Mado emerged from the kitchen to join them. The dogs immediately roused themselves to circle around, toenails clicking on the wooden floorboards.

Mado, a statuesque redhead with golden eyes and a creamy complexion that endless hours over a hot stove could not ruin, embraced everyone and squeezed in between Loulou and Julian. Paul kissed the women and shook hands with the men. Julian he slapped on the back.

"You tricky old dog. Married all this time," he chortled, voicing what everyone thought but did not like to say. Big and blunt, hair awry, stained chef's jacket hanging unbuttoned on his beefy frame, Paul was one of Julian's oldest friends in the region and the one most likely to put his foot in his mouth.

Mado gave her husband a look that he failed to see. Paul hooked a chair over with his foot and thumped down next to Mara.

Mado murmured in Julian's ear, "How are you holding up?"

"Better for your cooking," Julian rallied.

"So what was it like," grinned Paul, "being interrogated?"

"Julian doesn't want to talk about it," said Mara, Prudence and Patsy at the same time.

"Can you blame him?" sympathized Mado, dangling a backless sandal from a shapely foot. "*Le pauvre.*"

"Poor thing nothing," scoffed Paul. "He could probably sell his story for a packet. Wrongful arrest, police brutality, that kind of thing."

Mado shook her head. "Oh, do leave the man alone."

"If you must know"—Julian was finally goaded to speak—"I felt like a non-person. I was fingerprinted, given a mouth swab for DNA analysis, and interrogated by Adjudant—excuse me, Adjudant-*chef*—Compagnon until I wasn't sure of my own name. Then, when I thought they were about to charge me with a crime I did *not* commit, Laurent came in, had a word, and Compagnon got up and left the room. When he came back he said, 'Okay, you're free to go.' No explanation. *Point final.*"

"*Ah, ça.*" Loulou scooted forward in his seat. His cherubic face, topped by a large expanse of pink scalp, gleamed. "That information I can supply. You were released, *mon ami*, for sound reasons. *Primo*"—he stuck up a fat thumb—"you have, ahem, an alibi."

Mara and Julian exchanged a covert glance.

"*Secundo*"—the forefinger followed—"forensics couldn't link you to the crime scene."

At this, Julian felt vastly relieved. It was the first he'd heard of it. Blood began to course freely through his veins again.

"*Naturellement*. He wasn't there," said Prudence. "Julian, you've gone all red."

"*Tertio*"—Loulou held up his entire hand to signal that he had not finished—"the witness who saw the van, your Monsieur Boyer, when questioned again could not positively identify it as yours. He didn't have his glasses on. You're in the clear, *mon vieux*."

"*Et voilà*. You see?" crowed Patsy.

Mara felt almost dizzy with relief.

Charlie was staring curiously at Loulou. "I thought you said you were retired from the force. How do you know all this?"

Loulou tapped the side of his nose. "I have my sources."

"So where are the police at with the case?" asked Mara.

"The newspaper said it was a burglary," said Mado. "Something about her surprising her killer."

"Ah, yes." Loulou nodded. "But I happen to know there wasn't any sign of a break-in. Ergo, Véronique must have voluntarily admitted him. Besides, she had nothing worth stealing. *Entre nous*, the gendarmes are treating the perpetrator as someone known to the victim and the situation still as a possible *crime passionnel*, even though there was no evidence of sexual activity. One scenario is that the killer came, bearing a bottle of wine, and in the course of an argument struck her down with it. Then he trashed her flat afterwards to make it look like a break-in, took the bottle with him and dumped it in a recycling bin. It'll be in pieces by now. The police are keeping all this quiet, mind, and so should you."

Paul asked, "Boyfriends?"

"The occasional casual visitor, according to her landlady."

"*Et voilà*," growled Paul. "All the cops have to do is find out who they are, match up fingerprints and the like, and—*paf*!—haul the bastard in."

"Fingerprints, yes, and hair and semen samples belonging

to various unidentified males, including traces of the landlord, César Fargéas, a nasty little fellow who's always skated just this side of the law. Of course, being the landlord, he had legitimate reasons to go in there. He claims she wanted a lock changed. And whether or not he was having relations with her, it doesn't mean he killed her. His wife says he was with her at the critical time. Although, that's what she would say if her husband's the guilty party and she feels like backing him up."

Paul waved a finger. "*Ah, non*. She wouldn't. If the *con*'s been playing around, she'd want to nail his balls."

"Especially," put in Charlie, "if it was the jealous wife who did Véronique in. The killer doesn't have to be a man, you know."

Loulou dipped his head from side to side. "True." He poked his chin in Julian's direction. "You know, she was a mysterious one, your Véronique. For the past little while she lived almost like a recluse. Even her job, street miming, was a peculiar choice for a woman. Apart from her gentleman callers, which, *pardonnez-moi*, may have been a way of augmenting her income, she seems to have had no friends, no one she kept in contact with, no living family except you, who'd lost touch with her entirely."

"There was a rugby player from Bordeaux," offered Julian. "I told the gendarmes about him."

"Bordeaux!" snorted Paul, as if Julian had said something obscene.

"Ah, Victor Parizot." Loulou affirmed. "Second-string wing forward. The lads talked to him as well. Runs an abattoir in Les Eyzies nowadays. He claims he paid her a sum to take off years ago, never saw her again. Anyhow, he's in the clear. At the time Véronique was killed, he was celebrating his mother's ninetieth birthday in full view of twenty-three other family members and guests."

"What about work?" asked Mara.

"Various *boulots*. Between 2004 and 2005, Véronique worked at the Clinique Morange in Sarlat doing some kind of client follow-up. Then she had a job as a supermarket cashier for a few months, then cosmetics sales. That was before she started going to fairs and markets with her *mime automate* gig."

Julian stopped rubbing Edith's ears. "What's the Clinique Morange?"

"A sleep clinic," answered Loulou.

Mara laughed outright. "That's ironic."

Mado wrinkled her nose. "What does one do at a sleep clinic?"

"They wire you up and figure out why you can't sleep," answered Patsy.

"Anything there?" asked Mara.

Loulou tugged his dewlap. "Well, the director, Dr. Claude Morange, is a smooth character with a reputation as a lady-killer." Loulou seemed oblivious to his unfortunate choice of words. "His clinic, moreover, is said to be in financial trouble. It's Morange's wife's money that's keeping him afloat."

"So," broke in Paul, "if he was shagging Véronique, and she was pushing him to leave his wife and marry her or else, it could have been *tak*!" He slammed his right fist into his left palm.

"Indeed," said Loulou. "However, on the night in question Morange was at the clinic briefing patients who were there for sleep assessments. He stayed on until about half past nine, catching up on paperwork. His staff confirm this. After that, he went straight home, where his wife swears he arrived fifteen minutes later and where he remained for the rest of the night. If everyone's telling the truth, there's no way he could have committed the crime. However, the lads are also looking at a clinic technician who overlapped with Véronique and who was once charged with assault by a former girlfriend. Moreover, he has no alibi for the critical time. He says he was home alone with his cat."

Paul brought his fist down on the table, making the glassware rattle. "We live in a violent society!"

"Not really," murmured his wife. "You're the only one who breaks up the furniture around here."

"Used to be, it was just gangs nicking lawn mowers. Now, everywhere you look, it's robbery with violence." It was Paul's hobby horse, the rising rate of crime, even though the Dordogne, with its small villages and farms, still seemed at peace with itself. "Like that *merdeux* who snatched the old woman's purse in Bergerac last month. Broke her wrist. What do you call that?"

"Stupid," said Loulou with grim satisfaction. "Because when she wouldn't let go, he said, 'Hand it over, granny, or I'll smash you.' That constituted robbery with threats, a much more serious charge than if he'd said nothing at all."

"Or murder and perversion," Paul went on. "Take that artist, the one whose jealous lover shoved her out a window."

"Sofia Ventura," said Prudence. "Great stuff."

"Turns out she wasn't even a female," Paul nearly howled. "She was a man who'd had a sex-change operation. And the lover was a male model who went off his nut because this Sofia character was having it on with another woman. Now you tell me. What's the point of cutting it off if you're going to do it with women anyway?" Fingers splayed, Paul appealed to all of them. "I mean, does it make sense?"

10

"How is it," Julian complained as they turned into the rue de l'Angle, "that I can go from being prime suspect one day to the person responsible for clearing out Véronique's personal effects the next?" Their footfalls rang out on the cobblestones of the narrow alley that, even though it was nearly noon, still lay deep in shadow.

"You're her husband," Mara responded with some asperity. "That's why."

The forensic team had finished with the flat. Madame Fargéas, the landlady, had telephoned Julian the night before and demanded that he get out there *tout de suite* to deal with things.

"I have prospective tenants who want this place," she had screeched, implying that she was dealing with high-end real estate. "And she owed rent. I expect you to put that right."

There was a grinding noise overhead. The air suddenly shook with a thunderous tolling of bells emanating from the nearby Romanesque tower of the church of Saint-Germain.

Mara put her hands over her ears. "*Mon Dieu*, how can anyone live with this? Every hour on the hour?"

The last peal died out, leaving an aftershock of silence, as they reached number 17 *bis*. The door was ajar. Quite unexpectedly, a plastic garbage bag, stuffed full, came flying out to land at their feet. A woman appeared in the doorway. She was short and fat and wore a sleeveless dress out of which pale arms protruded like sandbags. Her hair was in pink rollers, and she had the head of a lizard, flattened, wider than it was long, with small mean eyes and a lipless mouth.

"Madame Fargéas?" Julian inquired.

"*C'est moi.* You the husband? About time you turned up." Madame was in a temper. "I've got someone coming to view this apartment in a couple of hours and I want this stuff out of here." She thumbed them in and marched off down the alley.

The space that had been Véronique's a week ago was now reduced to impersonal piles of rubbish, some of which had been bundled into the flying plastic bag. Chipped crockery, used toiletries, clothing and magazines littered the floor. The paltry odds and ends of a life.

A skinny runt of a man backed out of a curtained alcove, trailing a wet, filthy mop. He turned to stare at Julian and Mara, a cigarette stuck to his lower lip. The lizard's husband, they deduced. He confirmed it by transferring the mop to his left hand and wiping the fingers of his right on his trousers before extending them to Julian.

"César Fargéas. She was your wife? My condolences."

Julian nodded and took the fingers gingerly. "Julian Wood."

César leered at Mara.

"I'm helping Monsieur Wood," said Mara, keeping her hands behind her.

"The wife's very upset," César said.

"I suppose she would be," agreed Mara. "How long was Véronique your tenant?"

César scratched his ear. "A year maybe. Bad business, this." He tried to look solemn, but a juicy, racking cough ruined the effect. The cigarette jumped wildly. Improbably it stayed in place.

Madame Fargéas reappeared with an empty cardboard box and more plastic bags, which she dumped before Julian. "You can start by moving this stuff." She waved at the piles of junk.

To her husband she yelled, "Don't just stand there. Get on with it. Useless!"

Loudly she informed anyone interested, "Chases every bit of skirt going, that one. Just see where it's got him! The cops think he did it."

"I never," objected César. "You've got no right saying things like that in front of other people. Word gets round, you know."

"*Qui se sent morveux, qu'il se mouche*," pronounced his wife vindictively. Let him who feels snotty blow his nose. "As for her, she was nothing but trouble. Men in and out of here at all hours. I know she was your wife and all, monsieur, but frankly I'm glad to be rid of her. I have my reputation to think of."

Behind her back, César stuck out his tongue. He put his thumbs in the corners of his mouth and pulled his lips out wide in a remarkable parody of his wife's reptilian look. Then he held his nose. Julian was transfixed. Mara had to turn away quickly and hold her breath.

"To top it off," the landlady went on, "she owed rent. Hasn't paid me a penny for months. I want it settled today. A thousand euros. In cash."

"I don't have cash," said Julian, not at all inclined to believe her.

"I don't take cheques, if that's what you're thinking."

Julian said blandly, "What about plastic?"

She glared at him. "In your dreams." She sized Julian up sharply. "She had a car, you know. Orange hatchback parked at the end of the alley. Broken-down pile of tin. The keys and papers are there . . ." She jabbed her chin at the table and let the idea hang.

Julian remembered seeing a vehicle fitting that description in passing. It was probably worth more than the rent Madame claimed was owing, but it was an easy way out. "Okay. If I leave it with you, we're even?"

"Deal! But you'll have to take care of the *contrôle technique*," said the lizard. "I want things done proper."

"Forget it." Julian threw up his hands at the thought of getting the pile of tin through a safety inspection. "I'll sign it over, but you handle the *contrôle technique* or no deal."

Deciding to quit while she was winning, Madame Fargéas gave a grudging jerk of the head and turned her ill temper on the mime stage. "And do something about that *maudit* contraption. It's of no use to me." She stomped away again.

By the time the church bells bonged out one o'clock, they had packed up Véronique's belongings and were loading everything into Julian's van. They left the mime stage to last. It was heavy, being made of solid wood, but at least manoeuvrable, folding down on itself and fitted out with handles, a wheel and legs, like a wheelbarrow. César accompanied them as they rolled it down the alley.

"*Écoutez*," he said. "You being the husband and all, I want you to know I had nothing to do with it." He helped Julian lift the stage into the back of the van. "The *flics* questioned me, but they couldn't make it stick, you know."

Julian slammed the rear door shut. As a declaration of innocence, César's denial lacked conviction.

"Also I just wanted to say your wife wasn't as bad as the T. Rex makes out. Sure, she had a few visitors. No harm in it. And in case you're wondering, maybe we got a little friendly from time to time, she and I, but it was just a bit of fun. I was helping her out, wasn't I? I swear I never did her."

Nervously he passed a hand over his greasy scalp. "There's something else you ought to know. I got the impression Véronique was afraid. I told the cops, but those *cognes* never listen. Just because I've had—well, a bit of trouble in my day—they want to pin it on me. Why me, I ask you? Anyway, as I was saying, she was nervous like, definitely lying low. *Ouais*! The night she died, she asked me to change the lock on her door. I thought maybe a violent husband, but that would be you, wouldn't it?" He blinked uncertainly at Julian. "Whatever, someone or something definitely had her spooked."

"Spooked?" Julian echoed.

Mara was keenly interested. "Do you have any idea who? Or what? Or why?"

César drew scrawny shoulders up to his ears and turned a pair of grubby palms skyward. "Dunno. She never had a chance to say, did she!"

•

"I think he did it," said Mara as they drove away. "His wife thinks he's guilty, he had means and opportunity, and, according to Loulou, his traces were all over the flat."

"Motive?"

Mara shrugged. "Maybe it was unpremeditated. He admitted he and Véronique were occasionally friendly. He brought a bottle, she didn't feel like coming across, he got pushy, she threatened to tell his wife, he lost his cool, and, like Paul said, *tak*!"

"But what about his claim that Véronique was frightened?"

"An attempt to divert suspicion from himself?"

"He even had the nerve to imply *I* had something to do with it!"

"Well, you are an obvious choice."

"I wish you wouldn't keep on about it."

They rolled up to an intersection. Julian braked. "If I had to choose between the pair of them, I'd pick the wife. She's as vicious an old trout as I've ever met. Say she found out her husband was fooling around. I could see her hitting someone over the head."

He turned right, opting for a network of minor roads in preference to the main highway back to Ecoute-la-Pluie. Their way ran between ranks of shady poplars, breaking out into a tender landscape of newly planted fields of wheat and corn. Cattle grazed peacefully on the sloping pastures. Old stone buildings dreamed timeless on their sunny hillsides.

Eventually, Julian slowed and pulled off on a grassy verge colourful with wildflowers: daisies, purple sage, Tassel hyacinth, and here and there tall, elegant Lady orchids.

Turning to Mara, he said, "I just want you to know that I'm damned grateful to you for standing by me. I know our relationship has been—well, badly compromised by everything that's happened."

"Yes," she agreed, not giving him any wiggle room. "It has."

"I've made a cock-up of everything, and I've landed you in it as well. Even though the police have cleared me, until they find Véronique's murderer, people will continue to think of me as a possible wife killer. You'll be the wife killer's *petite amie*."

Mara relented. She knew exactly how he felt. Three years ago, she had found herself living in the shadow of something similarly unpleasant.

"Then it looks like we're in this together." She reached out and took his hand. His eyes, spaniel brown, met hers in melancholy interrogation.

"There's only one solution," she said. "Do everything you can to prove your innocence."

He drew his hand away. "By finding Véronique's killer? Isn't that a job for the gendarmes?"

She gave him an encouraging smile. "Look, just put *Cypripedium incognitum*, Horatio Kneebone and Charlie Perry on hold and take Véronique as a starting point. Loulou said it had to be someone known to her. Ask questions, dig into her life.

You're the husband. It'll seem natural coming from you. Maybe you can uncover something the police have overlooked. Besides, I'll help you."

Now he shot her a worried look. "Thank you very much," he said insincerely.

11

Footwear always told a story, Mara thought. The red stiletto slingbacks were not cheap, but they were much used, the grubby imprint of Véronique's feet deeply embedded in the curling insoles. The left heel was coming loose.

So what did these shoes say about the dead woman who had worn them? That she had liked the colour red—red to lure, red to warn? That at some time in the past she'd had the money to buy an expensive pair of shoes that had imparted their touch of glamour until the leather had begun to crack, the stitching break apart, a heel give way? That even after life had let her down and she had been reduced to doing street gigs for money thrown in a hat she had clung to this memento of better times?

She and Julian sat on the floor in the middle of the studio sorting through Véronique's belongings, salvaging usable clothing and household items to be donated to a local thrift shop. So far, they had consigned almost everything to a growing pile of garbage. Perhaps Madame Fargéas had already picked through Véronique's things. Perhaps Véronique had possessed nothing worth taking.

"She had so little." It was Mara's requiem for a woman she had never known.

Julian had known her once. But he was going through Véronique's effects wordlessly, offering nothing.

"And I find it odd that she left behind no information on

herself. No personal papers, no letters, no address or bank book, no diary, nothing at all that would tell us about her life."

"I expect the gendarmes took all that," said Julian, tossing a torn paperback on to the reject pile. "Plus her cellphone."

"But it leaves us nothing to work with. We need to get a picture of her, what her life was like, how she spent her time, what turned her on—"

"Money to burn and a good time."

Mara glanced up at him. His expression, more bitter than sad, did not invite sympathy.

She went on, almost to herself, "Loulou said she knew her killer. Was it someone from her present? Or her past? And how did she wind up earning her living jigging about on a portable stage?" Regretfully she relegated the red shoes to the trash.

"Speaking of which, what the hell should we do with the damned thing?" asked Julian.

"Firewood?"

He got to his feet and wandered over to it. "Be a shame to scrap it. It's solid and cleverly hinged. I wonder how Véronique came by it."

"Maybe she had it made."

"I doubt it. It looks quite old. Look at the patina of the wood. My guess is she had it off another street entertainer."

Mara raised her head sharply. "Of course! The Marquis! The old guy who used to dress up in an eighteenth-century costume and a powdered wig. He went about to all the markets with a little fold-up stage like this. Don't you remember him?"

"Vaguely. Seems to me he hasn't been around for awhile, though."

Mara came over to study the contraption. "Well, I couldn't swear to it, but it looks like the same stage. Maybe Véronique took over his act. Julian"—she suddenly became excited—"if she got it from the Marquis, maybe *he* can tell us something about her and why she became a street performer." When he looked unenthusiastic, she went on, "Well, it's worth a try. What was his name?" She closed her eyes, doing a mental sweep. "He used to hang a placard on the stage advertising himself as Le Marquis du Something. Dubois? Dupuy? Damn. It escapes me."

"Hello." He had crouched down and was examining the stage closely. "There's something under here." He searched around the studio, found a length of wire and coaxed a sheaf of papers from beneath the stage platform. It was a stapled five-page list of names in alphabetical order. Opposite each name was a telephone number. At the top right-hand corner of each page was the word *Pronole* followed by a hyphen and the number 2.

"What's Pronole-2?" he wondered aloud, passing the list over for Mara's inspection.

She studied it. "It looks like some kind of call sheet. Wait. Didn't Loulou say Véronique sold cosmetics? Maybe she was a telemarketer and these are customers she was supposed to sell a product called Pronole-2 to. Cosmetic companies are always naming their creams after revolutionary skin-care formulas. Regenera-93, that kind of thing."

Julian looked doubtful. "Pronole-2 doesn't sound very regenerative."

"True. Well, there's one way to find out." She went to her computer and logged on to Google, her fingers moving swiftly over the keyboard. Her search did not match any documents.

"*Flûte*!" She sat back, frowning.

Julian, who was still examining the stage, said, "Anyway, why the concealment? What's so important about a list of customers that she'd want to hide it?"

"If she was hiding it, it must have been important."

They fell silent, grappling with this tautology.

"There's another way around this," Mara said eventually, and reached for the phone.

"What are you going to do?"

"Make a few calls."

Julian was aghast. "You can't do that!"

But she was already keying in the first number on the list. It triggered a *répondeur* informing her that no one could take her call *chez Allard*, please leave a message. Mara disconnected. Her next attempt got a live person.

"*Bonjour*. Is this the Bonnet residence?"

"*Oui*." The woman's voice sounded like a creaky gate.

"Are you"—Mara squinted; the first name looked like Louise, but she did not have her glasses on—"er, Madame Bonnet?"

"*Oui*."

"Madame Bonnet, my name is, um, Marie." Mara took a leap of faith. "I'm phoning from the Pronole-2 call centre, and we're doing a follow-up survey—"

"*Comment*?" rasped the gate. "Are you calling from Canada?"

Damn. Her accent always gave her away.

Improvising wildly, Mara plunged on. "I believe you used our product, Pronole-2. This is just a survey to see if you were satisfied—"

Madame Bonnet cut in. "I don't know what you're talking about."

Then Mara realized that the name on the list was not Louise but Louis. "Oh, I'm sorry," she amended. "It's actually Louis Bonnet I want to speak with. Is he available?"

"No, he's not," snapped the woman. "Not now. Not ever. Don't you have anything better to do than bother people with stupid questions?" She hung up.

"Well, that went nowhere," said Mara.

"Maybe Pronole-2 isn't a product," suggested Julian. He had

filled a plastic bag destined for the thrift shop and was tying it off. "Maybe it's some kind of classification or code. It looks rather scientific to me."

"Well, you might have said so earlier."

"I didn't think of it earlier."

Mara sighed and ran her eyes down the columns of names. A moment later, she said in a puzzled voice, "Julian, you know that painter whose lover pushed her out a window?"

"Yes?" He was stuffing another bag, this one for the Dumpster. "What about her?"

She handed him the list, flipped over to the last page. "See for yourself. It's there. Under *V*."

He read the name and raised his gaze to hers. "Sofia Ventura?"

•

"Why should Sofia Ventura's name be on here?" Mara asked.

"Maybe it's a list of artists," Julian suggested. He hoisted the bags and carried them out the door.

"Pronole-2 doesn't sound very artistic," she said when he returned. "And anyway, why hide a bunch of artists' names?"

Julian squinted at the stage. "The platform's warped. It's possible she wasn't hiding anything. Perhaps she just shoved the list under the floor to level it. Besides, we don't know that it was Véronique who put the list in there. It could have been The Marquis." He went out again, carrying a box this time.

"Then we should find him and ask him," Mara concluded, following him outside. "Damn. I wish I could remember his name."

They stood on the walkway, staring undecidedly at each other. In the next moment, she exclaimed, "I've got it! The *placiers*!"

"What about the *placiers*?"

"They organize the open-air markets. They assign the sellers their spots. They would know who The Marquis is. We'll ask them. And if we find The Marquis, maybe he can tell us what Pronole-2 is."

"If we find The Marquis"—Julian grinned, seeing another possible upside to her idea—"maybe we can return this contraption to him."

12

"It's my bladder, you see," bawled the sausage vendor. She leaned forward, confidential-like, but her voice carried. "I keep telling you, I need an *emplacement* near the public toilets."

"Madame," said the small man with the smudge of a moustache under his nose. He was a good head shorter than the woman he addressed, an amazon in boots and an apron, but he held his ground. "I'm sorry about your internal problems, madame, but I am not God. You've got to have seniority for those spots, and only *le bon Dieu*, whom you must also talk to about your bladder, messes around with seniority."

It was the strawberry seller who informed Mara and Julian. He rubbed his nose with a juice-stained finger and said, "Oh, it's Philippe Milac you want. You'll find him around, probably at the other end of the market arguing with Madame Auberdier. Now, how about a nice basket of Cérafines? They're very good this year. *Très parfumées*. I also have Gariguettes if you like them a little tarter."

"We'll come back," Mara promised, and they made their way through the throng in search of the *placier*.

The market in this town occupied the length of the main street. It was anchored at the fountain end by the refrigerated stands of a butcher, who wiped his fingers on his apron before shaking hands with customers, and a *poissonnière*, whose fish on ice were displayed like works of art. Nearby was a brasserie-pizzeria. Its sidewalk tables were always crowded. A Brit crowd tended to gather at this end. At the other end of the market, across from the fruit and flower sellers, just after the spice table, the maker of take-away paella, and before the soap and lavender stall, the made-in-China clothing, and the North-African leather goods, was another brasserie-pizzeria patronized by the Dutch. Why it should be that way was a matter of time and custom. In between were vendors of locally produced vegetables, berries, cheeses, bread, wines, *confiture*, honey, wild mushrooms, eggs, spit-roasted chickens and sausages.

In any case, Philippe Milac would not have been hard to spot because he wore the uniform of his function: black trousers, white shirt with epaulettes, a leather satchel slung diagonally across his body, two cellphones hooked to his belt, and a permanently frazzled look from many years of organizing busy open-air markets. He seemed vastly relieved to be approached by a foreign couple, *anglais* from the look of them, nice people who were bound to be more reasonable than Madame Auberdier and her bladder.

"So how can I help you?" he inquired, ushering them quickly away from the sausage seller to a place of safety a little beyond a vendor of air-cured hams who greeted him in passing.

Julian introduced himself and Mara and explained that they were trying to locate the *mime automate* who used to perform at the market. Not the Polichinelle, he clarified. The one before. "I'm sure you remember him. He wore a powdered wig and danced on a little stage. Called himself The Marquis of Something."

"*Bien sûr.*" The *placier* nodded. "Le Marquis Du Pont. His real name is Pringault. Du Pont was a kind of pun because he lives just near the bridge outside Bigaroque. What do you want with him? Or maybe you didn't know he's retired now. Doesn't do his gig any more."

"We have something for him," said Julian.

"Oh. Well, you're sure to find him in the phone book."

•

They did, and Julian made the call. It was Madame Pringault who answered. At first she was wary when he mentioned the stage, but when he explained that all he wanted to do was to return it, there was a muffled exchange at her end and Monsieur Pringault came on to say that they would be happy to receive them. They lived just across the river from Le Buisson. He gave directions.

Mara and Julian found the Pringaults working in front of their house. She was deadheading roses; he was standing on a ladder, making a bad job of hacking at an overgrown hedge with a pair of shears. The couple apologized for the appearance of their garden, which was large and weedy and in need of a good cleanup. It was all getting beyond both of them. They were elderly, short and stout, a matching pair, like bookends. She had bright eyes and apple cheeks. He had overlarge dentures that gave him a slightly braying look.

"*Que c'est incroyable*! I never thought I'd see the old thing again," Pringault chortled, exposing an expanse of incisors as Julian unloaded the stage from his van and wheeled it up to the door. "It has a history, you know. The floor"—he stroked the platform—"was made from an old walnut tabletop that stood in my granny's dining room."

Madame Pringault insisted they come in for coffee and prune cake. Julian broached the subject of Véronique.

"We were wondering if you could tell us anything about the, um, woman who bought the stage from you."

"Véronique Rignon," said Madame promptly. "She's dead." She cocked an eye at him, intelligent, like a parrot. "Surely you knew that?"

"Er, yes," admitted Julian, abandoning all pretense. "I'm—I was her husband."

"We assumed as much," said Monsieur. "We read about you."

Everyone had, of course.

"Our condolences," murmured Madame. "And they still haven't caught the *canaille* who did it."

"Terrible affair," said Monsieur.

"The truth is," Julian said, nudging things back on track, "I'm trying to piece together a picture of Véronique's life. Why, for example, did she take to street entertainment?"

"Oh." Madame Pringault bridled slightly. "You may call it street entertainment, but really what Charlie did was art."

"Miming's not that easy, you know," the ex-marquis informed them. "Especially when you've got to make your movements stiff, like an automaton, and then stand there motionless when the music runs down, not even moving your eyes."

"Could she have earned a living that way?" put in Mara.

"Well," said Pringault, "if you did special events in addition to the markets, you might get by. But it would be hard, and it would depend on the season. Summer's always best, with all the tourists. Me, I wasn't doing it for the money. I have my pension. It was for fun. I worked on the trains all my life, you see, but an actor is what I've always wanted to be." He made an apologetic grin that caused his teeth to start slightly from his mouth. He pushed them back. "My little show let me tread the boards, *n'est-ce pas*, Nanette?"

"Right. And he was good at it. People used to clap him."

"They did," Pringault reflected happily.

"And anyway"—Nanette took up the tale—"your Véronique didn't have to buy the stage off Charlie. He gave it her. She heard he was winding up the act, and she just turned up at the market one day last year and said she was interested in continuing his show. Charlie said if she was really serious she could have it free."

"I liked the idea of the act going on, you see," Charlie explained. "So we settled, just like that."

"But you were asking why someone like your wife would have wanted to go into the business?" said Madame. "It's a good question. We wondered ourselves at the time, didn't we, Charlie? Because, *voyez-vous*, it's not the kind of thing you'd expect a woman to do. The stage was heavy for one thing, and it needed a lot of lifting."

"She never gave you a reason?" pressed Julian.

"Never." Pringault shook his head. "And we didn't like to ask."

"More coffee?" his wife offered.

"*Non, merci*," Mara and Julian declined together.

"Nevertheless," said the husband, "I helped her as much as I could. Took her through the routine, how to work the sound system, who to talk to about appearing at the markets. Because you can't just set up like that wherever you like, you know." He snapped his fingers.

Madame added, "He even had her here to the house and gave her tips on miming, how to jolly the public along, things she wouldn't have known about. And he gave her his costume, which I made."

Pringault nodded. "But she had a flair for it, I have to say. We saw her not long after in Saint-Cyprien, didn't we, Nanette? She'd changed the act, of course. Polichinelle with a hump and a great big nose, which I didn't like as much as Le Marquis Du Pont, but I expect she found my costume didn't fit her after all."

"More cake?" asked Madame.

Again Mara and Julian shook their heads.

"We also wondered if you knew anything about this." Mara showed them the Pronole-2 list. "We found it wedged under the floor of the stage. We thought you might have put it there, monsieur."

They both held their breath while Pringault put on a pair of wire-rimmed glasses and studied the list. He sucked his teeth and shook his head. "Not me. Never seen it before." He passed it to his wife, who also shook her head.

"Then Véronique must have put it there," Julian concluded. "What I can't figure out is why."

Pringault burst out laughing. "That's easy! The platform's uneven. Always used to bother me, too. Could be your wife just stuffed whatever was handy in there to level things up."

Julian shot Mara a meaningful glance.

Mara left her telephone number in case the Pringaults remembered anything more about Véronique. Julian left his business card in case they wanted help with their gardening. Monsieur walked them out to the van.

"By the way," Julian ventured as they shook hands, "Véronique never said anything to you about being afraid of anything, did she?"

"Afraid?" Pringault seemed genuinely surprised. "*Mon Dieu, non*! She certainly didn't suffer from stage fright, if that's what you mean. Although, she did say a funny thing, haw, haw!" He gave them the full benefit of his big white uppers. "She said the *mime automate* show had one advantage over ordinary *boulots*."

"What was that?" asked Julian.

"Why, it let her earn her living in disguise!"

•

"She was hiding," Mara concluded as they drove away. "That's twice we've heard it. First from César, and now Pringault. But why? And from whom?"

Julian shook his head.

"What about this." Mara sketched out a scene: "She's standing there between acts on her stage, not moving, and she overhears something she's not meant to. It's easy to forget she's there. I know. I've done it."

"Someone plotting a crime?" Julian was not quite convinced.

"Or she sees something."

"You mean a murder? *Have* there been any unsolved murders at the markets lately?"

"I wish you'd take this seriously."

Julian grinned. "I'd rather take you out to lunch."

•

When they returned to the house at the end of the afternoon, Julian strolled out to the studio to see if there was any news from Ms. Hsu. He was delighted, as he logged on to Mara's computer, to find a message:

> > *Dear Mr. Wood, How are you? I have e-mailed your description of* Cypripedium incognitum *to all my botanical colleagues in the hope that they have information on it. I am sure that someone will come up with something . . .* <

He clicked on reply and began a clumsy, one-fingered response.

> > *Dear Ms. Hsu, I can't thank you enough for your efforts on my behalf . . .* <

Mara, who had followed him into the studio, nursed her irritation. Here he was, chatting on-line about orchids, leaving her to do all the thinking about Véronique.

"Julian," she cut in rather severely after a few minutes, "what was that you said about Pronole-2 being a reference code?"

He hit send and leaned back in the chair. "Well, it looks rather codish, don't you think?"

"I do, and it's what's got me thinking. Loulou told us that Véronique worked at a sleep clinic. Maybe Pronole-2 has to do with that. Say it's some kind of patient classification. What was it called? The Clinique Morin?"

"Morange."

"Right." She shooed him away from her desk.

Google gave her what she wanted.

"Okay. Here it is. Clinique Morange. Established in Sarlat in 1987. A leading centre for diagnosing and treating dyssomnias. Sleep apnea, narcolepsy, movement-related sleep disorders, blah, blah, blah. Damn. Nothing on Pronole-2." She sighed and paged down. "I suppose it was a long shot. Oh, here's a photo of the director."

Julian joined her at the monitor to peer at a head-and-shoulders image of a handsome, middle-aged man with dark, curly hair. Dr. Claude Morange did not look as if he had lost a night's sleep in his life.

"A real *séducteur*," Julian observed with distaste, remembering Loulou's lady-killer comment.

"Definitely the sort who'd chat up his female staff," Mara agreed. "At the very least, I bet he knows a thing or two about Véronique. I think we should do some nosing around."

"At the clinic? We can't just walk in there and start interrogating people, Mara."

"Who said anything about interrogating? I'm talking about subtle undercover work."

"Undercover?" Julian almost laughed. "Don't run away with this."

"You're forgetting," retorted Mara with some exasperation, "they're a sleep clinic. I have a legitimate sleep problem. What's more logical than me going there and while they're fixing my insomnia seeing what I can dig up?"

•

But when Mara called the clinic, the woman who answered the phone informed her curtly that she needed a referral from her family doctor and, *non*, *impossible*, she could not get an appointment to see the clinic director without first being assessed. When she got her referral a few days later, she learned that the clinic assessed patients only on Tuesdays and Fridays, and the earliest appointment she could have was in seven weeks. This time she spoke with a man. Could she be put on a wait-list? Mara asked. Sure, said the man. If that was what she wanted. Mara could almost see the shrug. The front-line staff, for a leading sleep centre, seemed curiously unsympathetic to her needs.

"Yes, definitely," Mara said. "Put me on your wait-list."

•

"It would look fishy," said Patsy, her large frame overtopping a dainty stool. She, Mara and Prudence were having coffee at a trendy new place off the Place d'Armes in Belvès. They sat at a little marble-topped table. Their green demitasse cups had gilt rims. In the background a pale young woman with long fingers stroked languid music out of a Celtic harp.

"Not at all. You're a psychoanalyst. You have the bona fide credentials. I have to hang around for seven weeks before I can even get my foot in the door. They may be able to squeeze me in faster, but then, they may not. You can walk right in there. And you know the right kinds of questions to ask."

"Oh, that part's no problem, kiddo," said Patsy. "Sure, I can trump up a professional reason for meeting this Morange guy—say, what incidence does he see of sleep disorders coupled with diagnosed psychiatric illness, yada, yada, yada. But how do I get from there to Véronique and this Pronole-2 thing? It would be pretty embarrassing to be caught seeking information under false pretenses. I have my professional reputation to consider."

"You have to admit it's a long jump," put in Prudence, astonishing Mara by dunking a pink macaroon. Never in all the years that Mara had known her had she ever seen Prudence dunk anything.

It *was* a stretch, Mara had to admit, and she could think of no reasonable bridge. She was aware that her friends were waiting for her to come up with something. She conceded gloomily, "Well, maybe just go in there and do a bit of ferreting. Get a general impression of the place."

Patsy looked doubtful but did not refuse outright.

Knowing when she was ahead, Mara changed the subject. "Are you still intending to retire with Stanley to an ashram?"

Her friend's shoulders lifted slightly. "That's the plan."

Mara said impatiently, "Why are you doing this, Patsy? You know you don't want to. Stanley may be the love of your life, but he eats nothing but lentils, and you hate lentils."

Patsy's head with its spark-plug curls jerked up. "Actually, they're a very complete food."

"Like kibble," observed Prudence. "But what about lifestyle? This Stanley of yours will sit around meditating in a diaper and what will you do? I can't see you levitating, no offence intended."

Patsy looked hurt. "What you two don't get is this isn't some kind of wacky mid-life deviation. Stanley for me is the real thing. His quest for enlightenment is genuine. And—and it's catching."

"We just want to be sure you're sure," said Mara more gently. "Admit it, Patsy. You told me there were times when you were trekking around together in Nepal that you wanted to shove him off a mountain."

Patsy sighed. "I know, I know. But we came through it, and in the end, he taught me something."

"What?" asked Prudence, still skeptical.

"About my inner life."

"And?" In went a purple macaroon.

"I don't have one."

"Nonsense," said Mara. "Everyone has an inner life. Mine's a junk room where I store all the bits and pieces I don't want to look at. Julian's is a frigging warehouse of left luggage. Even Prudence—"

"Not me," said Prudence quite sincerely. "I got rid of mine years ago. Traded it in for Vuitton and Fendi. What you see is all you get."

"That's not what I mean," sighed Patsy. "I'm not talking about the incubus of our darker selves. I'm talking about peace and lightness. I've been digging around in other people's heads so long there's nothing left of *me*. Sometimes"—she sketched a gesture of despair—"I feel like an empty garbage bag, blowing in the wind."

"Lightness," Prudence nodded, reaching for the last macaroon, a lime-green one. "There you go."

"Look, Mara. About this clinic." Patsy seemed to want to drop the matter of her inner life. "Leave it with me. I'll see what I can do."

"Well, thank God that's settled," said Prudence. "Because I'd really like some more of these yummy cookies."

13

Ms. Hsu, the Chinese botanist, was becoming an increasingly frequent correspondent. Nowadays her messages popped up every time Mara went on-line.

"Julian, you've got e-mail," was Mara's current refrain.

Occasionally Mara opened Ms. Hsu's messages by mistake, frequently enough to have noted that her salutation had gone from "Dear Mr. Wood" to "Dear Julian."

Usually, however, he beat her to it. In fact, he was more at her computer nowadays than she. Therefore, it annoyed her enormously on Thursday afternoon (she had returned from another trying session with the Serafim brothers), to find him once again in her space.

"Mara, have a look at this," Julian called out as she entered the studio. He was eating a wizened-up apple, a Belchar, also called for some reason a Chantecler, that was sweetest if you left it until the skin went all wrinkled. "She's dug up more information on Yong Chun Hua, the Eternal Youth Flower."

Mara peered over his shoulder at the monitor screen, which showed another message from the Chinese botanist:

> I write to say that so far I have not heard from any of my colleagues about your orchid. However, I am very interested in the information you sent me on Mr. Perry and his ancestor's diary . . . <

"I thought you didn't want to give out information on Horatio Kneebone," said Mara testily.

"Well"—Julian took a final bite of apple and tossed the core into a wastebasket—"Ms. Hsu is different. I feel I can take her into my confidence. But this is what I really wanted you to see." His finger directed Mara's eye to the rest of the message.

> . . . *Nevertheless, I have some interesting news. I read in a 16th-century medical treatise that Yong Chun Hua has a pungent odour that arouses the sexual appetite in men and enables swooning ladies to recover to their senses. Therefore, if Yong Chun Hua and* Cypripedium incognitum *are the same thing, smell may be a characteristic to look for. I, too, would like to solve this puzzle. I have devoted myself to the study of orchids for 10 years now (I am 32 and quite tall for a Chinese woman) and this is the most interesting thing I have come across orchid-wise. Like you, I am very fascinated* . . . <

Mara thought sourly that tall Ms. Hsu sounded as crazy about orchids as Julian and probably wore a cheongsam slit up to her shapely thigh. This time she signed off as Hsu Fang, adding coyly: "*You may just call me Fang if you wish.*"

"I thought you agreed to put all of that aside and focus on finding Véronique's killer," Mara said with a slightly aggressive lift of her chin.

"No, that was you. Be reasonable, Mara. I can't stop Ms. Hsu—"

"You may call her 'Fang' if you wish." Nastily, Mara wondered what Ms. Hsu's teeth were like.

"—from writing. Besides, I think it's damned decent of her to try to help me, a perfect stranger, half a world away, to get information on my orchid. Anyway, what can I do that the police can't?"

To mask her irritation, Mara changed the subject. "I was thinking about going to a *vide-grenier* in Cadouin on Saturday. I'm looking for more bits and pieces for the Billons' house. Why don't you come too?"

"Can't. I still have to make good on Charlie's orchid walk, and I promised to do it then."

"There you go again!" She gave vent to a minieruption. "Orchids. Always orchids. You can't stay away from them."

"I stood Charlie up once, you know, and I can't back out a second time."

"Oh, yes? You were telling me just the other day you were finding him to be a downright nuisance. You said you couldn't imagine anything less enjoyable than dragging a neophyte around by the nose, showing him how to distinguish a *Dactylorhiza* from a daisy. What's changed your mind?"

"Nothing."

"I know that look, Julian. Your eyes have gone all shifty. Come clean."

Sheepishly, Julian confessed, "I'm afraid he's getting cold feet. If I don't strike while the iron's hot, he'll lose interest, and I'll have no more chance of seeing the Kneebone diary than flying to the moon."

"Another thing that gives you away is when you resort to clichés."

"Look, will you stop picking me apart? What I'm trying to say is, if I don't show him some orchids soon, he's bound to turn to someone else, and the only other person is that *chameau* Géraud. Then where will I be?"

Mara challenged, "Charlie also wants you to show him where *Cypripedium incognitum* grows. Are you going to do it?"

"Um." Julian glanced away uncomfortably.

"You snake. You expect him to come across with the goods,

while you have no intention whatever of keeping your end of the bargain. Is that fair?"

"I wish you'd stop calling my integrity into question. It's not that I won't take him into my confidence, it's just that I need to be cautious. Fact is, I'm not sure I entirely trust Charlie."

"What's not to trust about him? I think he's been perfectly straightforward with you."

Julian shrugged. "It's just a feeling I have. And about Saturday"—now Julian looked more than sheepish—"I, er, was hoping to ask for your help." He reached for her hand. She snatched it away. "I'm just trying to kill two birds with one stone, Mara."

"More clichés, Julian?"

"Well, it's all your fault, really," he burst out. "You put the wind up me by suggesting the embroidery was patterned on a drawing. I haven't had a good night's sleep since."

"Ha! Now you know what it feels like."

"Please. I've got to read that diary. Surely you understand how important it is for me to know whether Horatio Kneebone actually found the orchid he sketched, or if he simply copied it from another source."

"So? Where do I come in?"

"Well, I was thinking, I was hoping, while Charlie is out with me, you could, er, slip into the cottage and—"

"Steal the diary?" Mara looked thunderous.

"Borrow. Make a photocopy. Put it back. He'll never know."

"In a pig's eye!" Furious, she stalked off. When she reached the studio door, she swung about. "I refuse to be a part of this, Julian Wood. I never knew you could be so downright sneaky. I'm going to the *vide-grenier* in Cadouin. Get someone else to do your dirty work."

•

In the end, very unwillingly, she agreed to help him.

14

The flower was small, one of an inflorescence of perhaps twenty clustered on an upright stem. Violet-blotched on a white background, it had the comical appearance of a tiny humanoid, with a disproportionately large head and skinny arms and legs ending in purple-tinged hands and feet that were curled up, so that the little creature looked as if it were jumping.

"This," said Julian, handling the flower with care, "is *Orchis simia*, the Monkey orchid. It's the first I've seen this year."

"Yes," breathed Charlie, crouching beside him to study it closely. "It does look like a little monkey. You can even see the nub of a tail."

In a spiral-bound notebook he entered: "*Orchis simia*. Monkey orchid."

"Can I just write *O. simia* for short? But maybe then I'd get it mixed up with *Ophrys*. That starts with an O, too. It's all a bit confusing."

"Here the monkey's head is made up of the dorsal sepal, which curls over to form a kind of hood, and the two much-reduced lateral petals which are hidden inside the hood."

"Remind me again about sepals?"

Julian sighed. "The sepals look like petals but aren't. They lie behind the petals and protect the flower when it's in bud. The monkey-shaped form you see is actually the highly specialized middle petal, or labellum."

"Labellum. Right," said Charlie, jotting down more notes. "Tell me again why the labellum is so specialized?"

Julian gritted his teeth. The man was insatiable. "It's one of the ways many orchids attract pollinators. Some produce nectar, some mimic other nectar-bearing flowers and often grow among the plants they mimic. Others use visual lures, while others use scent lures, for example, pheromone smell-alikes that attract male insects. I suspect both are the case for the Monkey. Its labellum offers an interesting landing platform, and it's supposed to have a nasty odour, rather like feces, which may attract certain flies. If you bend down, you can smell what I mean."

Charlie crouched low to sniff. "I can't smell anything. And *Cypripedium incognitum*? What does it use?"

Julian shrugged. "Generally speaking, Slipper orchids use scent and visual lures. The pouch, of course, plays a role. It's shaped in such a way that insects that fall into it are able to escape only by passing by the stamens and getting covered with pollen, which they carry off to another flower."

"In other words, it's all about—ha! ha!—getting it on?" Charlie guffawed.

Julian would have liked him more if he had said the F-word.

But he had to admit, the man was keen. It wasn't even noon and already he had taken countless photos with a rather spiffy digital camera that Julian coveted and was filling his notebook with copious notes.

"Speaking of *Cypripedium incognitum*, don't forget you promised to show me where it grows."

"Where it *might* grow," Julian corrected crossly. It was the third time Charlie had mentioned it. "Besides, there's no guarantee it'll be in flower, and without the flower, we won't know what we're looking at."

"Why not? Isn't this the right season?"

Julian wanted to wring his neck. "It's just that they don't necessarily bloom every year, and without the flower, it'll be hard to locate it."

"Ah, but you do know roughly where that photo was taken? And I'm sure you've made some educated guesses based on the embroidery? So you must have narrowed it down a bit?"

"Come on," said Julian gruffly. "There's something in this field I want to show you."

•

Mara stood in the middle of Julian's kitchen. It was the obvious choice for an office, and Charlie was clearly using it as such. One end of the counter had been cleared to hold a small reference library: a Larousse French–English dictionary, city guides to Bordeaux and Paris, a collection of *Série bleue* maps for the Dordogne, showing in detail every feature of the landscape. Prominently displayed were Julian's books on wildflowers of the Dordogne and wild orchids of the Dordogne. But nothing resembling a diary. In fact, she had no idea what she was looking for. Was it big? Small? Loose-leaf? Leather-bound as a single volume fastened with a brass clasp? Or contained in several dog-eared notebooks?

The kitchen table served as Charlie's workstation. On it stood his laptop, printer and stacks of notes written in a firm, tidy script, evidence of work in progress. The topmost page read: "Horatio returned to Europe in October 1861, having bid farewell to the country of his botanical dreams and to a people he was never again to see . . ." Everything was neatly arranged: a stapler, a box of paper clips, a clutch of pencils, each sharpened to a point and standing at the ready in a mug. She saw none of the creative scatter one might expect of a writer, no scribbles on the backs of envelopes, no half-written wadded-up sheets of paper on the floor indicating creative frustration. Charlie had chosen, she noticed, the most comfortable of Julian's non-matching dining-room chairs, the only one with a padded seat.

On the floor under the table was a plastic hanging file containing coloured folders, each labelled by subject. Feeling like the thief she was (Charlie was a decent sort; she should not be doing this), Mara worked quickly through the folders. They held a variety of material: reproductions of nineteenth-century publications such as *Gardener's Chronicle* and William Cook's *Physiomedical Dispensatory* as well as modern issues of *Kew Scientist*.

And then she found it. Filed with no attempt at concealment in a folder clearly labelled "Kneebone China 1861." It was not the manuscript itself, rather loose, photocopied sheets of dated entries written in a tight copperplate hand with occasional annotated floral sketches, the whole thing faint to the eye, leading her to assume that the original was much faded, probably fragile, undoubtedly safely archived somewhere back in Ontario.

She took the entire folder and drove as if pursued by demons to the Brieux's emporium. Paul and Mado had recently installed a photocopier, self-serve at twenty-five centimes per page.

"What are you up to?" asked Paul when she requested change.

His casual question hit her like an inquisition. To put him off the scent, Mara bought a pot of Marmite and a jar of Branston Pickle—Julian liked Marmite on his morning toast and cheese and pickle sandwiches for lunch—from the "English" section of the counter, stalling until Paul was distracted by another customer before doing her photocopying.

An hour later, she had returned the diary to its place, locked the cottage, and was speeding away.

•

That evening, footsore and exhausted, Julian stumbled into the house. He found Mara in the kitchen, attended by the dogs, preparing her mother's foolproof recipe for spaghetti Bolognese.

Her mother, a very good cook, frequently sent Mara recipes that Mara generally found anything but foolproof.

"Any luck?" he asked eagerly.

Something made Mara want him to pay for what he had put her through.

"How did Orchids 101 go?" she asked, ignoring his question. Her voice was like honey dripping from a knife.

"Oh," said Julian, reading her temper correctly. He aimed a kiss at her cheek that she neatly sidestepped. "Give me strength," he muttered, and went to liberate a beer from the refrigerator. "If you must know, Charlie was like a sponge and indefatigable."

"You must have loved having such an attentive student."

"You know very well I didn't. Our boy took photographs and notes every step of the way and drove me round the twist with questions. I dragged him uphill and downhill, through field and forest, into bogs, across streams, and damn me if he didn't stick to me like a burr. And he was surprisingly able to follow all the botanical jargon I threw at him." Julian dropped on to a stool and drew a long swig straight from the bottle. "He wants me to take him out again next week."

"And will you?"

"Once is enough," Julian grumbled. He watched as she overturned a pot of steaming pasta into a colander. "Look, Mara, I'm sorry. I know I shouldn't have involved you—"

"No, you shouldn't have." She banged the pot down and swung about on him, fists on hips, eyes blazing. "And yes, I got it, since that's all you really care about. Your precious photocopy's there." She pointed to a buff-coloured envelope lying on the counter.

"Mara, you're brilliant!" He lurched to his feet.

She shoved him back. "Not until you hear me out, Julian Wood. For your information, I didn't feel good about what I did, going through Charlie's things. You know, the diary wasn't locked in a briefcase or stuffed under the mattress. It was right out in plain view. Why? Because he trusts you, Julian. He knows you can let yourself into the cottage anytime you like, but it doesn't occur to him that you won't play fair. You, on the other hand, think the imperative of your damned orchid excuses anything. Well, let me tell you something, Mr. *Cypripedium Über Alles*, you are going to give Charlie everything he asks for. You are going to take him out on walks 'til you drop, if that's what he wants. You are going to assist him in every way in researching his book. And you are going to tell him *exactly* where you think *Cypripedium incognitum* is to be found. Because if you don't"—she paused to draw breath—"I will."

"Mara!" Julian was flabbergasted and outraged.

"I mean it. I know all about Les Colombes, Aurillac Ridge and the Sigoulane Valley. I was there with you, in case you've forgotten, beating the bushes. You have your damned diary. Now pay up."

Their eyes locked. Julian was unequal to the contest. He looked away, ashamed.

"You're right, of course," he mumbled. "Sorry. I've behaved like a right pillock. I'll—I'll do everything you said."

"No holding back?" Her lips were still tight.

He shook his head. "No holding back."

"Promise?"

"Promise. Now can I read the bloody diary?"

15

Julian put on his glasses, took a long, satisfying swig of beer and pored over the first page of the diary. In early March 1861, Horatio Kneebone, accompanied by his servant Pung, left Shanghai aboard a Russell Company steamer that took them up the Yangtze River as far as Hankow. There the two men boarded a series of smaller boats to make the perilous month-long journey to Ch'ung Ch'ing. Horatio's entries during this leg of his travels related mostly to the dangers of river travel, the constant threat of pirates, the numerous rapids and gorges through which the boat had to be hauled by men using rocky, precarious footholds, and the occasional necessity of going overland when certain stretches of the river were impassable.

18 March. Our journey continues to be slowed by the strong current against which the boatmen row, or occasionally, when the winds are favourable, raise sail. Fortunately for me, the winter and spring have been unusually dry, otherwise the passage would have been impracticable at this time . . .

23 March. Continuously encounter dangerous rapids through which our boat must be towed by hauliers. Warned of river pirates, but fortunately have encountered none so far. The country through which we pass much deforested . . .

29 March. Broke our hawser in violent rainstorm today. But for the quick action of the hauliers, would have been carried away by the current and undoubtedly smashed to pieces . . .

On 5 April, they reached Ch'ung Ch'ing:

Arrived at last at Ch'ung Ch'ing where Pung and I disembarked and where we now enjoy the hospitality of Monsieur Dunaud, with whom I have communicated these several years and whose reports of fabulous flora have drawn me to these parts.

6 April. Dunaud is an even more knowledgeable botanist than his letters have led me to believe and would accompany me on my explorations but that his duties require him here, for he runs a small Catholic college in the city. He is deeply committed to the work of making converts of the heathen Chinese. I am careful to play the devout believer in his presence. Will reprovision here before continuing overland to Ch'eng Tu.

"Do you have an atlas?" Julian called from the dining table where the diary pages were spread around him.

"Bookshelf under the window," Mara answered, assembling the Bolognese at the stove.

A moment later he groaned. "Sod it. I can't find Ch'ung Ch'ing."

"The spellings are all different. They've changed since Horatio wrote that. Everything's in Pinyin now."

"Oh. Then maybe what he calls Ch'eng Tu is now Chengdu. That's the capital of Sichuan Province."

"Hot-pot and Mama Deng country," said Mara.

She was giving the sauce a final stir when Julian's sudden shout of triumph almost made her drop the spoon.

"Eureka! This is it!"

"What?" She came to the kitchen door.

"Just listen:

'7 April. I asked Dunaud if he had heard about Yong Chun Hua, the so-called Eternal Youth Flower, purported to grow in these parts, for it is what I especially am eager to find. He laughed, dismissing it as a pagan myth, but advised that I explore the mountains to the north and west, for he has heard reports of rich orchid sites there.'

"That answers one of my questions, Mara. Horatio knew about Yong Chun Hua, alias *Cypripedium incognitum*. The big question is, did he find it?" He continued reading aloud:

"'8 April. Alarmed and disgusted to find Tarquin Foster also arrived in Ch'ung Ch'ing! He is backed by "Mad" Harry, Lord Masterman, and boasts of having an open purse at his command. Is it coincidence or, since my intention to travel up the Yangtze was bruited in certain circles, has Foster purposely followed me? I know him of old, a poacher of other men's discoveries, a human hyena, too cowardly to bring down its own prey but quick to drive the legitimate hunter from its kill by the lowest means. Last night he courted my company with flattery and fawning, but I watched his eyes, burning with curiosity as he sought to know my intentions in these parts. Said nothing to him of Yong Chun Hua, of course, and will beg M. Dunaud to keep silent on this point . . .'"

"Sounds like bloody Géraud!"

"Sounds like you!"

"I hope you're not calling me a hyena."

"Of course not. I meant the burning eyes part."

Mara returned to the kitchen, and Julian continued devouring the diary.

9 April. Through the good offices of M. Dunaud, able to procure a cash advance from a local merchant, who has also agreed to send word ahead to provide me with a similar service in Ch'eng Tu.

11 April. Much precious time wasted in procuring porters and a closed chair in which I will travel, for though I dress as a Chinaman, I am discernibly not one, and people in these parts are not well disposed to Europeans, whom they consider spies and devils. I find I must watch Pung closely, for I have discovered him dishonest. He hired four men to carry my chair and a further three porters for our things for an outrageous amount of cash, some of which I suspect he pocketed . . .

A few minutes later, Julian called out, "He's a cagey old dodger, is Horatio. Foster proposed travelling together for safety against bandits. Horatio pretended to agree, then gave Foster the slip by setting up a rendezvous with him and going ahead without him. It took him twelve days to get to Ch'eng Tu on a road that sounds like it was mostly up and down steps, with him in a right sweat to shake Foster all the way."

Julian read on:

24 April. In Ch'eng Tu forced to pay an unconscionable amount for two miserable, ill-tempered ponies, and after much haggling finally found two men willing to guide me as far as Lantin. Must be away well before first light tomorrow. Tarquin Foster will have had no difficulty following my trail and surely gains on me with every minute lost . . .

"Dinner coming up," announced Mara.

Julian read avidly through spaghetti in sauce *à la maman* followed by salad and fruit, scarcely noticing what went into his mouth. When Mara rose to clear the table, he informed her, "They're heading into the mountains now."

30 April. Porters left us at Lantin, insisting that I pay them an additional 600 cash as a 'present,' of which I suspect Pung pocketed his share. After much difficulty engaged a guide to take us into the mountains, a savage-looking fellow dressed in a cloak made of some kind of fibrous material resembling tree bark. Pung, who somehow manages to communicate with him, says the fellow knows of high places where there are many "pocket flowers" in this season, by which I take him to mean Cypripediums, *but claims ignorance of anything resembling Yong Chun Hua . . .*

2 May. Set out early. Terrain extremely rugged and ponies skittish on the narrow paths. Today, we covered some twenty miles, our supplies going horseback, I, Pung and Tree Bark, as I've taken to calling our guide, on foot . . .

5 May. This morning, from the vantage of the foothills, I looked with my binocular telescope back across the distance we had come and saw a convoy of men and beasts winding up the valley. It had to be Foster who, I am certain, saw us, too. He is at most half a day's march behind us. When Pung explained to Tree Bark the importance of outdistancing Foster's party, the man said we would lose the "snake's tail" (as he calls it) easily enough but warned that we would have to keep our wits about us once in the mountains, for there are bandits about. On this score, I am confident, for I am an excellent shot and carry with me not only my gun but two loaded four-shot revolvers, very much in evidence to deter would-be brigands. Less sure of losing the "snake's tail." Mountains rise before us, exceedingly wild . . .

"Damn!"

"What's wrong now?" Mara was loading the dishwasher.

"There's a break. Horatio's entry on 5 May has him about to go into the mountains, trailed by Foster, but the next page puts him—I don't believe this!" Julian's voice rose to a piercing wail. "Back in sodding Ch'eng Tu on 2 July! From there"—Julian pawed feverishly through the remaining pages—"he travels back down to Ch'ung Ch'ing, and the diary ends in August with him back in Shanghai!" More pawing. "He talks about preparing plants for shipment back to Europe, and here he mentions an orchid—a single plant that must be *Cypripedium incognitum*. But what happened in the meantime? Are you sure that's all there was? You're positive you copied everything?"

Mara came out from the kitchen to peer at the scattered papers. "Absolutely. Anyway, why are you so surprised? Charlie told you there was nothing more than the sketch in the diary. Besides, it's nearly a century and a half old. Some of the pages probably got lost."

"You don't understand. The drawing of *Cypripedium incognitum*'s not here either." Julian slammed his fist on the table. "So where is it? And if it's gone, what else went with it? It's not just the occasional page missing, Mara. A whole bloody section's been taken out!"

"Maybe Horatio removed it himself."

"Or Charlie did. Don't you get it? That rubbish about Horatio not wanting anyone else to find out about the orchid—it was Charlie not wanting *me* to get the information, and he planned it from the start. So much for trust and fair play!" Julian's face was white with anger.

"But why would he do that? And please don't shout."

"Because he's a sneaking little stoat, that's why. He knows I'd kill for information on *Cypripedium incognitum*, and he wants to make me twist in the wind. What's so funny?"

Mara had fallen back into a chair, shaking with laughter. "You're the one who doesn't get it," she gasped. "Charlie's outfoxed you. He took out all the stuff he figured you'd be interested in because he knew—oh, God, it's so ironic—you'd try to steal—sorry—*borrow* the diary, and he's teaching you a lesson. He read you right from the get-go, and he's been one step ahead of you all the time! Face it. You've met your match. And it's no better than you deserve."

Julian looked dumbfounded. A moment later he said drily, "*Touché*." His lips curled in a curious smile.

Mara sat up. "What?"

"At least I know one thing. Kneebone not only found *Cypripedium incognitum*, he made diary entries on its location as well. Charlie wouldn't have removed the pages if there was nothing more on it and the drawing was just a copy. This means the important bits have got to be somewhere in the cottage."

"You don't know that. Maybe Charlie didn't bring them. Maybe, guessing what you'd be like, he left them in Canada."

Julian ignored her implication. "Oh, I think he has the entire manuscript with him. He needs both the drawing and Horatio's habitat notes. Don't forget, he wants to find *Cypripedium incognitum* too." He gazed speculatively at Mara.

She threw up her hands. "No way! Don't even think it. I refuse to be used by you again. Do your own thieving."

"Okay, okay. I'll do my own thieving. But this lets me off the hook."

"What do you mean?"

"Charlie's not as innocent as you like to believe. I'm damned if I'll take the bugger near another orchid, let alone show him where I think *Cypripedium incognitum* grows."

Mara jumped to her feet. "Oh no, you don't, Julian. Charlie did nothing more than protect what's his. Just because he outsmarted you doesn't mean you can wriggle out of your promise. If you don't come through, I swear I'll tell him everything you don't want him to know."

"Mara, for Chrissake, see reason. Charlie's behaviour changes everything. He—you can't—I'm not—"

The phone rang. Still spluttering, Julian went to answer it.

"Yes, what?" he bellowed. Then he said in a calmer tone, "*Ah oui. D'accord . . . Okay . . . d'accord . . .*" He grabbed pencil and paper and began writing swiftly. "*Okay. C'est bon.*" By the time he hung up, he seemed to have forgotten all about Charlie.

"What was that all about?" Mara asked suspiciously.

"Eh? Oh, that was Jean-Luc Jarry. I told you about him. He's the head of ActionTerre, the organization that's spearheading the challenge of the BoniSom patent." Julian looked excited. "The demonstration for Baixi rights is set for Wednesday at noon outside the Bonisanté headquarters in Bordeaux. They've got media coverage. I promised I'd go, do my bit for the orchids." He paused. "I was rather hoping you'd come too. They need all the bodies they can get."

"Oh great," said Mara in disgust. "First I'm a burglar. Now I'm a body. Thank you very much."

16

Mara downloaded information from the Internet and discovered, once she saw the logo, that she was more familiar with Bonisanté S.A. products than she had thought. The company's three entwined leaves were a familiar display in most pharmacies, which carried its phytotherapeutic treatments for everything from ailing livers to benign prostate hyperplasia, obesity to compromised immune systems. And insomnia.

"Says here Bonisanté began as a small herbal medicine company founded in 1955 by Jules Boniface," she read from her printout while Julian negotiated the congestion of Place Saint-Michel in the old quarter of Bordeaux, looking for a place to park. For the second time, they circled the soaring spire of the Flèche Saint-Michel, the fifteenth-century stand-alone belfry of the basilica of the same name that dominated the square. "It's now Europe's largest herbal pharmaceutical company with offices, research units and partners in North and South America, West Africa, China and Japan. And it sounds like its bioprospectors are as busy as ants, crawling about the planet looking for plants with healing properties."

"We're in luck," declared Julian, as a red Citroën vacated a space just large enough for his van.

They went on foot to arrive a little before twelve at the fringes of a crowd milling about in front of a narrow building. True to its roots, the company's administrative headquarters had remained in the Boniface family home, an old stone structure to which a raised portico—an obvious add-on—gave a certain presence.

Mara had expected something much grander. Then she noticed that the modest frontage masked considerable expansion into abutting properties.

The size of the gathering, for a weekday, was not bad. Demonstrators waved boldly lettered placards: DON'T TAKE WHAT ISN'T YOURS and YOU CAN'T PATENT PEOPLE. In the middle of the road a purple-faced policeman blew his whistle and directed traffic around the crowd spilling off the sidewalk. Arms crossed, a pair of private security guards stood nervously at the top of the portico stairs. Below them a large man addressed the crowd through a sputtering microphone. Around him clustered reporters, photographers and a TV cameraman.

"That must be him." Julian indicated the man to Mara. "Jean-Luc Jarry."

She saw a Promethean figure with a beard, a deeply lined face and a ponytail. His stomach hung out over his jeans, and he wore a T-shirt that read: *Justice Pour les Baixi*. Then her eye was drawn to a well-dressed man standing not far from them at the perimeter of the crowd. Something about his *beau garçon* face seemed vaguely familiar. Searching her recent memory, she realized with a sense of surprise that she was looking at the real-life, somewhat meatier version of a website photo.

"Hey." She tugged Julian's sleeve. "Isn't that What's His Name?"

"Who?"

"The sleep clinic director. Claude Morange."

Julian squinted in the direction she was pointing. "So it is."

"What's he doing here?"

"Maybe he's come to join the demonstration."

Mara did not think so. Morange, in his tailored suit, looked out of place, even a little ill at ease.

Jarry was working the crowd, citing case after case of what he called "blatant biopiracy," where big companies obtained monopoly patents on indigenous food crops, medicinal plants and germ plasm, stealing in the process the traditional know-how of the real innovators, many of them remote tribal people and rural poor in developing countries.

"Every time you turn around, they've taken out another patent on a naturally occurring plant or plant compound," he warned. "Soon nothing growing will be patent-free. Next it will be the water we drink, the air we breathe.

"These patents threaten all of us," Jarry boomed into the microphone, which squawked and whistled in response. "They're also an outright theft of intellectual property. They cut off market opportunities to the original and true developers, and they strip those same people of the right to their own creations. At the very least, the real inventors should get a share of the royalties—"

"And we all believe in *Père Noël*!" a young woman with a nose stud, also in a *Justice Pour les Baixi* T-shirt, shrilled.

"You got it, Danielle!" Jarry cocked a forefinger at her. "Companies like Bonisanté get fat by stealing other people's biological resources and know-how. The patenting of the Baixi's Sleep Tea is just one more flagrant example. And that is why, my friends"—he was on a roll—"we are here to call on the World Intellectual Property Organization to condemn the monopoly patents underlying the sleep medication BoniSom, and to appeal to the French government and the French people to take a stand against the practice of predatory patents. Let me be very clear. Today we make history. France is our test case!"

There was a sudden eruption as a shoving, struggling phalanx of bodies rushed the stairs. Others joined in. The media representatives swung away from Jarry to focus on the crowd. The security guards, legs and arms outspread and backed up against Bonisanté's front door, tried to hold off the surge. By then more people had joined the demonstration, occupying half the street. The policeman with his whistle was drowned out by drivers blasting their horns. Jarry, abandoned, was left mouthing at no one in particular. Julian, dragging Mara with him, chose that moment to make himself known.

"*Qui*?" Jarry, momentarily thrown by losing the limelight, shouted over the noise. "Ah, Monsieur Wood." He gave Julian an intensely speculative look before clapping him on the back and seizing his hand. "Yes, you're joining us. That's good. And—?" He fixed a red-rimmed adrenalin-charged gaze on Mara. "You an orchid specialist as well?"

"I'm here with Julian," said Mara, aware that Jarry was frowning at her chest. Her T-shirt, one that Patsy had made especially for her, read:

ORCHIDSMA
KEYOUR
EYESGOF
UNNY

"No matter. We need all the support we can get." He had the grace not to call her a body. He waved at the crowd swarming the portico. "A damned good turnout. And the media are behind us. This time, I really think we've got them."

Danielle of the nose stud seized the microphone. "Come out, come out, come out!"

The crowd picked up the chant and began a slow, ironic clapping.

Bonisanté's doors remained implacably shut.

"You see?" Jarry boomed, taking the microphone back. "They won't face us. They huddle inside like corporate cowards. They fear exposure."

Suddenly, the doors did open, and a startled-looking young man popped out, rather like a rabbit thrown to the hounds. The air was thick with derisive whistles and catcalls. The rabbit's glazed eyes swept the faces around him before fixing on Jarry. He mouthed something and began pushing his way down through the press of people to the ActionTerre leader's side, where he squeaked a few words in Jarry's ear.

"*Mes amis*," Jarry bellowed, pumping a fist. "You are witnessing the first crack in the dam. They will not come out, but we—just a select few, mind you—are being admitted into the inner sanctum." He said the words sardonically, eliciting a mixture of cheers and jeers. "What does that tell us?"

"They're pissing their pants," someone yelled.

"That, too. It tells us they haven't the courage to face us out here. It tells us they need to pare down our numbers to a manageable few in order to deal with us. Stand fast, I beg you. We will win this battle on behalf of the Baixi."

The crowd roared. Handing the mic back to Danielle, Jarry beckoned to a core of perhaps a dozen people to follow him, sweeping Julian and Mara along with them.

"They're inviting the media in as well," Jarry confided rapidly to Julian. "I want you with us to do your endangered orchid bit. That kind of thing always goes down well. And don't be taken in. You can be sure Bonisanté has its guns loaded, otherwise they wouldn't consider opening their doors like this."

17

The scene that greeted them when they entered the premises bore out Jarry's prediction. In the foyer, chairs had been set up auditorium style. Smiling Bonisanté staff were on hand to greet and seat them and hand out press releases. At the back of the area, more security guards discreetly blocked access to a pair of elevators and corridors leading to other parts of the building.

"*Putain*!" Jarry spat out in disgust.

The doors of one of the elevators opened on an imposing woman in her sixties, impeccably dressed and groomed. Her sensible heels rang out sharply on the terrazzo as she swept forward. A pair of glasses swung with the energy of her stride from a lanyard around her neck. Slightly behind and partly obscured by her, hurrying to keep up, was a thin young man with a tight mouth below a toucan's bill of a nose. His black hair, slicked to his scalp, looked painted on.

"Madame Juliette Thory, company CEO," Jarry muttered to Julian and Mara as the pair sat down at a table at the front. "She's the heavy artillery. Father founded the business, but she has a Ph.D in biochemistry and in the early days used to do a lot of the actual R and D herself. Now the company farms out its work to labs worldwide. It was their North American unit that developed BoniSom."

"Who's the man?" asked Mara.

"Edgard Papineau, marketing and PR. Son-in-law. Took over the position after Thory's husband died. It's a close, family-run business. There's a sister who co-owns the company with Thory and is a member of the board, but she keeps mostly in the background."

Thory brought the room to order simply by clearing her throat. She did not need the tiny static-free microphone that Edgard Papineau tried to clip to her lapel; her voice projected well.

"Welcome everyone. Welcome to our media corps and"—a swift movement to set the glasses on her nose, a glance at a prompt sheet—"representatives of ActionTerre, FemNova, Vilmondo, Social Justice Coalition and Ecovent."

"Econvert," a scowling young man in tattered jeans corrected.

"Econvert, of course."

Mince! Julian could not help a surge of admiration for the way the Bonisanté boss assumed command. She was like royalty granting an audience.

Thory smiled and took in the room with a cool, blue gaze. "Have I forgotten anyone?"

"The Baixi National Minority People," someone growled.

Her smile remained riveted in place. "I'm Juliette Thory, president and CEO of Bonisanté, and this is Edgard Papineau, our director of marketing." The hi-gloss head inclined slightly. "Our objective in asking a representative group of you in is to clear up what I'm sure is an unfortunate misunderstanding of Bonisanté's actions—"

"Cut the crap and tell us what you plan to do about the patents," another voice said, more audibly.

Unperturbed, Thory went on, "And to ensure that members of the media have the opportunity to ask questions so that they can take away an informed picture of the situation." She nodded to various faces that she seemed to recognize. "So I'd like to start out by telling you briefly what Bonisanté is all about, and then we can open up the floor to discussion. Is that acceptable?"

"We know what you're all about—money," the Econvert man shouted, this time to jeers, but beyond that no one openly disagreed with her plan.

"The story of Bonisanté is really the story of my father, and it's perhaps already known to some of you. As a child, my father was very sickly. He was treated with all kinds of medications, the so-called wonder drugs of the day, none of which helped him, and one of which nearly killed him. Finally, he was given a traditional herbal remedy by an old farming woman. It restored his health. My father's interest in natural medicines stemmed from that point. He was convinced that the rich store of herbal medicinal knowledge of France—indeed, globally—should not only be preserved, but documented, tested and developed. With the founding of Bonisanté more than half a century ago, his sole objective became to produce the best, most effective herbal medicines in the world. Simply put, our mission is to offer people healthier natural alternatives to the negative side effects of modern synthetic drugs. Our motto is 'The Purest and the Best.'"

At this Jarry rose. "Sounds noble, but you're omitting to say your overriding concern is your profit margin. So how are you different from the hundreds of other companies and research outfits that screen plants for their exploitable properties and develop them for the market? You also seem to have no problem robbing people of their traditional know-how when you find something you want. Your slapping a BoniSom label on the Baixi's Sleep Tea doesn't make it yours. So why do you think you have the right to a monopoly patent?"

Thory kept her cool. "First, I'd like to point out that the Baixi's so-called intellectual property claim on the soporific power of their Sleep Tea is undocumented—"

"Doesn't the fact that they've made it for centuries count for anything?" a woman called out.

"Second"—Thory ignored the rising tension in the room—"their claim is hardly exclusive. Many cultures have traditionally used related orchid species for their soporific properties, not only in Asia but in the western hemisphere as well. Our North American R and D unit, for example, has done extensive study on the use of *Cypripedium pubescens* as a calmative by native Indians."

Jarry shouted triumphantly, "You've just proved our point. You don't have the right to claim what many other people have discovered. That's what this challenge is all about."

There were cries of "Go to it, Jean-Luc!" and "*C'est ça*!" Two reporters scribbled furiously. Two others held up tape recorders.

Thory shook her head. "You've got it wrong. The Baixi's Sleep Tea is of no interest to us. It's nothing more than a simple infusion of glycosides, volatile oils, tannin and resin. What we've patented is Bonisanté's isolation and innovative formulation of cypronoline, an alkaloid found in the source plant and the active ingredient of BoniSom."

Papineau, ready to do his stuff, slid in. His voice, honked out of his prominent nasal chamber, was loud and piercing. "Look, we don't deny the Baixi people's claim to Sleep Tea. What Doctor Thory is saying is BoniSom's a completely different product. And while we sometimes springboard from traditional knowledge, our objective *always* is to produce something *better*. *That's* what we're patenting—our research and development, our testing—"

A woman in green rose to cut him off. "I represent FemNova, an NGO concerned with the economic rights of women. It's the Baixi women who invented Sleep Tea. For generations they and their mothers and grandmothers before them have gathered the plants and boiled the roots to make their medicine. Your so-called sophisticated isolation and formulation has been reviewed by Professor Beaudoin of Montpellier University, who found it's not a lot more than grinding, soaking and boiling the roots and extracting what you want—no different really from the traditional method. Where's the innovation?"

The sphincter of Papineau's mouth tightened. "The innovation is *how* we do it, our R and D, our quality control. Look, hundreds of millions of people all over the world, most of them rural poor in developing countries, rely on traditional plant therapies that are produced with absolutely no quality control and no benefit of research. Even in the industrialized world, consumers buy herbals on faith. Most are untested for efficacy or safety and in many countries are sold as food supplements because they can't label themselves as legitimate medicines. That's where Bonisanté comes in. We engage in extensive pre-clinical testing and product trials."

Although Mara instinctively disliked the gel-head marketing director, she thought he had a point.

But the FemNova woman merely snorted. "The Baixi have been taking Sleep Tea for generations with no ill effects, so the safety of the product is hardly something you've had to worry about."

Laughter and jeers, which Papineau overrode. "Do you have any idea how many negative events, including deaths, are caused every year by the ingestion of so-called home-made remedies? In BoniSom, we offer sufferers of sleep disorders an effective, trustworthy product that, I might point out, is now the world's fastest growing sleep medication."

"Yeah, and you offer it at a price most of the world can't afford," said a heavy-set fellow who identified himself as being with the Social Justice Coalition. "Or maybe you think the poor don't have trouble sleeping? Face it, your target market is insomniacs in rich countries able to fork out fifteen euros a packet. That's a week's wages for some."

Papineau opened his mouth, but Thory suppressed him with a look.

"And what about *our* wage earners?" she segued smoothly. "You seem to see us as a monolithic enterprise, Bonisanté S.A., multinational corporate enemy number one. You forget that we're made up of people. We employ directly and indirectly nearly two thousand individuals. Exploring the plant frontier is a slow and costly business. Of the million or so higher plant species on earth, at most a third have been identified, and only a small number of these have been studied. We provide a livelihood for our bioprospectors, our botanical advisers, our researchers, our technicians, our rank-and-file employees. We also provide incomes for many of the world's poor that you seem so worried about. We pay our plant hunters and gatherers, we reward them well for *their* effort and expertise. I take it you have no trouble with that?"

"So how much do you pay them?" piped up a Vilmondo representative.

"Centimes," shouted the Social Justice Coalition man. "While Bonisanté rakes in the big money."

Papineau blasted through him. "Maybe you should ask how the Baixi themselves feel about it."

Jarry guffawed. "It should be obvious. They're suing you."

Laughter rippled across the room. The media types joined in.

Papineau's complexion darkened. His voice became even more nasally shrill. "No. A small group of villagers, stirred up by people like you, want to overthrow our legal patents. You forget that we and our Chinese partner, Double Joy Natural Products, have the willing cooperation of the people in the growing areas in bringing a quality product to market. You forget that many Baixi households now derive steady income from providing us with harvested roots."

"Oh sure," the FemNova woman scoffed. "You've got it all sewn up, the source plants and cheap female labour. You're the monopsonistic buyer, the sole purchaser. You call the shots. If you feel like lowering the price per kilo by fifty percent tomorrow, who's to stop you?"

Jarry elbowed Julian sharply and said, *sotto voce*, "Come on, man. What are you waiting for? Do your thing."

Julian, who had been mesmerized by the rapid exchange, started. "And what about the impact on the orchids?" he spoke up. His voice, echoing in the stony foyer, sounded unnaturally thin.

Thory's eyes narrowed as she sought Julian out. "And you are?"

He rose, took a deep breath and said with more authority, "My name is Julian Wood. I'm here to speak on behalf of the only player in this sorry drama that can't speak for itself, *Cypripedium somniferum*, an orchid that grows in only one place in the world, the mountains of southwest China."

Thory frowned at the prompt sheet and consulted swiftly with Papineau. Neither seemed prepared for this wrinkle.

Julian thundered on. "What I'd like to know is how many tons of roots you harvest every year. Your demand could wipe out the entire natural population, you know. And how have you managed to get permission for the mass exportation of orchid rhizomes? You're surely aware that *Cypripediums* are protected under CITES II regulations?"

Papineau's lips twitched in a tight smile. He waved a hand. "Monsieur Wood, let me assure you. Not only do we have the necessary permits to export the roots, the amount we use in no way threatens the sustainability of *Cypripedium somniferum*. Believe me, Bonisanté is as concerned as you about the ecological impact of long-term harvesting. We strive, after all, to be eco-friendly—"

"What about people-friendly?" the Vilmondo person challenged.

Papineau trumpeted through the interruption. "First of all, we only harvest in the fall, when the plants are dormant. Second, we're using other parts of the plant that also contain the alkaloid we're interested in, to take pressure off the root system."

"Are you saying you no longer harvest roots?" demanded Julian, wanting to be absolutely clear on this matter.

"Let me put it this way. We hope to reduce substantially our reliance on the roots in the near future."

"How near?"

Papineau ducked the question and plowed ahead. "Most important, we're working on ways of cultivating the orchid commercially. As we speak, we're negotiating with the Chinese authorities and individual farmers to set up plantations in the growing areas so as not to exhaust the wild supply. This will provide the Baixi people with even greater sources of income. So you see, monsieur, all of your concerns are being addressed."

"God in heaven, man," Julian objected. "Orchids aren't wheat that you sow in spring and harvest in autumn. They take time to establish, they can be bloody temperamental, and they don't respond well to commercial cultivation."

Thory, who had been frowning at Julian with growing disfavour, spoke up. "Surely someone like you must have heard of *Gastrodia elata*, which has been cultivated commercially for years with great success." Her tone was condescending.

"What's that when it's at home?" the Econvert representative sang out.

"A woodland orchid traditionally used by the Chinese to treat hypertension," Thory responded with cold satisfaction.

Julian, who had never heard of *Gastrodia elata* either, shook his head. "I'm not convinced. As far as I know, it's not that easy to grow orchids in sufficient quantity for the kind of commercial cropping you have in mind. It'll take you years to get up and running. In the meantime, you'll continue digging up more and more wild plants to meet demand. By the time you figure out your experiment doesn't work, you'll have exhausted the natural supply. What then? Will you find another species of orchid to exploit to the point of extinction?"

Papineau's nostrils flared. "That won't happen. It wouldn't be in our interest—"

"Which is all that counts." Éconvert again.

"The question is," Jarry broke through, sensing that the ecological argument was beginning to see-saw, "will Bonisanté respect the rights of the real creators of BoniSom? Will it waive its existing patents and cease to attempt to extend its patent rights in other parts of the world?"

The answer to this was flatly negative, and Juliette Thory was giving no one the time to dwell on it. She brought the meeting to a close with a rapid summing up of the good Bonisanté did in the world, its outstanding reputation, the benefits it brought to consumers and suppliers alike. Then she and Papineau, like hosts slipping away from a boring party, thanked everyone for coming and strode quickly to one of the elevators, where they turned to smile and wave obligingly at the TV cameraman who followed them. The metal doors slid shut. With flawless timing, the second elevator doors parted, and a well-stocked trolley was trundled forth by a remarkably nubile female.

"By God," Jarry fumed, "the *salauds* are even serving food and drink! What the hell is this, some kind of *maudit* sales convention?"

More like an instance of stomach persuasion. Julian was forced to admire their tactics. The noon hour had come and gone, and the media people were hungry. They swarmed the trolley. He himself longed for a beer but noticed that the protestors, drawing together in an indignant huddle, stood well away from the refreshments. All momentum lost, the meeting broke up. The FemNova woman suggested a sit-in, but Jarry nixed the idea immediately. A reporter with his mouth full approached Julian, asking how to spell *Cypripedium somniferum.*

It was then that Jarry played his master stroke. Charging the trolley, he scooped up a handful of hors d'oeuvres and held them aloft.

"*Mes amis*," he roared. The media types, sensing a photo-of-the-week in the making, stopped chewing and reached for their cameras. "My friends, we came today to ask serious questions that merit serious answers. What did we get? We got *bouchées à la reine*!" The queen's mouthfuls, as the savoury pastries were called. He threw them into the air. Vol-au-vent cases with their creamed chicken fillings went flying. The TV camera caught the action, and those who got the play on words broke into noisy laughter.

Jarry bellowed on, "This tells you Bonisanté has no answers to give, nothing that it dares admit publicly. It has shamefully stolen and patented the intellectual property of the Baixi, and it fully intends to secure its profits through the monopoly patent process. Our course of action is clear. We will fight them in the international courts, and we will win. As of today, we urge a total boycott of all Bonisanté products. Tell your friends, tell your neighbours, tell your colleagues at work, tell your families. Let your euros speak for you. You wouldn't buy a hot car from a thief, would you? Then why buy a hot product from a corporate crook?"

•

"Well, that went well." Jarry looked around him in satisfaction. "How many do you think turned up, Danielle?"

Danielle fingered her nose stud and reckoned maybe five hundred at the peak. People had drifted away when the action had moved indoors.

The core group, including Mara and Julian, were now at a sidewalk café. They had pushed tables and chairs together and shouted out orders for food and drink. Mara had an omelette and iced tea, Julian a sandwich *jambon* and a Leffe.

Jarry, sitting across from them and also downing a beer, wiped foam from his whiskers with the back of his hand. "*Pas mal*," he chuckled. "Not bad at all. And this is just the beginning."

Mara wondered at his buoyancy. He had carried off a media coup with the *bouchées a la reine*, but the demonstration itself had produced nothing definitive. Thory and Papineau had had answers for everything. A lot of the wind, she felt, had been taken out of the protestors' sails. She glanced at Julian beside her, but he was thumbing a waiter for another Leffe.

As if guessing her doubt, Jarry addressed her personally. "This is how a social movement starts. Small drops converging into a stream"—he banged his glass down to knit his fingers together—"then a river, then an ocean, you see? And never doubt that this is a social movement. It's not just the Baixi we're fighting for. It's all part of a bigger thing." He nodded at Julian. "As for you, *mec*, you did your part well. You've a gift for the gab when you get fired up."

"I do?" Julian, feeling excessively pleased, took a hungry bite of ham sandwich. Then he realized that Jarry had stopped smiling and was studying him closely. The speculative look with which he had first greeted Julian was back.

"Okay." The other man planted his forearms, like a challenge, on the table. "No more games. I know why you're here. The question is, what do you have for us and how much?"

"Wha—what?" A splotch of mustard dropped onto Julian's shirt.

"Come on. Your name was in the news. You're the husband." And when Julian continued to look bewildered, Jarry said impatiently, "I'm talking about Véronique Rignon."

Caught off guard, Julian almost blurted out, *I didn't do it*. He changed it to, "What about her?"

Jarry glanced around quickly and lowered his voice, speaking into his flowing beard. "She approached us. A couple of weeks ago, as I'm sure you know. She'd heard about our case against Bonisanté and offered to sell us information she said would blow the company out of the water. Her very words. But she wanted a lot of money, and—no offence intended—she didn't sound like the kind of person who could deliver what she promised. I put her off. I needed to be sure who and what I was dealing with. Next I heard, she was dead. Then, when you got in touch, I realized it was no coincidence. You know what your wife was up to, don't you. And you've got more than orchids on your mind. So what is it?"

"I assure you I have no idea what you're talking about," said Julian, much alarmed. "I haven't—Véronique and I split up years ago. And I *didn't* know she'd contacted you."

"You'd be striking a blow for good," Jarry pressed, switching on his adrenalin eyes and his full powers of persuasion. "For justice. For people who can't defend themselves. For ecological conservancy. We really do need to know what she had on Bonisanté. Does it have something to do with orchids? We can't pay much, not nearly what she demanded, but I sense you genuinely care about your *Cypripedium* whatever, and it would help us enormously if you could give us something that would pull the legs out from under Bonisanté's case."

"I tell you, I haven't a clue!"

Prometheus sighed and sat back, crossing his arms before his chest. "Julian, as you must be aware, a lot is riding on the outcome of this patents challenge. The stakes here are enormous, man. Not just for the Baixi, not just for us. We're locked in a global battle against big-business greed and exploitation, and we need every weapon we can lay our hands on. So . . . I'm asking you again. Join us. Be part of the fight."

Julian gestured helplessly. "Look, I would if I could. But I'm afraid the only thing we found—*oi*!" Under the table Mara had cut him off with a swift kick to the shins that made his eyes water.

"—is that nothing related to Véronique makes sense," she finished for him. "Julian's telling you the truth, Jean-Luc. He really knows nothing."

•

"Why did you stop me when I started to mention the Pronole-2 list?" Julian asked as they left the café to walk back to the van. His shin still hurt.

"Honestly, Julian. You have no sense of self-preservation. Oh, I'm sure Jarry's concern for social justice is genuine. But a conspiracy theory involving you and Véronique is the last thing you want the police to get hold of."

"But what if the list was what Véronique wanted to sell to ActionTerre?"

"Then have you considered it might have been what got her killed? And if it's linked to something as big as Bonisanté, don't you think before you go public with it we'd better find out what the hell we're dealing with?"

18

Patsy Reicher was cursing herself. Perhaps because she had been puzzling over the impressions she had taken away from the clinic, she had missed her turn onto the D57 coming out of Sarlat. Things looked different after an absence of so many years, her old landmarks gone or no longer recognizable. She now found herself in Carsac, on the D704, heading in the wrong direction. Eventually, she managed to reconnect with the D703 and was now bearing west, as she had intended. The brash afternoon light made her squint. She wished she had brought her sunglasses. She took a curve too fast and slid with a squeal of tires across the narrow departmental road that wound along the cliffs high above the Dordogne River.

"*Merde*!" she muttered aloud, downshifting to regain control of the car. Thankfully, it was early May and there were no oncoming vehicles. Had it been July or August, the traffic would have been crazy.

Her meeting with Claude Morange had started well but ended abruptly and decidedly oddly. Early for her two o'clock appointment, she had hung about the empty reception area until a tall blonde walked out of an office, stared at her in surprise and asked rather rudely what she wanted. Patsy explained that she had a meeting with the director.

"Wait here," said the blonde. She disappeared into the same office and re-emerged a moment later.

"He'll see you now." She gestured abruptly with her head before stalking off down the hall.

"Dr. Reicher!" A big man, dressed in linen trousers and an avocado-green silk shirt, came forward from behind a desk. "*Enchanté*, *madame*. Claude Morange." He gave her the benefit of his massive handshake, his smile, his thrusting jaw, his aggressive aftershave. His furnishings—teak, black leather—matched his macho presence. In one corner of the room there was a patient couch, also in black leather.

"Please." Morange waved her toward one of a pair of armchairs and offered her coffee, an aperitif if she preferred. She accepted coffee. He stuck his head out the door and called down the hall, presumably to the blonde, "*Deux cafés*, *s'il vous plaît*, Sandrine."

"From New York, you say?" Morange settled into the other armchair, drawing it nearer and leaning his dark, curly head forward as if to impart greater intimacy to their conversation. They exchanged standard pleasantries until Sandrine reappeared a few minutes later with their coffees.

"We're out of sugar," she announced sourly.

Now it was down to business. Carefully—her French had grown rusty with disuse, but she had taken the precaution of looking up terms in advance—Patsy explained her reasons for coming.

"You see, many of my patients suffer from insomnia. Of course, I treat mainly depression and post-traumatic stress, so disturbed sleep isn't really surprising in such a population. But I'm beginning to wonder if lack of sleep isn't more than just a symptom."

"Ah." Morange was all attention. He sat even farther forward, hands on thighs, his boulder of a jaw cracking into a celebrity smile. "You think it may be an underlying pathology? Now *that* is very interesting. Very interesting indeed. Because, you see, it is exactly the line of study I have been pursuing. It's a well-known fact that people who sleep badly are more irritable, more emotionally unstable, and research is beginning to show that there is a neural basis for this." His dark eyes bored into hers.

"So you think lack of sleep could actually trigger psychiatric illness?"

"*Exactement*! It's what I've been saying for years. In fact, I'm of the opinion that insomnia should be regarded as a serious, discrete disorder, not just a by-product of stress or some other underlying health problem. The entire field of sleep study needs to be reassessed from this perspective."

Patsy nodded gravely. "It's an intriguing idea."

Morange threw up his hands. "My dear Doctor, the world is literally going crazy from lack of sleep! In the last fifty years average sleep time has decreased significantly in the industrialized world. Stress and environmental factors have driven our internal clocks haywire. Billions are spent annually on sleep drugs. And the cost of sleep-related dysfunction is skyrocketing."

He fielded all of her questions enthusiastically, managing at the same time to promote the clinic's international reputation. He seemed hungry for business. Perhaps he was hoping this American psychoanalyst would refer streams of sleepless New Yorkers his way.

Patsy asked for a tour of the premises. Morange was delighted to oblige. Making appropriate comments along the way, he led her through the area where patients were fitted up with biophysiological sensors, then into the wing where the sleep chambers were situated. Here the decor was beige, beige walls, beige carpeting. Was beige, Patsy wondered, the colour of sleep? She noticed that sounds had a curious, muffled quality, as if the very air was swathed in cotton batting. She was certain that if she gave the wall a sharp rap, the result would be not a *whack* but a *thud*.

"The Clinique Morange has long been at the forefront of treating sleep problems," Morange declaimed as they stepped into a glassed-in room equipped with a battery of monitors where Sandrine and a swarthy man, built like a wrestler, paused in their work to glance their way. He lowered his voice. "I really can't say too much at this point, but I should tell you I'm about to launch research into dyssomnias that I'm certain will lead to groundbreaking medical approaches."

Sheer instinct caused Patsy to ask, "It wouldn't be Pronole-2, would it?"

"Eh?" said the doctor blankly. "Of course, one of our strengths is our human resources. We have the services of an excellent respiratory therapist, and we count among our associates physicians trained in all the complementary specialties. Many of the leading names in the field work with us. And Francke and Sandrine here are our two highly trained polysomnographers, who aid us in our diagnosis of sleep disorders." He gave a nod of acknowledgement to the pair.

It seemed to Patsy that if the clinic were such a centre of excellence, the place ought to be a hive of activity. So far, apart from Sandrine, who shot Morange a sulky look, the wrestler, who fixed Patsy with eyes the colour of lead, and Morange himself, there seemed to be no one else on the premises.

"Speaking of staff," Patsy said, seizing the lead Morange had provided, "maybe you can tell me something about a friend of mine. Véronique Rignon. I know she used to work here. Unfortunately, we've lost touch over the years. I'm back just for a short visit, and I really don't know how to get in contact with her."

At this point, Morange was supposed to look grave, tell her, *désolé*, Véronique Rignon is no longer with us, tragic circumstances, and this would have provided the opening for a distraught Patsy to ask lots of questions about her deceased friend, what kind of work she had done at the clinic, and did anyone there know her well?

Instead, Morange clapped his hands and declared, "Well, that's the tour, I'm afraid. And that, my dear Dr. Reicher, is also the end of my time." He pivoted her around and walked her rapidly back the way they had come. "Regretfully, I have another appointment. However, it has been a great pleasure meeting you. Perhaps, if you have more questions about our work, we could talk further on another occasion?"

He escorted her back to his office, allowing her just enough time to retrieve her things, and then out of the building, even right out to her car. Her last glimpse of him, captured in the rearview mirror, was of his large frame, planted on guard, as it were, making sure that she left.

•

A loud honking brought Patsy back to the moment. A truck, coming up suddenly on her tail, followed her closely around a bend, then rattled by as they hit a straightaway. Patsy braked to let it pass.

The doctor's complete closing down at the mention of Véronique made no sense. It was known that Véronique had worked at the clinic, so why had he stonewalled her? Had he simply not wanted to upset her by telling her that her supposed friend was dead? Or, Patsy amended, given Véronique's alleged proclivities and Morange's overt sexuality, maybe the director had wanted to avoid discussing something that must have gone far beyond an employer–employee relationship. She wondered to what use the patient couch was put. And then there was his obvious evasion when she had asked about Pronole-2. What was he hiding? She guessed Sandrine and Francke, given half a chance, could tell her quite a bit. Sandrine looked like a tough cookie, but she wondered if there was a way of getting Francke, who had given her a very odd look, on his own.

Another car behind her gave a blast of the horn, recalling her sharply to her driving and the fact that she had slowed to almost a snail's pace. She sped up, but it tailgated her aggressively until it, too, was able to pass. Far below, the Dordogne River looped like an old, gold serpent, scales glinting in the mellow sunshine.

As she rounded a tight curve, the tunnel took her completely by surprise. Her only thought as she plunged into it was how dark it was, with no interior lighting. Good God, didn't the French have any notion of road safety? She fumbled to activate the headlights. It was Prudence's car, and she was unfamiliar with the features.

Then, just as suddenly as she had entered it, she emerged from the tunnel into a world of blinding light. Again she wished she had remembered to bring her sunglasses, for she was dazzled by the view, a panorama of the river and the valley that she had never seen before. It was truly magnificent, limestone cliffs and woods and water, everything spinning like a giant kaleidoscope as her car crashed through the metal guard rail and soared momentarily like a bird before plunging down to the water below.

•

"Her condition's extremely critical. Internal injuries, multiple fractures, in a coma. To be honest, she's lucky to be alive," said the young doctor. He added, avoiding their eyes, "I'm sorry," and strode off, shoulders hunched, head down, not wanting to hear their questions or their grief.

Prudence had been contacted first because the car was hers. She had phoned Mara on her land line and cellphone and left messages on both. She had then called Loulou. Mara had not picked up either of Prudence's messages until the end of the day. She and Julian had jumped into Mara's Renault and driven straight to the hospital in Sarlat where Patsy had been taken after being pulled from the wreckage. There they had found an unusually disarranged Prudence and a very grave-looking Loulou in the Intensive Care waiting room.

"A freak accident," said Loulou. "Road conditions were good, light traffic, no other vehicles involved, *grâce à Dieu*, and it didn't look as if she had been speeding. They think she simply misread the turn—it happened on that very winding stretch around the Cingle de Montfort—and drove straight off the road."

"She had a meeting with Dr. Morange at that sleep clinic in Sarlat," added Prudence. "She must have been coming back from there, although why she didn't take the direct route down the D57 beats me." She gestured helplessly. "I'm sure it couldn't have been anything mechanical because I just had the car serviced last week. The brakes were fine."

"I talked with one of the SAMU crew," Loulou said. "Fellow told me Patsy mumbled something before she lost consciousness. She said, 'It shouldn't have been there.' What do you suppose she meant by that?"

Mara shook her head, staring numbly at the opposite wall. She had sent Patsy to the clinic on a ferreting mission, and Patsy had gone, ignorant of the consequences that her mention of Pronole-2 and Véronique could unleash. Now she was fighting for her life. Extremely critical, the doctor had said. That meant not likely to make it. The thought of a world without Patsy was more than Mara could bear. She wanted to cry, to wail, but her emotions remained stifled in her chest, leaving her parched and soundless. Also she wanted to rage. Because if road conditions had been good, if the car had been mechanically sound, if Patsy had not been speeding, then someone or something must have forced her over the cliff.

•

The waiting was terrible. Mara paced. Loulou drank endless cups of coffee. Prudence made a pretense of reading a magazine. Julian sprawled listlessly in a chair.

"Look, why don't you two go home?" Prudence finally suggested, seeing the state Mara was in. "Loulou and I can hang around here. We'll let you know if—if there's any change."

"She's right," reasoned Julian. "No point in us all staying. We can come back to relieve you later."

"No," said Mara. "You go, Julian. I'm not leaving."

•

When Julian arrived back at the house, he found Jazz and Bismuth barking frantically. Mechanically, he let them out, let them in, and fed them. All he wanted was a stiff drink, a shower and bed, in that order. *Mon Dieu*, he thought, as he stripped off in the bathroom. Véronique murdered, and Patsy fighting for her life. Véronique had worked at the Clinique Morange. Patsy had crashed coming away from the clinic. Was there a link there? He stood long in the shower, letting the water beat down on him, struggling to find a way of bringing the two events together.

He ate a perfunctory meal while staring at the eight o'clock televised news, which carried a brief mention of the accident. Some time later, when the ringing of the phone awoke him, he realized that he had fallen asleep in front of the TV that was now showing a dubbed American western. It was twenty past two.

"It's me." Mara voice sounded bleakly in his ear.

"How is she?" Julian croaked, afraid of the worst.

"Still in a coma. They told us to go home. Loulou is bringing Prudence and me back. I'll see you in a while."

He turned off the television and walked restlessly about the house. Mara wouldn't be back for at least half an hour. No point going to bed. Eventually, he wandered out to the studio and flipped on the computer. There was a message waiting for him from Fang.

"*Dear Julian*," it began. His eyes moved dully down the screen, scarcely taking in what the Chinese botanist had to say.

Suddenly, as he made sense of her message, his heart began to thunder in his chest. Shaking, he hit *reply* and began to tap out a one-fingered response.

19

The dogs had taken refuge behind the art deco sofa, away from raised voices coming from the bedroom.

"Stuff your tea and toast!" Mara was not mollified by breakfast in bed. "I can't believe you're doing this. Patsy may be dying."

"The doctor said her vital signs have stabilized. They've moved her to the general hospital in Périgueux. She's in good hands."

"She's still unconscious. She has tubes coming out of every orifice. She's been in a coma for three days."

"You know I'd move mountains to help her, but there's nothing I can do. I wish you wouldn't take it like this."

"For God's sake, Julian, how do you expect me to take it? First, you ask me to steal the Kneebone diary. Now you want me to go back for the missing pages, while you—"

"I'm just saying try to find them if you can. There's no point in my asking Charlie again, and you know I can't very well confront him for removing the critical part!"

"Moreover, Véronique's killer is still running around free."

"Well, the gendarmes know it's not me, and that's the important thing. Anyway, they're okay with this."

"And to top everything off, you expect me to help you bankroll this crazy scheme!"

"Lend, not bankroll. Don't you see? I've got to do it, and I've got to do it now. I know the timing's bad, but every day could make a difference. Besides, it'll be an opportunity to get information on the BoniSom patent suit. Jean-Luc Jarry's very enthusiastic. He says ActionTerre—"

"And stuff BoniSom, Jarry and ActionTerre! It's friendship I'm talking about. Solidarity. And not just Patsy. I might like a little support from you at this time too, you know. You expect a lot of me, but where are you when I need you?" Her subtext was: *Have you ever really been there for me? Am I wrong to wonder if it's always going to be this way?*

Julian sounded pained. "Look, I'm sorry. I'd hoped you'd be more understanding."

Mara sounded angry, deeply hurt and disgusted. "You don't need understanding. You need psychoanalysis."

•

Perhaps because Monday was usually a slow night (for that reason the only one the Brieuxs had free), there were only four other customers besides Mara's party at La Pagode.

"*Bonsoir, bienvenus.*" Linus Chen bowed them in like a sapling in a wind. "Big event tonight, eh?" Mara had informed him in advance that the dinner was in honour of Paul's birthday. "We got a new menu. Very good."

They sat down, and Linus distributed the new *cartes*, which came in shiny green plastic holders with a bamboo design.

"Foie gras? *Magret de canard*?" Paul, scanning his, was bewildered. He frowned at Mara. "I thought this was supposed to be a Chinese restaurant."

"It is," said Mara, also puzzled. "It was."

"*Tout à la chinoise*," explained Linus.

"I don't want to be rude," rumbled Paul, "but how can foie gras be *à la chinoise*?"

"It is rather strange," agreed Loulou, also studying the menu.

Linus said evasively, "We use sweet-sour sauce."

"*Des conneries*!" Paul, who took French food very seriously, half started out of his chair in disbelief. Mado subdued him with a look.

Mama Deng emerged from the kitchen to wrap everyone in her motherly smile. She suggested they forget the *carte* and leave everything to her.

"Hot-pot?" Charlie asked hopefully.

She shook her head. "Only special demand. French don't got stomach for it."

"*Dommage*," said Prudence, genuinely sorry.

"Bummer," said Charlie.

Linus grinned. "How about aperitifs? You want to see the *carte des vins*?"

"Oh swell," grumbled Prudence. "Foie gras. *Magret*. Aperitifs. Wine list. Another promising Chinese restaurant gone west."

Linus insisted they try the La Pagode cocktail. It came frothy pink with little paper parasols in tall glasses borne aloft by Linus on a tray, true *garçon*-style.

"*Bon anniversaire*!" they all toasted Paul's forty-third.

"And long life," added Loulou for good measure.

"Thanks," said Paul, looking pleased. He scanned the room and checked his watch. "Julian's late."

Mara said stiffly, "No. Julian's gone."

"Gone where?" asked everyone together.

Mara threw down her paper parasol. "Oh, I suppose I may as well tell you. You'll find out soon enough. Julian's in Paris picking up his visa for China. Then he'll fly to Chengdu. He's going to hunt for his damned *Cypripedium incognitum*. And"—it pained Mara to admit it—"he borrowed money from me to float this little expedition."

"China?" Paul gawped. "He's gone to China to look for his crazy orchid?"

Mara shrugged in a show of great indifference. Since Paul and Mado knew nothing about Horatio Kneebone, she informed them: "That's where it originated. Tell them, Charlie."

"Er, yes," said the writer. "My great-great-great-grandfather found it and brought it back with him to France."

"Julian's meeting a female Chinese botanist named Fang"—for a nanosecond Mara's eyes flickered dangerously—"who said she's located a possible growing site somewhere in Southwest China, and Julian and she are going with a team of botanists to hunt for it."

"He's taken off with a woman named Fang?" Charlie sounded shocked.

Prudence said, "If Julian's in China, who's going to cut my grass?"

"He said to tell you he's fixed it up with Bernard." Bernard was Julian's assistant, a young man with big arms and heavy thighs; also the Brieuxs' weekend waiter.

"Why, the randy old dog," grinned Paul. "Fang, eh?"

The food came quickly, dish after dish with not a hot pepper in sight. Noodles with chicken and aromatic mushrooms. A sizzling platter of succulent pork ribs. Stir-fried vegetables. Braised eggplant. Stuffed tofu. Mama Deng's pan-fried dumplings. An aromatic steamer of rice. Served with a chilled rosé. Linus gave them none of his "wine doesn't go so good with Sichuan food" mantra on this occasion.

"Never could get the hang of these things," Paul remarked, clutching chopsticks that in his large paw looked like matchsticks.

"So do you think Julian will find his orchid?" asked Mado. She did not bother with chopsticks but used a fork.

"Frankly," snapped Mara, "*je m'en foutre*."

"You're not serious," said Mado, taken aback.

"Of course she isn't," soothed Loulou, helping himself liberally to spare ribs, which seemed to be his favourite dish.

"I am." Mara's chin firmed up. "I really no longer give a damn. Let him stay in China. And in case you're all wondering, as far as I'm concerned our engagement is off. It would never have worked anyway. I mean, how do you live with a man who hides the fact that he's married, then takes off altogether to chase a flower? I'm sick of playing runner-up to *Cypripedium* frigging *incognitum*. I'm sick of him. As of now, consider me a free woman."

There followed a long, awkward silence. Charlie looked especially uncomfortable, as if he had been caught eavesdropping on a private conversation.

"I, ah, heard Patsy was in a bad car accident," he said eventually. "How is she?"

Mara shook her head.

"Still no sign of life, eh?" Paul, with his typical disastrous choice of words.

"Stanley calls every day, asking the same thing. He was going to fly out. I told him to hold off for now."

"But we heard she's stabilized," Mado said. "At least she's out of danger?"

"She's on life support," clarified Prudence.

"If you can call that *hors de danger*," said Loulou gravely.

"*Putain*!" uttered Paul.

"Bummer," said Charlie.

•

The following evening a tired, rumpled Julian arrived at Chengdu International Airport. It was a small facility, but crowded and noisy. He stood in the arrivals area, senses reeling, jostled by the press of bodies and luggage trolleys. He had never particularly believed that all Chinese looked alike, but here he felt swamped by a sea of indistinguishable faces. Eventually he came to focus on a cardboard sign with his name on it, then the person holding the sign, a long, slim youth in jeans and a black baseball cap skewed sideways. Julian looked again and saw it was a woman.

"Hello? Julian Wood? I'm Fang." She had said she was unusually tall for a Chinese, but he had not expected her to be almost on a level with him. She shook his hand and grinned, showing very nice teeth.

Fang helped him with his bags and led him to a waiting taxi. Sitting next to her as they roared down the motorway into the city, he saw that while she was not exactly pretty, she was striking. Her biscuit-toned skin was smooth, her neck graceful, her mouth small and full. Her almond eyes were topped with heavy masculine eyebrows that struck him as somehow very sexy. Julian could not guess if her hair was long or short; it was tucked under the baseball cap. She regarded him teasingly, as if amused to be the object of his obvious intense curiosity.

"You tired? Hungry? You want to eat or sleep?" Fang asked him, omitting to make the usual polite inquiries about his trip. The fact that he had arrived was good enough for her. Her spoken English was as good as her written.

"Sleep, I think," he said honestly. The flight—he had boarded at an ungodly time and had been wedged in the middle of a row of five passengers—left him wanting nothing more than to get horizontal for about twelve hours. He felt as if he were floating in a bubble of unreality.

"No sweat," she said, and yelled something to the cab driver, who yelled back and made a sudden left turn against three lanes of oncoming traffic. Julian threw up his arms, warding off certain death. Fang laughed heartily.

Forty minutes later he was checked into a hotel. Fang took him up to his room to make sure things were satisfactory.

"This mattress is okay," she said, bouncing on one of a pair of twin beds pushed under double headboards fixed to the wall with a built-in central control panel for the lights and the television. She looked particularly teasing as she bounced, and Julian began to see trouble ahead. He hoped the search team she had assembled consisted of the typical serious, obsessive, botanical types.

"Leave your key card in the slot by the door when you're in the room," she instructed, continuing to bob up and down on his horizon. "If you take it out, the lights go off. Saves electricity. There's air conditioning, but they don't turn it on. Open the window if you get hot. If you're hungry, the restaurant is on the first floor. If you want room service, ask for the manager, Mr. Tang. He's the only one here who speaks English, except for the women who call you up at night offering massage. That's up to you, but I don't recommend it."

"Okay," he said. "Thanks for the warning. And for all your help."

"No sweat," Fang laughed.

To his surprise, she did not linger but shot up abruptly, propelled by a final bounce.

"Here is my telephone number if you have problems. And this is your voucher for breakfast." She handed him two slips of paper. "I'll come for you tomorrow at ten o'clock. We have an appointment with the director of Double Joy Natural Products Company at ten thirty, okay?" Before he could speak, she was out the door. Stunned, he sat down on the bed. He checked the time: 19:04. That meant it was four minutes past one in the afternoon, Mara's time.

•

"Hello?" Her voice sounded groggy.

"Mara? It's Julian." There was a pause that he hoped was the natural delay of a long-distance phone connection from China to France.

The pause went on. "Well," he said, scrambling to fill it, "I just wanted to let you know I arrived in Chengdu. I'm at the Golden Phoenix Hotel." He had showered, unpacked minimally, opened the window to let in a moist, lukewarm breeze, and was now sitting on the very hard mattress of one of the twin beds. "I, ah, didn't expect to find you in. How are you?"

"Do you really want to know?" Groggy had changed to grumpy.

"Well, yes, of course."

"Wiped out. I didn't sleep at all last night. I was having a nap when you called. You woke me up."

"Oh, look, I'm really sorry."

"Yes, Julian. Sorry is what you should be." Grumpy was now decidedly unfriendly.

"Ah." Again Julian groped for words. "Listen, Mara, I want to tell you again how much I appreciate your helping me out. Money-wise, that is. I'll pay it all back the minute I get back." His voice echoed tinnily against a wall of silence. "Er . . . how's Patsy?"

"Still unconscious."

A pang of guilt hit him. "Her condition hasn't deteriorated, has it?"

"No. But her brain is on hold. And until she wakes up, they won't be able to assess how much damage was done. And we won't be able to find out what caused her accident. Prudence, Loulou and I have been taking it in turns to sit with her. The doctors think it helps to have someone talk to her. It's pretty discouraging because the conversation is one-sided, of course, and I'm running out of things to say. Prudence is going with me later today. But I'm sure you don't want to hear about all this."

"No, no. I mean, yes, I do."

She made no reply.

He rummaged around for another subject. "I thought you'd be interested to know I'll be meeting Yang Xiaoxi tomorrow. He's the head of Double Joy Natural Products Limited, Bonisanté's Chinese partner. Their headquarters are in Chengdu. I told you Jean-Luc Jarry asked me to get as much information as I can at the Chinese end about BoniSom, anything that might help them with the patents suit. Fang set the meeting up." And since Mara still did not engage, he babbled on, "She really is tall. Damned near six feet. In fact, I'm seeing lots of tall young Chinese. Must be the improved nutrition. Anyway, we'll meet Yang in the morning. Then, the day after, Fang and I will travel by car to join up with a team of Chinese botanists to look for *Cypripedium incognitum*. One of them has mapped out the areas for our search."

"How nice."

"Um, Mara, you haven't by any chance . . . ?"

"Found the missing diary pages?"

"Well, yes. As it is, the search zones are pretty extensive, and we'll have to cover them on foot. If Horatio noted a precise location, mentioned a geological feature, say, or anything that could give us a lead, it would be tremendously helpful. I've only got a thirty-day visa—"

Mara broke in sharply. "Julian, I don't know how you have the nerve to ask me this. I mean, do you honestly think you can just walk out on me—"

"Walk out!" Stung, he jumped to his feet. "Christ, Mara, be reasonable. It's just a trip. A minor detour in the trajectory of life—"

"Oh, don't try to play the philosopher. It doesn't suit you. If you need it spelled out, I no longer care what happens to you, your bloody orchid or Kneebone's diary. And, just in case you're remotely interested, the police still haven't found Véronique's killer. Not that you should concern yourself, of course. Nor have they been able to determine what caused Patsy's crash other than she simply drove over a cliff. You know as well as I do that she uncovered something about the Clinique Morange and was run off the road to keep her from talking. Apropos of which, I've just been given a fast-track appointment for a sleep disorder assessment this Friday. I'm going to use the opportunity to find out what Patsy discovered. Who knows, since you're not here to do it, maybe I can even learn something useful about your dead ex-wife."

Julian sat up abruptly. "Mara, listen to me. For Chrissake be careful. Don't go jumping feet first into something you know nothing—"

A steady hum told him he was holding a dead connection. He stared helplessly at the receiver in his hand. The words *I no longer care* rang ominously in his ear. Then reason reasserted itself. Mara was simply upset about Patsy. Surely she'd see that she was overreacting to his departure. He'd call her again in another day or two. *She'll come round*, he tried to convince himself. *She'll come round.*

That night, Mara and his orchid slipped in and out of his uneasy dreams. And in the way of dreams, the two had somehow become interchangeable.

20

Julian's first experience with breakfast Chengdu-style left him wondering if he was looking at a truly Chinese breakfast, last night's leftovers or a dotty international committee's decision on what breakfast should be. There were cornflakes, hard-boiled eggs and doughy little croissants; trays of stir-fried green beans, savoury steamed buns and noodles; some kind of yellow sponge cake, a vat of thin rice gruel and plates of pungent, pickled vegetables; oranges, watermelon slices and, if you felt like a salad first thing in the morning, lettuce and tomatoes. There was no coffee, tea or milk, but you could have soy milk, hot or cold. Or, if you preferred, something that resembled Orangina. He was ravenous, and he tried a little of everything. Eventually he discovered that he could also have a fried egg, prepared on a hot plate by a handsome sous-chef in a white uniform. Unfortunately the fellow insisted on cooking the egg both sides to the toughness of leather. Julian understood why a moment later when he realized that a runny egg would have been impossible to eat with chopsticks. He had a slippery enough time with it as it was. In the end he did what he was sure was an unacceptable thing. He cut the egg into pieces by spearing it with one chopstick while sawing at it with the other. A few of his Chinese co-breakfasters watched this operation in fascination.

Julian had risen early and had time to kill before Fang came for him. He was curious to see what he could of Chengdu. His guidebook informed him that this thriving capital of Sichuan

Province had a population of 15 million and that the Sichuanese were a friendly, individualistic lot, sure of themselves and committed to their own ways of doing things. It did not warn that they were murderous drivers.

He strolled out into an overcast, humid morning. The broad sidewalk outside the hotel was teeming with people going to work, children on their way to school and grannies already coming back from the market with shopping bags loaded with vegetables and fish. Some passersby glanced at him curiously. Most ignored him. Foreigners were no longer that unusual in Chengdu. The divided thoroughfare along which he walked was jammed with traffic, the curbside lanes filled with herds of bicyclists and motorscooter riders. Young women puttered past in fluttering dresses, high heels and large tinted plastic visors pulled down over their faces.

The main challenge was crossing the streets. Although Julian had long legs and could sprint, he thought it best to do as the natives did. Safety in numbers seemed to be the principle. The traffic lights, which flashed the countdown of seconds remaining before going red, generally controlled things, but there was a lot of dodging and weaving to be done around turning vehicles that seemed to consider pedestrians the sport of the day. At one point, Julian found himself stranded with a ragged knot of people in a centre island between six lanes of roaring traffic. Here it was every man for himself, he realized, as one by one his fellow pedestrians made a dash through impossible gaps in the traffic. He saw a break, started across, and pulled back just as a bus came roaring around the corner. A sharp shove from behind, however, sent him sprawling right into the bus's path. He landed on his hands and knees and somehow managed to vault himself up and out of the way just as the bus shot past, missing him by centimetres. There was a cacophony of horns as other cars braked and swerved. Miraculously, he found himself scrambling on to the opposite sidewalk. His hands were cut, his trousers torn, but he was otherwise intact.

The spectacle of a long, tall westerner on his hands and knees drew an amused crowd. A gentleman in a dark business suit stopped to help him up. He grinned and said in very good English, "Oh, well done, sir, well done! Welcome to Chengdu."

•

"You're late," said Fang when he appeared in the hotel lobby some time later. She eyed his dishevelled look and bandaged hands. He had changed his trousers, but his shirt was imperfectly tucked in. She wore tight black slacks with loopy spangled designs on the back pockets, a matching bolero with spangled loops on the front panels, a red low-cut blouse and snappy black leather high-heeled boots. She had made up her eyes, which glinted beneath her velvety brows like twin pools of Coca-Cola. Her hair, without the baseball cap, proved to be shoulder length. It was stylishly blunt-cut, parted on one side.

"What happened to you?" she asked.

"I was nearly roadkill."

"What?" She wrinkled her brow, not understanding.

"Someone tried to push me under a bus."

She was unimpressed. "Why would anyone want to do that?"

"Let's talk about something else," muttered Julian, deciding he did not want to explain. "Like Mr. Yang Xiaoxi."

"Director Yang," she corrected him as she ushered him into a waiting taxi.

"Is that what I call him?"

"Better that way. More respectful because he is the Double Joy director. A very important man. You'll see when you meet him." She gave him a smile layered with significance that made Julian understand the meaning of the word enigmatic.

"How do I say, 'How do you do?'"

"*Ni hao. Ni*—like 'knee' in 'Kneebone,' so you should remember that—means 'you.' *Hao*—like 'how' in 'how do you do?'—means 'good.' So '*ni hao*?' means 'you good?' If you are asked, you answer, '*hao*.' You can also say '*hen hao*,' 'very good.' But not to worry, Director Yang's English is excellent."

"Knee haw," Julian practised. "Is that right?"

"Not exactly."

Their taxi driver, a young man with a toothy smile, turned the air conditioning and the radio on full blast and drove with attitude. To the strains of Chinese rock, he shot recklessly into a busy stream of cars, crossed an intersection, nearly taking out a mob of pedestrians, and sped westward across the city. The wide streets were choked with everything on wheels—cars, cabs, mopeds, motorcycles, bicycles, buses, trucks and even the occasional horse-drawn cart. The buildings they passed looked new, the cars looked new, the people looked prosperous. Finding the air conditioning too much, Julian rolled down the window to be hit by a blast of muggy air. The sky was the colour of tin.

"Will it rain?" Julian asked.

"No. It's always like this," replied Fang. "That's why Chengdu women are famous for their fair complexions. The sun shines so rarely in Chengdu, they say dogs bark when it comes out. By the way, that plant hunter you told me about, Horatio Kneebone? I told Director Yang you are his descendant."

"But I'm not," objected Julian. "Why did you do that?"

"Better that way," said Fang and once again smiled her smile of many meanings.

En route, Fang elaborated on the plans for the Wood Expedition. Julian experienced a thrill on hearing her call it that. She had hired a car and driver to take them the following day to Mingdan about 250 kilometres to the northwest. There they would spend the night and continue the day after to another place called Kanglong, where they would meet the rest of the team. Camping gear and provisions had already been organized, but Julian was expected to provide his own sleeping bag, backpack and plant press.

"Check," said Julian. "What about expenses?"

"We'll talk about that later," said Fang evasively.

She went on to say that in Kanglong they would load everything on to pack mules and hike into the foothills of the Crouching Tiger Mountain Range, the very mountains Kneebone had explored. Julian's heart soared as he heard those words. He was about to walk in the footsteps of Horatio Kneebone! They would spend in total three weeks there, searching different sites, coming down only to reprovision. They were going to find *Cypripedium incognitum*. He was certain of it, felt it in his gut. A local botanist named Zhang Shugang, who was familiar with the area, would lead them.

But how did this Zhang Shugang know how to retrace Horatio Kneebone's path? Julian wanted to know. Fang said that local stories passed down from generation to generation described a European named Nie Bo who had come to those parts a century and a half ago looking for plants. When Zhang read her message about Horatio Kneebone, he had reasoned that it must be the same man. Fang pointed out how different this journey would be from Horatio's, referring to the current ease of travel—even though most of the roads they would use were under construction—the vastly improved communications, to say nothing of the fact that Julian as a foreigner was allowed to move about quite freely, compared with Horatio, who for most of his time in China was forbidden to penetrate into the interior of the country.

Their taxi left them at the gate of what looked like a modern industrial park surrounded by a wall. Fang spoke with the uniformed guard at the gate, who checked their identification, telephoned, then waved them in toward a two-storied, white brick building bearing large Chinese characters over the doorway as well as the English words DOUBLE JOY NATURAL PRODUCTS COMPANY LIMITED.

"*Ni hao*?" said the very pretty young woman who greeted them in the reception area.

"Gung ho." Julian grinned. The words did not sound quite right, even to his ear.

Fang and the receptionist conferred. The latter got on the telephone, saying "*dui*, *dui*," and dimpling at them all the while. Then she hung up and invited them to follow her. They walked up a broad flight of stairs to the upper floor. At the head of the stairs, the receptionist threw open a pair of double doors.

Julian's mouth fell open. The room they entered was more greenhouse than executive office. They were surrounded by orchids. In racks, on stands, in hanging baskets, they were everywhere: *Dendrobiums*, *Paphiopedilums*, *Cymbidiums*, *Cattleyas*, all in spectacular bloom. Ceiling fans turned slowly overhead. One wall was entirely tinted glass. Another was given over to an immense tank full of colourful tropical fish.

"Hello," said a roly-poly little man. He was standing on tiptoe on a stool feeding the fish that swarmed to the surface of the tank. When he climbed down from the stool, Julian could see that he barely topped five feet. The man put the container of fish food on the stool and waddled over to them, puffing slightly at the exertion.

Abandoning her normal casualness to stand on ceremony, Fang announced, "This is Director Yang, founder and director of Double Joy Natural Products." In a lesser voice, she said, "Julian Wood."

"Knee hi." Julian bobbed.

"*Ni hao*," Fang corrected swiftly, adding in an undertone. "He's not that short."

"Ah, happy to meet you," said the director, who resembled a koala bear. His face was broad and smiling and dominated by a thick, flat nose. Hair sprung up around his ears, and he had round moist eyes backed nevertheless by an underlying gleam of cleverness. He was dressed in capacious trousers and a purple short-sleeved shirt, open at the neck. It was hard to guess at his age. Fifty? Sixty?

"Sit, sit." Yang Xiaoxi urged them toward a cluster of armchairs in the middle of the room, where he himself plopped down.

The dimpled receptionist entered with tea and soft candies that she placed before them on small tables. She gave a slight bow and left.

"This is Double Joy Health Tea." Yang raised his cup to Julian. He inhaled the steam arising from it as if it would do him good. "Specially blended by my company. We started marketing it a few years ago, and it has sold very well. Clears the lungs and cleanses the blood. I hope you like it."

"Mmm," said Julian, impressed by the director's command of English but thinking that the tea tasted like grass cuttings.

"You know," Yang went on, "I started life as a simple country boy. It's true!"—with a pudgy hand he waved away any attempt by Julian to disagree with him—"I grew up in a poor mountain village and would never have made it past middle school except that during the Cultural Revolution I earned"—here he paused to wheeze—"what you call 'brownie points' as a member of the Red Guard. I helped expose and punish a number of capitalist roaders. That got me into university where I studied languages and science. My training enabled me to become the head of a state-run chemical factory." Yang took a few shallow breaths. "Later I started my own herbal medicine business. I have been very successful. Now"—his koala bear face shaped into an engaging grin—"I myself have become a capitalist roader, a Mr. Big Bucks, as we say today. I am a wealthy manufacturer of pharmaceuticals with profitable interests in the export of natural products. I drive a Mercedes, I have two houses, a wife, a son, a mistress whose credit card expenses I pay and a lifestyle totally corrupted by your western values." He found the irony of the turnaround highly amusing and laughed windily, like a broken accordion.

"A Chinese success story, in short," said Julian, forcing a smile. "In fact, that's one of the reasons I asked to meet with you. I'm very interested in Double Joy's involvement with Bonisanté and BoniSom. What can you tell me about that?"

Yang shrugged. "Very simple. Double Joy supplies pharmaceutical companies around the world with a range of natural products. In the case of Bonisanté, it's the dried roots of the plant *cuimin cao*, sleeping grass in English, otherwise known as *Cypripedium somniferum*. The Baixi villagers gather and dry the roots, we buy it from them and ship it to France where the active ingredient, cypronoline, is extracted and formulated into the sleeping tablet BoniSom. A very successful product."

"The roots?" Julian pricked up his ears. "I was given to understand, Director Yang, that you're using other parts of the plant in order to take the pressure off the root system."

Yang shook his head. "There was some talk of that. No good. The greatest concentration of the alkaloid is in the roots, and given the amount needed, it is much more cost-effective to stick with the roots."

"And what exactly is the amount needed?"

"More than we can get. To meet galloping demand."

"I see." Julian was very interested in what this talkative director had to say. "What about commercial cultivation? Is it true you're planning to cultivate *Cypripedium somniferum* on a commercial scale?"

"Ah, yes. That is something we are working on. But it will take time."

"And meanwhile you'll go on harvesting wild plants?"

"Of course. But not to worry. We hope to have a system of plantation production in full operation before we run out of wild sources."

"Before you run out!" Julian half started out of his chair. He sank back, wishing he had a means of capturing the director's frank admission. He put his teacup down and tried for a neutral tone. "I also understand that Bonisanté learned about cypronoline from the Baixi and that its method of extracting the compound is actually not that different from the Baixi's method of concocting Sleep Tea."

"Maybe." Yang waggled his head. "Actually, it was Pei Li Boshun—Dr. Pei Li—who spotted the commercial potential of Sleep Tea a number of years ago. He travelled among the Baixi and brought their use of it to the attention of Bonisanté. He also was instrumental in identifying and isolating the active alkaloid."

Julian leaned forward. "So you *are* confirming that BoniSom is based on the Baixi's knowledge and extraction method?"

"Of course."

How Jean-Luc Jarry would have loved to be here! Julian decided it was time to come to the point. "Director Yang, are you aware that the Baixi, supported by a coalition of international NGOs, are challenging Bonisanté's patent rights to cypronoline?"

For the first time Yang looked a little evasive. "I think you should not take that seriously. As Dr. Pei Li says, it is very difficult to get patents overturned."

"But what about the Chinese government itself? Why isn't it supporting the Baixi's claim?"

Yang looked puzzled. "Why should it do that when it has already granted Double Joy the patent for China? We will be releasing the drug here under our own label quite soon, but as a tincture. We're calling it An Min Yao, Slumber Drops. We, too, have insomniacs, and our domestic market is huge, as I'm sure you are aware."

Damn, thought Julian gloomily. He should have known it would come down to something like that. So much for the Baixi's chances. He decided to play the devil's advocate. "It would be quite an opportunity for Double Joy though, if Bonisanté's North American and European patents were overturned. I mean, you control the source material, and you're already on stream to produce the drug. You'd be in an excellent position to take over the BoniSom market worldwide."

Now Yang's expression turned foxy. "Ah, but the patents haven't been overturned. And our mutually beneficial partnership with Bonisanté at present works very well. As we say, *ni peng wo, wo jui peng ni*—you praise me, I praise you. Or, as Dr. Pei Li might put it, 'We scratch each other's back.' Everyone's happy."

"Who is this Dr. Pei Li?" Julian said, barely concealing his irritation.

Yang looked astonished. "You don't know him? I'm very surprised. He's like you. He, too, searches for orchids."

Julian exchanged a wary glance with Fang.

"Now," said Yang, changing the subject. "What about you? Miss Hsu tells me you are the great-great-great-grandson of the plant hunter Horatio Kneebone who led an expedition into the interior of China in 1861."

"He's not really my—" Julian demurred, but Fang overrode him with a nervous laugh.

"History repeats itself, Director Yang."

"So it does, Miss Hsu. So it does. And here you are, Mr. Wood, in search of the orchid your ancestor found and took with him to France. Yong Chun Hua, the legendary flower of eternal youth, or what you call *Cypripedium incognitum*. It is a fascinating story."

"Well, we don't know for certain that Horatio actually found Yong Chun Hua," said Julian, letting the misrepresentation stand. "I mean, isn't Yong Chun Hua more fable than fact?"

Yang smiled. "It is and it isn't. Just because you can't find a thing doesn't mean it doesn't exist. Besides, Yong Chun Hua was real enough many centuries ago for our ancient scholars to write treatises on its restorative powers. Did they make it up? Was it here with us once, and has it been lost? Or has it yet to come into existence? Do you follow my meaning?"

"Not really."

"It's simple. I am a successful businessman. And"—Yang gestured about him—"as you can see, also an orchid collector. A serious one. So, I propose to you the same deal I made Miss Hsu and Dr. Pei Li, although I should warn you, *he's* been looking for Yong Chun Hua for years. Make Yong Chun Hua exist, Mr. Wood. Find me the orchid. I offer the finder one thousand dollars for every live specimen in good condition he or she brings back. Less costs, of course."

"The same deal as you offered—? Less costs?" Julian stared in dismay at Fang, who turned her head quickly to look at the fish.

"Certainly," Yang nodded. "Who do you think is financing your expedition? Why do you think I agreed to see you? But I warn you. You will have stiff competition from Dr. Pei Li. Nevertheless, I am banking on you. You have the advantage because you have read your ancestor's diary, and, as Kneebone's descendant, I think there is a kind of correctness that you should be the one to find it. I believe in fate, you see. If you wish to share the reward with Miss Hsu and her colleagues, that is up to you. Of course, I will also need verifiable information on where the flower grows. There is a fortune to be made here, Mr. Wood. We Chinese are very superstitious. We believe in things like eternal youth flowers. Moreover, it's not just us." Yang chortled breathlessly. "Do you have any idea how much just one plant of Yong Chun Hua would fetch on the international market?"

21

Julian strode out of Double Joy in black silence, Fang hurrying in his wake. They stopped outside the compound gate to hail a taxi.

"You angry with me?" Fang asked, trying to make eye contact.

He averted his head. "What do you expect? You set me up. This is nothing but a commissioned plant grab." Streams of cars, some of them empty taxis, whizzed past.

"No." Fang seized his arm to pull him around with surprising force. Her heavy brows were fiercely drawn in a way that reminded him of Mara. "It's not true. I want to find Yong Chun Hua, which I believe is the same thing as your *Cypripedium incognitum*, but for science, not for money, not to sell it to Yang. I think by working together we can succeed."

"Then why involve Yang?"

"You asked to see him."

"Oh, pull the other one. That was in connection with Bonisanté. You didn't have to tell him about the orchid or the diary or that lie about my being the descendant of Horatio Kneebone." Julian had brought the diary with him, had intended to let her read it, incomplete though it was, but now he was damned if he'd let her anywhere near it.

She turned sulky. "How else could I get money for the expedition? It's okay for you. You're rich—"

Julian snorted.

"Do you know how little I earn as a junior botanist?"

"That's my point. Behind your lofty protestations, you and your cronies are in this for the cash. And you brought me in because you think I have information you need." It was on the tip of Julian's tongue to tell her how wrong she was, but he decided to string her along just as she had led him by the nose into this sorry mess. Instead he said, "Has it occurred to you that if this orchid still exists, it's probably extremely rare? It might be down to a handful of plants. Delivering it into the hands of the likes of Yang, who's no better than a poacher, will just ensure its extinction. Oh sure, maybe he'll succeed in breeding it, but it will be wiped out in the wild."

"If we find it, I won't hand it over to Yang."

"I see. You and your pals plan to set up a little private orchid enterprise of your own?"

"Never! I told you. We are interested in Yong Chun Hua for scientific reasons."

"And what about Dr. Pei Li? I assume he's part of your botanical team?"

"No." Fang looked surprised. "Today is the first time I heard of him."

"Then who the hell is he?"

She shrugged. "I think some bigwig from Beijing."

"Who's also only interested in Yong Chun Hua for reasons of unadulterated science? He isolated cypronoline, don't forget, so he's more than just an innocent botanist." Julian's tone oozed sarcasm. "Well, you've made your pact with the devil, Fang, but I want no part of it."

Fang shook her head impatiently, her glossy black hair swinging from side to side. "You don't get it. It's not just Pei Li and Yang. China is the botanical promised land. Pharmaceutical companies and plant breeders and nurseries all over the world are sniffing around us like dogs. Everyone is looking for rare plants and natural products they can exploit. Every villager, every farmer, every goat herder is a potential plant hunter. As for orchids, do you know how many tens of thousands of wild orchids are dug up and smuggled out of China every year and sold to foreign collectors and nurseries and breeders? Then there is development. Pollution. China's economy is taking off. The air in our big cities is becoming unbreathable. Our rivers are becoming sewers. And tourism. China has a billion people. Everyone wants to be a tourist. Plus all you foreigners. We're building hotels and roads everywhere. There's a superhighway going into the Wolong Panda Reserve now. In a few years, thousands of kilometres of natural habitat will be wiped out, just like that." She pointed to a squashed orange lying in the gutter. "How long do you think your orchid will survive? The only way to make Yong Chun Hua safe is to find it before anyone else does. And then force the government to protect its habitat."

"In my experience," said Julian icily, "that never works. By the time the government gets around to slapping a protection order on it, Yang and his like will have poached every living plant. The minute something rare is found, it's endangered."

"Then why are *you* looking for *Cypripedium incognitum*?" Fang glared at him scornfully. "You're not even Chinese. Aren't you part of the problem? Your peoples' reputation for habitat destruction is worse than ours, you know. And the environment! You're the ones exporting your high-polluting industries to other countries. You're the ones driving SUVs and gobbling up fossil fuels. You're the ones pumping out greenhouse gases"—She slammed him with every violation of God's green earth she could think of.

He wanted to say that with a billion people, all wanting to drive SUVs too, China was making up for lost time, but the truth of her accusations struck home. Everyone on the planet was doing a terrific job of soiling the nest.

To avoid an all-out brawl, he began flagging down taxis.

•

They rode in prickly silence back to the hotel, where Julian got out. Fang told him she would meet him again in the lobby at seven for dinner. Julian almost said, *Don't bother*, but realized that without her, speaking no Chinese, not knowing his way around, he was lost. He did not even know how to order from a Chinese menu. So he said curtly, "Fine."

He slept for most of the afternoon.

The place she took him to for dinner was a simple restaurant that offered cuisine typical of the region.

"Please," said Julian, "no hot-pot."

She did the ordering. The strain between them gave way as plate after plate of food began to appear. Fried rice paddy eels, a platter of mushrooms and green peppers, slick potato slices cut very thin and quickly cooked, beef braised in soy sauce with Chinese broccoli. It surprised Julian that they had to ask especially for rice. He drank beer—he found he quite liked Chinese beer—Fang bottled water.

By the time the meal ended with a tureen of watery vegetable soup, Julian had come to believe that her interest in *Cypripedium incognitum* really was scientific and decided that he wanted to be part of the expedition after all. Now they were talking like friends. Maybe he would let her see the diary after all. He asked Fang how she came to speak English so well. Had she studied abroad? No, she had studied English in middle school and university and read a lot in English. Many of her technical references, for example, were in English. And she practised whenever she could. Like now. Fang was hungry for details of Julian's life in France. He told her about his landscaping business and his books on local orchids and wildflowers.

"And do you have a sweetheart?" she asked, eyeing him coyly.

Abruptly he changed the subject. She did not push for an answer, but she laughed.

Fang in turn told Julian about her life. She taught basic plant physiology at the Chengdu Institute of Plant Sciences and did a little research. But with small chance for advancement, she felt wasted where she was. A lot of her colleagues felt the same way. Single, she lived with her mother and younger brother, the three of them crammed into a small apartment on the other side of the city. Compared with many, they were not badly off.

She spoke with affection of her father, who died when she was seven. He, too, had been a botanist. As a university-trained intellectual accused of rightist thinking during the Cultural Revolution, he had been beaten, made to self-denounce, and sent to do heavy labour on a fruit farm. The peasants there had been kind to him because of his heart condition and had allowed him, when possible, to perform lighter tasks. But she was sure the strain had shortened his life.

"It was from my father that I got my love of plants," Fang said. "He used to take me out to look at flowers. He made up stories about them for me." Momentarily, she looked a little misty eyed.

Her brother, on the other hand, had no feeling for growing things. Sports was his thing, but he was in a dead-end job as a postal worker and giving both her and their mother grief because of his frustration. You had to have *guanxi*, connections, to get ahead, and the Hsu family was short on *guanxi*. Fang and he were among the last generation of Chinese to grow up with siblings. Under China's one-child policy, the generations after them would never know what it was to have brothers, sisters, uncles, aunts or cousins.

By now, Julian felt comfortable enough with her to remark on her unusual height. Not just nutrition—she grinned—but genes. Both her parents, northerners from Liaoning, were quite tall. Her brother, who had been a crack basketball player in his day, was even taller.

"How were you able to get time off to go in search of *Cypripedium incognitum*?" he asked.

"Oh, my work-unit head liked the idea. If I find it, he's hoping to take all the credit."

•

"Okay," said Fang, as the cab dropped Julian off at the hotel once again. "I will come by with a car and driver at eight in the morning. Get a good night's sleep. The road tomorrow will be very bad."

•

Julian, suffering from jet lag, was still awake at around midnight when the telephone rang.

"Good evening," sang a falsetto voice. "You order massage? Massage on way up now. Please you let in."

"No, I did not order a massage," Julian barked, remembering Fang's warning about middle-of-the-night offers, but the party at the other end had already hung up.

A moment later there was a light tap on the door. Julian ignored it. The tapping continued. Irritably, he switched on the light, got up and stomped barefoot across the room.

"Go away," he called through the door.

"You order massage. You take now please."

"Listen," Julian growled, flipping the lock and yanking the door open to a not particularly feminine form standing in the hallway. Its face, surrounded by golden curls, looked weirdly artificial, with dark eye-holes and a red mouth fixed more in a grimace than a smile. "What is this? I told you—"

A foot hit him in the groin. As he pitched forward with a howl of pain, something heavy crashed down on the back of his head, causing a supernova in his brain.

•

"You okay? You okay?" The question, insistent, in English, was the only thing that Julian was able to make out against a scramble of unintelligible noises. He opened his eyes and closed them immediately, aware of a cracking pain at the base of his skull and a dull, throbbing ache in the balls. He groaned. When he opened his eyes again, he saw that he was on the floor, half in, half out of the doorway of his room. A young man in a dark suit was bending over him, looking very concerned. Behind the man hovered other faces.

"I'm hotel manager, Mr. Tang. What happened?"

"Attacked," Julian managed to mumble. "Masseuse. Kicked me in the—hit me on the head." He experienced, in a rush, the dubious pleasure of full recall.

"Attack?" Mr. Tang sounded deeply shocked. "You say masseuse attack you?"

There followed several simultaneous conversations in Chinese.

"This is Mr. Chu," said the manager, gesturing at a thin man in a paisley dressing gown. "Next door to you. He say he hear shouting. When he look out, he see person running. Then he see you. He think it must be robbery."

"Don't know. Dark. Wore a mask." Julian had difficulty believing it had even happened.

Mr. Tang and Mr. Chu helped Julian into his room and on to his bed. Mr. Tang then escorted Mr. Chu out, shouted something at the small crowd of staff and other hotel guests gathered in the hallway, and hurriedly shut the door.

"You want doctor?" Mr. Tang asked, returning to Julian's side.

"No," said Julian. He remembered reading in his guidebook that this was to be avoided.

Mr. Tang surveyed the room. Julian's suitcase lay open on the other bed.

"You check please. Anything missing? Wallet? Money? Passport?"

Julian felt very dizzy, but with the help of Mr. Tang, he stood up and went through his things. He was alert enough to judge that everything seemed accounted for. Much relieved, he fell back on the bed. It would have been damned inconvenient to be robbed on the eve of the Wood Expedition. Nor did he want the involvement of the Chinese police.

"Just let me sleep," he muttered.

"Okay. Okay. You want anything, you call Room Service, ask for me."

He heard the sounds of withdrawal, the door shutting. Julian fumbled with the headboard controls, found the light switch and sank thankfully into darkness. The last thought that flickered in his mind before he went unconscious was that he'd had two close calls in one day. He had considered his encounter with the bus an accident. Now he wasn't so sure. Had tonight's assault really been a robbery attempt? Or if robbery had not been the intention, what had?

Suddenly, he remembered Kneebone's diary. With a sick feeling that had nothing to do with his head, he flipped on the lights and stumbled out of bed. To his immense relief, he found the diary in its folder, undisturbed, at the bottom of his carry-on bag.

· 22 ·

"Oh, give the man a break," said Prudence. "Find him his missing pages."

"No," replied Mara. "I told you, I've finished with all that."

They were driving back in Mara's car from the hospital where Patsy was still unconscious, locked in an existence bounded by the dimensions of her bed and the tubes that fed in and out of her. Mara, exhausted and stressed, was in no mood to oblige Julian.

"Who are you calling?"

Prudence had pulled out her cellphone and was pushing numbers.

"Julian. Or his cottage." Prudence listened. "No answer. That means Charlie's out. Maybe he's away. Didn't he say something about doing research in Paris and Bordeaux? Why not swing by Grissac for a quick peek around? The dogs and I will be your lookout." Bismuth and Jazz were asleep in the rear of the car. "That way at least you can tell Julian you tried."

"I doubt I'll be speaking to him again. He phoned from Chengdu yesterday. I"—Mara's voice broke slightly—"I dumped him."

Prudence turned her sleek head to stare at Mara. "I don't believe it."

Mara gestured despairingly. "Why is it so unbelievable? It's over, Prudence, finished."

"But you love each other. Don't you?" Her friend peered so searchingly into her face that Mara had to turn away. *Love*? she thought. There was a time when she had hoped that love was the glue that held them together. Now she realized that what they shared was fondness. *We're friends. We're two lonely people in France who'd rather be together than apart. It's not the same thing.* And in a moment of clarity, she felt inexpressibly sad.

"Look," she said evasively, "I'm a presentable, competent professional with a few clicks left on the odometer. I have my own business, a house, friends, interests. I have a dog—"

"You have two dogs at the moment."

"I'm even able to cook a halfway decent meal when required. Why in God's name would I need an unreliable, egocentric orchid freak in my life?"

"Is this about Julian being gaga about his *Cypripedium* thingy, or his not telling you he was married, or his going to China, or what?"

"All of the above, but mostly it's about him not being there when I need him, Prudence. He uses me, he takes me for granted. He doesn't mean to, but he simply walks on another planet where flowers are more important than people. And I'm afraid it'll always be this way with him." Mara was finally able to meet Prudence's questioning look with tired eyes underlain by shadows the colour of bruises, the colour of hurt.

"And you want to teach him a lesson?"

Mara shook her head wearily. "I'm not trying to teach him anything. I just want my life and my money back, sans his agenda, sans his botanical obsessions, sans him. Is that so hard to understand?"

"Okay." Prudence raised an eyebrow. "I understand. You can still swing by Grissac. If Charlie's in, you can say you were just feeling caring. Canadians are very caring people, aren't they?"

•

Charlie's car was not parked outside the cottage.

"See? Not there. Go on," urged Prudence. "Now's your chance. If I spot him coming, I'll honk the horn."

"Oh, for pity's sake," said Mara, climbing out of the Renault.

Charlie really was out, or at least he did not respond to her knock. She glanced around, saw Prudence waving her on. Unwillingly, she jabbed the key into the lock and let herself in.

The cottage looked and smelled unoccupied. She was tempted to throw open the windows to air out the musty odour of damp stone. Charlie's workstation in the kitchen was much as she remembered it, books and notepads neatly arranged, pencils at the ready. Nor had Charlie made much progress on Kneebone's Dordogne period. The handwritten draft she had seen earlier still read: *Horatio returned to Europe in October 1861 . . .*

"I don't know why I'm doing this," Mara grumbled to herself.

She searched through his papers again, and when this proved unproductive stood staring around her. Where would be the most likely place to hide the missing diary pages? The kitchen cabinets? A quick rummage turned up nothing. In the refrigerator she found a bottle of milk gone sour and a mouldy cheese.

Resentfully she addressed an absent Julian, "You don't deserve this," and moved into the front room, scanning shelves bulging with books. The drawers of his battered desk were crammed with bills, bank statements, old nursery catalogs. She shook her head. No one as fastidious as Charlie would even consider putting important primary source material in with that mess.

She went into the bedroom where the bed was made and clothes hung tidily in the armoire. There was none of Julian's all-over-the-place disorder. She stood on a chair to inspect the top of the armoire. Dust. The nightstand held throat lozenges and a flashlight. The medicine cabinet in the bathroom contained nothing but toiletries; the wicker hamper was empty. Charlie evidently kept on top of his laundry.

There was a spare room that Julian used as his "tidying up" area, a place where he tossed junk, empty boxes, battered sports equipment, old magazines. A matching pair of handsome, aluminum-sided suitcases—obviously Charlie's, Julian had never owned anything so grand—stood just inside the door. She popped the catches. The larger one was empty; the smaller contained a folder of travel documents, an inflatable neck cushion, keys. She closed the cases and set them back in place.

There was a dented metal cabinet where, higgledy-piggledy, Julian stored his floral slides, photographs and notes, taken over a lifetime. It was the only thing in the house that he normally locked, so Mara was surprised to find it unsecured. Of course, anything pertaining to *Cypripedium incognitum* had gone with him to Ecoute-la-Pluie, but she suspected that Charlie had been doing a bit of prying and poking himself. Fair enough. It served Julian right. The missing diary pages were not there either.

So where were they? Running out of places to look, Mara went out to the furnace–laundry room attached to the house. Surely not, she thought, but she checked inside the washing machine and dryer all the same.

She returned to the house. The fireplace? She crouched down and opened the damper, releasing nothing but a drift of soot. Puzzled, she flopped down into Julian's worn leather armchair. The cottage was dim and quiet. His chair smelled of him and bore the impress of his body. She closed her eyes, breathing in deeply, striving to capture a sense of him. Sadly she wondered what he was doing. Did he miss her? Probably too busy with tall Fang to give her a thought.

Suddenly, she sat forward. There was one place she had overlooked. Her alcoholic ex-husband Hal had sometimes hidden bottles of scotch there. She returned to the bathroom and lifted the top of the toilet tank. Pay dirt! Not immersed in the reservoir but stuck with duct tape to the underside of the lid and double sealed in Ziploc bags. She opened the bags and riffled through the contents. In addition to the missing pages, she found a monograph on Kneebone's China travels written by someone named P.K. Chapman.

Before she left the cottage, her eye fell on a notepad by the telephone. The top sheet bore a name and number written in Charlie's neat hand. An ironic smile flitted across Mara's face. A minute later, she was in the car.

"Got it," cried Mara, tossing the Ziploc package on to Prudence's lap. "Let's get this photocopied and back in place *tout de suite*."

"Where was it?" asked Prudence, as Mara started up the car and accelerated down the road toward Chez Nous.

"You'll never guess."

•

Mara had a new *femme de ménage*. Her old one, a sour-tempered person named Madame Audebert, had never got on with Julian and had been replaced by a good-natured Alsacienne named Colette. She was an energetic woman with arms like a stevedore who sang while she scrubbed and who took Julian's potted plants, which dropped leaves, and his dog, whose hairs covered everything, philosophically. Colette had been in that day, and Mara returned to a tidy, spotless house redolent of beeswax polish.

"No litter," she told the dogs, who pushed in the door past her. She added, addressing the unaccustomed silence, "Peace."

Later she ran herself a bath, adding a dollop of her favourite *bain moussant*, and sank in it up to her chin, submerged in foam and surrounded by the tiny crepitation of millions of bath bubbles giving up the ghost. She was half asleep when the clicking of the dogs' claws on the bathroom tiles roused her. They stared at her over the rim of the bath, noses twitching, eyes asking if dinner was on its way.

"Fix it yourselves," she said, and flicked foam in their faces. They lay down on the bath mat and gazed at her reproachfully.

Tonight I will sleep, she promised herself. *Tonight I will sleep. I have my life back. No more orchids. No more socks on the radiators. No more newspapers all over the place. When he returns from China, I'll give him the rest of his damned diary—unread by me—and tell him to pack up and move out. He can bunk with Charlie, like it or lump it. Tonight I will sleep like a baby.*

A little later, by way of celebration, Mara, barefoot and in her favourite silk pyjamas, loaded up a tray with a tub of *rillettes d'oie*, bread and a bottle of chilled Monbazillac, and carried it to bed with her.

"*Liberté*!" she toasted her new-found freedom. The dogs, having been fed, let out and let in, jumped up beside her.

"Hey, *égalité*," Mara complained as they crowded in.

"*Maternité*," she laughed, and cuddled them. It was as close as she would ever get to motherhood.

For dessert, she offered herself a bowl of dark, ripe strawberries that she ate with her fingers.

Outside, evening was settling in on soft, dove-coloured wings. Cool air drifted through the open windows, carrying with it the fading scent of roses and lilacs, the many-layered chirr of crickets. Her house, old, solid and kindly, enfolded her.

But sleep came fitfully. Perhaps it was the *rillettes d'oie*, a rich concoction of potted goose, that brought on a dream in which she stood in the middle of a vast, windy square and Julian walked right past her on the arm of a woman with very long legs whose face she could not see. She awoke with indigestion. She switched on the light, climbed out of bed over Jazz's immovable form and stumped grumpily into the bathroom for an antacid, reflecting sourly that Bismuth's name figured prominently on the label. His bad behaviour as a puppy had often made Julian reach for the bottle of Pepto-Bismol. She chewed two tablets. For good measure she took a third. They calmed her dyspepsia, but she could not fall back to sleep. Eventually she got up again and walked restlessly around the house. She thought of a paperback thriller that she had started, but it was not what she wanted at the moment. She wanted, she was annoyed to admit, to find out what secrets Horatio's missing pages held.

•

The diary entries began where Julian's section broke off and contained an account of an arduous journey into what Horatio called the "western mountains," accompanied by his servant Pung and Tree Bark the guide.

> *7 May. Path extremely rocky. Have seen no further sign of Foster or his party since I last spied him two days ago, but in these narrow twisting passes, that does not signify. All day we followed the course of a dark, rapidly flowing river choked with the debris of mountains looming all around. Progress slow. Covered at best fifteen miles this day.*

The writing, faint and cramped, was hard to decipher, but that was also because Mara's glasses were the varifocal type that she had never learned to read with properly.

> *9 May. Reached a village, the local name of which is unpronounceable for me, but which Pung says is Si Li Ting in Chinese and which I take to mean Fourth Li Pavilion. Inhabitants stared at me as if at a monster. Pung and Tree Bark had difficulty explaining I was harmless, that I only wanted to collect plants, which seemed beyond their comprehension. Eventually, after much persuasion and promises of generous payment, we were offered food and shelter for the night.*

10 May. After more negotiation, three men who claimed to know the terrain well agreed to take me up into the mountains. I asked them if they had ever seen the flower Yong Chun Hua, describing it in detail, but they shook their heads.

11 May. Reprovisioned, Pung buying rice and millet, vegetables, loquats, apples, strips of dried takin flesh and several chickens that we will carry live in baskets, slung on bamboo poles across the ponies' backs. Tree Bark left us to return to his own village, assuring me that we had lost Foster, the "snake's tail," which I do not for a minute believe.

12 May. Set out again, this time a party of five.

The next several entries described an upward trek through groves of blooming rhododendrons, virgin forests of towering oak, ash and maple, dense stands of bamboo and, higher up the mountainside, many species of conifers. Once a terrific rainstorm drenched their encampment, nearly blowing away their tents. By the sixth day, they were beginning to run out of food, and Horatio grumbled at having to waste daylight hours and ammunition shooting small game to keep the men fed. He himself seemed content to live on nothing but rice and millet. Along the way, he found many plants that he sketched and described, recording that his presses were growing full.

Then Mara read something that made her heart race:

22 May. The Luck of the Kneebones holds! Today I found it, a prize so rare, so stupendous that all pales beside it. It surely was destiny that led me along the cliff base while my men were making camp, that caused a shaft of light to break like a celestial arrow to illuminate a cleft in the rock face. Curious, I slipped in through a narrow passage that opened at the other end into the head of a hanging valley. The place was full of plants unknown to me and had an otherworldliness about it that seemed to put it beyond all human experience. I wandered in a daze. And then, two hundred feet or more in, I saw them, scattered across the steep east wall of the valley, several hundred in all, perhaps a third still in bloom, each exactly as described in the ancient texts: a tall stem bearing a single flower with a dark pink pouch flanked by two exceedingly long, spiralling, blackish-purple petals. The sepals, of which there were three, were of the same blackish-purple hue. I stood incredulous for above a quarter of an hour before I could let my mind believe what my eyes were telling me. I had found Yong Chun Hua, the mythical flower of eternal youth!

"My God!" Mara exclaimed so loudly that the dogs jumped. "He found it! He really found it!" Despite herself, she wished Julian were there to read Horatio's words.

Does Yong Chun Hua truly impart immortality? I am ready to believe it has magical powers of some sort, for it is almost sinister in its beauty and gives off a pungent odour to which small, iridescent flies seem much attracted. The orchids appear to be confined to this place only, for although I combed the entirety of the valley, which ran on for perhaps another half a mile and led off into a number of dead-end ravines, I found nothing more, in fact no other orchids of any kind. Took several flowering stems which I pressed and from which I prepared a detailed drawing. One of these plants alone will be worth a king's fortune to the right buyer. What, I wonder, would "Mad" Harry Masterman pay? And how to measure Foster's envy, indeed his fury? My problem for the moment is what to call it. A discovery of this magnitude requires a worthy name. Cypripedium splendidum? C. pulcherrimum? *For the moment, I will be forgiven for naming it after myself,* Cypripedium kneebonei.

The following page was the annotated sketch, the copy of which Charlie had given Julian.

23 May. Slept not at all last night. Rose at first light and returned to do a thorough search of the area surrounding the valley. By day's end, I confirmed that the orchids are highly localized, growing only in this one place, for I encountered absolutely no further evidence of them elsewhere. As I searched, I struggled over what to do. I will of course take as many plants as I can carry. But Tarquin Foster forces my hand. Contrary to Tree Bark's assurances, I am certain he continues to dog my steps, and should he come upon my find, with "Mad" Harry's resources behind him, he will have every advantage of speed and facility to claim what is rightfully mine. It is unthinkable that he should bring my prize to the attention of the world before me. God forgive me what I must do.

24 May. This morning led my men to the passage in the rock face. At first they were reluctant to enter, disliking the enclosed feeling of the place, but I drove them in, and when they came upon the orchids, they marvelled, for even they, and certainly Pung, had some inkling of the significance of what they saw. Thus I ordered the taking up of the plants, as many as could be carried, with great care to avoid damage to the roots. The promise of so much cash per plant was sufficient to set them digging with a will. Precious cargo then carried out and packed in damp mosses, taking extreme care that each plant was loaded on the ponies so as to ensure protection of each as well as sufficient circulation of air. I know from sad experience how few of these splendid beauties will withstand the journey down from the mountains and thence to Shanghai, to say nothing of the long sea voyage before them. Then, against my will and before quitting the valley, I did the necessary, making sure I left behind nothing that could profit Foster.

Stunned, Mara reread Horatio's words. Surely this was the source of Charlie's tale of the plant hunter who had taken what he could carry and destroyed the remaining plants to protect his find from claim-jumpers. Charlie had been referring to his own great-great-great-grandfather!

"The bastard!" she shouted, and again the dogs jumped. "The malignant, greedy bastard!"

The next few entries, sporadic and written over the ensuing eight days, were brief and in an increasingly unsteady hand:

25 May. Slow going with the ponies, path dictated by the need to stay near water, a narrow tumbling stream that leads over extremely difficult terrain.

26 May. Very hot during day, bitterly cold at night.

28 May. Supplies and water running low. Today parted company with the stream, which suddenly disappeared underground, as if by some evil sorcery.

31 May. Supplies exhausted. Parched, but every drop of water must be reserved for the orchids. I fear greatly for my plants, many of which look in poor condition. I would gladly give my life's blood to sustain them. These endless, God-forsaken mountains! Is there no easy way down from them?

And then:

1 June. Once again the Luck of the Kneebones holds! Met a party of hunters whom I initially took for brigands but who proved honest men. They directed me to water and, for a consideration, were willing to part with some of their game and lead the way down to a village where provisions could be purchased.

The last entries, written over the next six days, put Horatio en route to Ch'eng Tu, where the final portion of the diary that Julian had already read took up the account.

As her anger subsided, Mara wondered if Horatio's destructive deed was the reason Charlie had been unwilling to let Julian see the diary, and why, suspecting that Julian would find a way of reading it anyway, he had taken the precaution of removing Horatio's account of his time in the mountains. She thought she understood the writer's dilemma: to lay before the world an awful truth, or to let sleeping dogs, and Horatio's reputation, lie?

She, who only hours earlier had celebrated her freedom from one orchid freak, now found herself intrigued by another. Horatio was driven, greedy and ruthless. He had the white man's arrogance typical of his times, and yet there was also something almost pathetic about his obsession with his orchids. And familiar. Did Kneebone, a plant hunter from another era, hold the key to Julian? She wanted to know more about Charlie's ancestor. Her only other source of information was the Chapman monograph that she had copied along with the missing pages. She read it now.

"Horatio Kneebone," it began, "was without doubt one of the most determined, single-minded and intrepid of the early China plant explorers." But it dealt only with his activities around Canton and Peking and told her little about the man that she did not already know. Undeterred, she put on her bathrobe, went out to her studio, and Googled "Chapman" together with "Kneebone." What came up surprised her enormously.

"Why the cunning devil!" Mara did not know whether to laugh or cry.

• 23 •

"Mara?" Julian spoke into the receiver. He was still in his pyjamas, sitting on the edge of the bed, still feeling rocky from the night before.

"Julian, do you know what time it is?" Her voice was thin and slightly shrill, with the ghost of an echo trailing after it.

"I know. I'm really sorry. I hope I didn't wake you. I'm still in Chengdu, and it's just that we're leaving soon and I may not have the chance to call again for a while." When she did not respond, he volunteered, "I was nearly run over by a bus yesterday, and then someone coshed me in the middle of the night. In my hotel room."

"Coshed! Are you all right?"

He was gratified to hear the spike of concern in her voice. Fang, when she had been informed, had merely sniffed, implying that he had been done over by a midnight masseuse whom he had unwisely invited in.

"Sure. Just a knock on the head, and you know how hard that is." His pause was not rewarded by laughter. "Nothing taken, thank God. Fang wanted to put off travelling until tomorrow, just in case I had a concussion—"

"Oh well, good for Fang."

"But I insisted on keeping to schedule. I must say, I feel fine." It was not true. His head still ached, his nuts were sore and his throat felt raw, as if he had swallowed sandpaper.

There was another pause.

Then Mara said coldly, "I suppose you're calling about the diary?"

"What? No. Not at all." Julian felt genuinely hurt by her assumption, her accusation really. When all he had wanted was to make contact, to be reassured that some threads of their relationship still held. "I was just wondering how you are. And Patsy, of course."

"I'm fine, there's no change in Patsy, so why don't we cut to the chase? There's good news and bad news. The good news is I found your missing pages."

"You found—?" It was absolutely the last thing he had expected to hear her say, and he felt immediately that all had been forgiven, that she still cared—must care—for him. Why else make the effort? He jumped up, ignoring his swimming head, his voice breaking with excitement. "Mara, bless you! That's brilliant! I knew you'd do it. I knew I could count on you. What was in them that Charlie didn't want me to see?"

"Oh, not much. Only that Horatio really did find your orchid. In fact, he stumbled on a colony of several hundred plants, a third still in bloom."

Now Julian stood stock-still. Had he heard correctly? Several hundred plants? A third in bloom?

She went on, "And the drawing he made, the one Charlie gave you, was done from a living model. Moreover, Horatio was convinced that the orchids he found were Yong Chun Hua."

"My God!" Forgotten were the nasty events of the last twenty-four hours. "This is absolutely the best news you could have given me. Did he say where he found them? Does he give any site information?"

In response to Julian's flood of questions, she read him all the entries: Horatio's journey to the western mountains, the race to lose Tarquin Foster, the departure from Si Li Ting, the ensuing days as Horatio filled his plant presses and shot game to feed his men, his tremendous discovery, and his descent from the mountains. Julian took frantic notes.

"Wait a minute. Ten days out from—what was the name of the village again? Can you spell it? Okay, let me see if I've got this right. Cleft in rock face, narrow hanging valley, a couple of hundred feet in, east valley wall? Look, can you fax the pages to me? We'll be leaving in a couple of hours, so you'll have to send them off right away."

"Julian, are you out of your mind? For your information, it's past midnight here, and if I wasn't asleep when you called, I'd like to get some sleep before the night is out—"

"Sorry, sorry. Stupid of me. But you're absolutely sure he didn't give any other clues as to location? Mention any other place names? Geological formations?"

"Quite sure. What I gave you is what there is. Now"—her tone was ominous—"do you want the bad news?"

"What? Oh, fire away." After the splendid news she had just given him, who cared?

"Once Horatio had taken all the plants he could carry—you'd better brace yourself for this—I think he destroyed the remaining orchids because he didn't want Tarquin Foster, who was closing in on him, to find them. Hello? Julian? Did you hear me? I said he destroyed all the remaining orchids. He probably left Foster nothing but ashes."

"Destroyed?" Her words hit him far harder than the blows delivered by his murderous masseuse. Julian stumbled backwards onto the bed. Grown men did shed tears, and he was as close as he had ever come to crying. Sadly, he realized it was the age-old story of greed and insolence that led men to violate the very earth on which they stood.

Mara, responding to his distress, said sympathetically,

"Well, if it's any consolation to you, he had a rough time coming down from the mountains, and you know that all but one of his orchids died."

"Of course they died!" Hyperventilating, Julian jumped up again and paced the length of the phone cord. "He dug them up at the wrong time. He should have left them and gone back later when they were dormant and in seed. What the hell did he expect?"

"This was 1861, don't forget. It took him months to make his way into the interior. He had to take what he found when he found it. Anyway, the point is, you now have the missing diary information on *Cypripedium incognitum*."

Julian fought to get his breathing under control. "Yes. At least there's that. And listen, Mara, what you've told me is immensely important. I can't thank you enough for this. I'll pass it on to the other members of the team. You're—" He was overcome for a moment. "Let me just say you're wonderful," he finished off huskily.

She brushed aside his gratitude. "Right. Now for the really bad news, if you think you can handle it."

"What can be worse than what you've just told me?"

"Just this. Charlie isn't who he says he is. In addition to the missing diary pages, I also found an article by P.K. Chapman on Kneebone's travels in China. Out of curiosity, I looked up Chapman on the Internet and found a hit, an interview with a Perry K. Chapman in *The Journal of Historical Botany*, complete with photo. I didn't recognize him at first because of the beard, but when I looked closely, I realized that Chapman is none other than our boy Charlie K. Perry!"

It required a moment for Julian to take this in. "Well, what's wrong with that?" he asked cautiously. "The man uses a pseudonym. Lots of writers do that."

"True. But they don't lie about *what* they are. He may be a writer, Julian, but he's no botanical neophyte. Like his ancestor, he's a full-blown professional plant hunter, a bioprospector and, like you, an orchid freak. What do you bet the *K* in both cases stands for Kneebone? Moreover—you're going to like this even less—he's hooked up with Géraud. I found a notepad at the cottage with Géraud's name and number on it, in Charlie's handwriting."

Julian heard a ringing in his ears, as if something was about to go off inside his head. The detonation came seconds later: "The bastard! The lowdown duplicitous bastard! I knew there was something fishy about him from the start! Just wait 'til I get my hands on him. I'll murder the piece of shite. I'll drop him head first in a swamp. Don't you see? Charlie didn't come to France to research Kneebone's Dordogne period. He came to screw out of me where *Cypripedium incognitum* grows!"

"Oh, do be fair." Mara tried to calm him down. "You weren't planning to tell him, were you?"

But Julian was past hearing, riding the tide of his fury. "And he's probably been in touch with Géraud all along. Which means it was Géraud who put Charlie up to it in the first place. And like an idiot I fell for it. I've left the field wide open to the pair of them by taking off for China!"

"So you have," said Mara with heavy irony. "Although they may be hedging their bets. While Géraud is here looking for your orchid, Charlie seems to be mysteriously absent. His car's gone, he doesn't answer the phone, and I found sour milk and mouldy cheese in the fridge. I think he came to France because he knew from the diary that Horatio had destroyed all the orchids in the valley and he believed their only living representative was here in the Dordogne. However, the minute I mentioned you'd gone to China to hook up with Fang, who had a lead on a possible growing site, he realized that maybe Horatio hadn't wiped out all the orchids after all."

"Oh, bloody hell, you didn't tell him!"

"Why not? And please stop yelling."

"So are you suggesting he's followed me here and is dogging my steps like Foster dogged Horatio's?"

"Or else he's trying to get to that valley ahead of you."

"Good God," groaned Julian. If his head had not been so sore, he would have banged it against the wall. "Mara, look, I hate to ask you this, but can you talk to Iris? Find out what you can from her about what Géraud knows and what he's up to. And most important, check to see if Charlie really has left. Go to the cottage, search around for his passport—"

Mara cut him off. "Julian, there's a one-syllable word you don't seem to understand. No. In French it's *non*. I don't know how to say it in Chinese. Let me put you straight on something. I went after those missing diary pages not for you but to get Prudence off my back, and because, quite frankly, I was curious. But that's it. No more. Finished. Over. You and I are history. I've done everything I'm going to do for you. So good luck with your orchid hunt—"

"Mara—" Julian broke in desperately.

"And"—she paused, perhaps to impart greater meaning to her final word—"goodbye."

Julian heard again the heart-sinking drone of a dead connection. Stunned, he cradled the receiver. He could not believe it. After four years and as many orchid springtimes, after endless skirmishes about relationships, she had done it. She had walked away. She had cleaned up the one piece of unfinished business between them, the missing diary pages, and she had said goodbye. It was not the word itself, but the way she had said it that made him realize that she had finally let go her end of the piece of elastic that held them together, finishing it not with a snap but a limp memory of how they once had been. Sadly, he pondered the nature of relationships. Risky. Bound in the end to fail. All of his did, at any rate. Perhaps it was the blow to his head, for Julian, normally not an introspective man, was suddenly struck by perhaps the most profound insight he had ever had. Love was measured by degrees of loss. And he, Julian, was at the losing end.

•

He had plenty of time to reflect upon his situation during the journey the next day. Initially they passed through a wide fertile plain that stretched away in fields of mixed vegetables and rice paddies. The toll road they travelled was straight and smooth and signed in English: OVERTAKING LANE, CARRIAGEWAY, HARD SHOULDER. Or sometimes HARD SOLDER. Speed limits were posted in Arabic numerals. Fang, too, seemed content to remain with her thoughts, so they travelled mostly unspeaking but not in silence. Their driver, a grizzled chain-smoker named Mr. Jin, drove fast and passed everything in sight, blaring his horn all the way.

They ate lunch at a roadside stand where a single cook manned four sizzling woks with the panache of a symphony orchestra conductor. Throughout the meal, Julian remained uncommunicative, his mind taken up with Mara (how was he to get her back? *could* he get her back?), inevitably circling around to the awful truth: in pursuing the thing he most wanted to find, he had lost the one person he most wanted to keep.

"You all right?" Fang peered at him over a bowl of pork and steamed noodles.

"What? Oh fine," said Julian with a deep intake of breath. He sat up and squared his shoulders. "I'm just fine."

All too soon, they turned off on to the awful road that Fang had warned Julian about. Everything was in a state of construction or deconstruction, reduced in places to a single rubble-strewn track. Mr. Jin smoked and grumbled about the constant holdups as heavy earth-moving equipment lumbered about, and the even longer waits while oncoming traffic had the right of way. Julian swallowed two aspirins and held his head in his hands. The jolting and lurching had brought on another Thumper.

The rich flatlands through which they had come now narrowed to a landscape of rocky, scrub-covered hills ringed by distant, looming mountains. Everything had a wild look. Civilization here was invested in isolated Han and national minority villages, each with its particular architectural expression, and, incongruously, the occasional slender finger of a China Mobile tower pointing ironically skywards. Whereas the toilets along the toll road had at least been clean (you paid five *jau* to use them), the facilities along this stretch were primitive and smelly. One Julian encountered, a long cement trough spilling directly out over a cliff, adjoined a pigsty inhabited by a lumbering sow who eyed him suspiciously through a chink in the plank wall.

They spent the night in a noisy hotel in Mingdan and continued in the morning to Kanglong, which they reached toward the end of the day. It was a village of perhaps a hundred souls built upon a hillside stepped in terraces of maize, barley and groves of what Fang said were Sichuan pepper trees. The sudden appearance of a car bearing a *lao wai*, as foreigners were politely called (there were other, less respectful terms, but Julian had not learned them yet), caused an impromptu welcoming committee of sorts to form. One by one people began to appear until the car was surrounded by a ring of faces. Julian grew uncomfortable as he realized that the dominant expression was not friendliness or even curiosity, but hostility. Maybe not that much had changed since Horatio's time after all.

"Are you sure this is the right place?" he asked.

"Don't be stupid," snapped Fang. She, too, seemed unnerved by their reception. She conferred with Mr. Jin, who took his cigarette out of his mouth long enough to say emphatically, "*Dui*, *dui*!"

"Come on," said Fang, and got out of the car.

A small wiry man was coming down the steep, unpaved main road of the village at a rapid pace, braking with his heels against the slope. He talked on a cellphone as he came. In the misty distance, high on a mountainside, Julian saw the ghost of another China Mobile tower. This was a country, he realized, the remote fastness of which had totally skipped the land-line era. The man snapped the phone shut and pushed through the crowd. He had a brief conversation with Fang, all the while sizing Julian up in an unfriendly, speculative way.

"This is Mr. He," Fang said to Julian. "He's the headman of Kanglong. The rest of the team is waiting for us at his house."

"*Ni hao*," said Julian, to which Mr. He made no reply.

Fang saw to the unloading of the car and paid the driver off. Then she and Julian, carrying their things, followed Mr. He up to his house, a mud-brick structure built around a courtyard where chickens pecked in the dirt.

The rest of the team was two people. Fang performed the introductions. Zhang Shugang, their guide, proved a tough-looking fellow in his thirties. Xing Weiming was a mere kid, maybe seventeen or eighteen, dressed in Hilfiger jeans, a Gap T-shirt, and Nike runners, or else knock-offs of the same. They all sat down in Mr. He's small front room on child-sized wooden stools around a low wooden table. Tea was served by an older woman whom Julian took to be Mrs. He.

Julian did not know what to make of Zhang or Xing. Zhang made it clear from the outset that he disliked Julian intensely, glowering at him from under a broad-brimmed leather hat as if Julian were the object of a long-standing grudge. Xing was thin, looked no one in the eye, and behaved peculiarly, sometimes marching about stiff armed, or breaking off to weave and duck, or whirling around to fire a finger pistol with accompanying explosive mouth noises at unseen enemies. Both spoke passable English, although Zhang did little more than grunt in answer to Julian's attempts at conversation. The most Julian was able to elicit from him was that he was from Kanglong and that he worked as a plant protection officer in a provincial forest preserve a hundred kilometres away. When Julian tried to pry out of him information on their intended botanical itinerary—could he see it on a map? for example—Zhang got up and stalked out of the house. Xing had no qualifications whatever to justify his participation in the team, his sole interest in life being video games. His favourites were *Hero*, *Blood War* and something called *Dragon Warriors*, which perhaps accounted for his odd behaviour. He was acting out, Julian decided, endless, imaginary, computerized battles.

"How did you come across those two anyway?" Julian asked Fang later when Mr. He, Zhang and Xing had gone off on business of their own and they had a moment alone. Julian's confidence in the expedition was waning by the minute.

Fang shrugged. "Zhang I know from university. After we graduated, I got a job at the institute, but he got stuck up in the north. We lost touch until I contacted him about *Cypripedium incognitum*."

"Passing me off as Horatio Kneebone's great-great-great-grandson?"

"Better that way." Fang smiled her unreadable smile. "Anyway, Zhang e-mailed me about the stories his grandmother used to tell him about the European, Nie Bo. Like I said, he figured Nie Bo and Kneebone must have been the same person. So he suggested the expedition, and he insisted you be included."

At this, Julian brightened. However, he felt moved to observe, "That surprises me. He doesn't seem to like me very much. He called me something—it sounded like *dabeezee*. What does that mean?"

"Oh, it's just another name for foreigner." Fang waved the word away.

"It didn't sound very nice the way he said it."

"Actually, *dabizi* means big nose. Pay no attention," Fang advised him. "He could have called you *yang guizi*, foreign devil, which is even worse. Zhang is hard to get along with because he's frustrated. He's in a dead-end job. But he knows orchids, and he knows the area around here like the inside of his own elbow. If anyone can find *Cypripedium incognitum*, Zhang can."

"But what earthly good is Xing?" Julian complained. "Why is he along?"

Fang shrugged. "Xing is Zhang's cousin. That's why."

•

Dinner, served at the same low wooden table, was simple. Braised mutton, rice, vegetables, dumpling soup with green onions and tea. From the kitchen, Julian could hear shouting and banging. Mrs. He and a younger woman, a daughter-in-law, did the serving. Occasionally he saw an old man's face, weathered as eroded stone, peering at them from around a door jamb. Once or twice a young child ran into the room, chased by the daughter-in-law. But that was as much as he saw of the He family.

Relations did not warm much at dinnertime. Everyone ate in silence. Julian had purposely saved the information Mara had given him on Horatio's discovery until he could announce it to the entire team. He had also thought to make an impression by whipping out the diary, but his hopes were deceived. The team was hardly a team, and the diary and his news fell flat. Zhang did not seem interested. Xing was lost in a world of his own. Mr. He, to whom the information was translated by Fang, merely picked his teeth. Only Fang was excited about the mention of Si Li Ting, the fissure in the cliff face and the hanging valley, which she said were important indicators. Julian did not tell them that there might not be any orchids left to find. He had been counting on at least a few plants surviving Horatio's scorched-earth policy. Now, with everything turning out so queerly, he had no reason to feel at all optimistic.

"Okay," said Fang as they all stood up from the table. "Zhang has organized our equipment and provisions. There is a mule to carry everything. We pack up and set out after breakfast tomorrow morning." To Julian she said, "Get a good night's sleep." She added, half seriously, "Don't open your door to anyone."

A cot had been made up for Fang in the front area of the headman's house, but Julian was given a small room to himself. He had no idea where Zhang, Xing and the members of the He family planned to put up for the night. He sat on the edge of a narrow iron bed and pulled off his boots. The room smelled of straw and camphor. Too exhausted to undress, he fell back, pulling a rough woollen blanket over him. Despite the fact that the mattress was lumpy and hard and, as he was to learn later, full of bedbugs, he slept soundly.

24

Mara arrived at the Clinique Morange at eight in the evening. *This is for you, Patsy,* she messaged mentally, sensing somehow that her friend, wandering in the twilight zone, received her. *I'm going to find out who drove you over a cliff, and when I do, I'm going to bring hell down on the bastard.*

In order to do that, first she had to find out what Patsy had seen, heard or said to make her accident necessary.

As instructed, she wore loose clothing and had abstained from caffeine and alcohol. She was checked in by a tall, good-looking blonde in a lab coat who told her rather snippily to sit down in the waiting area. Then a muscular fellow, also in a lab coat, appeared and gave her a questionnaire to complete. A faint, bitter odour of body musk drifted from him. He walked about, cracking his knuckles, while Mara filled in her name, date of birth, gender and profession, and gave information on her general health and sleep pattern. Did she experience delayed sleep, broken sleep or was she unable to get to sleep at all? All of the above. Did she suffer from tinnitus? Did she work shifts? Was she willing to be contacted for possible participation in future sleep drug trials? She ticked yes.

Other patients arrived, two men clad in track suits and an exhausted-looking woman wearing a raincoat over a frilly nightgown. She clutched a lavender-scented pillow.

"Can't sleep either?" The woman addressed Mara after she had filled in her questionnaire. "I've tried everything. Pills, melatonin, chamomile, yoga, acupuncture, sheep."

"What about names?" asked one of the men. "I say them alphabetically. Alice, Benoît, Claude . . ."

"It's the change of life," the woman whispered to Mara. "Your hormones let you down."

"Dianne, Edouard, Fernande . . ."

"Mine's sleep apnea," said the other man. He was bald and overweight. "I'm a long-distance trucker. A lot of my mates have the same problem."

"Georges, Hébert, Ivan . . ."

Claude Morange came bustling out of an office. Whereas in Bordeaux, hanging about at the fringes of the demonstration, he had looked ill at ease, here he was in his element. His gestures were large, he filled the space. Mara was able to study him up close: his clothes (expensive), his bonhomie (too suave by half), his dark curly hair (dyed?). His aftershave rode over the muscular fellow's body odour and had to be called something like Stallion or Machissimo. He looked outgoing, ambitious, sexually predatory—but was he dangerous?

"*Bonsoir, messieurs, 'dames.*" He swept them with a twenty-four-carat smile, shook hands with everyone, jollying them along. "I'm Dr. Morange. I see we're all ready to go."

"Where are we going?" quipped the names man. No one laughed.

"You, *mon cher monsieur*, are going to sleep," said Morange genially. This drew skeptical snorts from the woman and the truck driver. "Now, what will happen is this. Our two very able polysomnographers, Sandrine"—he waved at the blonde who flashed him a look that was hard to decipher—"and Francke, will wire you up. No, there's nothing to be alarmed at, *madame*. It's painless and it allows us to track you during sleep, you see. Your movements, brain activity, heart, respiration, everything will be recorded and carefully watched by Sandrine and Francke in the monitoring station. They, unlike you, will get very little sleep tonight. All you have to do is lie back and relax." Claude Morange bowed. "We want you to behave exactly as if you were at home. You may read if you like, but we do ask that you shut off your lights by ten thirty. Or earlier, of course, if you find yourself growing drowsy. Our beds are very comfortable. Then in the morning we will unhook you, give you a nice *petit déjeuner*—our coffee is excellent—and you will be free to go. In a week or so, after we've had a chance to study your data, we will call you back for a follow-up appointment, at which time we will be in a position to make a diagnosis and offer some helpful suggestions for treatment." The doctor's voice was reassuring, chocolate smooth, modulated perhaps to induce sleep. "Now, before I leave, are there any questions?"

There were none.

"*Alors, bonne nuit, et dormez bien.*" On that exit line, Morange raised a hand and left the building.

Sandrine followed him out at a run. Through the glass door, Mara could see them talking, she gesticulating angrily, he placating. At one point, he took her arm. She shook him off. He threw up his hands. She whirled about and stomped back into the building. He stood, his face momentarily illuminated by the light from the doorway, his bonhomie gone, replaced by a look of nervous perplexity.

"Okay, you first." Sandrine, in a temper, jerked her head at Mara. "Bring your things." She marched Mara like a kindergartner first to the toilet and then into an area of cubicles divided by curtains.

Francke followed with the sleep apnea man, whom he took into a neighbouring cubicle.

"So," said Mara conversationally as Sandrine yanked the curtains closed. "What happens now?"

"Sit down," was the terse reply. "Roll up your sweatpants."

Mara did as she was told. "Been working here long?"

"Awhile."

"What do you do?"

"Too much," snapped Sandrine, taking a tube of gel from the drawer of a little cabinet. "Extend your legs." She squatted down, gelled the outsides of Mara's calves and pressed on a pair of electrodes. Mara's view of the top of Sandrine's head told her the blonde was not a natural; dark roots lurked at the scalp line.

"On the questionnaire we had to fill out there was a question about participating in future drug trials. I ticked yes. So does that mean I'll be a guinea pig?"

"Trial subject. And it's not that simple." Sandrine stood up. "Unbutton your top." She continued to gel and place electrodes on various parts of Mara's upper body. "Even if you agreed, you'd still have to meet certain criteria."

"Such as?"

Sandrine shot her a look of annoyance. "You'd have to be diagnosed with a sleep disorder for a start, and it's not just insomnia. The study might focus on things like sleep apnea or narcolepsy. Then, they might want people of a certain age or physical profile or profession. They also check into your medical condition and history. If you pass the screen, you'd have to sign an informed consent form and agree to take an experimental medication—or it might be a placebo, but you wouldn't be told which—for a certain length of time. You might be asked to keep a daily log, or there might be restrictions on your diet or other medications. Your progress would be monitored, and you'd have to come in for an on-site assessment. Raise your chin." Sandrine taped something to the base of Mara's throat and added electrodes to her head, behind her ears and above her eyes.

Something detached itself from the jumble in Mara's brain. "Come to think of it," she improvised, "a friend of mine used to work here, and that may be what she did. Called people, scheduled their assessments. She told me she was once involved with something—what was it called?—Pronole-2, I think. Do you know anything about it?"

For the first time Sandrine looked at Mara directly. She wore cobalt-blue eyeliner that gave her a hard, ceramic gaze. "Never heard of it."

"Are you sure?" Mara was now bristling with loose wires.

"Listen," Sandrine said impatiently, "the clinic does a lot of testing of sleep products, okay? Our patients are a natural population for that kind of thing. But it's not my area. Besides, nine out of ten drugs never make it past the experimental stage."

"Why not?"

"You ask a lot of questions."

"I'm interested. Why not?"

"All kinds of reasons. They don't work. Or they produce bad side effects. Rashes, nausea, that kind of thing. Hold your head still." Sandrine was now taping something under Mara's nose to measure airflow.

"But you must have known my friend. Véronique Rignon."

Sandrine's hand froze. A hint of fear showed in her eyes. "What about her?"

"Well, it was awful, what happened. I expect the police talked to you about her?"

Now Sandrine's expression was positively hostile. "Who are you anyway? Are you a cop?"

"Good heavens, no. I told you. A friend."

Sandrine continued to glare at Mara. "You may have been her friend, but I wasn't. I hardly knew her, and what happened to her had nothing to do with me." She moved away, breathing hard. "Okay," she barked. "You're done. Watch your wires, take your things, follow me."

Sandrine led Mara to one of the sleep chambers, a narrow soundproofed room with a bed, a chair and a nightstand. On the stand were a lamp, a box of tissues and a bottle of water. Once Mara was settled in the bed, Sandrine inserted her leads into a box over the head of the bed.

"All right. This is your light control. If you need to go to the toilet or get out of bed for any reason, speak up. I'll hear you." She indicated an illuminated button below a circular grille in the wall that indicated a live intercom. "I'll have to come in to unhook you. Or Francke will. He has the graveyard shift from two to seven." She left, almost slamming the door behind her.

"I doubt," Mara spoke to the air, "you'll get much data on me in sleep mode."

How anyone was supposed to sleep under such conditions, wired and taped, in a claustrophobic space, was beyond her. Besides, Sandrine had given her plenty to think about.

25

As Mara had predicted, she did not sleep. Questions rolled around in her head like steel balls in a bearing. Was Pronole-2 a drug the clinic had tested? If so, what kind of drug was it? Something to help people sleep? Or to keep narcoleptics awake? Had Véronique's job been to follow up with trial subjects? And was it their names on the list? Restlessly, Mara tossed about, suppressing a desire to tear herself free of the ensnaring wires. It galled her to know that Sandrine was in the monitoring station, probably taking a grim satisfaction in her discomfort, aware of every move she made.

"*Merde*!" she exclaimed, as a wire got entangled with her watch. Exasperated, she sat up.

"What?" Sandrine's disembodied voice crackled from the grille.

"Nothing," said Mara, feeling like a delinquent. She lay back again, staring into darkness. The silence was oppressive.

She must have slept after all, because she dreamed that someone was tinkering with a machine, like a fan, that produced a humming noise. It blew out a kind of snow that blanketed everything, trees, bushes, houses, cars, people. "What are you doing?" she murmured, but the person—a man—put his finger to his lips, and he, too, was lost in swirling whiteness. Then something dark moved across her line of vision. Gradually it grew in size, taking on a hulking, threatening shape. She jerked awake.

It required only a split second for her to realize that someone was in the room with her. She could not see, but she could feel movement at the head of her bed.

"Who's there?" Her cry was stifled by a hand clamped over her mouth. She struggled and tried to claw free but was pushed back forcibly.

A voice said, "Shut up. For the love of God, I'm not going to hurt you."

She knew who it was by the smell even before the bedside lamp was switched on. In the sudden illumination, Francke's face surged out at her, his mouth open as if miming the scream he had just smothered.

"Okay," he said. "You're dead." The hand came off her mouth.

"Dead!" She scrambled away from him, nearly tumbling off the other side of the bed. Then she saw what he meant. The intercom button was dark, and he had disconnected all her leads. Loose wires trailed from her like winter vines.

"What are you doing in here?" she demanded, badly frightened. Belatedly, she realized that this might be the clinic technician Loulou had mentioned, the one who had been charged with assault, who was a possible suspect in Véronique's death. The bed between them made an inadequate barrier.

"*Chut*! Calm down." He backed off, hands up, palms forward. "I have to talk to you."

Mara glared at him distrustfully. "Well, you have a damned funny way of going about it." But he did look harmless, as frightened as she, in fact. "Why did you unhook me?"

"Had to, didn't I? As long as you're wired up everything is recorded. You saw how you reacted. Your readings would have gone crazy, and how would I have accounted for that? For the record, you're taking an unofficial toilet break. And I've got to make this fast because I'm supposed to be watching the monitors." He gave his knuckles a crack.

"Where's Sandrine?" Mara demanded.

"Forget Sandrine. It's my shift. Look, I heard you asking about Véronique and Pronole-2. You're an undercover cop, aren't you?"

It was on the tip of Mara's tongue to deny it again, but Francke's question came out less as an accusation than as a matter of urgent interest.

"And if I am?"

"Then maybe I have information for you."

Her heart beat out an arrhythmic tattoo. "What kind of information are we talking about?" She tipped her head back to size him up through narrowed eyes, like the tough undercover *flic* he seemed to want her to be, adding what she thought was a nice touch: "And what do you expect to get out of it?"

"Protection, *quoi*! Plus money. Because what I have to sell is worth buying."

"About Véronique?"

"Yeah. Her and that American doctor."

Again Mara's heart stuttered. "Dr. Reicher? What do you know about her?"

"I was here the day she came. I heard her pumping Morange. Same questions you were asking. And then she crashed."

"You know something about that?"

"Me? *Putain*! I didn't have anything to do with it, if that's what you think. I never left thc clinic."

"Well, who did? Morange?"

"You're saying did he go after her and drive her off that cliff?"

"You tell me."

Francke shrugged, an odd twisting motion. He said darkly, "Well, someone must have."

"Meaning?"

"Meaning, I don't know." His pulled his fingers and his knuckles went off like minor fireworks. "Look, are you going to help me? *Merde*. First Véronique, then the Reicher woman.

I don't want to be the next in line!" The whites of his eyes were vitreous in the lamplight.

"Why should you be next in line?"

"Because I've figured out what's going on, *quoi*."

Now Mara's heart slammed wildly in her throat. "And just what"—she pulled the blanket from the bed and drew it around her, realizing too late that a real cop probably would not have done that; Francke seemed not to notice—"do you think is going on?"

"I need to know first if it's a deal. You'll see me right? You'll tell them I cooperated?"

Mara nodded.

It came out in a rush. Pronole was an experimental herbal sleep medication tested by the clinic. It was planned as a three-phase study. The first phase, Pronole-1, in 2004, was a short, dose-escalation trial in which a small number of subjects took increasing amounts of the drug until a maximum tolerance was identified. The second, Pronole-2, carried out the following year, was a longer bigger study. In both cases the clinic was the study site and Morange the principal investigator. The third phase was to have been a twelve-month multi-site study involving a much larger number of people.

"Are you saying the clinic also develops sleep drugs?" Mara asked in surprise.

Francke looked at her as if she had become unhinged. "*Merde*! Don't you know anything? Use your brain. Herbal medications? The *promoteur*, the sponsor, was Bonisanté. Morange's wife owns half the company, *quoi*."

Juliette Thory's sister, the one who kept in the background. *A close, family-run business*, Jean-Luc Jarry had said, and Mara found herself wondering if the sister were anything as daunting as the company CEO. Then she recalled Morange's presence at the demonstration in Bordeaux and realized that he had not come to join the action against the pharmaceutical company. He was on the other side, there for business or personal reasons.

The second phase of the study was to have run from January to June 2005, but was discontinued in the fifth month. Francke didn't know why. He'd had nothing to do with the project, had not joined the clinic until July, after the study had been terminated, but he suspected something had gone very wrong, because phase three was never carried out.

"One of the nine out of ten that don't make it past the experimental stage," Mara mused. "But how do you know all this if you weren't involved with the study?"

"Véronique told me a bit. She did the follow-up for the first two phases, mainly clerical stuff, calling testers, reminding them to fill out their logs, booking their on-site assessments. Plus I had a look at the study protocol. When I got into the files to get her a copy of the Pronole-2 call list."

"You got her the list?" Mara was beginning to feel confused. "Why would you have needed to do that? If she was phoning people, wouldn't she have already had it?"

"Because by then Morange had fired her. He'd been shagging her, hadn't he? But when Sandrine came on the scene, Véronique had to go. She didn't like being dumped like so much garbage, I can tell you."

"Wait. When was she fired?"

"*Ouais*!" Francke seemed increasingly astonished at her ignorance. "September. Your lot already know all this."

"And she asked you for the list when?"

"Not until February the following year. One day, out of the blue, she called me up and said, 'Remember me, Franckie?' Well, I remembered her all right. She was the kind who came on to you, *quoi*! Then she said she had a proposition for me. She wanted a copy of the Pronole-2 list, and she said she'd pay me to get into the clinic files and get it. I said, 'How much?' and she said, 'I can be very generous with people who do me favours.' So I did it. But she never paid me."

"Then what?"

"Then she had a meeting with Morange. That was in March. I saw her just as she was going into his office. She looked like she'd won the *loto*. I said, 'What about my money?' She gave me a wink and said, 'Patience, Franckie, and remember these names: Marsaud, Soulivet, Bonnet. They're worth gold.'"

Bonnet? Louis Bonnet? Mara wondered, recalling her phone conversation, under the guise of Marie of the call centre, with Madame Bonnet.

"But when she left, she didn't stop to talk. She was running like all the devils of hell were after her."

"You're saying she was excited and confident when she went in but scared when she came out? Do you know what went on in that meeting?"

"Are you joking? But Bonisanté's honchos turned up as well, so figure it out for yourself. It must have been important."

"Bonisanté's honchos?"

"Thory. And a gelled-up, smarmy *type*. I didn't know him."

"Edgard Papineau, Bonisanté's marketing director," Mara was able to inform him. "Also Thory's son-in-law. Véronique never told you what happened?"

Francke shook his head. "I tried calling her. She still owed me, didn't she? Besides, I was curious. But her phone was dead. I went by her place. Her landlord said she'd skipped, without paying her rent. I never saw her again. Then, right after that, Morange got us all together. He was furious. He gave us a lecture on patient confidentiality and how we were jeopardizing our jobs, possibly committing a criminal offence, by letting drug trial information leave the clinic and all that. He knew someone had slipped Véronique that list, see? And he was trying to narrow it down. He knew it wasn't Sandrine, because they were already like this." He held up two fingers together.

"That's not how they seemed earlier tonight." Mara recalled the scene outside the clinic door.

"Hunh, you saw that, did you? Well, Sandrine's just pissed off because she has to work double shifts. Morange is downsizing, and we're short-staffed. But don't let that fool you. Sandrine calls the shots where he's concerned. Anyway, to get back to what I was saying, that just left me and the rest of the staff. Morange is no dummy. I'm sure by now he's figured out it was me. And then"—Francke broke off to release more knuckles—"a few weeks ago I heard Véronique had been murdered."

"And you concluded the list had something to do with her death?"

He shook his head. "Not at first. I mean, they said it was a burglary, *quoi*. But when that Reicher woman turned up asking questions about her and Pronole-2, I started thinking maybe she was some kind of medical investigator and something had gone wrong. Then I remembered the names Véronique said were worth gold. My sister works for a news database service, so I asked her to do a search for those people. It was a long shot, but I figured they were Pronole-2 testers, and if there'd been a problem with the study, some kind of irregularity or tester complaint, say, I thought it might have made the news. My sister found them, all right"—Francke took a gulping breath—"in the obits! *Merde*!" The whites of his eyes flashed again. "They're dying."

"Dying!" Mara thought immediately of Madame Bonnet's "*Not now, not ever*." Add to that the name of Sofia Ventura, whom Francke had not yet connected to the list. A crazy thought flashed through her mind. "Are you saying someone's going around killing testers?"

"No!" Francke ran the back of his hand over his face. He was sweating, and his body odour, filling the small sleep chamber, was oppressive. "I don't know! But they're dead, aren't they?" He shook his head. "I was thinking"—he made a writhing shrug—"maybe some kind of chronic toxicity."

He saw that she did not understand him. "Look, there's two kinds of problems you have to look out for in drug trials. One is acute toxicity, where you take a drug and right away or in a short time you develop side effects. The other problem is chronic toxicity, where the effects result from repeated exposure over a longer period. They may not be felt until later, and even not for a long time. Those three testers died between five and eight months after the trial ended. But they died in funny ways. I had my sister check them out. That Soulivet woman committed suicide by jumping in front of a Paris *métro* train. But she went holding her baby. What mother does that? Marsaud, a fishing accident, fell out of his boat and drowned in water not deep enough to drown a cat. Bonnet was a single-car accident. He crashed into a tree." Francke took a gulping breath and plunged on. "Véronique must have recognized the names from her call sheet. She might not have thought much about the first death, or even the second, but by the third she would have started getting suspicious. I think she figured pronole had something to do with why these people were dying. I think she tried to blackmail Morange over it. Bonisanté, too, which would explain why the honchos turned up."

"And was murdered for her effort?" Mara had to sit down on the edge of the bed. "But would Morange and Bonisanté have taken her seriously? How could she hope to establish a link after so much time? I mean, you said between five and eight months."

"Months, years!" exploded Francke. "Do I have to explain everything?" His doubts about her investigatory capacity seemed to ratchet up. "With chronic toxicity, the effects can take a long time to develop, even after a person has stopped taking a drug. Maybe pronole has some kind of cumulative effect in the body or the brain, or the damage takes a long time to show up—I don't know—but those testers had been taking the drug every day for five months. Sure, Véronique might have had a hard time making a case, but the publicity alone could have created bad fallout for the clinic, and especially Bonisanté. Don't forget, their motto is 'The Purest and the Best.'"

"And," Mara added, "the company also has its hands full at the moment with a patents challenge." She now had a pretty good idea what Véronique had wanted to sell Jean-Luc Jarry.

"Yeah. That, too. And I'll tell you something else. The day after that Reicher woman was here I looked through the files. All the documentation on pronole, including the second study call list, was gone."

"Which makes the one you gave Véronique the only remaining copy?"

Francke nodded. His chest was heaving, as if he had been running hard. "So maybe now you understand why I need protection? And money. Because I can't go on working here, and I've got to come out of this with something."

"I can't promise anything, but I'll do what I can."

"Do what you can?" Francke's voice rose to a panicked treble. "Listen, I need better than that. I've spilled my guts, haven't I? I've handed it to you on a fucking platter. Because you didn't have a clue what was going on before—" His expression changed abruptly as the truth opened up before him like an abyss into which he had already stepped. "*Putain*! You're no goddam cop!" He advanced on her around the end of the bed, looming aggressively large. "Who the hell are you, and why are you here?"

Mara retreated hastily before him. "I have a genuine sleep disorder." It was the only answer she could think of.

"Shut it! Are you some kind of private investigator?"

She was now backed up against the wall. He blocked her way to the door. The room was soundproofed. If she screamed, would anyone hear her? Would Sandrine come to her rescue? Then, to her surprise and relief, Francke suddenly deflated. His shoulders sagged, his arms dropped to his sides and he became a very frightened man.

"Listen, Francke," Mara said, needing to maintain the precarious rapport she had established with him. "It's true I'm not a cop. I'm not even a private investigator. Like you, I'm looking for answers. And you've given me plenty. But I do have connections. Trust me. I'll do everything I can to help you."

Francke stared at her haggardly. "Trust you!" His face in the lamplight had gone a greenish-grey. "You don't know what you're dealing with here. Bonisanté's big. They can crush the likes of you and me like flies. And Morange won't stop at anything."

"We can work together, Francke," Mara pleaded.

"And wind up like Véronique and that doctor? Forget it. Forget everything I said. I'll deny I ever talked to you." Roughly, he shoved her on to the bed. "Get back in there. I have to make this look good."

Rapidly he reconnected her leads. A moment later, without another word, he switched off the lamp and was gone.

Mara lay in darkness, trying to sort through the jumble of information Francke had spewed up. She now knew what pronole was, that it linked Bonisanté and the clinic, that testers who had taken it had died, and that Véronique had tried to blackmail Thory and Morange over the deaths. But neither had been willing to pay up. On the contrary, they had intimidated her sufficiently to force her into hiding. *Afraid and lying low*, César Fargéas had said. *Making a living in disguise*, Charles Pringault had joked. Then Véronique had seized on the Baixi patents challenge as an opportunity to sell her information to the people who were mounting the suit against the pharmaceutical company. But Jarry had been wary of making a deal. So what would Véronique have done next? The answer stood out a mile: she must have had one more crack at levering money out of Bonisanté and the clinic. However, she had not reckoned on the ruthlessness or the speed of her adversaries. Maybe Thory and Morange had lured her out of hiding by making her believe that this time they would pay up, or maybe they had simply hunted her down. Either way, they had silenced her. And when Patsy had come to the clinic asking questions, they had attempted to silence her as well.

Suddenly, the sleep chamber door flew open. Mara had no time to react before Francke was on her. But he was pulling electrodes off her, yanking wires as he found them, heedless of her squeal of pain as tape was ripped from skin.

"Get up!" he whispered hoarsely. "Get out of here! I just heard Sandrine on the phone to Morange. She told him all about you. He's probably on his way here right now!"

"But what about you?" Mara asked as she scrambled off the bed, stuffing her feet into her shoes. She grabbed her purse and raced after him down the hall. "I have to talk to you again, Francke. How can I get in touch with you? I can't call you here."

"Are you crazy?" Francke gave a choked, mirthless laugh as he unlocked the front door of the clinic and shoved her out into a swirling pre-dawn mist. "Don't even try it. I've told you enough. As of now, I'm gone. I don't exist. You never talked to me!"

26

Julian awoke to find himself sucking on a blanket that had somehow migrated up over his head. His arms were covered in bites. Where the hell was he?

Gradually, the smell of camphor gave him his clue: he was in a room in Headman He's house, in the remote village of Kanglong, Sichuan Province. He sat up groggily, put his boots and jacket on and wandered into the main part of the house. He appeared to be the last up. Fang was nowhere to be seen, but the old man with the weathered face was there, eating a breakfast of thin rice gruel and pickled vegetables that Julian decided to pass on. He stumbled out to the communal toilet.

Later, he found Fang at the other end of the village with Xing, Headman He and what seemed like the entire local population, watching Zhang load the mule, a starved-looking animal with dainty hooves, loose lips and a defeated look that spoke of a life of abuse. The mule was called Xiao Lajiao, Little Pepper. True to her name, she was small as mules went, more the size of a donkey, an impression heightened by the mountain of gear that Zhang was piling on her. In addition to their camping and cooking equipment, plant presses, supplies, backpacks and a jerrycan of water, he slung on such necessaries as a crate of Pepsi-Cola and a dozen vacuum-sealed packages of barbecued chicken's feet. Quixotically, Julian insisted on carrying his own pack, a gesture that won him more unfriendly stares and, as the sun grew hotter, that he later came to regret.

They were seen off in silence. At one point, Julian looked back. The villagers stood grouped together in a frozen tableau, all eyes, it seemed, focused on him.

Zhang, with Little Pepper, led the way along a path that cut through a wooded valley where cattle and the occasional yak grazed. They walked among golden primulas, wild iris, bright pink peonies and, to Julian's delight, scatterings of *Cypripedium tibeticum*, a magnificent magenta orchid with a fat inflated slipper as big as a pigeon's egg. When he stopped to take photographs and make notes in a small binder he had brought for the purpose, Zhang dropped Little Pepper's lead and came back to see what the delay was about.

"What are you doing?" Zhang barked. "These things are common like grass."

"You don't have to be rude about it," Julian snapped. "And I wouldn't mind knowing where you're taking us. We're part of a team, aren't we? Shouldn't I know where we're going?"

For answer, Zhang hawked and spat, depositing a milky globule almost at Julian's feet. He turned away, muttering something that sounded like the *dabizi* word.

This exchange left Julian with a keen desire to punch Zhang out. His anger dissipated only when some time later Zhang, perhaps by way of apology, handed Little Pepper's lead to Fang and grudgingly called Julian to follow him off-trail and up a steep embankment.

"You want photograph," he said sourly as Julian scrambled up behind him, "this is better."

At the top of the embankment, growing under light shrub cover, was a group of five plants. Each was anchored to a pair of bright green leaves by a short, hairy stem; each bore a single, small, pure white blossom marked with red dots, like droplets of blood.

"*Cypripedium wardii*!" Julian, who had seen only pictures of the flower, recognized it at once. You did not forget an orchid like that. Named after Francis Kingdon-Ward, the famous English plant hunter who first reported it to the West in the early twentieth century, *wardii* was rare and a true botanical gem. Julian's estimation of Zhang went up enormously.

"You foreigners think you name something, it belong to you." Zhang's tone was scornful. "Chinese botanists know plenty about orchids too. They write books centuries before you people even know what orchid is."

"Whatever you say." Julian was too busy fiddling with his camera to argue.

In his excitement, he lost his footing and stumbled backwards into Zhang, who, purposely or not, gave him a hard shove forward that nearly sent him sprawling. Julian barely noticed. He was prepared to forgive anything of a man who could lead him to something as precious as *wardii*.

For the rest of the morning, Julian held things up by peering under bushes, looking behind rocks, darting off to walk among the trees. He felt lucky. Who knew what else there was to discover? He was rewarded by a dense colony of diminutive, purple-splotched *Cypripedium guttatum* sheltering under some thorny bushes.

"We'll never get anywhere if you keep doing this," Fang eventually complained.

Xing said something in Chinese that sounded uncomplimentary. Zhang laughed bitterly and ground out the butt of his cigarette.

And to hell with all of you, Julian retorted mentally. He was in China, *Cypripedium* capital of the world. Of the forty-six known species of *Cypripediums* in the world, China had thirty-two. You couldn't get much better than that. It was his own version of heaven, walking among orchids he had never seen except in books. The lot of them—he threw Mara in for good measure—be damned. He was going to relish every minute of it.

Their path dwindled to a goat track, well-used judging by the quantities of droppings they encountered, that led up to a high escarpment. As usual Zhang went first with Little Pepper, followed by Julian, then Fang and lastly Xing, who wandered in a video-game world of his own. At the top, they had a view of a deep valley on the other side, the head of which was blocked by a massive rock slide. It was a bleak, endless prospect of stones, the lap of the Crouching Tiger Mountain, a great weathered hump that pushed out of the earth like a petrified backbone.

At the leading edge of the rockfall, they stopped for lunch. It was an uncomfortable place. The heat was oppressive and the flies persistent and biting. As they rested in the shade of a stunted copse of trees, Fang gave Julian a lesson in counting: *yi*, *er*, *san*, *si*. One, two, three, four and so on. *Si* (four) sounded too much like *shi* (ten) to Julian's ear, and he could not make his tongue form the distinction.

"It's a common error," Fang laughed. "*Si* is often mistaken for *shi*, even by Chinese themselves."

Julian also could not get the hang of the high, low, rising and falling tones of the language.

Teasingly, Fang proposed giving him a Chinese name. The trick lay in finding two words that sounded like "Julian" but that also made sense in Chinese.

"For example," said Fang, "I knew an American woman whose name was Alma. The closest Chinese words to Alma are *ai ma*, but that means 'love a horse' and what woman wants to be called that?" After some joking around, she settled on Zhu Ren, which translated roughly as lord or master. Julian was quite pleased with this. It seemed a propitious name.

"What does your name mean?"

"Fragrance," answered Fang.

"What about you?" he asked Xing, who hunkered low to the ground, a posture that Julian tried unsuccessfully to copy—his legs were not made to fold in the same way, and his knees cracked like gunfire.

"Xing means 'wake up,'" said Xing.

"Yeah," Fang said, and reached out to poke Xing in the shoulder. "Hey, wake up!"

"But you can call me Joystick," Xing offered unexpectedly.

"It's a deal," declared Julian, encouraged by this small intimacy. "Are you from Kanglong?"

"No." The youngster looked disdainful. "I'm from Chengdu. I only stay in Kanglong at my uncle's house until I fix up."

"Fix up?"

"Rehabilitate," Fang clarified, which made Julian wonder if the Chinese still practised some form of "sending down" of political undesirables. Xing did not look much like an enemy of the state.

"Because my parents say I'm addicted to video games," explained the youth. "So they send me here to live with goats and chickens until I get over it."

"And how long will that take?" asked Julian.

Xing shrugged. From the look of him, disheartened and indignant, it might not be for years. Julian stored up this little exchange. It was the nearest he had come so far to establishing rapport with the young man.

Zhang took no part in the conversation. He perched on a rock a little way off, smoking and staring moodily into the distance. Little Pepper stood in what shade she could find, head down, tail swishing, pendulous lips searching for a single blade of grass on the barren ground.

Their way over the rockfall was extremely rough. Little Pepper slipped and skittered on the broken surface and picked her way gingerly around boulders as big as cars. Julian could keep quiet no longer. He insisted that the others also carry their own packs at least until they were on to smoother ground. This his companions, Fang included, refused to do, but at least Zhang agreed to stop and rebalance Little Pepper's load, which was listing heavily to one side.

"It's only going to get worse," said Fang, by way of explanation and not very reassuringly.

It took them more than an hour to work their way over the rocks. After that their path became easier in the sense that they no longer had to scramble around boulders, but harder because now they began to climb in earnest and there was no goat path to follow. Zhang set a killing pace, perhaps to make up for the time Julian had wasted photographing. Julian did his best to keep up, but he was gasping for breath from the altitude. His head ached, the sun beat down on him mercilessly and the weight of his rucksack nearly brought him to his knees. Soon he was the last in line, trailing even behind Xing, who went along jerkily firing finger bullets at rocks and bushes. From this position, Julian pondered his life. Dumped by Mara, here he was in the back of beyond with a man who called him names, a video-game addict and a woman who owed, if not her soul, a lot of money to a greedy orchid collector. He wondered, not for the last time, what he was doing in such company.

· 27 ·

Mara sat at her kitchen table drinking not the murky brew of tea Julian preferred but coffee, straight up, hot and strong. Was that, she wondered, what getting Julian out of her life amounted to? A decent cup of coffee? Were it not for the Pronole-2 list that lay before her (and in which Marsaud's and Soulivet's names figured along with Bonnet's and Ventura's), her nighttime experience would have seemed surrealistic, the stuff of bad dreams.

"All right," she told the dogs, who were just emerging from the bedroom. "Time to prioritize. Forget Julian, forget Fang, forget Horatio Kneebone. Focus on how to bring a nasty cover-up out in the open."

Jazz and Bismuth padded sleepily past and went to point their noses at the back door. With a sigh, Mara rose to let them out. The air was cool and damp, the sky swollen with clouds. Bismuth disappeared immediately into the bushes at the bottom of the garden. Jazz lifted his leg just outside the door and then stood sniffing the air. Suddenly, he gave a low *gruff* and shot around the side of the house. The neighbour's cat, Mara thought, and hurried after him just in time to see a sleek, black Citroën pull up in the drive. To her great alarm, Claude Morange got out of it.

"Madame Dunn!" he hailed her. All solicitude, he came striding up. "My dear madame. I had to assure myself. Are you all right? But why did you run away?" Of course he understood the experience could be a little unnerving, all those wires and electrodes, but surely it was not as terrible as that? They could not have patients fleeing in the middle of the night. All he wanted to do was help her cure her terrible insomnia, but how could he if . . . ? The doctor did not look as smooth and assured as he had the night before—his hair was on end, and he appeared not to have slept much—yet he seemed in earnest.

"Look, it's impossible talking out here like this." He waved a hand at the rain that was starting to fall. "Can't we go inside?"

Reluctantly, Mara led him around the back and into the kitchen, hoping that for once Jazz, who followed them, would do his duty, if not as a guard dog, at least as a deterrent. The Pronole-2 list lay on the table. Hastily, before Morange could see what it was, she threw a dishtowel over it and swept it into a drawer. The doctor sat down on a wooden stool. Jazz rested his big head in the man's lap. Morange tickled his ears.

"I'll get straight to the point, doctor." Offence, Mara decided, was her best defence. Sandrine had already tipped him off, so there was nothing to gain by holding back. "I have information that a drug trial sponsored by Bonisanté and run by your clinic proved fatal to testers, and that the clinic and Bonisanté have been engaged in a cover-up." She swallowed hard. "I should also tell you I've already notified the gendarmes."

Morange might have sagged a little, but he recovered quickly, almost regaining his normally genial expression.

"Madame Dunn," he said, looking as if he doubted her sanity, "are you quite well? Fatal to testers? Cover-up? Gendarmes? I have no idea what you're talking about."

"Do the names Soulivet, Marsaud, Bonnet and Ventura mean anything to you? They should. All of those people took the experimental drug pronole that your clinic tested for Bonisanté. All of them are dead. Under suspicious circumstances."

"Ah," said Morange. "Véronique." His face reshaped itself into an expression of resigned candour. "Look, I may as well tell you that she did approach me with a fantastic story about pronole being responsible for trial subjects dying. However, I assure you this was something she cooked up in an attempt to extort money from the clinic—and Bonisanté—she wasn't fussy where it came from. The more the merrier! As you obviously know, Véronique used to work for us. What you may not be aware of is that I had to fire her because her work was sloppy, she was unpunctual, sometimes she didn't show up at all. Worst of all, she was quite an unstable person. I'm sorry she was killed in that awful way, but what we're dealing with here is simply an opportunistic vendetta and a crude attempt at blackmail."

"Call it what you will, people have died as a result of your drug trial."

"But this is insane," Morange objected. "The drug was a benign herbal soporific."

"Do you deny there were side effects?"

"Of course I don't deny it. There are always side effects with any drug. That's why we do these studies, to establish the level of benefit versus risk. But with pronole the negative events were well within the range of tolerance and safety—a few cases of dry mouth, mild headaches, one or two instances of slight nausea. And the trial itself was highly successful. Pronole proved to significantly increase stage three sleep and in many cases helped to restore healthy sleep structure."

"Then why was the study stopped?" challenged Mara. "I'm betting your so-called negative events were a lot more serious than you're admitting."

"This is ridiculous." Morange, beginning to lose his cool, rose to his feet, gesticulating largely. "The side effects were absolutely negligible, and as for those testers, there is no way on earth you can attribute their deaths to pronole. They occurred months after the study ended."

"There's such a thing as chronic toxicity."

"Chronic toxicity? I don't know who you've been talking to"—he looked as if he had a good idea whom to suspect—"but that's just not possible. Pronole simply could not have remained in the system that long. One of its benefits is that it has a short half-life and is eliminated within hours. Besides, one of the people you mentioned wasn't even on the drug. Bonnet was taking a placebo!"

"Placebo!"

"That's right." Morange took immense satisfaction in her discomfiture. He got technical. "Look, Pronole-2 was a study we carried out a couple of years ago involving subjects with diagnosed primary insomnia. Its objective was to demonstrate long-term safety and effectiveness. It was a randomized, placebo-controlled, double-blind trial—" he broke off, at her look of incomprehension, to explain. "Double-blind means that neither the subject nor the investigator, nor any of the study personnel, know who is taking the drug or the placebo until the study is over. In this case, a quarter of the subjects were given a harmless sugar pill made to look and taste like the actual drug. Louis Bonnet was among that group. Véronique had no way of knowing this, otherwise she might have thought twice before coming across with her crazy accusations. As for the others, although they took the drug, Marsaud died in a fishing accident, Soulivet was a suicide. And Ventura, as you must be aware, was killed by her lover."

"And what about Véronique? She was murdered too. So who killed her?" Mara gave him a brief moment to think about it and continued, "You've just admitted she tried to blackmail you and Bonisanté. Whether or not she had a case, a public inquiry would have been bad PR and potentially costly for you, and especially for Bonisanté at a time when they also have a patents suit on the table." She stopped short of an outright accusation but let it hang heavy in the air.

Morange, however, was not as impressed as he should have been. He seemed to have his counter-arguments ready. "Absolute rubbish," he snorted. "The trial protocol was rigorous and impeccably followed. Most important, since drug testing is never without risks, all of our subjects gave us their *accord signé*, their signed informed consent. Bonisanté's lawyers wrote it, and, if I say so myself, the document is as close to lawsuit-proof as you can get. If damage claims *were* initiated, and they wouldn't be because there are absolutely no grounds, Bonisanté and the clinic would have nothing to fear."

"Then why is Patsy—Dr. Reicher—lying in a coma after asking questions about Véronique and pronole?"

Morange stared at her. "Dr. Reicher? What has this to do with her?"

"You tell me," Mara raged. "What did she see or hear while she was at your clinic that made it necessary to drive her off the road? Or can you explain that away, too?"

He seemed caught between indignation and a genuine hilarity that shook Mara's confidence badly and made her want to sock him.

"Explain it? I don't need to. Dr. Reicher's unfortunate accident was just that. An accident. I'm not sure what you're accusing me of, madame, but I'm afraid you have been grossly misled. Now really, I think I've heard enough science fiction for one morning, and since there is clearly nothing more I can do for you, I'll take my leave. I urge you to continue to find a cure for your insomnia, but I suggest you try another sleep clinic. There's an excellent centre in Montpellier I can highly recommend. However, I warn you that if you attempt to go public with any of your deluded accusations, the clinic and Bonisanté together will hit you so hard for defamation you'll be left with nothing but what you stand up in. Give my best wishes to your gendarmes. Should they wish to contact me, I am always at their disposal."

He strode out of the house.

"Damn," Mara uttered, aware that her knees were shaking.

•

Mara poured herself another cup of coffee and stood watching rain track down the windowpanes. The dogs had gobbled their breakfast. Jazz was now sleeping in his accustomed place on a costly Aubusson rug in the front room. Bismuth lay in the middle of the kitchen floor grooming himself. First he nibbled fleas, then he cleaned his feet, picking delicately between his toes with his teeth. Lastly, he began a wet and loving toilet of his private parts.

"Damn," said Mara again.

Morange's self-assurance told Mara what she should have anticipated. Morange and Thory were no fools. The minute Véronique had approached them, they had prepared their case. Every angle had been covered. What she needed was something they weren't prepared for, anything to put a dent in Morange's glib self-confidence. But what?

She pulled the Pronole-2 list from the drawer, staring at it as if willing an answer to emerge from the ranks of names. There were 150 in all, 146 if you excluded the dead testers.

"All right," she whispered to Patsy. "Let's up the ante."

•

After the first twenty-six calls, she found that three people were not home, two refused to speak to her, two lines were busy, and one number was no longer assigned. Eighteen individuals, very much alive, remembered being part of the Pronole-2 trial. Most recalled having experienced improved sleep while on the drug. One person, in response to Mara's questions about adverse reactions, said he remembered having a dry mouth, another recalled slight dizziness. Another admitted that he'd been suffering from a great deal of flatulence lately and did Mara have anything for it? A Madame Derain said her husband had been a pronole tester, but there was no point in talking to him because his mind was going. She sometimes found him standing in the middle of the room, staring blankly into space. And then the other day he complained about the unlit cellar stairs, only they didn't have a cellar. But he refused to see a doctor about it.

A Madame Quichaud said that she'd had no problem whatsoever with pronole, it really helped her sleep, but nowadays her eyesight was going. She bumped into walls. "Old age, I'm afraid," she told Mara plaintively. "I think the doors are there, but they're not. It's what I told the other woman who called."

"What other woman?" Mara asked.

"Oh, the one like you. About a year ago. Said she was doing some kind of study follow-up."

Véronique, Mara concluded.

There were 120 names left, but Mara, tired of misrepresenting herself and uncertain of what she had turned up, decided it was time to try another approach.

•

"On your own, eh?" Géraud Laval bellowed as he opened the door. The retired pharmacist peered suspiciously past her as if expecting Julian to pop out of the bushes. "Where is he?"

When she had first met him, Mara had wondered if the tufts of hair that grew profusely out of Géraud's ears obstructed his hearing. Since then, she had concluded that he shouted because he liked the sound of his own voice.

"Away," she replied minimally, and stepped inside.

"Humph! That charlatan! I hold him responsible for Iris's going off, you know."

Iris still seemed to be "off." At least, she was nowhere in sight.

"Would you like"—Géraud's leer, a ferocious squint with a display of teeth, Mara knew of old—"to see my Lady of the Night? It's in very good scent right now."

It was de rigueur. Géraud always had something to show off. He steered her into a glassed-in area at the back of his house that was crammed with orchids, many in bloom. Flamboyant—for Géraud went in for tropical hybrids—they filled the entire space.

"This beauty," he announced, bringing her up to a handsome plant bearing several large, spade-like, greenish-white flowers, "is *Brassavola nodosa*. They call it Lady of the Night because of its wonderful nighttime fragrance. Put your nose here."

Mara did, breathing in a truly heady sweetness.

"I don't let just anyone smell it, you know. Wouldn't have done if that poseur had been with you. Had your supper yet? I haven't."

He sat her down in his front room and bustled around, putting out bowls of nuts and olives, a creamy pâté, a basket of bread. He even produced a chilled bottle of champagne that he opened with great ceremony. *Brassavola nodosa* had obviously improved his humour.

"*Tchin tchin*!"

Mara got down to business.

"Pronole?" Géraud, blinking like a querulous toad, plopped down on the sofa next to her. "A sleep medication, you say? Never heard of it. Anyway, pronole sounds more like the drug name, not the brand name." He laid a thick slab of sweating pâté on a round of bread and popped it into his mouth.

"What's the difference?" Mara asked.

He chewed and gesticulated with fat fingers. "A drug usually has three names: a nonproprietary or generic name, a systematic name that relates to its chemical structure and a brand name that's designed to appeal to consumers. For example, the sleeping drug zolpidem, which has a systematic name as long as your arm, is marketed in France as Stilnox. In the United States it's called Ambien. But if you look closely, you'll also see zolpidem in small print somewhere on the label."

Mara asked him about sleep medication side effects.

Géraud stuck out his lower lip. "Well, typically you might get morning-after drowsiness, dizziness, loss of coordination, confusion, even memory loss. It's all spelled out on the labels. That's why they tell you to take the stuff just before bedtime and warn you not to overdose or operate heavy equipment after use. With benzodiazepines, you can also become addicted if you take them long enough."

Mara turned her champagne glass round and round between her fingers, setting up a tiny sparkling vortex. "What about something more serious? Like death."

"Death?" Géraud's eyebrows jumped. "These things are meant to help you sleep, not kill you. Unless, of course, you overdose. Although"—he considered—"some drugs, like zolpidem, have been associated with hallucinations, sleepwalking and even sleep-driving, which could, I suppose, lead to death. *Mon Dieu*, there have been cases where people have jumped in their cars in the middle of the night, driven off, and woken up only after they've smashed into something. Have some pâté."

Mara helped herself. He tipped more champagne into her glass, and she sipped it.

"Could you have a problem like that with an herbal medicine?" she asked.

He hiked his shoulders up. "Why not?"

"It's just that I thought herbals were supposed to be safer. Isn't that one of their benefits?"

Géraud negated this vigorously. "Any drug, synthetic or herbal, can produce adverse events. Take BoniSom. It's an herbal that came out a year or so ago, amid a lot of hoopla, and it's supposed to be one of the best and safest sleep medications around because it acts on a different part of the brain than other drugs and can be used long term. That's why it's so innovative and such a big seller. But you still have to use it as directed. The bottom line is that there's always some degree of risk with any drug."

"I suppose that's why you often read about people suing drug companies."

"Ha!" Géraud boomed. "Pharmaceutical lawsuits are the new spectator sport."

"But what chance do claimants have of winning, especially against the big pharmaceutical companies?"

For answer, Géraud threw up his hands. "It depends on the strength of the case. You'd have to prove the adverse effect can be attributed to the drug in question, to begin with. And that the drug was used according to instructions. Anyway, these things often wind up being settled out of court. Faster and cheaper that way because it's a legal jungle out there, especially in America, but then, *les américains*, they love lawsuits. It's starting to happen in France too." He carved off more pâté, balancing it on the tip of his knife, which he pointed at Mara. "And it's not just drug companies that are the targets. Nowadays lawyers are dragging in everyone and their cat, investigators, study sites, even upstream researchers and research companies involved in the development of a drug."

"What about cases where people die as a result of taking an experimental drug?" Mara asked, feeling her way. "That would be a different situation, wouldn't it?"

"Drug trial deaths?" Géraud applied himself to loading up another piece of bread. "Well, yes, that is a different matter because there the test subjects knowingly act as human guinea pigs. But again whether or not a lawsuit is successful depends on a lot of things. The *accord signé* for one. How well was it worded?

Were the trial subjects fully informed of the risks, and did they really understand the risks? Then there are other issues, like did the exclusion criteria adequately screen out vulnerable, inappropriate subjects? Did people comply with the study protocol? Was there proper monitoring of subjects? Can negligence be proved?" He sighed gustily, chewed and swallowed. "It's not a simple, straightforward matter."

He gave her a canny look. "Funny questions for you to be asking. What's this all about, eh?"

"Just curious," murmured Mara, unwilling to say more.

Before she left, she asked a final question.

Géraud looked highly amused. "No," he said, "I'm not in league with Charles Perry, or Monsieur Chapman, if that's his real name. Never heard of him until last week. But, yes, he has approached me. With a very interesting proposition."

•

Later, when she had returned home and after a great deal of thought, Mara punched in the number of the Brames Gendarmerie, briefly considered speaking with Sergeant Laurent Naudet, but in the end asked to speak with Adjudant-chef Compagnon.

28

By the end of the first day, Julian's legs were cramping. They were now at an altitude of over three thousand metres. He was grateful when they finally made camp on a hillside where there was grazing for Little Pepper. Wandering off for a moment's privacy, he walked through a scattering of narrow-leaved Helleborine, an orchid with white bell-shaped blossoms that commonly graced footpaths in the Dordogne. This set him wondering, as he released a long stream of urine, about the forces responsible for the migration of plants over the millennia: the wind, bearing seeds and spores, the drifting apart of continents, each carrying with it the germ plasm of the original land mass. And the diaspora caused by man, who uprooted things from their natural habitats and took them all over the place.

He thought about the intrepid European plant hunters who had gone before him in this part of the world, men like Abbé Armand David who tramped thirty miles a day over mountainous terrain in bamboo sandals, who was one of the first westerners to comment on the nutritive value of tofu, and who sent back to Paris a wealth of plants, seeds and animals. The French missionary-botanists Soulié and Bourdonnec who met gruesome deaths at the hands of rampaging Tibetan monks. Or "Chinese" Wilson who nearly starved to death on one of his plant-collecting expeditions, yet who insisted on lugging a cumbersome full-plate camera, complete with tripod and black headcloth, wherever he went.

His mind was continuing in this vein when he glanced up and saw a flash of colour. It looked like an orchid, clinging precariously to the eroded face of a nearby ridge, but in the gloomy light, he could barely make it out. Climbing up to investigate, he found a flower that took his breath away. It was creamy yellow with a dentated edging to the slipper lip. Pronounced maroon striping marked the dorsal sepal and lateral petals. The orchid was totally unknown to him, and he stared in wonder.

"Fang!" he bellowed. "Zhang! Come see this!"

•

"It's what you people call *Cypripedium farreri*," said Zhang.

Named after Reginald Farrer, Julian assumed, another *dabizi*, but even Zhang was too overawed to be nasty about it.

Fang was hopping about with excitement. "Do you know it's been reported only few times in the last century? Some people even thought it had been wiped out." She, too, had hurried back for her camera and was now setting it to flash.

"That makes two in one day," Julian crowed. "And I wasn't even looking for it. I just happened to be"—he broke off hastily to check his fly—"when I spotted it."

"Sometimes it happen like that," said Zhang in an almost collegial tone. "You don't look for something, you find it. Especially when you make water."

•

The second day brought more climbing. Julian, stiff from the rigours of the trek and puffing from the altitude, found himself again in last position, but he was too elated by the discovery of *Cypripediums wardii* and *farreri* to care. Never in his most lunar moments had he expected to encounter two rare orchids that very few other westerners had ever seen in the wild. Things happened in threes, and it augured well, he thought, for *Cypripedium incognitum*. He did not care that Zhang no longer bothered to wait for him each time he had to stop to catch his breath (more and more under the guise of taking photographs). It did not even embarrass him that Fang on numerous occasions had to walk back to make sure he did not lose the rest of the party.

"What's the matter, Zhu Ren?" she teased him. "Got no iron in your legs?"

That night it rained heavily. The next morning they had to pack the tents wet, which, because they were canvas, added significantly to the weight Little Pepper had to carry. However, the weather was cool and breezy, and Julian felt that he was finally toughening up, acclimatizing. They covered, by his reckoning, at least twenty miles that day. It gave him a sense of real accomplishment.

In the late afternoon, they set up camp in an alpine meadow that offered tree shelter. Little Pepper was unloaded and left to graze. They were now at about 3,500 metres. An immense panorama of mountains rolled away before them. Clouds, wind driven, threw their moving shadows over the land. The sun lingered redly on the distant peaks.

Xing made a fire, and they all pitched their tents around it. The canvas of Julian's was still quite damp, but he hoped the wind, which was picking up, would dry it out. After supper (greasy flat bread, apples and a soup made with the chicken's feet, which Julian found tasty but visually unappealing), sitting around the fire, Zhang turned uncharacteristically jovial and produced a bottle of *mao tai* from the recesses of their supplies. He filled Fang's and Julian's cups to the brim. Xing preferred Pepsi-Cola, swigging straight from a litre bottle.

"*Gam bei*! Bottoms up!" Zhang nodded at Julian. "You did good today."

The man was definitely mellowing. Julian glowed at this unexpected praise and drank deeply to everyone's health. The raw liquor made his eyes water and brought on a coughing fit. Zhang gave a scornful snort, undoing the benefit of his compliment. Through his tears Julian thought he saw Fang and Xing laughing. Then he looked up and saw a boundless vision of the sky, bright with wheeling constellations, and suddenly no longer cared what his Chinese companions thought of him. He forgot everything but the enormity and beauty of the night, the clean, piney scent of the wind rushing down the mountainside, and the whispered imperative of his orchid: *Find me*!

"Top 'er up!" he cried, holding out his cup.

Zhang obliged. "What you say, 'down the hutch'?"

"Hatch," Julian corrected, and tossed the *mao tai* back. He was emboldened to ask once more about his orchid. "Come on, Zhang, I think it's time you told me what you know about it and how you intend to find it."

Zhang shrugged. "Only that your great-great-great-grandfather—"

"Look," said Julian. "I really ought to set you straight—"

"You want to hear or not?" Zhang snapped with the unpredictable belligerence of the drunk.

Julian raised his hands in a gesture of submission. Xing fired a round of finger bullets.

"Okay," Zhang continued petulantly. "Long time ago Nie Bo hunt plants in these mountains. Some people think he searched the west side. For example, that botanist, Pei Li Boshun, he came looking for Yong Chun Hua nine, maybe ten years ago—"

"Wait a minute," broke in Julian, considerably rattled. "Dr. Pei Li also knew about Kneebone?"

Zhang shrugged. "Nie Bo was the first European people ever see in these parts. Story pass down, get around. So Pei Li Boshun search and search the west side of Crouching Tiger Mountain, up above Si Li Ting, but he find nothing. So"—Zhang pitched a log into the fire, releasing a shower of sparks—"we search the east side."

Julian stared at Zhang in dismay. "But that's not right! How can you say that? In his diary Kneebone clearly wrote that he reprovisioned at Si Li Ting and from there went up into the mountains." At that moment, he dearly wished Mara had faxed him the missing pages so he could wave them in Zhang's face. "He found the hanging valley ten days' walk above the village. If Si Li Ting is on the west, you're taking us up the wrong bloody side!"

"Not wrong bloody side," Zhang said stubbornly. "Because I know something Pei Li don't know. I know Nie Bo didn't start from Si Li Ting. He actually start from Shi Li Ting, which is on east side."

"Where did you hear this?" demanded Julian.

"People from Shi Li Ting say so," said Zhang.

"Pow-pow!" exploded Xing.

Fang started laughing. "Si Li Ting, Fourth Li Pavilion. Shi Li Ting, Tenth Li Pavilion. Li is an old measure of distance. Like I told you, Zhu Ren. *Si* and *shi*, it's confusing. Nie Bo mixed up the names, and Pei Li also got it wrong."

"But we"—Zhang belched loudly—"will get it right." He leaned forward and topped Julian up again.

By the end of the evening Fang was tipsy, Zhang almost maudlin and Julian blind drunk. Head swimming, he found his way to his tent and sprawled face down on his sleeping bag, going unconscious almost immediately. In the middle of the night, he woke up freezing, with stomach cramps and loose bowels. Teeth chattering, he crawled out of his tent. The act of standing up almost made him pass out again. He managed to stagger a decent distance from the camp to relieve himself among the trees, but in the middle of it, with his jeans around his ankles, he felt a bout of nausea coming on. He was losing it shamefully from both ends. The cramps hit him in powerful waves. He wondered if the *mao tai* had poisoned him. He pitched forward on to his face, wanting nothing more than to die.

He might have lain there for minutes or for hours. When he awoke it was to shouts. Fang was screaming something. It sounded like his name. His mouth tasted like vomit, and he smelled the stench of his own mess. He rolled over on to his knees, pulling his jeans up and stumbling forward. Through the trees he saw a bizarre scene: the campfire, much brighter and smokier than he remembered it, and black shadows dancing crazily around it. Only when he came within the circle of light did he realize that his tent was aflame.

•

"Too close to campfire," said Zhang. "The wind must have blow a spark on it." He had something in his mouth. It was not a cigarette. For some reason, he was chewing on a match.

"You're lucky you weren't inside!" exclaimed Fang, stamping energetically on the still-smoking canvas. "You could have been cooked."

"Damned right." Julian was entirely sober now and feeling quite shaken.

"*Lao wai* barbecue," sniggered Xing.

Julian glared at the young man, then turned on Zhang. "My tent is downwind of the fire. How could a spark have set it alight?"

Zhang shrugged. "Wind change."

On inspection they found that although one corner was badly burned, the tent might still be usable with some creative rerigging of the guy-ropes. But Fang, quick to act, had thrown an entire jerrycan of water on it, and the bottom of Julian's bedding was soaked.

"You can sleep with me for now," Fang said generously. She laughed. "We will have to squeeze together." Then she caught a whiff of him. "Whew."

He cleaned himself up as best he could and pulled on a change of clothes that had fortunately escaped dousing. They crowded together in Fang's tent. Fang put a plastic rain-sheet on the ground and opened out her sleeping bag to cover them both against the cold night air. If she showed signs of friskiness, Julian was still feeling too ill to register that he was lying up close to a very sexy woman.

"You not sleepy, long legs?" Fang said invitingly at one point as she snuggled up against him "You got something on your mind?"

"Yes," said Julian. "I think someone is trying to kill me."

She rolled over on to her elbows. "What?"

"Think about it. I was nearly shoved under a bus, someone attacked me in the hotel, and now this. If I hadn't left my tent to be sick, I'd have been burned alive."

"That's stupid. It was an accident. Who would want to kill you?"

Who indeed? Was Charlie really out there, willing to do anything to beat out a rival? Suddenly Julian remembered that there was someone else in the race for Yong Chun Hua, someone who had been searching for the orchid for years, the man who got it wrong, the mysterious Beijing botanist Dr. Pei Li. But—he checked himself—how would either of them have known where to find him, here or in Chengdu, a city of millions? Only Fang . . . Good God!

Julian sat up abruptly. He couldn't credit it. Fang was the one who had raised the alarm, who had put the tent fire out, and Julian was convinced that her desire to find and protect *Cypripedium incognitum* was sincere. Unless she had decided that the orchid's best chances were under the aegis of Charlie or Pei

Li. But then why lure him, Julian, to China just to get rid of him? The thing was becoming as convoluted as a Chinese box puzzle. And why had Zhang been chewing on a match?

"You tell me," Julian said in tardy answer to Fang's question.

Fang let a number of seconds pass before she said, "We better get some sleep."

They both settled back, but there was no more snuggling. And certainly no sleep for Julian.

29

"Quite frankly, Madame Dunn, you haven't given us much to work with," said Adjudant-chef Compagnon. His pockmarked face was grim, and his tone implied that she had wasted police time.

Mara had been summoned to the Brames Gendarmerie where she now stood before the commanding officer like a wayward schoolgirl. Compagnon had invited her to be seated, but since he remained standing in front of his desk, scowling down at her, she decided to remain standing too. She would much rather have been dealing with Laurent Naudet. However, the beanpole of a sergeant, also on his feet, was positioned slightly off to the side, clearly peripheral to the conversation.

Compagnon rocked back and forth, heel to toe, "First we checked into the deaths. Bonnet hadn't even taken the drug, so we can eliminate him right off the top. The fisherman, Roland Marsaud, died in October 2005. The fact that he toppled out of his boat and drowned in shallow water is not so much suspicious as consistent with his having a blood alcohol level twice the legal limit. Not enough to make him blotto, but enough to help him sink. Maryse Soulivet, two months later. Single mother, having trouble coping after the birth of her baby. Witnesses said she simply walked off the platform into the path of an oncoming train. No one was even near her. Her death was judged a suicide, the result of postpartum depression. As for Sofia Ventura, March of this year, if you've read the news lately you'll know the boyfriend has been charged with the murder for motives of sexual jealousy. He was about to be replaced in Ventura's affections by another model."

"He denies that he pushed her," Mara said with spirit.

Compagnon snorted. "Believe that if you want. He had a motive, and he was the only person in the studio with her at the time. Ventura's works were selling well, she was preparing for an important *vernissage*. She had no reason to jump. The point is, Marsaud died five months, Soulivet seven months, and Ventura twenty-one months after the pronole trial was stopped. That's too long in my book. Moreover, none of the autopsies turned up anything pointing to chronic toxicity."

"But were the *médecins légistes* specifically checking for it? Would they even know what to look for?"

The adjudant-chef squeezed his eyes shut and pinched the bridge of his nose.

"It would be best, Madame Dunn"—when he opened his eyes again, Mara noticed that the whites were filamented with red—"if you let the experts do their jobs."

She stuck her chin out. "Well, at least you have to admit it's damned suspicious that when Francke went into the clinic files recently, all the documentation on pronole, including the second trial call list, was gone."

Compagnon sighed heavily and turned to his subordinate. "You tell her, Laurent." He flapped a hand as if driving off flies.

The sergeant cleared his throat. "Both Dr. Morange and Dr. Thory were very cooperative in making the study documentation available to us. Although, Morange did say all confidential material had been moved because of security concerns. Francke just didn't know where to look, and in any case he would no longer have had access." Laurent's bony shoulders hovered in a shrug.

"Okay," said Mara, "but that doesn't do away with the fact that something bad happened during the Pronole-2 trial. There was a third phase planned, don't forget. But Morange stopped the study. And then he tried to cover up—"

"And that"—Compagnon smacked the flat of his hand down on the desktop with the impact of a small explosion—"is where you're completely off track. In fact, it was the other way around. The Pronole-2 trial was a whopping success."

"Come on, you don't believe that."

"I do. I've seen the study report with my own eyes. A clinical trial isn't terminated only for negative reasons, you know. It can also be wound up early because an experimental drug *is so clearly effective there's no need to continue*. There are precedents, and that was the case here. And if you think Morange is lying, let me tell you he'd be stupid to try it, because a forensic audit would easily pick up any attempt to fiddle with the data. So what was there to cover up?" The brigade chief glared at her triumphantly.

"Maybe not then," Mara, rather shaken, conceded. "But after."

"Or after. Thory and Morange had no motive to kill Véronique. The only thing they did was threaten to have her prosecuted to the full extent of the law. Blackmail's a criminal offence, in case you didn't know. They rightly sent her off with her tail between her legs."

"So they say. But I think Véronique shook those two up more than they're admitting. I'm pretty sure she did some investigating of her own before she approached them, and Thory and Morange took her seriously enough to hit her with more than the law. She was badly frightened when she left the clinic. People I talked to said she was lying low, scared. But still greedy, or maybe desperate enough, to have another go when Ventura died. This time she tried to sell her information to the people who are launching an international patents challenge against Bonisanté. Then"—Mara paused to draw breath—"she made the mistake of trying to play one side off against the other."

Compagnon's jaw twitched and his colour heightened. "I've spoken with Jean-Luc Jarry. He said he never cut a deal with Véronique, and he has no idea what she was trying to sell him."

"But Thory and Morange didn't know that, did they. For them, with ActionTerre in the picture, the danger Véronique posed was of an even higher order. The last thing either of them wanted was a coalition of NGOs getting hold of that tester list and making an issue of the deaths. Think of the leverage it would have given them against Bonisanté. Other testers might be prompted to remember symptoms and come forward. People are getting more litigious, even here in France. The nuisance factor and bad press would be huge, to say nothing of the costs. Bonisanté could lose a lot. Morange even more. He was the principal researcher. His precious clinic was the centre for the drug trials, and plaintiffs nowadays are going for everyone involved in the development and testing of an experimental drug. Regardless of what those two say, Véronique had them in a corner. The second time around, they knew they had to kill her. Then they tore her place apart looking for the Pronole-2 list because it was the one thing linking the clinic and Bonisanté with her death."

Compagnon's complexion was now the hue of a blood orange. "Before you go down that road, you'd better bear in mind that Morange has an international reputation for his research into sleep disorders. Thory's the head of Europe's largest herbal pharmaceutical company. *Mon Dieu*, even my mother-in-law takes BoniSom! Finally, both Thory and Morange have solid alibis for the time of the murder. She was at a meeting in New York. He was at the clinic from seven until nine thirty. Staff confirm this. After that, he went straight home, where his wife swears he arrived around nine forty-five and where he remained for the rest of the night. It takes over an hour to get from Sarlat to Le Verger, so there's no way he could have gone there, committed a murder, and driven back, all in fifteen minutes. So which one do you think did it?" His voice was smeared with sarcasm.

"Edgard Papineau," Mara threw out furiously, just to goad him. "He's Thory's son-in-law. She calls the shots, he does what she says, and as Bonisanté's marketing director he has a stake in the family business." Recalling the man's gelled head, his arrogance, Mara decided that she liked the idea.

Compagnon swivelled his eyes heavenward and blew air out his nose.

Mara saw the eye roll and wanted to kick his shins. "What about Patsy Reicher?" she demanded. "She was at the clinic asking questions about Véronique and pronole. She could have been seen as presenting a danger too. I think someone went after her and ran her off a cliff."

"Madame Reicher's crash was an accident," the adjudant-chef growled. "There's no evidence to the contrary. As far as I'm concerned, until she wakes up to tell me differently, she simply misjudged her turn. The road is very dangerous in that part."

"And Francke?" Mara was close to shouting with frustration. "He's terrified he'll be the next victim because of what he knows. Or do you dismiss his evidence as well?"

Compagnon barked out a laugh. "What evidence? First, your Francke's a nutter. Everyone at the clinic says so. Second, far from dismissing him, the information you gave me makes me want to have another word with that *type*. There are quite a few more questions I'd like to ask him. But he's not around for me to talk to, is he."

"Not around?" The news hit Mara like a body blow.

"That's right." Compagnon's expression reassembled itself into a triumphant grimace. "Gone. *Disparu*. His sister says he left his cat with her and took off. But rest assured, we'll pick him up.

In the meantime, help me out. What is it exactly that you want me to do about Francke's so-called evidence?"

"Nothing," said Mara, knowing when to cut her losses. She gave the adjudant-chef a long reproachful look. "Forget it."

•

"What do you think, Laurent?" Compagnon said after Mara had gone. He dropped into his chair and waved Laurent into another.

The gendarme sat. With his long legs, to avoid the appearance of sprawling, he had to draw his knees up almost to his chest. "She argues a good case, sir. The threat of Jarry and his crowd getting into the act may have tipped the balance. Morange or Thory could have hired someone to do their dirty work. Or maybe the idea of the son-in-law is worth looking into."

Compagnon harrumphed. "I'm not convinced. This pronole thing might have given Jarry and his lot something to wave around, but it wouldn't have affected the patents challenge. ActionTerre isn't going to win this one, and Thory knows it. Moreover, even if the company and the clinic have to weather a bit of bad press, legally they're pretty well covered." Compagnon puffed out his cheeks and shook his head. "No. There's simply not sufficient motive for murder."

Laurent shifted in his seat. "There is another possibility, sir."

The brigade chief waited, scowling.

"What if pronole has nothing to do with it? What if it was Morange acting alone for purely personal reasons?"

"Go on." Compagnon looked wary but interested.

"Véronique was a blackmailer. She wanted money. When her attempt related to the tester deaths didn't fly, what if she simply threatened to tell Morange's wife about his affairs? From what we've heard, she was in a position to speak from first-hand knowledge. We know the clinic is in financial trouble, and it's only the wife's money that's keeping things afloat. The doctor might have had no choice but to silence Véronique. The fact that she invited her killer in also goes against him."

"This assumes Madame Morange doesn't already know about her husband's philandering, and in my experience, the wife generally does."

"Knowing is one thing, sir. Having it aired in a publicly humiliating way is another."

Meditatively, Compagnon gnawed the inside of his lip. "And Thory? Where does she fit in this? You think she'd sanction murder to keep the family linen out of the gutter?"

"She has a vested interest. Morange *is* married to her sister. And the sister owns half of Bonisanté. On the other hand, Thory may not know what her brother-in-law did."

The adjudant-chef rumbled, "Oh, she'd know all right. Those Bonisanté people strike me as very tight, the kind that would want to keep everything, even murder, in the family. Maybe we'd better take a closer look at our good doctor after all. And Madame Morange. She says her husband came straight back from the clinic, and she alibis him from nine forty-five onwards. Let's see if we can't break her down. Papineau as well. Give him a good shake. Maybe something will fall out. In fact, let's shake up the whole damn lot of them!"

30

"You have to trust Zhang," said Fang. Their leader was far up the trail with Little Pepper, Xing was bounding around in the middle ground, and she and Julian were bringing up the rear. "Why would he want to burn you up in your tent?" It was a continuation of a conversation they had already had.

Julian gave Fang a sideways glance. The morning air was cool, and she wore a sweatshirt that said *Harvard Men*. Her hair was bundled up again under the baseball cap. Stylish sunglasses blanked out her eyes, lending prominence to her jaw and eyebrows and giving her face an androgynous look. He did not want to tell her that at this point crazy Xing was the only one of the team he halfway trusted and that was because Xing was the only one who had no interest in Yong Chun Hua. Fang wanted to find it, so did Zhang. So did Charlie, Dr. Pei Li and Director Yang, who sat like a fat lazy spider in its web, waiting for deliveries of juicy prey. Everyone, including Julian himself, had their motives and agendas with respect to the orchid, and it seemed that at least one of those agendas included the disposal of a certain Brit orchidologist who at the moment was feeling paranoid and very out of his depth.

"I don't think Zhang's being straight with us," Julian said, deviating slightly. "This Si Li Ting, Shi Li Ting thing sound fishy to me. If Nie Bo's exploits in these parts were so well known, why didn't someone set Dr. Pei Li right about which side of the mountain he went up? I think we're being led on a wild goose chase."

"Maybe Pei Li never asked. Maybe he wanted to keep things secret. You know what orchid hunters are like. Anyway," Fang said firmly, "Zhang knows what he's doing. If he says the orchid is up here on the eastern side, that's where we'll find it. He has—how do you say it?—an eighth sense about orchids."

"Sixth," corrected Julian.

"Eight is better. It's a lucky number for us."

•

In an alpine meadow, they found sprinklings of *Cypripedium calcicolum*, a slipper species related to the splendid specimens of *tibeticum* they had seen earlier. These, because of the harsher, more exposed conditions, were smaller and grew lower to the ground, as if to shelter from the unrelenting wind. Normally plum coloured, many of the blossoms were almost black.

"My father used to tell me stories about these orchids when I was little," Fang said. "He said birds laid their eggs in the pouches. Colourful finches came out of yellow and purple orchids like *Cypripedium flavum* and *tibeticum*. But if the birds were bad birds, they'd lay their eggs in black *calcicolum*, like these, and they would hatch into crows."

They came across a field of *Meconopsis*. A relative of the poppy, its delicate, deep-blue petals fluttered in the breeze like silken handkerchiefs. And then, to Julian's delight, he found himself walking amid nodding bells of Snake's Head fritillary. Handsome, with white and purple reticulated markings, they were one of his favourites and an increasingly rare plant in Britain and Europe. To see them growing in abundance in the highlands of China was almost a religious moment for him. He was moved to admit as much to Fang, who laughed.

Across a valley, on another mountainside, strings of colourful Tibetan prayer flags snapped in the wind. Below them, he made out people kneeling on the ground.

"Are they praying?" he asked Fang.

She pushed her sunglasses up on her head and raised her binoculars. "Digging up plants," she said after a moment. "They sell them to herbal medicine companies, like Double Joy."

That made him think of the Baixi, harvesting the roots of *Cypripedium somniferum*, the raw material of BoniSom. It all began here, on a hillside like this.

He decided to push ahead to overtake Zhang. The matter of his tent was still not answered to his satisfaction, and he was fed up with the man's reticence and not at all convinced they were on the right side of the mountain.

"I want a word with you," Julian said harshly as he came abreast of the team leader. "I don't know how my tent caught fire last night, but I want you to know I don't believe this nonsense of a spark setting it alight. What is it you have against me?" His underlying question was: *why are you trying to kill me*? The only thing that prevented him from articulating this question was a slender hope that he, Julian, was as mistaken as Fang seemed to think he was.

Zhang walked, eyes forward, as if Julian did not exist.

"All right. Have it your way. But just get it through your head that I'm capable of defending myself." It was a weak warning, and both of them knew it. Julian did a quick mental inventory and came up with a Swiss Army knife as his only weapon. Briefly, he fantasized about having a gun.

"Okay, let's say you're right." Julian tried conciliation. He was finding the silence between them unnerving. "Nie Bo started out from Shi Li Ting. His diary puts his discovery ten days out. Let's say his progress was half as fast as ours, because he obviously stopped along the way."

Zhang spoke up at last. "Like you."

"Because he talked about his presses being nearly full, so he must have been gathering plants as he went. And from the sixth day on he had to shoot game to keep his men fed. So let's say he found Yong Chun Hua five-days' straight march out from Shi Li Ting. This is our fifth day on the trail. We should be there by now, don't you think?"—wherever "there" was—"Shouldn't we be looking for Nie Bo's hanging valley? Those cliffs we just passed, for example. We could have stopped to have a good look around."

"I did already," said Zhang, not giving Julian a glance.

"You did? When?" Julian demanded. He had been within view of Zhang for the whole morning and had not seen him checking anything out.

"Before," said Zhang uninformatively.

Julian remembered that Zhang knew these mountains well.

"Ah, but you didn't know what to look for then, did you."

Zhang kept walking, eyes straight ahead.

"Look," Julian burst out in exasperation, "I don't know what your game is, but I think you're purposely misleading us—*me*. For all I know, we could be going around in circles. You have absolutely no proof that Nie Bo left from Shi Li Ting and went up the east side of Crouching Tiger Mountain. The diary clearly said *Si* Li Ting, not *Shi* Li Ting. Why do you assume that Nie Bo confused the names? If the people of Shi Li Ting are claiming he left from their village, maybe they got it wrong. All this happened nearly 150 years ago. How do I even know Shi Li Ting exists?"

At last Zhang turned to meet Julian's eyes directly. "It exists," he said in a flat voice, "because in old days, before administrative changes, Kanglong used to be Shi Li Ting. And I'm right because my many-times-great-grandfather was one of the men who took Nie Bo up."

Julian gaped. "Kanglong used to be—? How—What—?"

Despite his rush of questions, he could get nothing more out of the man. With a jerk at Little Pepper's lead, Zhang moved briskly forward. Julian had to jump out of the way to avoid being knocked over by the mule's swaying load.

•

In fact, before day's end, they did stop on several occasions to investigate various rock faces. None offered a telltale cleft or fissure of any kind leading into a hanging valley. The sun was sinking behind the western mountain peaks by the time they made camp in the lee of a high ridge. Thoroughly disgusted, Julian left the others to prepare supper and strode away to work off his frustration by doing some independent exploration. To the two outstanding finds of their first day, perhaps he could add a third. After poking about for a while, he was surprised to find that Xing had followed him. The youth looked glum, totally out of his element.

"What's wrong?" Julian asked.

"Nothing," replied Xing, stuffing his hands into his jacket pockets. He seemed to have holstered his finger pistol for the night.

More for protection than for company, Julian invited Xing to ramble with him. They discovered a spot where they could climb up to the top of the ridge. From there, to their left, they had a sweeping vista of foothills and valleys already deep in shadows, and beyond them a succession of mountains peaks momentarily illuminated by an angry, blood-red sun. To their right was a precipitous drop-off into a ravine.

"I suppose you miss your family and friends in the big city?" Julian said after they had followed the line of the ridge for about fifteen minutes in silence.

"This is stupid," said Xing by way of reply. Their way, heavily overgrown, was quite narrow, and they had to move with care.

"What's with Zhang anyway?" Julian asked, thinking they had better turn back soon. The colour was beginning to drain from the sky, and the wind was picking up.

Xing shrugged. "He's okay."

"Is it true that Kanglong used to be called Shi Li Ting?"

"I guess so." Xing sniggered. "Before my time."

"And is it also true that Zhang's many-times-great-grandfather was one of the men who guided Nie Bo up the mountain?"

"Yeah," said Xing. After a pause he added, "Mine, too."

Julian looked at him in surprise. "Yours as well?"

"Sure. Everyone in Kanglong is related."

Xing glanced about nervously. Suddenly, he broke off, pointing. "Look!"

Julian looked. He saw nothing but clouds banking up in the north. Rain, he thought.

And then Xing shoved him. The move, a frontal schoolyard attack, was almost laughable, but it came so unexpectedly that Julian found himself flat on his back, the wind knocked out of him. Then Xing was pushing him toward the edge of the ridge. Frantically, Julian grabbed Xing's jacket, pulling the slim youth down on top of him. They locked in a scrambling struggle of arms and legs—Julian was much the stronger but Xing was determined—rolling this way and that. Julian felt the earth give way beneath him. Half of him was now hanging in space. In desperation he clung to Xing, holding him in a death embrace. Then they both pitched into the abyss.

It seemed to Julian that they fell for a long time, crashing through branches, bumping off rocky projections, before they hit bottom.

•

When Julian regained his senses, he was aware of lying on something. Or someone. Beneath him, Xing groaned. Dizzily, Julian pushed himself off the youth and sat up. His right shoulder throbbed painfully, but other than that he seemed to be intact. Xing had taken the brunt of the fall, in fact, he had cushioned

Julian's landing. They were lying at the bottom of the ravine, the sides of which looked impossibly sheer, the top a long way up.

"You little bastard!" was Julian's first utterance. "It was you! You tried to push me under a bus, and when that didn't work, you attacked me in the hotel. And then you tried to burn me up in my tent. Why?"

Xing only groaned again, so Julian shook him. Xing yelped in pain.

"Sure," Xing whimpered. "Pick on those who can't defend himself. I need a doctor. I think my leg's broken. Maybe my ribs too."

"It'll be your neck if you don't start giving me some answers fast. Once again, why?"

"Okay, okay. I want to get it over."

"Get what over?"

Xing coughed weakly. "You. I figure if I kill you right away, I don't have to do this crazy orchid hunt. So I took Zhang's motorcycle and went to Chengdu. I knew what hotel you were at from Fang. You were easy to spot and follow. *Dabizi*! Besides, we agreed to do it away from the village so no one there got blamed."

"Bloody hell! You knew from Fang? 'We agreed!' So Zhang and Fang are part of this crazy plot too!"

Xing shook his head. "Not Fang. Just me and Zhang. Although he said to wait until we got more information out of you. The tent was his idea. Because by then you already told us everything about Nie Bo's valley, so now he knew where to look."

"But why? Why do you want to kill me? What have I ever done to you?" And when Xing maintained a stubborn silence, Julian threatened, "Talk, you murderous little prick. Or I'll leave you here to be eaten by wolves or tigers or whatever you have up here."

Xing, really frightened, squeaked, "You wouldn't do that!"

"Try me!" Julian roared.

•

In the failing light, Julian made a quick reconnaissance of the ravine but could find no way up the steep sides. He now knew that neither Pei Li nor Charlie had been behind the attempts on his life. He also reasoned that if Fang had not been part of the plot against him, she was potentially in danger as well. He needed to warn her against Zhang, but to do that, he first had to get out of the ravine. By then darkness had settled in, and he was barely able to find his way back to Xing, locating him less by sight than by the sound of his breathing, an eerie rasping in the dense silence. Maybe the kid wasn't lying about his ribs. Julian imagined Xing's lungs filling up with blood and, perversely, began to worry.

Then, because he could think of nothing better to do, he yelled for help. He kept it up until he was hoarse.

"Save your breath," Xing muttered. "They don't hear you."

"You'd better hope they do. My shoulder feels like it's dislocated, and if you can't walk, I'm not going to be able to carry you out of here."

Xing sniffed.

Eventually he said, "I hate being stuck in that village."

"My heart bleeds."

"Well, would you like it? Nothing to do? My uncle scold, scold all the time, food very bad. I was going to become a videogame tester, you know? They hire people for things like that."

"Good luck, Joystick," snarled Julian. "I hope you succeed, because you make a piss-poor assassin."

It began to rain, big fat drops smacking down on leaf and stone. Supporting Xing as best he could, Julian moved him under the shelter of an overhanging rock, where they settled down to spend a miserable night.

31

Julian awoke wet, stiff, freezing and in pain. His right shoulder throbbed horribly, and the drummer in his head was performing a blinding virtuoso percussion solo. He was also thirsty and weak. When had he last eaten? Xing, whose teeth had clattered like castanets throughout the night, now lay silent and inert. Seriously concerned, Julian reached out with his good arm and shook him gently. A wheezing cough burst from Xing's lips, followed by words in Chinese that Julian could not understand. His face was ashen, his skin clammy, and he looked in very bad shape.

"Don't leave me," croaked his would-be killer, as Julian staggered up to take stock of their predicament.

"Don't tempt me," snapped Julian. More kindly, he added, "I'm going to find a way out of here. Hang on. I'll be back."

The ravine was deep and steep-sided, a challenge for a man with a dislocated—maybe even broken—shoulder. After the night's rain, everything was soaked and cloaked in mist. However, the sky above was brightening, promising fair weather.

Julian hallooed loudly as he explored. By his reckoning, they were some forty minutes from their camp. He knew that Fang, if she were able, would try to find him, and he expected Zhang to come searching for his cousin at the very least. But would either of them hear him? The ravine trapped his voice. Would they even know where to look?

After about fifty metres, the ravine led into a canyon, wider but with walls just as sheer. Nevertheless, Julian found a place where he thought he might be able to scramble out. He tried hauling himself up one-handed, using rocky projections and branches, hoping that Xing could last until he returned with help. However, it proved impossible. Gritting his teeth with pain, he slithered back down amid an avalanche of stony soil.

He continued for another half a kilometre down the canyon. The sun was now high enough to illuminate its western rim, the mist was lifting, and the air was warming perceptibly. As he looked about him, the botanist in him became aware of plants, underfoot and clinging to the rocky walls, that he had never seen before. There was a fern with flat silky fronds, several types of tiny unidentified sedum, a flower whose pale, elongated petals were still tightly closed. Higher up were stunted bushes covered in small magenta blooms, some kind of dwarf rhododendron, he reckoned.

Then he saw a way out. Ahead of him, part of the east side of the canyon had collapsed in a massive rock slide, leaving a steep but possibly manageable ascent. Eagerly he clambered up a few metres before he realized that the slide was recent and quite unstable. The debris had not had time to settle into the land. His movements loosened small boulders that rocked and tumbled away beneath his feet, setting others above him bouncing dangerously down on him. Julian decided to find a less perilous exit.

But there seemed to be no other way out. Farther ahead the canyon narrowed to rocky defile that ended in a cul-de-sac of stone. He peered hopelessly down the defile, concluding that it would have to be the rock slide or nothing, when he noticed a shadow in the cul-de-sac face, partly obscured by vines and bushes. He made his way forward and pulled the vegetation aside. The shadow resolved itself into a narrow fissure, wide enough to accommodate a man, running forward perhaps five metres through solid rock and finishing at the far end in a blinding sliver of light. Julian gave an echoing shout of triumph.

In the next moment, his heart was in his throat. The canyon was, he realized, a hanging valley very much like the one Horatio Kneebone had described. But if this were Horatio's valley, there should also be orchids. He whirled around and retraced his steps. What was it Mara had said? The orchids had been growing up the east side of the valley, two hundred feet or so in? Feverishly, he raised his eyes and gave a cry of despair. Two hundred feet in, the east wall of this valley was a rocky ruin where nothing grew and where nothing that had ever grown there could have survived.

Frantically, he searched the ground for any remnant of Horatio's splendid colony. Several hundred. A third in bloom. Then he remembered Xing, and stopped.

Thirty minutes, he bargained with himself. *The little toe-rag can hold out for thirty fucking minutes.* After all, Xing had tried twice to kill him, hadn't he? Torn between common decency and his aching desire to find at least one living remnant of Yong Chun Hua, Julian knew his priority had to be to get the injured youth off the mountain.

"Shit!" he yelled in frustration, and kicked a mossy stone.

It was lighter than he expected and dislodged easily from the gravelly earth in which it was partly buried. Rolling sideways, it revealed something that nearly made Julian choke with fright: eye sockets plugged with earth that stared up accusingly at him above a semicircle of yellowed, broken teeth. A human skull. Stained and weathered, it lay alone. Gingerly, Julian turned it over with the toe of his boot. The back of the cranium showed a jagged hole.

Searching forward, nearer the entry of the defile, he found another skull, this one more deeply buried. And, lodged beneath a rock, another. In total, four skulls, all with similar ragged holes, lying in a random pattern. Whoever these people were, each appeared to have been killed by a single or multiple shots to the head. And here and there, now that he was looking for them, he discovered other skeletal remains: a greenish hump of vines proved to be a human rib cage heavily wrapped, like a ghastly package, in flowering convolvulus; the shattered head of a femur slanted like a bleached stick out of the ground.

Slowly, he came to understand that Horatio's crime had not been to destroy the orchids. Julian of all people should have guessed this. The plant hunter had done the other unthinkable thing. He had killed those who could reveal the secret of his splendid find to Tarquin Foster, who was coming hard on his heels. The men's remains told their story. Horatio had shot them from behind as they filed out of the valley. The first kill, before the men understood their danger, was a clean shot to the back of the head. The rest was carnage. Trapped in the defile, the men would have had nowhere to run, and Horatio, an excellent marksman, had his rifle in addition to two four-shot pistols. He did not even bother to bury the bodies, leaving them where they fell to be picked apart and scattered by scavenging animals, trusting to the inaccessibility of the valley to hide his crime. He had then quit the mountains, taking all the orchids he could carry.

Back in France, Horatio had pursued his master plan. He targeted rich sponsors whom he approached, using the lure of Yong Chun Hua to attract financing for a return mission to China to bring out a payload of plants, for only one of the orchids had survived the arduous overland and river journey back to Shanghai and the sea voyage to Europe. Did he envision first selling a limited number of rhizomes amid great fanfare at a select auction, say in Brussels or London, realizing thousands of pounds or even more in francs per plant? This to be followed by a larger auction to satisfy any latent demand and to mop up a secondary windfall? However, Tarquin Foster's smear campaign, based perhaps on something he had heard or suspected about Kneebone's expedition, or springing from nothing more than jealousy and malice, had warned off potential funders. The return mission never materialized. Ill, desperate and penniless, Horatio had in the end sold Yong Chun Hua to a French collector in the Dordogne. That plant was the ancestor of *Cypripedium incognitum*. Horatio had died as he deserved to die, alone, in poverty, and by his own hand.

Faced with the enormity of Kneebone's crime, Julian understood fully why Zhang and Xing wanted him dead. Sadly, he abandoned the valley, slipping through the crevice in the rock and emerging from it into the bright light of day. He was still trying to get his bearings when Fang and Zhang came upon him.

Fang gave a great shout. "Zhu Ren! You okay? What happened? Where were you? We were looking all over. You had us worried."

"You maybe. But not him." Julian pointed an accusatory finger at Zhang. "Your cousin pushed me off a cliff last night. He got the worst of it and needs help. And I have something to show you."

•

Zhang said very little as he stared at the skulls that Julian had collected and laid side by side on a flat boulder.

"This is what you were really looking for, isn't it?" Julian demanded of their expedition leader. "Proof that Nie Bo killed your ancestors?"

Zhang glanced away. "We don't need proof. We already know. But we have to find their bones. Put their souls to rest. Until we do, everyone has bad luck. All the families of the men."

"And you figured where the orchid was, there you'd find their bodies?"

"What's this about?" Fang turned from Zhang to Julian and back to Zhang. Her voice was shrill, partly from anger, partly from fear. She avoided looking at the skulls. "Whose ancestors? Whose bodies?"

Zhang pushed his hat back on his head. "What you do with Xing?" he asked.

•

They gave Xing rudimentary first aid, crudely splinting his leg with sticks tied with strips of cloth torn from Zhang's own undershirt. Fang said she would remain with Xing while Julian and Zhang returned to camp to pack up their gear and come back with the mule. There was no question of searching for orchids.

Before they left, Julian said to Fang, "By the way, I think you'd better tell him. I'm not Nie Bo's descendant." And then to Zhang: "She said it for effect. Up until a month ago, I'd never heard of the bastard."

•

"You owe me an explanation," Julian said as they made their way back to camp.

As a way of ignoring him, Zhang lengthened his stride and concentrated on getting a signal on his cellphone. In the heart of the mountains, it was impossible.

"I'm talking to you!" Julian yelled.

Zhang pushed on ahead, walking even faster.

"You and your crazy cousin tried to kill me," Julian panted, trying to keep up. The exertion reminded him painfully of his injured shoulder. "Attempted murder. Assault at the very least. The hotel manager in Chengdu can back me up. So can Fang. I could report you to the police."

At this Zhang stopped and turned. He glowered at Julian. "Okay," he said finally. He pulled out his cigarettes, lit one, sucked deeply on it. "I tell you."

They fell into step.

Zhang spoke, smoke trailing out of his mouth and nose, eyes forward as usual. "Many years ago, three Kanglong men took Nie Bo and his servant up into these mountains to collect plants. My ancestor, Zhang Xinyou, was one of those men. Nie Bo promise them lots of cash plus bonus if he find what he especially look for. None of the men, including Nie Bo's servant, returned." Here Zhang paused to pick a shred of tobacco from his tongue and to spit.

"After a few weeks, when they don't come back, the villagers get worried, go to look. They search and search, come down, go up again. They never found anyone. Then, one day they hear about a European with two horses and lots of plants who got lost in the mountains. Some hunters found him. He told the hunters bandits attack him and his men. His men ran away, but he scare bandits off with guns, save himself and horses. The hunters gave him food and water and help him down from the mountain."

Zhang smoked in silence for a moment, coughed, and resumed. "Long time later, Zhang Xinyou's wife, my many-times-great grandmother, have a dream. She see her husband lying dead. Nie Bo stand over him, pluck an orchid from his mouth. Then she know that Nie Bo had kill him and the other men. Zhang Xinyou's ghost visit her many times after that, demanding proper burial and vengeance on Nie Bo and his line. This obligation pass down through generations." For the first time, Zhang faced Julian squarely. "*Yi ya huan ya*," he declared emphatically. "You say eye for eye, tooth for tooth."

Julian growled softly, "So you and Xing—"

"Not just us. Everyone in Kanglong is related."

"I heard. So the whole village is behind this, and you two are just the designated hit men. And the only reason I wasn't murdered as soon as I told you about Nie Bo's hanging valley was because, as Xing said, you needed to dispose of me away from Kanglong so none of you would be blamed. Well, I hope you intend to call your people off. Your revenge is wasted on me. As Fang told you, I'm not related to Kneebone. A man named Charlie Perry is the fellow you want. He's Horatio Kneebone's great-great-great-grandson, and he just happens to be living in my cottage in France. So if you have any grievances, take it up with him. I can give you the address. Hell," Julian offered, "I can give you a letter of introduction!"

•

They loaded Xing on to Little Pepper and backpacked the rest of their gear out. Along the way, Zhang kept trying his cellphone until he was able to get a signal and put through a call. By the end of the second day of their return journey, they encountered a party of Kanglong villagers, including Headman He and a rural health worker, who had come up to meet them. They had a second mule, loaded with provisions, sacks and digging implements. The health worker, a stocky woman with short-cropped hair, resplinted Xing's leg, examined his ribs but did nothing to them, and gave him something for his pain and fever. She also treated Julian's shoulder by giving it a tremendous yank. He howled unmanfully, but something clicked into place. Then the health worker and a thin man with glasses, who proved to be Xing's uncle, returned to the village, leading Xing on Little Pepper. Mr. He and another man named Deng said they would go back with Zhang and the second mule to the hanging valley to bring out their ancestors' remains. The entire village was preparing to give them a proper burial in a more propitious resting place.

Perhaps by way of apology, Zhang said to Julian, "You can come too. Maybe you find your orchid." He smiled sourly, lighting one cigarette from another and grinding the butt of the first under his heel.

Julian, who had been reflecting on nature's irony—she gave with a generous hand, destroyed with the other—shrugged bleakly.

"It's up to you, Zhu Ren," Fang said, promptly excluding herself. "Maybe you'll get lucky." But she said it without conviction. The valley for her was tainted with death, and she, too, had seen the rock slide.

•

He found no orchids. Back in Kanglong, Xing was taken to the local dispensary where his leg was put in plaster, then he was sent to recuperate in his uncle's house. The ancestors' bones were washed and given their due interment, a noisy ceremony that neither Julian nor Fang were invited to join. Zhang left immediately after the burial, without a word of farewell, to resume his work as a forest ranger in the north of the province. Now that the villagers knew that Julian was not their man, they were no longer hostile. But they were not amicable either. Some turned away from him in embarrassment. Most treated him simply as if he had ceased to exist. Only Xing showed signs of friendliness.

"You okay for a *dabizi*," he said, his mouth stretching into a rueful grin when Julian came to say goodbye. Mr. Jin had arrived to drive Julian and Fang back to Chengdu. Xing lay on a narrow bed looking bored, his plastered leg raised by a rope-and-pulley affair that had been strung up from the ceiling. "You hard man to kill."

"Luckily for you," said Julian.

"Pow-pow!" said Xing, firing off a round of finger bullets.

32

Mara, clad in shorts and a tank top, lay face down on a chaise longue on the terrace. Late afternoon sun fell through the foliage of the cherry tree, composing shattered patterns of light and shadow. The tree always released its fruit prematurely, dense, green little nuggets that pelted anyone beneath it, sometimes quite hard. Unperturbed by the precocious rain, Mara appeared to be asleep, but she was not. She was thinking about the different ways people died.

Marsaud had tumbled out of his boat and drowned. Soulivet had stepped off a *métro* platform in front of a train. Ventura had gone out a third-storey window. If all of the deaths were linked to pronole, shouldn't there be some common element? What? She rolled over on her back, staring up into the canopy of the tree, quarrelsome with unseen birds. An unripe cherry struck her on the forehead. And then she had it: *falling*.

Each of the cases had involved a fall of some kind or other. But what caused people to fall? That was the million-euro question.

Her cellphone rang. She swung a hand down to sweep the ground for it.

"Hello?"

"Mara, it's Prudence. I'm at the hospital."

Mara's gut tightened. She sat up abruptly, fearing the worst, hardly able to bring the words out. "It's Patsy, isn't it."

"And how!" crowed Prudence. "She's back! She's regained consciousness!"

•

A small crowd had gathered around the bed: Mara, Prudence, a nurse and the neurosurgeon in charge of Patsy's case. There was also a large woman, another specialist, who came and went. Eventually she, the neurosurgeon and the nurse withdrew, leaving only the friends.

"Five minutes," they were told.

"Welcome to the land of the living," said Mara, stroking a hand that felt papery, almost weightless in her own. Corkscrew hair lay limp and faded about Patsy's face, grown shockingly thin. Even her eyes seemed to have lost colour.

"They said . . . you've all been here . . . every day . . ." Patsy's voice was indistinct as she tried to articulate around her tubes. "Good of you."

"Nothing better to do," said Prudence, quite sincerely.

"Likewise," Mara said, and turned away to blow her nose. When she could control her voice again, she asked, "Did they tell you you've been out two weeks?"

Patsy smiled weakly. "Time flies when you're having fun."

"Glad someone was enjoying herself," breathed Prudence.

"It's good to have you back," Mara said.

Patsy released a wheezy sigh. "I could kill for a burger."

Her friends laughed. Then her eyes lost focus and her eyelids began to droop. Mara squeezed her hand, willing her to stay with them, but she was drifting.

"Maybe we should let her sleep," murmured Prudence, beginning to gather up her things.

Unexpectedly, Patsy said, "Flying." Her eyes were open again.

"Flying?" Mara exchanged a startled glance with Prudence.

"In the air. Going over. The view was so beautiful."

"Patsy"—Mara leaned forward—"are you talking about your accident? Do you remember what happened?"

Remembering came with an effort.

"You were driving away from the clinic," Mara prompted. "You were going through that stretch of winding road above the Cingle de Montfort. Was someone following you? Did someone run you off the road? Please try to focus, Patsy. This is important."

A slight shake of the head signified either no, or that focusing was too hard. Patsy seemed to slip away from them again.

"That may be all we'll get out of her for now," whispered Prudence, touching Mara's arm.

They were turning to go when Patsy's voice rang out: "It was the tunnel . . . suddenly in front of me . . . No lights . . . So dark . . . so dark."

Mara stared. She looked at Prudence for confirmation and saw in her expression the mirror of her own bewilderment: *There was no tunnel on that stretch of road.*

It shouldn't have been there. With sudden clarity, Mara understood the meaning of Patsy's words as she had been pulled from the wreckage. *Like Monsieur Derain's cellar stairs, like Madame Quichaud's doors in the wall*, Patsy's tunnel did not exist. And Mara began to have an idea of why people fell.

But Patsy had not been a Pronole-2 subject, had no knowledge of the drug, had not even been in France when it was being tested. Unless, Mara pondered, there had been a similar study under another name conducted in the States?

"Patsy," Mara said urgently, returning to the head of the bed. "Think carefully. Have you ever participated in a sleep medication trial?"

"Trial?"

"Clinical trial. Have you ever been a tester for an experimental sleeping drug?"

Patsy frowned. Her words came thickly. "Trouble sleeping. Only Xerafus. Buy it over the counter."

Mara turned to Prudence. "Xerafus. Isn't that the American version of BoniSom?"

"*N'importe quoi*!"

"Please hear me out."

She was in Adjudant-chef Compagnon's office again. Laurent was at the front desk dealing with a woman about a goat, so it was just the two of them, both seated this time, the brigade chief pushing back in his creaking swivel chair as if seeking to maximize the distance between them, Mara leaning forward in an upright wooden model. Compagnon closed his eyes. Mara took this as permission to continue.

"I think pronole was a chronically toxic drug that provoked bizarre behaviour. At a guess, I'd say it caused hallucinations that made people walk on water, step off *métro* platforms and maybe even go out windows."

"Pure conjecture." The expression on Compagnon's moonscape face was wary. "You don't know what Soulivet and Marsaud saw, or Ventura for that matter, unless you propose to question the dead. Besides, if pronole causes 'visions,' why haven't any other testers complained?"

"It may not affect everyone. And, as you've already pointed out, there's the time element. So much time has elapsed that people don't link their experiences to it. But you can talk to Monsieur Derain and Madame Quichaud. Ask them what they see. Contact the rest of the testers. You might just turn up a 'vision' or two."

The brigade chief shook his head. "The study protocol was strictly followed. Those testers knew they were part of an experiment. They gave their signed, informed consent, all of which covers Bonisanté and the clinic legally. Thory and Morange may face some hassles, some embarrassment, but nothing they would kill for. So where does this get us?"

Mara ran her fingers through her hair, making it stand up in spikes. "It gets us to the real motive for murder. Look, just go with me through the logic. Pronole was an experimental sleep drug. It was put through two phases of testing. The second phase was to have run six months, and a bigger twelve-month third trial was also planned because the drug was intended for long-term use. However, the second phase study was stopped in the fifth month and the third phase never undertaken because, as you said, pronole had proved so successful it was felt there was no need to continue."

"Nothing wrong with that. Lots of drugs companies do much less testing."

"Yes, but what happened to pronole after that? Francke thought it had been scrapped. You tell me, would Bonisanté have scrapped something that worked?"

Compagnon made a noise, like a growl, in the back of his throat.

"I think testing of pronole stopped because it was fast-tracked on to the market." She tossed a dark blue packet on the table. "Read the label for yourself."

He picked up the packet, a twenty-four-pill format. "BoniSom?"

"And the small print underneath."

His mouth shaped the word: "Cypronoline."

"It's the active ingredient of BoniSom, a powerful alkaloid found in an orchid that the Baixi people of southwest China have traditionally made their Sleep Tea from. I read all about it on the Internet. What do you bet pronole is short for cypronoline?"

Compagnon's nostrils flared. "Are you saying pronole was the prototype of BoniSom?"

Mara nodded. "And if it is, you see the problem. Véronique's first blackmail attempt was in March 2006, shortly before BoniSom was due to be released on the market. You can imagine the position she put Bonisanté in. Even if her proof wasn't conclusive, the company couldn't risk launching the miracle insomnia cure with her threatening to tell the world the drug was a possible killer. Buying her off wouldn't work. It would be an endless bleed. That left two options: to delay the launch, do further testing and lose time and money, or shut Véronique up and press on. Thory and Morange chose the latter. They say they threatened her with criminal prosecution, but I'm guessing they did more than that. I think they left her fearing for her life. She went into hiding. She even took a job that let her work in disguise.

"If only she'd stayed hidden she would still be alive. But she was broke and desperate, and she resurfaced to make a second attempt a year later when another tester, Sofia Ventura, died. This time, the stakes were much higher. BoniSom was making a big impact on the market at the same time that the ActionTerre coalition was challenging the company's patent rights to cypronoline. For Thory and Morange, it was no longer a question of frightening Véronique into silence. This time, they hunted her down, and they killed her."

She paused. The adjudant-chef's mouth was hanging slightly open.

Mara went on. "It's too bad Morange and Thory didn't carry out the pronole study as planned. If they'd continued with the third phase, they might have caught the problem before BoniSom hit the market. But they were in a hurry. Bonisanté thought it had a winner and wanted to get its product on the shelf as fast as possible. BoniSom's been out there for almost a year now, and it's a huge seller. More and more people are switching to this effective and 'safe' herbal alternative."

Now Compagnon breathed out slowly and scratched his stubbly chin with a rasping sound. "This is still in the realm of supposition. You don't know for certain that pronole is the same thing as cypronoline, and even if it is and supposing you can link the tester deaths to the Pronole-2 trial, how do you know there's a problem with BoniSom? The drug could have been fixed—reformulated—before it was launched."

"Why would they have done that?" Mara regarded him intently. "Like I said, Bonisanté was in a hurry, and the prototype was a huge success, wasn't it? It did everything they had hoped for. People were sleeping. Their normal sleep patterns were restored. At that point, it was just a matter of cosmetics, finding a catchy brand name, packaging, marketing. But the main reason I *know* pronole wasn't reformulated before it became BoniSom is Patsy Reicher."

"Madame Reicher?" Compagnon jerked up, startled.

"She, too, experienced a hallucination. She saw a tunnel where there is no tunnel. It made her drive off the road, and it nearly killed her, but at least she's one witness you don't have to bring back from the dead. Patsy wasn't a pronole tester, but she *is* a long-term user of a product called Xerafus. It's the North American version of BoniSom. Her hallucination tells us the problem is also present with the marketed drug. So how long do you think it will be before other users start reporting similar symptoms?"

"*Putain*!" A vein in Compagnon's temple pulsed. He shoved back his chair, scrambled to his feet, moved with surprising speed around his desk and shot into the hall.

"Naudet," he bellowed. "My office. On the double!"

33

Director Yang received Julian and Fang philosophically.

"Win some, lose some," he said, his placid koala bear face untroubled by their failure.

His office-cum-greenhouse was even more abloom with orchids than when Julian had first seen it. In their oceanic tank, even the fish seemed to glow like rare underwater flowers.

"So now," Yang addressed Julian with a certain regret, "I suppose it is up to Pei Li Boshun. This is too bad. I was counting on you."

"He won't find anything either," Julian retorted, stung. "There's nothing left to find."

Director Yang smiled. "You don't know Pei Li. He has the instinct of a born hunter, and he's a very determined man. Also clever. I told you he discovered cypronoline, the basis of BoniSom? Once he sets his mind to something, he usually achieves it."

Enjoying Julian's discomfiture, Director Yang pushed the needle deeper. "Come on, Mr. Wood. You would not be so ungenerous as to deny a fellow orchid hunter success?"

Julian subsided sulkily.

Before they left, Yang asked Fang to stay behind for a moment. Julian left them talking and followed the pretty secretary downstairs.

•

They had dinner—Fang's choice, Julian's treat—at a vast seafood restaurant in downtown Chengdu. An army of cheerful hostesses greeted them at the door, the decor was aggressively gold and red, and everything on the menu was live on view—sea bass, sturgeon, flounder, eel, lobster, giant clams, grouper, even small crocodiles floating balefully in a glass-sided pool. There were tanks of turtles, a basin of pink sea worms, and, to Julian's fascination, a tub of scorpions. There were also seals, but they were not on offer. They were an attraction; they barked and cavorted, and indulgent parents bought packets of fish for their children to throw to them.

"What did Director Yang want to talk to you about?" Julian said as they were seated, just the two of them, at a large, round table, an island in a sea of other diners. He had hesitated to question Fang about this earlier, but his curiosity had finally won out. "I hope he wasn't asking for his money back?"

Fang shook her head, black hair swinging seductively. She wore a hot-pink dress of some kind of clinging material that hung well on her long frame and showed off a pair of stunning legs. "It was a business deal. He's a businessman. Money's not the issue for him. He wants Yong Chun Hua. If he can't get it, he'll move on to something else." Momentarily she looked undecided, then conceded: "He wants to send me to Yunnan on another expedition to find a rare *Paphiopedilum*."

"And?" Julian asked guardedly.

Fang laughed. "I told him I have to go back to work."

They had a round of *mao tai*, and then another.

"*Gam bei*!"

Fang became quickly drunk. Leaning sideways, she bumped shoulders with him. "We make a good team, huh, Zhu Ren?"

He bumped her back, and they laughed.

"I like my Chinese name," he said. He also liked the way she said it, as if it came with exclamation marks. "I think your system of giving foreigners Chinese names to match the sound of their own names is a good one."

"It doesn't work in reverse," she said. "Fang in English would be Fang, and that isn't so good." She glanced at him flirtatiously. "You give me an English name."

"Well." Julian thought for a moment. "How about Samantha?"

"Sha Manta," she intoned. "I like it. You know, I could fall for someone like you, Zhu Ren." She giggled.

Julian decided it was time for them both to switch to green tea.

Given the menu options, their order was fairly conventional—lobster, a deep-fried crispy fish that crackled in the mouth, shrimp in hot sauce. Over their meal, they discussed what Julian would do in the days remaining before he had to return to France. Fang still had time off and volunteered to act as tour guide. She proposed a bus trip to Huanglong National Park, which she praised as an example of excellent nature conservancy.

"You'll approve of it," she teased. "Tourists are strictly made to stay on raised wooden walkways, and they provide oxygen for people who can't handle the altitude. But you should be toughened up by now."

In the park and surrounding areas they would see hosts of *Cypripediums*, among them purple *tibeticum* and yellow *flavum*, tiny hairy *macranthum*, bronze *shanxiense*, coy *bardolphianum*, and pointy-chinned little *plechtrochilum*, Chinese cousin to the North American Ram's Head orchid. Many kinds of *Epipactis* and *Calanthe* would also be in bloom, also *Calypso bulbosa*, although they might be a bit late for the golden, red-spotted *Cymbidium faberi* that Fang loved. Julian listened with interest to her description of the main attraction of the park, the amazing travertine system that had formed over thousands of years into breathtaking steppes of tufa pools ranging in colour from azure to turquoise to sandy gold.

To his surprise, Julian found himself feeling homesick. Huanglong sounded wonderful, and he knew he ought to be glad of a chance to sightsee properly without the threat of being murdered, but he felt that something was missing. Without meaning to, he found himself telling Fang about his troubles with Mara.

Fang took it well, listening to him sympathetically.

"You should make it up with her," she counselled generously. "She sounds like a very nice woman."

"She is," Julian agreed, and decided to call Mara that night.

•

I love you, he would say. He would put it to her: *Can we leave all this behind us and start again*?

But as soon as Mara picked up the phone and heard his voice, she poured out the flood of latest developments. She had just had a further update from Laurent, and her news would not wait.

Julian was equally swept away by what she had to say.

"Pronole was the prototype of BoniSom? Damn! Cypronoline! I should have made the association." He shook his head in wonder. "It'll be open season on Thory and Morange now that word of Patsy's tunnel hallucination is out."

"It's only been a few days but already other Xerafus and BoniSom users in the States, Canada and Europe are coming forward with stories of their own. All of the testers from both pronole trials are being checked for symptoms. Bonisanté and the clinic could be facing massive lawsuits. Everyone up the line could be dragged in, including the person who developed cypronoline."

"They'll have a time pinning him down in China," Julian sniffed. "He's a Beijing botanist named Dr. Pei Li, and I doubt he'll answer a court summons."

"I thought Jean-Luc Jarry said Bonisanté's North American lab developed it."

"Well, he got it wrong. I suppose Compagnon's in his glory?"

"Like a bloodhound on the scent. He's circling around Thory

and Morange, trying to work up a charge of conspiracy to murder. But breaking down those two isn't going to be easy because she was out of the country when Véronique was killed, and Morange's wife swears he came straight home after leaving the clinic. So it's down to the unknown third party who did the actual deed. Compagnon suspects it's someone in the family. Right now he's focusing on Edgard Papineau. Laurent thinks Thory and Morange simply bought themselves a professional hit man."

"Why does it always have to be a man?" Julian asked a little testily. "Why not a woman?"

And then, not to be outdone, he told her his news.

Mara was stunned by Julian's discovery in Horatio's valley.

"He shot them?" she gasped. "Just to prevent them from leading Foster to the site?"

"Look at it from his perspective. Foster was backed by 'Mad' Harry Masterman. He had the resources to take out all of the remaining plants and beat Horatio back to Europe. By the time Horatio returned with his single surviving orchid, the market could have been saturated with Yong Chun Hua."

"I hope you're not excusing him!"

"Not at all. Horatio was a greedy, obsessive bastard."

"And a killer. You know, in a way, what he did is just a more extreme version of Bonisanté's patent of the Baixi's Sleep Tea."

"Eh? How's that?"

"Well, they're both driven by the same things—a desire for monopoly control and a well-developed disregard for people's rights. Or human life," she added.

"Or human life," he echoed.

Mara, who found herself thawing slightly, said, "And so in the end you found no trace of *Cypripedium incognitum*?"

"Not a leaf. It really was disappointing. This whole sorry story has ended in nothing."

Not just for him. For Fang. For Director Yang, although Julian had no regrets there. For Dr. Pei Li, who had been searching for the orchid for years longer than Julian and with whom Julian, if he were generous, ought to have some kindred feeling. Even perfidious Charlie. The only ones who had come down from the mountains with something were the Kanglong villagers, with their tragic pile of bones.

"I'm sorry," she said. There was a kindness in her voice.

"I suppose"—encouraged, he ventured a peace offering—"you're going to say it serves me right? It's what I get for bouncing off to the other side of the globe to chase a flower?" At his end of the line, he gave a rueful smile.

"Not at all," said Mara, unable to see the smile. "No longer any of my business, is it." A cold snap freezing out the thaw.

"Ah," he said rather foolishly, and they both gave forced laughs.

Then she said, "But listen, Julian, if you told Zhang and Xing all about Charlie, you don't suppose the Kanglong villagers will try to get at him, do you? I mean, if they've sworn to avenge their ancestors' deaths?"

"Ha! I wish they would! I even gave them my address."

Mara turned serious. "Was that wise? Assassinations can be organized a world away with a phone call or the click of mouse, you know."

"Oh, I doubt they'd go to that extreme." Then Julian said reluctantly, "Look, Mara, maybe you ought to warn him. Just to be on his guard, I mean. He may be a lying little prick, but if anyone breaks his neck, I want it to be me."

34

Mara hung up the phone and stood thoughtfully in the middle of her front room. Losing his orchids to a landslide was tough on Julian, she knew. But he'd get over it to hunt flowers another day. She wondered if she ought to have a word with Charlie. He would probably think her crazy. And then another thought filled her mind.

"Why not a woman?" Julian had asked.

Why not indeed?

Who were the women of the case? Juliette Thory definitely, but she had an alibi. Whom could she have paid or persuaded to do the job for her? Sandrine? Madame Fargéas? Or her own sister, co-owner of Bonisanté and Claude Morange's wife? What was she like, Madame Morange? Mara wondered, and a shadowy yet substantial shape rose in her mind. Ruthlessness, she concluded, probably ran in the family. Speaking of which, if Juliet Thory had a son-in-law, presumably she had a daughter. Mara shook her head. The possibilities were endless.

The matter nagged her overnight and stayed with her until she arrived at the Billons' house the following morning to discover that Smokey and Theo were having trouble distinguishing left from right. She managed to avert another disaster, but it was a close thing. In her need to oversee the brothers, she forgot about the women in the case.

As for Charlie, she did not think of him again until toward the end of the afternoon. She called him on her *portable.*

The phone rang until Julian's recorded greeting clicked on.

"Charlie, it's Mara," she began, and switched off. *Someone's out to kill you* was not the kind of message one left on voice mail. Recollecting that she had not seen or heard from him for some time, since Paul's birthday party in fact, she began to worry.

"This is very silly," she told herself. Nevertheless, she left the Serafims to do their worst and drove to Grissac.

•

Her knock went unanswered. She let herself in with Julian's key, sniffing the same musty smells of an unaired cottage. Things on the kitchen table were exactly as she remembered them, the position of the laptop, the files and notebooks, the mug of pencils, the stapler—all unchanged. It made her think of a stage setting, where items were placed with purpose, for effect. The milk in the *frigo* had curdled to an unpleasant state; the cheese was furred with green mould. Charlie, wherever he was, no longer seemed to be living at the cottage. The frightening thought struck her: was he still alive?

Or was he simply away? Prudence thought he was in Paris or Bordeaux. She herself had suggested that he might be in China, trying to beat Julian to Horatio's valley. *Check for his passport*, Julian had said. She remembered the suitcases in the junk room.

They were still there. She opened the smaller one, took out the plastic travel folder and found a Canadian passport in the name of Perry Kneebone Chapman. Well, there was no question of Charlie, or Perry, having followed Julian to China. The keys, on a ring attached to a handsome metal fob, caught her attention. One side of the fob was embossed with the initials *PKC*. When she turned it over, the letters that jumped out at her made her sit back on her haunches in surprise.

•

Julian's day had begun with a real massage delivered by Fang's masseur, a blind man with brutal thumbs who caused him exquisite pain even as he worked out knots in muscles Julian did not know he had. Then he played the tourist with Fang, visiting the house of the eighth-century poet Du Fu, a leafy place of repose in the middle of the noisy city. Afterwards, they strolled up crowded Jin Li Street, sampling its many snack shops and finishing up with iced cappuccinos at Starbucks. They had dinner at a Korean barbecue restaurant. When the taxi dropped him off at his hotel, Fang reminded him that they had bus tickets for Huanglong National Park the next day and told him to get a good night's sleep.

Perhaps it was the spicy pork bulgogi that brought on Julian's dream. Both Fang and Mara were demanding that he give them names. Mara wanted a Chinese name, and he suggested something that Fang said, with a laugh, meant crispy fish. Mara was insulted. Julian tried to explain the Chinese way of naming westerners, using homophonic syllables.

"Stuff your homophones!" yelled Mara. Then she told Fang sneeringly that no one was called Samantha any more. Inexplicably, Charlie appeared on the scene. He had been running, in a hurry to arrive, and his owlish face was flushed and shiny with perspiration.

"Perry," he said, and stuck out his hand. His upper lip was sharply pointed, like a beak. "The name's Perry."

So how, Julian wondered, would the Chinese render Perry?

•

He woke with his heart hammering. He sat up, fumbling for the light. So how *would* the Chinese render Perry? Pei Li was a damned good guess. But Dr. Pei Li was a Beijing botanist, or so Fang had assumed, and because she had, so had Julian. However, Pei Li as Charlie made more sense. Pei Li was a plant hunter. So was Charlie, and he handled Sichuan cuisine like a native. Informed by Horatio's diary, Pei Li/Charlie had gone to Crouching Tiger Mountain to search for Yong Chun Hua ten years ago. But Horatio's orthographic mistake had sent him up the wrong side. Then Julian's book on orchids, with its drawing of *Cypripedium incognitum*, had brought him to the Dordogne.

Other things locked into place. According to Director Yang, Pei Li was also the man who had brought Sleep Tea to the attention of Bonisanté, the man who had identified and isolated cypronoline. And Jean-Luc Jarry had said that cypronoline had been developed by Bonisanté's North American laboratory. Julian recalled the Canadian saying dismissively, "My real background is . . ." Hell! It was probably the only truthful thing the bastard *had* said.

The implications of Julian's conclusions came crashing down on him like a landslide. Cypronoline linked Charlie to Bonisanté. As the inventor of the chemical, he not only had a stake in the patents, he also had exposure to any lawsuits launched by affected testers, their families and BoniSom and Xerafus users. Véronique's threats could have cost Bonisanté, the clinic and Charlie a lot.

Adjudant-chef Compagnon was looking for an unknown assassin, the faceless killer who had hunted Véronique down while Thory and Morange created their shatter-proof alibis. Who better than Charlie? Director Yang had called him a hunter. How simple for Charlie to have turned his skills on Véronique, cornering her in her hiding place? Or—the possibility hit Julian hard—had she delivered herself up to him? In a moment of terrible clarity Julian saw Véronique going unsuspectingly to the cottage in Grissac to look for the estranged husband she intended to blackmail. Instead she had found Charlie. And he had found her.

With a jolt, Julian remembered setting Mara the task of alerting Charlie to the Kanglong vendetta. Good God, he thought, and grabbed the phone.

He got her *répondeur*. He left a terse but clear warning and willed her fervently to call him back. He contemplated threading the intricate communication path to Adjudant-chef Compagnon, but realized that without help he'd never make it through Chinese directory assistance. He called Fang. It took a long time to get past her mother, who spoke no English, then her brother, half asleep, who spoke a little, and finally to her.

"Fang," he cried hoarsely. "You've got to help me. I need to get through to the French police, and I absolutely have to be on the next flight back to Paris."

35

PRONOLE.

Stunned, Mara stared at the word. The fob was clearly Charlie's. His initials were embossed on the reverse side. He was a writer, an orchid hunter. What was his connection with pronole? Puzzled, she dredged up the little that Charlie had actually revealed about himself. *A son of the Dordogne.* And something about chemistry, wasn't it? Slowly, she began to pick apart the web of Charlie's deceit to test the few remaining strands that might bear the weight of truth.

A sound behind her caused her to start and turn.

Charlie was standing in the doorway.

"Mara," he said pleasantly. He carried a bunched extension cord in one hand.

"I—I've been trying to get hold of you. Where have you been?" Guiltily, she slammed the suitcase shut, jumped up and backed away as Charlie took a couple of steps into the room.

"Away. Doing research on Horatio."

"Really?" Her tone admitted doubt.

"Of course. I really *am* writing the Kneebone biography, you know. A question for you: why are you snooping around in my things?" He saw the key fob, which she still held, PRONOLE side up. "Ah." He appraised her coolly. "A commemorative token. I had it made to celebrate the development of cypronoline. It's my discovery. I think I mentioned I'm a chemist? When I'm not writing about Horatio Kneebone, that is." He held out his free hand for the keys. Mara tossed them to him. He caught them and slipped them into a pocket.

She said accusingly, "You might also have told us that your real name is Perry K. Chapman, that you're a bioprospector and an orchid hunter, and that you've been looking for Yong Chun Hua ever since you read about it in Horatio's diary."

"You've done your research." Charlie sounded pleased. "Congratulations. One should never take people at face value."

"Especially in your case, Charlie. Or do I call you Perry?"

"Whatever. It doesn't matter." He moved toward the suitcases.

"Going somewhere?" inquired Mara, backing away as he picked up the one she had just closed. The door behind him beckoned. *Run*, a voice cried out in her head. But he stood between her and escape.

"A necessary departure." His tone was genial. "Unfortunate, just when my research was going so well. Your doing, I'm sorry to say. *Tante* Juliette told me you've been creating difficulties."

"*Tante* Juliette?"

"Juliette Thory. My aunt. On my mother's side. I didn't tell you that, either. We're very much a family firm. I run BoniGen, the North American research unit of Bonisanté, based in Mississauga, Ontario."

Mara's gut lurched, and she swallowed hard. Compagnon's third man, linking Bonisanté, the clinic and Véronique together. Again, she assessed her chances of making a break for it. She would never make it out of the house, much less to her car.

"Look," he said as if to put her at her ease. "I don't want trouble. My priority is to pack up and leave. I hope you won't present an obstacle?"

"Not at all. But what about *Cypripedium incognitum*?" she asked, knowing that she needed to keep him talking.

"Ah, yes." He gestured regretfully. "I *am* sincerely interested in finding it, you know. It's what I came for, but Véronique came up as a more pressing matter, and my aunt called on my"—he paused—"services, shall we say, when things started to go bad. Another day, perhaps?" He picked up the suitcase.

And then he hit her with it, a blinding blow on the side of the head that sent her sprawling. He was on her immediately, pushing her face down, jerking her arms behind her and securing her wrists tightly with the electrical cord.

"You killed her, didn't you!" Mara screamed as loudly as she could, hoping desperately that someone, a neighbour, a passing farmer, would hear her. "Véronique. You killed her!"

"Someone had to do it." His voice was matter-of-fact. "She was a liability. Claude's useless, and my aunt could hardly afford to be directly involved."

"Are you planning to kill me too?"

He stepped away from her. She craned her head around to see him searching for something amid the clutter of Julian's store of junk. He found what he wanted, Julian's old cricket bat, hard wood, weighty, the handle wrapped with sweat-stained tape. He turned back to her, holding it in his right hand, slapping it lightly against his left palm, testing its heft.

"Charlie, don't do this!" Mara pleaded, wriggling away, trying to work her wrists free. The cord held fast, cutting into her flesh.

"Save your breath, Mara," said her fellow Canadian. "No one's around to hear you, and Julian's in China. He's let you down badly, I'm afraid."

Yes, she thought with a bitterness that almost overcame her fear. Once again, when it mattered most, Julian wasn't here for her. In her head she screamed at him: *You got me into this, you loony flower freak. It's your fault I'm here with a psychopathic killer, and I am going to die!*

Charlie was saying something: "With your cooperation I can make this quick. Or messy. Which will it be?"

She twisted aside just as the bat crashed down, missing her by centimetres.

Anger gave Mara strength. She kicked out viciously at Charlie, making contact with his shins, sending him skipping back a step or two. This bought her enough time to get her legs beneath her, but as she scrambled up, Charlie knocked her back with a nonchalant shove of the foot. Her attempts to save herself seemed to amuse him.

"You bastard!" she yelled, as he brought the bat down again. Once more, to her amazement, she managed to roll out of the way of its deadly impact. He was smiling, stroking his improvised weapon, running his thumb down its leading edge. She realized that he was purposely aiming wide, not really trying to hit her, not yet, but rather dragging out the pleasure of the kill. And she knew that only she could save herself.

"You won't get away with this," she shouted. She was on her knees now, struggling to move away from him, frantically working her wrists against the electrical cord, which seemed to be loosening, allowing her slight freedom of one hand. She curled her fingers around, picking desperately at the knot.

"I think I will." Leisurely, he followed her, his smile widening. "It's a bummer, I know. When they find your body, *if* they find it, there'll be nothing to connect you to me."

Then the smile was gone, replaced by a look of intense concentration, his upper lip sharpening to a nasty point, his round eyes focused darkly on her. He raised the bat. This time he would not miss. She screamed again and rolled over on her back, drawing up her legs against her body, prepared with her final action to kick Charlie and the cricket bat all the way to hell.

Suddenly, there was a movement behind him, perceptible more as a rush of air than actual motion. Charlie sensed it, but before he could turn, his head snapped forward and all expression slid from his face. With a grunt of surprise, bat slipping from his hand, Charlie toppled forward, landing on top of Mara in a clattering free fall.

•

"You!"

"You okay?"

Charlie's body was pulled off her. Busy fingers loosened the cord that bound her wrists.

Mara stared dazedly from Charlie's motionless form to the dumpling-soft face of the woman who knelt beside her. "What—what did you hit him with?" was all she could think of to say.

"Frying pan, the dog's head," said Mama Deng with a measure of pride as she held up, like a winner's trophy, one of Julian's battered skillets.

Questions tumbled out of Mara's mouth like gravel down a chute. "Is he dead? What—? How—?" And suddenly Mara knew. "Sichuan pepper? Sichuan hot-pot? Mama Deng, you're from Kanglong!"

Solemnly, the motherly chef nodded and helped Mara to her feet.

"My nephew Zhang Shugang phone me from China," she said with a frown in Charlie's direction. "Look like I got here just in time."

Distantly, they heard the two-toned wail of police sirens, growing stronger, now pulsing in the air. And then, above the commotion, Adjudant-chef Compagnon roaring, "In here, lads. And hope to God we're not too late!"

36

Adjudant-chef Compagnon was not a happy man.

Thanks to an exceptionally hard head, Perry K. Chapman, alias Charlie, was concussed but deemed fit for questioning within twenty-four hours. He answered Compagnon's questions directly and concisely, assuming full responsibility for Véronique's death and stonewalling on everything else.

"It was unpremeditated," he said. "I met her for the first time when she came to the cottage looking for Julian. She stayed to flirt and left an open invitation that I took her up on. Things got out of hand. She was a sexual tease. I hit her. I didn't mean to kill her."

"Then why hit her twice? Why trash her place?"

"I panicked. Tried to cover up." Charlie, hardly the panicking type, shrugged. "*C'est la vie.*"

•

"*Putain*!" fumed Compagnon to Laurent, his case against Thory and Morange for conspiracy to murder left to flounder in the shallows of circumstantial evidence. Francke had been run to earth where he was working as a waiter in the Gers, but his testimony was not strong enough to outweigh Charlie's unequivocal confession. "Evasion! Obstruction! The *salaud* is as slippery as an eel. He'll have the best legal representation money can buy, plead sexual provocation, and get off with a reduced sentence."

"*Merde*!" declared Laurent more softly but with feeling.

•

Patsy occupied the seat of honour: a wheelchair. The friends were gathered not at Chez Nous, but in her private room, at the moment as crowded as a convention in an elevator, in the Bellevue Maison de Repos. Loulou and Prudence had brought chocolates, grapes and flowers; Mara and Julian champagne; Mado and Paul an enormous tray of hors d'oeuvres: *bouchées à la périgourdine*—puff pastry cases filled with truffles and foie gras in a Madeira glaze; smoked salmon rolls; artichoke hearts; crayfish-filled barquettes; quails' eggs; minibrioches stuffed with various kinds of tasty forcemeats.

"Thank God," said Patsy, wolfing down two of anything at a time. She drank champagne from a plastic cup. "I'm starving in here. The food, let me tell you, is not great."

"Mama Deng didn't come to the cottage to save me," Mara was explaining to the Brieuxs. "She didn't know I was there. She came to kill Charlie."

"With a frying pan?" marvelled Mado, who valued her cookware.

"Not exactly. She heard me screaming, and it happened to be handy. She said she came to the cottage to invite Charlie to a special hot-pot at the restaurant. But the gendarmes aren't to know that."

"Ha!" crowed Paul. "They took their time getting there. She could have chopped him up into little pieces and served him up as a stir-fry. No one would have been the wiser."

"Or just blown his head away with chilis," Julian recalled painfully. "Too bad you French have done away with the death penalty. I'd like to see the bastard guillotined." He added glumly, "It really looks like Thory and Morange are going to walk away from this. I wonder how much the family promised Charlie for taking the rap."

"Look at it this way," reasoned Paul, "if the cops didn't get him, your Kanglongers would. He's safer behind bars, and he knows it."

Loulou said, "Don't give up on Compagnon yet. He's like a terrier. Never lets go of his end. Meantime, have you heard? Class action suits are being launched against Bonisanté, the clinic and BoniGen Canada. All supplies of BoniSom and Xerafus have been pulled from the shelves, the sleep clinic is closing, the doctor is up to his neck in debt, and word has it that Juliette Thory and her sister are having to shore up their company with their own personal resources." Loulou stuffed an anchovy-filled brioche in his mouth. "The litigation alone is sure to sink them!" he exclaimed rather indistinctly.

"Somehow I doubt it," intoned Julian, untrusting of the way of the world. The buoyancy of slime meant that it usually managed to bubble its way to the top.

"The murder charge against Ventura's lover has been dropped," put in Prudence, "on the grounds that it was the drug that sent Ventura out her studio window. She wasn't just a Pronole-2 tester, she was also a long-term BoniSom user, so she got a double whammy."

Patsy nodded. "That's the problem. BoniSom and Xerafus are labelled as safe for long-term use, so people stay on it for months, like me. They're working on the theory that cypronoline causes changes to the brain chemistry that don't show up right away but go on getting quietly worse the longer you take it."

"But not all Pronole-2 testers and BoniSom or Xerafus users have had problems," objected Mado.

Patsy shrugged. "It affects people differently. Or maybe it just takes longer for some. Only time will tell. The symptoms can go unnoticed for a long time because they can be so fleeting. The brain just goes to sleep for a split second, like a miniseizure. In other cases symptoms can last up to several minutes and are experienced as a kind of hallucinatory black hole. With me it was both. Now that I think about it, I realize I've been having momentary blackouts for some time. I'd find myself switching off, forgetting what I was doing. I put it down to overwork or plain old absent-mindedness. Until I finally hit the big one: a pitch-black tunnel. I hear other testers have described similar hallucinations."

"It was an unlit stairwell and doors in walls for the two I talked to," Mara said. "Who knows what Sofia Ventura, Marsaud and Soulivet saw?"

Prudence frowned. "But if cypronoline is so dangerous, why hasn't it affected the Baixi? They've been taking it for centuries, haven't they?"

Julian said, "I suspect it's because the Baixi boil the entire root and drink it as an infusion, while BoniSom is a highly concentrated dose of the pure alkaloid."

"So," Paul asked Patsy in his typically blunt way, "is this brain chemistry thing of yours going to be permanent?"

Mado kicked him in full view of everyone.

"What?" Her husband looked hurt. "I just meant, is she going to go on seeing tunnels?"

"Who knows?" Patsy gave a wry grin. "Who knows when I'll be able to drive again and if any insurance company will cover me. There's some thought that the brain may be capable of healing itself, but, like I said, only time will tell."

"Think on the bright side," said Loulou cheerfully. "You are lucky to be alive."

"*Putain*!" uttered Paul.

"What about the patents challenge?" asked Prudence, delicately peeling a quail's egg.

"On hold," said Julian, "until the final word on cypronoline is handed down. Could be that the Baixi will be able to reclaim their rights over their Sleep Tea without recourse to the courts. Although Jean-Luc Jarry told me that he feels the current publicity against Bonisanté makes an excellent climate for continuing to push the coalition's case against predatory patents and biopiracy in general."

"It's all about timing," approved Prudence, with the experience of forty years in advertising behind her.

Paul gulped his champagne and slapped Julian on the back. "So, *mec*, after all that, you didn't find your whatsit?"

"It was wiped out by a rock slide," replied Julian briefly, experiencing a momentary pang.

"And this Fang. What was she like?"

"Too tall for you," said Julian, even more briefly. "More bubbly, everyone?"

Patsy pulled Mara aside while the others moved to the far side of the room where Julian, using the windowsill as a makeshift bar, had popped another cork.

"You look pale, kid. You okay?"

"Not really."

"Still can't sleep?"

"That too."

"Well"—Patsy gave a dry laugh—"I won't be recommending BoniSom again. How's Julian doing?" It was an oblique way of asking if they were back together.

"He says he's glad to be home," was the uninformative reply. At Patsy's raised eyebrows, Mara added, "He brought me a 'Shi Nu Bi' T-shirt. That's Snoopy in Chinese. Embroidered. With sequins."

"Give it time," said Patsy.

Mara shook her head. "No time. Look, Patsy," she burst out under the pressure of her friend's concerned gaze, "we're not on the same path. Never have been, if you want to know the truth. It's as simple as that."

"You are," Patsy murmured, perhaps too softly for Mara to catch her words. "It's just that neither of you knows it."

Mara changed the subject. "Are you still planning to join Stanley in an ashram?"

To her surprise Patsy shook her head. "I've had a lot of time to think things over lying on my back. Ceilings are surprisingly helpful in shaping perspective, and it's amazing how hungry for life a near-death experience can make you. Stanley's a sweetie, but, like Prudence says, it's all about timing. He called again yesterday. I told him I'm ready to retire from my practice but not from the world." Patsy grinned. "To be honest, it was Prudence's crack about sitting around in a diaper that did it. I'm too old for spiritual toilet training. And you're right. I couldn't stand the food." It was the old Patsy back full beam. "In fact, I'm seriously thinking of winding things up and moving back here."

Mara stared at her friend in disbelief. Suddenly, she was overcome by a lift of gladness such as she had not known for a long time. "Welcome back, traveller," she laughed, and gave Patsy a long and careful hug.

•

"Well, that's it," said Julian as he heaved the box into the back of his van. He scanned Mara's face, alert for any change of direction. But her chin was set, her dark eyes gave nothing away. "We'll see each other, of course?"

"Of course," she said. "Friday nights. For dinner. At Chez Nous."

"Yes. We'll have to keep that up." He spoke without conviction.

"It'll be like old times," she said with an awful brightness. "With the addition of Patsy, when she comes."

"Right."

"She'll stay here with me until she finds a place of her own," Mara told him unnecessarily.

He stood in the driveway, staring out at a view of hills and forests that by now he knew by heart. He thought of the path they had come down together, he and she, the good times and the bad, but mostly of the good, the meals they had cooked and shared, their petty disagreements, their lovemaking. Then he thought of his own cottage—his books, his favourite chair, his chimney that smoked—and had a presentiment of a sad homecoming. He gave himself an inward shake. He was only twenty minutes down the road, not as if he were in the next *département*. He realized that he might as well be on the far side of the moon.

She caught his expression. "We—*I* need to move on, Julian," she said.

Was he wrong, or did he hear regret in her voice? He waited. She looked away.

"I'm sorry it didn't work out," he said, with a tightness in his chest that was more likely the implosion of his heart. "It's my fault. I wish—" He broke off, earnestly searching for a sign.

"It's both our fault." Her eyes, her mouth, her chin were unrevealing, giving him little reason to hope.

He turned, closed the rear door of the van and whistled for Bismuth. Both dogs came galloping around the corner of the house.

Julian opened the driver's side door. "Up, boy."

Bismuth scrambled on to the front seat. Jazz attempted to follow. Mara grabbed his collar and pulled him back.

"Down! Sit!"

Jazz gave a sharp bark and a bewildered whimper, but sat.

"Well, be seeing you," Julian said.

Awkwardly, he put his hand out. She took it. It felt warm and sinewy in her own, a long live thing that she wanted to continue holding.

"Will you go on looking for *Cypripedium incognitum*?" she asked, and was surprised to find herself genuinely interested.

His shoulders rose on the updraft of a sigh. "I suppose I will. Although it's ironic."

"What is?"

"I went halfway around the world to discover that the thing I'm looking for, if it exists, grows only here."

"You never know." She tried to cheer him up. "Some plants might have survived the rock slide."

"I wasn't talking about orchids," he said, and withdrew his hand. He climbed into the van, slid the door shut and rolled down the window.

"Keep in touch." He managed, despite himself, a crooked grin.

"I will. You too."

Julian started up the engine. Jazz, indignant at being left, barked and strained forward, forelegs scrabbling in the air. Mara pulled him back again. Her glance met Julian's. Jazz gave another desperate lunge.

"Stay!" she said.

EPILOGUE

Somewhere in the Dordogne, on a sun-dappled slope, a flower bloomed. It had been a long time preparing itself, years coming to this point. Starting as an offshoot many generations removed from the mother plant, now long dead, it had worked slowly through its infancy and juvenile phase, to reach the critical size for flowering. Springtime after springtime it had put out leaves. Sometimes hopeful growth was trampled by deer, sometimes nibbled by rabbits. The flower itself was unhurried, heeding its own subterranean promptings, receiving whispered messages of sun and rain, until the right moment.

Leisurely, the flower head began to twist about on its stem. Its near-black sepals unfolded to reveal a tightly closed bud within. The bud swelled, exposing a vivid pink slipper. Long, dark, spiralled petals uncoiled. A breeze caught them. In a moment of playful celebration, they flew like party streamers in the wind. And then, as a gesture of completion, the slipper dropped down to expand, glorious and trembling, in the warm spring air.

NOTE ON THE AUTHOR

Michelle Wan was born in Kunming, China. She and her tropical horticulturalist husband, Tim, live in Guelph, Ontario, and travel regularly to the Dordogne to photograph and chart wild orchids. She is the author of three previous novels in the "Death in the Dordogne" series, *Deadly Slipper*, *The Orchid Shroud*, and *A Twist of Orchids*.

ALSO BY MICHELLE WAN

DEADLY SLIPPER

Nearly twenty years have passed since Mara Dunn's sister Bedie, an orchid enthusiast, disappeared while on a hiking holiday in southwestern France. Mara remains determined to find out what happened—but her only real clue is a sequence of wild orchids, including a mysterious, unknown Lady's Slipper, captured on a roll of film found in Bedie's long-lost camera. With the help of Julian Wood, a reclusive English botanist, Mara begins her search . . . stumbling into decades' worth of local secrets and putting herself in danger. Rich in lush descriptions of the Dordogne, and laden with savory details of French cooking, *Deadly Slipper* is rife with surprising twists and turns.

Anchor Canada / ISBN: 978–0-385–66118–8

ALSO BY MICHELLE WAN

THE ORCHID SHROUD

Something terrifying is stalking the Sigoulane Valley. When Mara discovers the body of a murdered infant in a wall of the manor house she is renovating, she also taps into a history of frightening family secrets. The discovery is a PR disaster for the house owner, wealthy Christophe de Bonfond, who is desperate to clear his family's name. But for Julian it is an amazing breakthrough—the baby's clothes bear an embroidery of the mysterious Slipper orchid he has been searching for. Then a new body is found, savaged by some kind of wild beast, merging the hunt for the orchid with a trail of murder spanning decades. As Mara and Julian uncover a past filled with greed and treachery, they must also unmask a present-day killer—before they become the next victims.

Anchor Canada / ISBN: 978–0-385–66120–1

ALSO BY MICHELLE WAN

A TWIST OF ORCHIDS

Mara and Julian's up-and-down relationship is troubled by frightening events. A neighbour plunges to her death. Another is terrorized by a murderous midnight apparition. A young man dies of an overdose. An elusive burglar baffles the gendarmes. And Julian's continuing search for his mystery orchid leads to a volatile mix of botany and illicit drugs in this compelling novel with a deadly twist. Michelle Wan weaves another delicate and exhilarating tale of mystery and intrigue.

Anchor Canada / ISBN: 978-0-385-66485-1